THE
AYLESFORD
SKULL

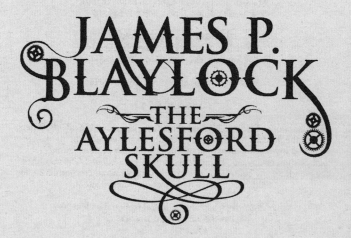

JAMES P. BLAYLOCK
THE AYLESFORD SKULL

TITAN BOOKS

The Aylesford Skull
Mass-market edition ISBN: 9781781167601
E-book edition ISBN: 9780857689818

Published by Titan Books
A division of Titan Publishing Group Ltd
144 Southwark Street, London SE1 0UP

First mass-market edition: August 2016

1 3 5 7 9 10 8 6 4 2

Did you enjoy this book? We love to hear from our readers.
Please email us at readerfeedback@titanemail.com or write to us at
Reader Feedback at the above address.

To receive advance information, news, competitions, and exclusive offers
online, please sign up for the Titan newsletter on our website.

TITANBOOKS.COM

For Viki, John, and Danny,
and for
John Berlyne

And these are the gems of the Human Soul
The rubies & pearls of a lovesick eye
The countless gold of the akeing heart
The martyrs groan & the lovers sigh

WILLIAM BLAKE
"The Mental Traveler"

PROLOGUE, 1883
RIVER THAMES, THE SEA REACH

The black smoke issuing from the chimney of the steam launch was nearly invisible under the cloudy night sky, although now and then the moon shone through a break in the clouds, illuminating the narrow launch, the streaming smoke, and the dirty canvas canopy that arched over the stern of the thirty-five-foot vessel. The river was empty in the early morning darkness, nothing to be seen ahead, and far behind them the shadow of the distant boat that they'd passed forty minutes back, low in the water, disappearing behind flurries of rain.

The launch wanted very little draft, and now she hugged the marshy Thames shore, running upriver toward Gravesend. The Pilot, Nathaniel Wise, stood at the wheel in the prow, his hat doing little to keep off the rain. Despite his time on the water, he had never learned to swim, and he meant to be as close in to the land as ever he could be if there were trouble, especially on this uncomfortably empty stretch of river. He owed nothing to the man who had hired him, and although the pay was good enough, it wasn't worth dying for, not by a long chalk.

"Those lights you see," he said to the dull-witted boy sitting by the furnace, "them's the lights of the Havens, as we call them, and over there the Chapman Light." The boy looked around, trying to make out what Wise was talking about. "There on the starboard shore, Billy. Not much farther now and we'll slant 'round into the Lower Hope, and then it's ten miles in all to Gravesend. In an hour by the clock you'll be dry again, with the tide beating against the stern like it is."

The boy nodded at him, but didn't speak. Too miserable, perhaps. The wind sprang up now, the rain beat down, and there was thunder downriver. In Gravesend, Wise would collect his percentage and find a warm berth at a handy inn, leaving the unloading of the launch to the four men who huddled in the stern beneath the canvas now, out of the rain and dry, drunk on gin they'd bought by the quart in Margate. Their singing was loud and tuneless when it wasn't drowned out by the rain and thunder. It had been worse when they were sober. Now and then one of them was taken with a fit of laughter that gave way to an explosion of coughing. That the man hadn't spewed up his lungs was a miracle.

Pilot, captain, and bleeding engineer, Wise thought, commanding a crew of layabout drunks dredged out of a Billingsgate tavern by the fool of a merchant who had hired the launch. Wise was a lighterman by trade, and carried cargo upriver and down, but he had signed on for this cruise across the Channel to France because he couldn't turn down the pay, which was five times what it should be. And it was the pay that was the two-edged sword, as the saying went – overlarge for the time spent, and that implied risk, although he was damned if he knew what sort.

The boy fed coal to the boiler with a big scoop, doing his duty, hunkering down in the falling rain and no doubt wishing he were lying abed wherever he called home. He had been sick on the Channel crossing, his first time at sea, he had told Wise. And the last, no doubt. He wasn't made for it. The boy set the scoop down, sheltering his face with his hand, and with the other he picked up a heavy iron poker and stirred the coals, which glowed orange, throwing out a welcome heat. He had done his work steadily enough, despite the rain and in between puking over the side.

The launch had come around through the Dover Strait from a no-name, ramshackle dock on a deserted stretch of shore below Calais, where they had loaded a round dozen of beef kegs in the dead of night. If the kegs actually contained beef, Wise thought, he would eat his hat. Contraband was more like it, although the kegs were too light for brandy. But it was none of his business – his commission was purely temporary – and he had learned to shut off any curiosity at the tap. Curiosity was a beehive of trouble. And he wasn't of the variety of lighterman who helped himself to cargo, either. Sooner or later that caper would spell the end of a man's livelihood, or the gibbet, like as not. He looked back downriver toward the east, trying to hurry the dawn, but it was early yet, and the thick clouds would hide the daylight until the sun was well up.

When the rain fell off and made talking easier, Wise said, "There on the larboard side lies Egypt Bay, Billy, and with the Cliffe Marshes beyond. You can see the black shadow of the rise there along the shore. When the moon looks out you'll make out the mouth of the bay, but on a filthy night like this it's all one. Nought but smugglers and river pirates since the dawn of time in Egypt Bay. I've heard stories of the old Shade House Inn, with signal lights in the top window, and an honest man as good as dead if he came upon it on a dark night. There were tunnels away under the marsh, full of plunder brought in from distant lands. Like as not the plunder lies there today, although you'd be a fool to search for it. It's still a den of cutthroats when the sun sets. What do you think of that, Billy?"

The boy looked out over the water, peering at the southern shore, but said nothing, although his eyes were wide and searching.

"There was a keg at the Shade House," Wise said, looking ahead at the river, "full of rum, with a severed head aswim in it that they say was the Duke of Monmouth, preserved in spirits these many years. The rogues would drink of it and then top off the keg so that the head was always a-brewing. Many's the time that the Duke's head would rise up out of the keg and have his say, a-dripping rum from his mouth..."

The boy shouted a startled, "There!" just as the rain beat down again. He stood up and pointed with the iron poker. Wise looked sharply back to port, seeing with shocked surprise that a black cutter bore down on them, already close – six men on the thwarts leaning hard into muffled oars, black kerchiefs over their faces. The cutter must have rowed out of Egypt Bay, meaning to take the launch – *What comes of speaking of the Devil*, Wise thought.

"All hands!" he shouted, although the singing continued aft as he swung the wheel hard to port, thinking to run in toward shore – to run her aground if he had to and damn the cargo. The crew could earn their keep if they chose to stay and fight.

But it was too late. He heard the thud of a grappling hook striking home, the launch slewing sideways with the weight of the cutter, which backed water hard, coming around and slamming sideways into the launch, the pirates shipping their oars and swarming over the low gunwale.

The flap of the canvas flew back, the singing at an end, but the first man out from under the canopy was shot in the chest at close range. He reeled backward, pushing the canvas toward the stern with his head and his flung-back arms, the heavy, wet canopy encumbering the other three men, who tried to fight their way clear – sober enough now.

Wise abandoned the wheel, looking hard toward shore, still a good distance away, the launch turning in a lazy arc. Pistol shots mingled with the crack of thunder, the two running together. The river pirates were intent upon murder, and Wise wondered again what was in the kegs and how the pirates bloody well knew.

He stepped in a low crouch to the starboard railing, meaning to throw himself overside and take his chances with the river, but he saw that the boy still stood as if frozen. Wise grabbed him by the shoulder and shouted, "Can you swim, Billy?" He looked up in the same moment to see one of the pirates, a huge man, whose long black beard flowed out from beneath his kerchief, leveling a pistol at him. Without waiting for Billy's reply, Wise picked the boy up bodily, spun around, and heaved him over the railing. The bullet punched Wise sideways, a searing pain in his left shoulder. He knew without question that the pirates would kill them all, and that he would just as surely drown in the river if he leapt in. With his good hand he snatched up the iron poker from beside the coal oven. It felt pitifully light to him now, but it was the only weapon within reach.

The big man who had shot him had turned away to club one of the crew with his pistol, the man crawling across the deck, as if he might yet slip beneath the railing and swim away. The pirate bent over the now-still form, placed the barrel against the back of the man's head, and pulled the trigger. Wise, knowing that it was futile even as he sprang forward, hammered the bar down upon the big man's head, heaving his full weight behind the blow, although already weakening from the bleeding wound in his shoulder, his left arm slick with blood. The bar tore itself out of Wise's grip as he was shot in the neck by someone unseen and thrown back against the oven, the red-hot chimney searing his flesh through his clothing.

Wise reeled away. His senses were uncannily sharp in that moment; he heard the rain beating on the deck and hissing on the hot iron of the oven, and he smelled the rain and the river, and saw with particular clarity the lights winking along the far shore. He felt the railing in the small of his back, and he heard what sounded to him like the murmuring of the Thames flowing in its bed toward the sea, its waters unsettled and agitated by the incoming tide. He found himself teetering backward, his weight levering him over the railing – the brief sensation of falling and of the dark waters mercifully closing over him as he drowned in his own blood.

* * *

The pirates heaved the bodies into the river, then yanked the fallen canvas free and dumped it over the side in order to unencumber the deck. The big man, his forehead running blood from the blow that Wise had delivered, took a heavy pistol from within his coat, aimed it into the air, and fired it, the bullet blazing white as it exited the barrel, shooting up into the sky with a long, flaming tail, like a miniature comet. He put the pistol away in his coat, stepped to the wheel, and turned the launch back toward the bay, towing the cutter now.

The rest of the pirates watched sharply for the boy who had gone overside, although by now he would have been swept away with the corpses and so there was little chance of finding him. Within minutes they had run in around the spit of land that hid the bay's northern shore, where they doused the glowing coal fire in the oven with buckets of water until the smoke ran white and then cleared away utterly. Taking to the cutter again, the rain beating down, they towed the launch toward the distant, farther shore, where there stood an acre or two of trees and dense shrubbery along both sides of a wide creek. They took the launch in under the trees and warped it in alongside a low, half-ruined dock with a boathouse built over it, a mere hovel of boards and tarred sailcloth, invisible from the bay.

A man in an Inverness cape stood on the dock, waiting for them, having seen the Fenian fire, as it was called, arc up into the sky. He was well satisfied with the behavior of the projectile, one of his more useful inventions, although he would experiment with it further in order to make very certain it wouldn't fail him when he had real need for it. He held a lantern up in front of him now, the light shining on his pale features. There was an evident hump on his back, the cape doing little to hide it, and his face was as pale as a moth, although his hair was black. He walked along the dock to where the kegs were being lifted out of the launch and set down on their sides, two of the men rolling them along the planks toward a wagon that waited on shore, the horses huddled in the rain. The hunchbacked man said nothing, his attention concentrated on the kegs, which he counted carefully. After hanging his lantern on a rusty spike, he took up a mallet and crowbar and pried a stave out of the barrelhead of one of them. He regarded the contents of the keg for a time, peering closely at the bones and bone chips that studded the rubble of coal – one of the bones entire, almost certainly a human clavicle. He dipped his hand into the mix and then withdrew it, looking at the grit on his palm: coal dust, certainly, mixed with dry soil and miniscule bone fragments. He smelled and tasted it, and then dusted his hand on his trousers.

He had been promised a mixture of decomposing coal and fragments of Neolithic human bone, and he was well satisfied with what he found in the keg. If he had been cheated, he would have taken his pound of flesh, quite literally, from the London merchant who had arranged the sale of the contraband coal, despite the entertaining fact that he had refused to pay for the coal until it was delivered to him in London, and so he had no real need to pay for it at all, given that it would never be delivered.

ONE

INTO THE DARKNESS

The Bayswater Club, frequented by members of the Royal Society, stood on Craven Hill, with a view of Hyde Park to the south, and, through the trees, the roof of Kensington Palace. The view of the palace improved in autumn and winter when the trees weren't so riotously green. What must have been half the population of London strolled up and down Bayswater Road and through the park today, sitting near the banks of the Serpentine, soaking up the sun's warmth like salamanders after the rains of late spring. There had been an anarchist bomb, reportedly Fenian, set off just two days ago near Marble Arch, with two pedestrians killed – murdered was the more accurate term – but the city seemed already to have forgotten it.

Langdon St. Ives looked out through the window, half lost in thought, a glass of champagne in his hand. Nothing was more likely to give an anarchist the pip, it seemed to him, than public indifference, and surely there was some small justice in that, although justice was in uncommonly short supply lately. It had been a perilous two weeks, during which St. Ives had foolishly attempted to recover three notebooks of botanical illustrations drawn by Sir Joseph Banks as a boy, which had been turned over to Secretary Parsons of the Royal Society for authentication. The man who had "found" the notebooks had offered to sell them to the Society for an astonishingly moderate sum. No fewer than four experts had signed affidavits authenticating the drawings. But then, as if a magician had waved a wand over them, the original notebooks were spirited away, replaced by forgeries, and the owner of the notebooks demanded recompense.

In the interests of the Royal Society, St. Ives had played the part of a devious and interested collector to flush the thief out by offering to buy the purloined sketches. The result of the ruse had been the violent death of the thief, who, by the wildest happenstance, had apparently recognized St. Ives, knew at once that he had been practiced upon, and had fled pell-mell into the street, running with a heavy limp and carrying the three authenticated notebooks, which, along with the thief, had been trodden under the wheels of an omnibus. The man was dead where he lay, his widow and two children were left to beg in the streets, several score of early drawings by Sir Joseph Banks were ruined for good and all, and the Royal Society owed the moderate sum – no longer quite so moderate, given that it had bought them nothing – to the owner of the notebooks. It was a mess in so many ways that St. Ives scarcely knew where to begin when he attempted to itemize his regret.

The worst of it was that in a fit of remorse St. Ives had given money to the unfortunate thief's widow when her husband lay dead in the street. The woman had unfortunately been hiding nearby with her children, she being almost certainly an accomplice as well as a witness. The money seemed to baffle her until she understood what it was for, which is to say, a guilt payment. She had loved her husband, just as St. Ives loved Alice, his own wife, and in the widow's eyes there was no price that could be put on her husband's bloody death. She had kept the money, however, clutching the five crowns in her hand, and had said to St. Ives, "There will be a time to judge every deed," in a scarcely audible voice.

"I pray it won't be soon," he had replied, and had turned away, feeling shabbier than he remembered having felt in his life up until that time. After a period of reflection, however, it seemed to him that he might have played the fool in the matter – not his favorite instrument. The complications of the whole thing were rather *too* complicated to seem quite right to him now, and it had the earmarks of a plot, although the nature of the plot was beyond his grasp. He caught sight of his image in the window glass now, and saw that he looked even more craggy than usual, his long face careworn and drawn. He sat up, taking his long legs from the ottoman, suddenly restless.

He heartily wished that he were at home in Aylesford, with Alice and the children. Soon he would be, he told himself, and he looked at his pocket watch for the third time in the last half hour. The next train on the Medway Valley Line of the South Eastern Railway left Tooley Street Station in two hours, and he meant to be on it. He wouldn't be home by suppertime, perhaps, but something very near.

He realized that his friend Tubby Frobisher was engaged in an argument with Secretary Parsons, heated on Parsons's side – Parsons being disagreeable by nature – and ironic on Tubby's, whose single-minded goal was to irritate Parsons. Parsons was an old man, humorless, stooped, and narrow-shouldered. His eyebrows were heavy and wild, which gave his face a fierce appearance. There was nothing at all fierce about Tubby, whose name was perfectly appropriate, although his enormous girth and cheerful demeanor sometimes mislead his enemies into thinking that he wasn't both quick and ready to act.

"I tell you that Quittichunk's Tablets have no virtue at all," Parsons said, his face flushed and his beard quivering with passion. "Complete fraud. Medicinally inert if not poisonous." He set his empty glass down and signaled for another bottle.

"Nonsense," said Tubby. "My Uncle Gilbert swears by them. He's an amateur sailor, you know. Docks his steam yacht in Eastbourne Harbour. He used to feed the tablets to me as a boy, before he'd allow me to go punting on the lake. I never suffered from a moment's scurvy. You can have my affidavit on it."

"On the bleeding *lake*?" Parsons sputtered. "The man was raving."

"Never," Tubby said. "Quittichunk's Tablets were efficacious there, too, you know – in the case of lunacy, that is to say. Uncle Gilbert ground them with a pestle and consumed the powder with a measured dose of whisky when he was tempted to run mad."

Parsons blinked, speechless, his heavy features frozen into a rictus of bewildered loathing. The waiter brought the fresh bottle, which was beaded with moisture and apparently steaming cold. He poured it into Parsons's glass, and the rush of ascending bubbles seemed to restore the man to partial equanimity.

"You remember Uncle Gilbert, Langdon?" Tubby said. "You can vouch for his sanity?"

"Indeed I can," St. Ives replied. "As sane as you or I and with a measure left over."

"I have no argument with that," Parsons muttered.

St. Ives, in fact, would not swear an oath on the matter of Uncle Gilbert's sanity, if it came down to it, although it was true that sanity was a difficult thing to define.

"Do you know that he's come up from Dicker on a birding expedition in the Cliffe Marshes?" Tubby asked. "He's keen on finding the great bustard, which have largely been shot out of existence."

"He intends to bag the rest of them?" Parsons asked.

"Not Uncle Gilbert. He intends to count them. Goes off hunting with his binocle and a notebook. The bird was allegedly seen in the brushlands in the marshes by an amateur birder, although it might easily have been an enormous pheasant. Uncle Gilbert means to sort the bustard out. He's setting up a bivouac above the bay. Another glass of this capital champagne?" Tubby asked St. Ives.

"No," St. Ives said. "It's wasted on me."

"You were off your feed at lunch, I noticed. Pining for home and hearth again?"

St. Ives nodded, started to reply, but was abruptly distracted when it came into his mind that he had been promised begonia cuttings, and that he might have time to fetch them before leaving for the station. The thought perked him up considerably. Something good might come of this damnable two-weeks-long detour after all. Alice was a slave to begonias – one of her chief hobbyhorses. She could plant a fragment of a leaf in a pot of sand, and it would put down roots and produce fresh leaves in a fortnight. She would be doubly happy to see him if he arrived with cuttings, and, it seemed to him at that moment, her happiness was his own.

He bent forward and looked back out of the window, where he could see the glass roof of the conservatory, a small palm house kept by an ancient gardener named Jensen Shorter, recently the secretary of the Royal Horticultural Society. Shorter had seemed to decline in stature over the long years and was now as old as Moses and as tall as Commodore Nutt. The interior of the glass building appeared to St. Ives to be inordinately dark, given the bright afternoon, as if the coal oil heater were smoking, although why the heater would be on in midsummer was a poser. Shorter was a begonia fancier of the first water: rhizomatous exclusively, no gaudy tuberous show-offs. He had been given two-dozen new species from Brazil a year ago, but he wouldn't hear of parting with any of the plants until his cuttings had flourished. Given that he hadn't taken the lot of them out to the gardens at Chiswick, it wouldn't take ten minutes for Shorter to snip off a few pieces of rhizome, which would ride home snugly in various coat pockets.

St. Ives stood up decidedly. "Good day to you both," he said. "I've got to see Shorter about begonia cuttings before I set out for Tooley Street."

"*Begonias*," said Parsons dismissively, "I don't fancy

them myself. Hairy damned abominations, like something out of a nightmare."

"I couldn't agree more," St. Ives said, shaking the man's hand. "Please convey my apologies to the Society for the way this business of Banks's notebooks fell out. I would have had it turn out in any other way than it did."

"As would I," Parsons said, shaking his head and scowling. "The loss in money is troubling enough, not to mention the reputation of the Society, but that's the least of it. Forty-seven original drawings by the greatest botanist of his age reduced to muddy rubbish! Still, no one's suggesting that you were careless in the matter. Time and chance happeneth to all of us, eh? Some of us perhaps more often than others. All the more reason to put it behind us, as they say."

"Time and chance it will have to be," St. Ives said, seeing that Tubby had a dangerous look about him, as if he were on the verge of committing an act of violence against Secretary Parsons. "I'll just be off, then. Tubby, give my best to Chingford."

"I'll do that," Tubby said. "I'm on my way out myself, though. I'll see you to the street." He drank off the rest of his champagne, nodded darkly at Parsons, and put on his hat.

They passed through the book room, which was nearly empty, although it appeared to contain a high percentage of luminaries among the several men lounging at the tables. Lord Kelvin sat alone near the window, sketching something out on a piece of foolscap. St. Ives knew two of the others by reputation, both mad doctors, who sat nattering away in Latin; one of them a wild-eyed French phrenologist and the other a crackpot criminologist from Turin University named

Lombroso, whose work with imbeciles had impressed certain members of the Royal Society, especially Secretary Parsons, who was happy with the idea that the greater part of the world's population suffered from imbecility. St. Ives was currently inclined to include himself among that number.

"There might be a bigger fool than Secretary Lambert Parsons alive in the world," Tubby said, "but if there is, he keeps himself moderately well hidden. The man is a humorless oaf. It's a marvel that air allows itself to enter his lungs."

They walked down into the entry hall, where Lawrence, the doorman, was propped against the wall just inside the open door, taking advantage of a warm ray of sunlight, his eyes closed.

"Do you have a coin for Lawrence?" Tubby whispered to St. Ives. "My pockets are empty."

St. Ives reached into his pocket, and in that instant there sounded a shattering explosion and he was thrown bodily to the floor, Tubby landing on top of him like two-hundredweight of sand. St. Ives was deafened by the blast, and he found himself looking up at the chandelier swaying dangerously overhead, plaster raining down.

"Move!" he shouted at Tubby, his voice sounding small and distant, but his friend was already pushing himself to his feet, and the two of them staggered at a run through the door, the chandelier crashing to the tiles behind them, glass crystals pelting them on the back of the legs.

Lawrence crouched on the footpath now, holding his palm over a bloody gash on the side of his head. There was the sound of screams, people shouting and running. The ground was littered with broken glass and wood, fragments of stone pots, and uprooted trees and shrubs.

Shorter lay folded in half, dead still, twenty feet away on the lawn, his neck and head canted back at an unnatural angle. St. Ives saw at once that the man's arm was missing at the shoulder, torn off in the blast. He looked away, his chest tightening.

The glasshouse had blown to pieces. Where it had been there was a stone foundation and little more. Along the base of the inside wall, between what had been the glasshouse and the Bayswater Club proper, a gaping hole looked down into the Ranelagh Sewer. Sunlight shone through the hole, revealing the shimmering surface of the Westbourne River moving toward the Thames through its immense brick tunnel.

Secretary Parsons appeared, looking stunned. "Thank God the force of the blast went out through the glass," he said. "Aside from the odd window and the chandelier in the entry, the club itself seems to be sound. Poor Shorter." He shook his head, looking across the lawn. "He was with Wellington at Waterloo, you know. Ninety years old if he was a day. And now he's done down by a damned anarchist in his own palm house."

"Do we know that?" asked St. Ives.

"Take a look at the man," Parsons said. "He's been blown to pieces."

"I mean do we know it was an anarchist's device? Why would anarchists blow up a palm house?"

"Because they're imbeciles. They exist to be imbeciles. No one but an imbecile would detonate a bomb in a hollow tree near Marble Arch, but the thing was done."

Parsons and Tubby moved away toward where a

policeman was just then laying a coat across Shorter's body. It occurred to St. Ives that the totality of the old man's begonias lay in fragments amidst the rubble. He would gather pieces of them up before he left, he thought, and Alice could carry on with them – something saved from this carnage. He stepped down onto the floor of the ruined glasshouse and looked around, seeing at once that there was a wash of fine black dust on the ground, despite the turbulence of the blast, which must have thrown most of it into the atmosphere. Several clay pots that had miraculously survived the blast burned with an orange flame, which was damned odd. He smelled a wisp of rising smoke. Greek fire? Sulfur, surely. He tried to recall the ingredients of the incendiary fluid – pitch? Resin? The smell of sulfur overrode the others. He recalled that the interior of the glasshouse had been uncommonly dark when he had looked out at it through the window. Coal gas was a filthy substance when it burned, but that scarcely explained things here, unless it had been leaking badly.

He stepped across and peered into the sewer, although it was too dark to see more than a few feet in either direction. The brick floor of the enormous pipe was so broad as to be nearly flat, with a depression in the floor along which the Westbourne rippled in its channel. There was a litter of wet brick lying about and more of the black dust. He crouched at the edge of the ragged hole and bent into the pipe, looking back upriver into utter darkness. A person could trudge all the way to Hampstead Heath in that direction, to where the Westbourne rose at Whitestone Ponds, but it would be a long and tiresome journey. He turned to look downriver, and immediately saw a light in the far distance: the mouth of the sewer, perhaps, where it emptied into the Thames below the Chelsea Embankment.

Abruptly the light shifted, however, then disappeared entirely, and then winked back on – not the mouth of the sewer at all, but a lantern some distance away, moving in the direction of the Thames. Perhaps a lone anarchist.

St. Ives stepped into the sewer, down the several feet to the floor, and set out into the musty air, the light through the hole in the sewer wall giving up almost immediately so that he quickly found himself in darkness. His going back after a lantern would simply waste time – no value in even thinking about it. And besides, a lantern would give him away. It was stealth he wanted. He trailed his left hand along the wall, watching the lantern light ahead, unable to gauge its distance. Thank God, he thought, that the moving water smelled as if it were more river than filth, but he was careful where he stepped – as careful as was possible in the darkness.

He hastened forward, emboldened by the comparatively smooth brick floor, but almost immediately he stumbled over an impediment and fell to his knees, scraping his palms on the bricks and letting out a muffled shout, cursing himself under his breath, and then staying very still. The lantern in the distance went on apace. He looked back, but could see nothing behind him now, the tunnel curving slightly to the west as it ran beneath Hyde Park. That he could still see the lantern meant that it was closer than he had thought; otherwise it, too, would be hidden by the swerve of the tunnel wall.

He pushed himself to his feet, flexing his bruised knees, and went quietly on, listening hard. The awful picture of

Shorter lying dead on the lawn came into his mind, and abruptly he wished that he had a weapon of some sort. He thought of Tubby Frobisher, who was as fearless as a water buffalo and nearly as vast. Tubby would have come along with him in a cold moment if only St. Ives had thought to summon him before setting out. But there was nothing for it but to go on. Nothing ventured, he thought, nothing gained – aside from a knife in the ribs.

It came to him now that he could hear a squeaking and rattling, like axles turning, as if the moving lantern were fixed on a cart. Had they brought machinery with them? To what end…?

He heard a sharp, scraping sound behind him now. He turned, seeing too late a moving shadow lunging toward him, a man's narrow face slightly pale against the darkness. St. Ives was borne over backward, the back of his head banging down onto the brick floor so that his skull rang with the force of it. Before he could come to his senses he was rolled bodily into the river, his assailant clutching him by the hair, pushing his head beneath the surface of the water.

St. Ives flailed with his hands, seeking a purchase on the brick, which scraped past beneath him as he was swept downward in the flood, pulled from the grip of the man who was endeavoring to drown him. He lurched upward, gasping in a breath of air and twisting around, getting his feet under him so that he managed to half stand up. Immediately he was struck hard on the right cheek with something heavy and flat – the blade of a shovel? – and he reeled back against the wall of the tunnel, his cheek throbbing with pain, holding out his hands to keep the blade away from his face, hoping that his assailant was equally blind and that it had been a lucky blow.

He saw that the distant lantern bobbed toward him now – almost certainly a second assailant, coming at a run to finish him off. The word "imbecile" was no doubt writ large on his own face where the shovel had struck him. Then he realized that he was looking upriver and not down – that the lantern was coming down from *above* – two lanterns, in fact, come to rescue him. He heard his assailant's splashing footfalls receding down the tunnel. There was no lantern to be seen downstream at all now, no sound of turning axles, nothing but dark silence.

TWO

HOME AT LAST

"You say that you followed these men into the darkness alone, Langdon?" Alice asked.

"Not *men*, do you see. One man."

"But you said that you believed one to be pushing a cart with a lantern on it while the other one lurked behind to waylay you. I count two."

"*Lurked*, as you so accurately put it. I had no idea of anyone lurking, not until he sprang out at me." St. Ives helped himself to a second slice of cold beef and kidney pie and poured more ale from the pitcher on the breadboard. Moonlight shone through the bullseye glass in the kitchen window, casting circular shadows on the wall behind him.

"Lurkers are clever that way," she said. "They've been schooled in the art of lurking. That's why one doesn't wade into dark tunnels to seek them out. You've still got black grit along the edge of the wound." She dipped a cloth in a basin of water and wiped gingerly at the dried blood.

The wind had come up outside, and the night beyond the wall was alive with moaning and creaking. It had been a hellish trip out from London – a three-hour wait outside

Gravesend for repairs to be made to the tracks, and with every hour that passed St. Ives had regretted not having taken a coach. Walking would have made considerably more sense than waiting, or at least wouldn't have been so wretchedly frustrating. Despite the noise of the wind, Alice had opened the front door the moment she heard him step up onto the veranda half an hour ago. She had been up waiting for him, perhaps watching from the bedroom window upstairs.

"You're quite fortunate that you were turning away from him," she said, peering closely at his face. "He might easily have disfigured you. You'll have an untidy scar."

Her dark hair was tousled from sleep, giving her a slightly wild air, and she wore a silk robe that made her appear... lithe, perhaps. She was tall, nearly six feet, and under certain circumstances could appear to be quite formidable – at the present moment, in fact – largely because of her eyes, which had the keenness of those of a predatory bird, and were intensely beautiful. It seemed to him now that he had been away a foolishly long time, and he wondered what she was wearing beneath the robe.

"What I feel most," he said, shifting the subject into a safer realm, "is the death of the book thief. I didn't want that. I'm certain that I behaved as a complete flat throughout. The escapade seems to me too contrived, elaborately choreographed up until the point of the man's death, which was a grotesque accident."

"But it's done now, if I follow your story correctly."

"Done and done, as was I – done to a turn."

"Indeed. First by this mysterious book thief, and then

by yourself, and then by a man with a coal shovel."

"By myself, do you say?"

"You went into the tunnel out of a sense of guilt, it would seem. You had failed to solve the first crime, and in fact blamed yourself for compounding it. So you set out into the sewer to put things right as a salve to your conscience."

He sat in silence considering this. It sounded logical enough to him, although equally unfair. Human motivation was surely more complex than this.

"At the time," he said to her, "it seemed to me that there was a man's murderer to catch, and it was within my power to do so."

"Good enough. But you're also telling me that you had Tubby Frobisher close at hand, but you failed to invite him to join you in the pursuit of this murderer, this anarchist?"

"I'm not persuaded that anarchy had anything to do with it," he said.

"Ah, surely that makes a great difference. Were you worried that Tubby would be discommoded, then?"

"Tubby? Of course not. He would have seen it as sport. You know Tubby."

"Indeed I do. I'm baffled that you didn't know him a little better yourself when you decided to go sporting in the sewer alone." She tossed the cloth onto the tabletop, stepped back, and gave him a steady look, staring not at the wound on his cheek, but into his eyes, holding his gaze. It wouldn't do to look away, and clearly it was best not to answer. "The next time you behave like an impulsive schoolboy and witlessly put yourself in danger, you won't have to go into a sewer in order to be beaten with a coal shovel. I can

34

accommodate you in that regard right here at home."

He had a difficult time swallowing his mouthful of pie, but he nodded his head with what he hoped was agreeable determination.

"There exist in London what have come to be called 'the police,'" she continued. "You seem already to be aware of that fact. I distinctly recall your mentioning only five minutes ago that at least one of them was there on the grounds of the Club not long after the blast, before you made your foray into the tunnel. Did it occur to you that they might take some interest in the very thing that was interesting you at that moment?"

"I... It seemed to me that..."

"It seems to me that I don't want a dead husband, Langdon, and your children don't want a dead father. Can you grasp that? I believe that the cat has sufficient genius to catch my meaning. Easier than catching a mouse, I should think. It's not your business to bring anarchists and book thieves to justice in any event. I honor you for your bravery and sacrifice, you know that, but... For God's *sake*, Langdon!"

"Of course," St. Ives said. "Of course. Quite right." He reached for his glass and was sorry to find it empty. It came to him abruptly that she was more distraught than he had imagined – more distraught than angry. He wondered whether she was on the verge of tears, something that was blessedly rare, but far worse than anger when it happened. He felt hollow and wretched. She glared at him now, shaking her head as if confounded by his antics. In that moment he knew that it was as good as done. She would let him down easily after all.

Alice picked up the pitcher of ale and filled his glass. "Drink it," she said. "You'll sleep better. You look done up."

"In a moment, Alice. Have a look at these." He reached into his coat pockets and began to haul out chunks of begonia rhizome. There hadn't been an opportunity earlier, but now that the storm had begun to clear, the promise of exotic begonias might chase it over the horizon. "I haven't any idea what species. Shorter had a recent lot from Brazil, and this could easily be them, or pieces of them, rather." He drew more from his trouser pockets, and then opened his portmanteau, which sat nearby on the floor, and picked several more from among his things. "They rained down over the lawn when…" Abruptly he pictured Shorter lying dead on the grass, and the enthusiasm went out of him.

"They'll abide here quite well until tomorrow morning," she told him, arranging them alongside the sink. "You, however, will do better in bed. I'm more than a little tired of it being empty."

~~ THREE ~~
THE AYLESFORD SKULL

D r. Narbondo watched as the woman, Mary Eastman by name, crossed the green and stepped over the stile into the Aylesford churchyard. Even in the moonlight he could see that there was an element of angry pride in her walk, nothing furtive or fearful, as if she had some hard words for him and was anxious to throw them into his face after all these years. "Careful you don't take a fall," he muttered, but at the same time he was aware that she still had a certain beauty, her hair still red, as he remembered it. He stepped clear of the shadow of the tomb behind him and stood at the edge of the open grave with its small headstone.

She stood staring at him, the grave standing between them now. "Of course," she said. "I knew it would be you. I prayed that you were dead, but my prayers clearly went unanswered. I wanted to be certain."

"Prayer is indeed uncertain, Mary. Flesh and blood are certain enough." He affected a smile. The night was warm, the air clear and dry. In the grave lay a broken coffin and a scattering of bones, the skull conspicuously missing. A high mound of soil lay heaped at the head of the grave, burying the foot of the headstone. Hidden behind the nearby tomb lay the body of the sexton, his coat soaked in blood. He had taken Narbondo's money happily enough, and had been richer for the space of some few seconds. Until Narbondo had made up his mind, he wouldn't let Mary see the dead sexton or the skull that he had taken from the grave.

"The years haven't been kind to you," she said bitterly, choosing to look into his face rather than into the grave. "You've grown a hump, which is as it should be. It's the mark of Cain, sure as I'm standing here."

"The years are never kind," he said. "But in any event I have no interest in kindness. As for the hump, I'm disappointed that you would cast such stones. That was never your way, Mary."

"My *way*? What do you know of my ways, then or now? I deny that you know me."

"And yet you knew that it was I when you received the note. Surely you did. Edward's ghost is restless, but it hasn't taken to writing missives. And yet despite your knowledge you came freely. That gives me a degree of hope." He kept his voice tempered. There would be no hint of pleading or desire – quite the opposite. Just an even-handed statement of the facts, such as they had undeniably come to be over the long years.

Abruptly she began to weep, the moonlight shining on her face. A breeze stirred the leaves in a nearby willow. Somewhere in the village a dog barked and then fell silent, and there was the low sound of a horse's whinny nearby and its hoof scuffing against loose stones. She looked up at the scattering of stars, as if searching for solace. He found the gesture tiresome.

"I thought that you would profit from seeing my half-brother's condition," he said to her, looking about to ascertain that they were indeed alone. "I won't say 'brother,' for he was never more than half alive to me. The flesh is gone from the bones now, and the skull, the salient part of his skeleton, is missing, as you can see for yourself. He was half a brother and half a man – half a *boy*, to be more precise – and in death he remains so. Your kindness to him was laudable, no doubt, but misconceived. Sentimentality pays a very small dividend."

She stared at him now with a loathing that was clearly written in her features. "What do you want?" she asked. "It's late, and I'm weary of hearing your voice."

"You ask a direct question. Excellent," he said. "I have a simple proposition. I want your hand in marriage. You're a spinster, with no prospects other than that doom that awaits us all, some of us sooner than others." He gestured at the grave by way of explanation. "I can offer you wealth and freedom from want. I won't press my affections upon you, however. In short, I desire what was rightfully mine thirty years ago when you were a girl of fifteen. Think carefully before you deny me."

"*Rightfully yours?* Do you say so? You hanged your own brother from a tree branch, leering at him as he swung there choking. It's my undying shame that I was too cowardly to come forward, although I still can, and you know that. You have no right to ask anything of anyone but forgiveness, which I can assure you you'll never find on Earth. Even your own mother despises you. I've been told that you've changed your name. No doubt you despise yourself."

"I have the right to do as I please, Mary, including abandoning a name that I had grown to loathe. And the truth is, as we both know, Edward would have hanged himself eventually, or some such thing, if I hadn't done him the kindness. He was a sniveling little toad. As for your not coming forward when you might have, that was simply good sense. Surely you recall our bargain, and so you know that your silence has so far gained you thirty years of life. Now I'm offering you that same bargain again, except that the life that I would grant you is considerably more handsome than the life you enjoy. You're a serving wench, or so I'm told, in my own mother's employ. Or is it a mere charwoman? It amounts to charity in either event. I tell you plainly that you might have servants of your own, if that's what you desire."

She stared at him as if he were insane. "I'd sooner die," she said.

He nodded, momentarily silent, and then said, "You've always been a woman who spoke plainly, Mary, when you chose to speak. One thing, though, before you take your leave…"

He turned and drew out his murdered brother's skull from where it sat atop the wall of the tomb behind him, holding it out to her as if it were an offering. She stared at it in horror, recoiling from it. Unlike the dry bones in the grave, the skull had a mocking semblance of life: the hollows of the eyes were set with illuminated silver orbs, the mouth agape, the skull itself trepanned, the opening fitted with a clockwork mechanism beneath a crystal shell. It sat on a polished wooden base, like a trophy.

"Your paramour has been well-treated, as you can see,"

he said. "In life he accounted for nothing, but in death, thanks to the skills of his own loathsome father, he has ascended to something very like the plain of glory."

Narbondo's interest was drawn to a movement beneath a heavy branch of the willow, a shifting glow like misty candlelight on the fine curtain of leaves. He peered at it, turning his head slightly to the side to see it more clearly. He returned the skull to its resting place, and then nodded for Mary's benefit at the figure that was slowly taking shape in the light that hovered within the wavering shadows. "The ghost walks," he whispered.

The semblance of a boy, Narbondo's murdered brother, paced silently toward them, his hand outstretched, the animated branches of the willow visible through his transparent body. He seemed to see Mary standing before him, and she put her hand to her mouth in happy surprise. The ghost flickered in the moonlight, winking away and then reappearing beneath the branch as before, walking toward them again over the same ground, reaching out as if there were something that he wanted – to touch Mary's hand, perhaps. Again he flickered away, and again he reappeared and set out. His mouth worked, as if he were trying to find words that had been choked out of him thirty years ago.

Mary started toward the ghost, sobbing aloud now, putting out her arms as if to embrace it. In that moment Narbondo sprang across the open grave like an ape, his black cloak flying behind him, a knife glinting in the hand that had held the skull only moments before. She heard him alight, and she spun around, looking in horror at the knife, reaching upward to stop the hand that swept toward her, but too late. The force of the blow knocked her over backward, blood spraying from her lacerated neck, welling out of her voiceless throat where she lay now on the ground beside the open grave. She tried to push herself up onto her elbows but fell back again and lay still.

Narbondo saw that there was a rose-shaped spattering of her blood on the headstone, shining crimson in the moonlight, which struck him as slightly theatrical, although entirely fitting. It would bloom there considerably longer than would a living rose, especially after the summer sun had baked it into the stone.

FOUR
THE WEIR

With two hours remaining before the tidal surge, the river below Aylesford was shallow, slow moving, and deserted. The day was warm and the breeze had dropped, so that the silent afternoon had a brooding and timeless air, the shadows deep and still along the wooded shore. Alice St. Ives, wearing men's trousers and India rubber wading boots over her shoes, moved farther into the river, throwing her fishing line into the deep waters behind the weir, jigging it hard, feeling it jerk once and then release. Something was interested in it.

She was fishing her own lure, tied up out of peacock feathers, silver wire, and a strip of green wool with a barbless treble hook. She had lost two big pike in the last twenty minutes, although it might have been the same pike twice. Both of them had thrown the hook, which was frustrating, but she was anxious not to do any damage to the fish's lips with a barbed hook, since her goal was taxidermy and not dinner. There was nothing wrong with pike stuffed with ground veal and tiny pearl onions out of the garden, though, and she might have Mrs. Langley roast one for the family after all if she caught nothing larger than the single fish that lay now in her creel.

She found that she was distracted by the silence, and her gaze was drawn again to the forest, her mind running on the unpleasant idea that someone was hidden among the trees, watching her. It was a foolish apprehension. She had actually seen nothing, and nothing stirred now in the dead air. The only sound was the tiny chatter made by small stones in the moving water that flowed out of the narrow passage in the weir. She looked back downriver at her creel – an oversized salmon basket, big enough to hold a pike. It was apparently still lodged securely among the stones on the river bottom.

She'd had to kill the pike when she'd caught it half an hour ago. Despite the damage from the gaff, the ten-pound fish was ferocious enough to tear the creel apart if it were given a chance. She had used a pike-gag to hold its mouth open in order to work the hook out of the tongue, but the creature had twisted in her grip, dislodged the gag, and lacerated her hand with its teeth. Now the fish rested in wet moss, which, along with the cool river water, would keep it fresh. She wanted a larger fish if she could catch one, for the sake of the head, which she intended to mount on a plaque and give to her husband. There was a particular giant living in the weir, which she'd had on her line more than once. Langdon had volunteered to persuade it to the surface with a nitroglycerin bomb, but Alice was a proponent of fairness, especially when it came to fishing.

Their friend Tubby Frobisher had brought the greenheart wood for her fishing rod back from an expedition to South America. It looked like English walnut, but was light and flexible, the ten-foot-long rod weighing only a couple of pounds despite the heavy fittings. It was too short for salmon or trout fishing, but perfect for the kind of coarse fishing that was Alice's passion. She had caught a heavy-bodied carp with the pole in the pond on their own property – an enormous thing with scales the size of twopenny pieces, black with burnished gold slashes on the side and a golden underbelly, quite the most beautiful thing she had ever seen. Unfortunately the fixative that St. Ives had developed had failed to harden the skin, and in the end the carp was ruined, which seemed an almost criminal offense to her. She would try his newly reconstituted fixative on the pike, if she managed to land him.

She threw out the line again, but in the moment of silence that followed she heard a snapping and stirring of underbrush in the trees. She looked sharply in the direction of the sound, holding her breath and making an effort to sort out the shadows and the mottled sunlight. A man was standing there – she saw his figure clearly now – some fifty feet into the wood among the oak and chestnut trees. He was tall and thin and was standing perfectly still, his green shirt illuminated by a ray of sunlight. Certainly he knew he could be seen.

She resisted the urge to wade to the opposite bank, retrieve her creel, and walk back downriver to the farm. She and her husband had only lived on the place for a couple of months, having inherited it from her Aunt Agatha Walton, but Alice had already come to consider this quiet stretch of the Medway her own, and she was damned if she were going to flee from a shadow. She could acquaint the man with the hook of her gaff, if it came to it. A gaffed wrist or neck would be a most unpleasant thing.

She realized now that the figure had disappeared, but she was still uneasy. She would far rather know where he was than not know. Her rod dipped, and there was a tentative jerk on the lure. Nothing. The pike was teasing her. She reminded herself that there was a path in the wood. It was no crime for people to use the path on their way to and from the village of Aylesford. One could walk all the way to Maidstone that way more quickly than along the road. That no doubt accounted for the man she had just seen. The sight of a woman dressed as Alice was dressed and fishing the Medway for pike might easily strike a foot traveler as amusing or curious. In any event, clearly he had moved on.

Her line jerked heavily now and instantly began to run through the eye on the float, taking her by surprise. The big pike exploded out of the lumber of driftwood along the shore. She could see it swim in the clear water, angling fast toward the top of the weir, perfectly enormous. She stopped the line from spinning out of the reel and set the hook hard, fixing the rubber butt of the rod into the leather depression in the belt below her waist, gripping the cork handle tightly and watching the tip bow and bend as the pike raced upriver toward her again, weaving through the water, then turning and heading back. She reeled in the line, heaving the rod back against the considerable weight of the fish, putting her back into it. The sun glinted on the surface of the weir, nearly blinding her despite her blue-tinted goggles as she worked her way backwards toward shore.

She heard a sharp cry from behind her, and she glanced into the trees but still saw nothing. It had been a man's voice, pained and high, as if he had been knocked on the head. She felt the pike turn abruptly, pulling heavily on the pole, which slipped out of its anchorage and twisted in her hands before the big fish yanked it entirely out of her grasp with a force that astonished her. The pole rocketed away across the weir. Alice staggered forward, stepping into a deep hole so that the river ran freely into her waders, which were leaden with the weight of the water in a matter of moments. She slogged to shore, climbed heavily up the bank, removed the boots, and drained them. She could see the pole right enough from her higher vantage point, its cork handle visible in the sunlight, its tip borne down by the pike, which was a monstrous thing, surely forty pounds if it were an ounce, taking into account the magnification of the water.

The fish disappeared from view, darting into the depths among the waterweeds and stones. Suddenly the pole shot forward, jammed into the stones, and the line snapped, the tip of the pole ascending slowly toward the surface, the base held down by the metal reel. She slipped her waders back on and went in again to fetch it, hooking it with the gaff in order to draw it to her. The peacock feather lure, the best she had ever tied, was no doubt lost forever.

At least she had the fish in the creel, she thought, removing her wading boots again and setting out along the bank. But the fish in the creel was small compared to the sea monster from the weir – definitely something to be eaten rather than hung on the wall. She bent over to pick up the creel, but stopped, her hand hovering over the handle.

She looked at it curiously, fear rising within her again. The basket was still firmly set among the stones on the river bottom, but one of the stones that should have anchored its handle had been pushed aside and lay now a foot away. She was certain of it. The stone was boxy, some dark stone. There it lay, where she hadn't put it. Someone else had put it there. The creel sat in shallower water, too. The pike lay inside the creel as ever, although the moss had been pushed aside and then rearranged, leaving the top half of the fish uncovered and dry.

Who had done this – the man she had seen standing among the trees? Why hadn't he merely stolen the fish, which could feed a moderately large family? He must have been remarkably curious if he had simply wanted to get a look at it. She stared at the fish for another moment, then hoisted the creel over her forearm and started off along the shore once again, looking into the wood with a heightened sense of suspicion. She unfastened the gaff from where it hung at her side and gripped the handle. Carrying the gaff in one hand and the creel in the other meant leaving the waders, but she would be less encumbered. The man would think twice about approaching her once he'd had a look at the business end of the gaff. Soon she was entirely out of sight around the swerve of the shore, and in fifteen minutes she was home again.

The sun shone through the intertwined branches of the wisteria alley, stippling the path. Away to her left the hop plants were shockingly green, climbing up their twining supports toward the heavens. She saw that Eddie and his sister Cleo were playing at tin soldiers on the broad veranda,

Cleo laughing and bowling through Eddie's troops with a siege engine towed by a mechanical elephant that was a marvel of moving gears, visible through a sort of Momus's glass set into the elephant's belly. The wind-up engine had been contrived for the children by William Keeble, the preternaturally brilliant London toymaker and inventor, who had long been Langdon's friend.

Young Finn Conrad, the gardener's apprentice, was cultivating the soil in the flowerbeds nearby, clearing fresh weeds from around a riot of pansies and foxgloves and marigolds. Finn had come into their lives a year ago, having endured a hard passage on the streets of London for a time before that, after tramping down the North Road from Edinburgh when he was eleven years old, taking six months on the journey. He had grown up in Duffy's Circus and had manifold talents, of which they knew only a small part. He spoke less of what he had learned on the road and shifting for himself on the London streets and docks than about what he had learned in the circus, although no doubt both of those worldly schools were colorful in their course of study. He could ride a horse as if he were born to it, which he had been, and he was an astonishing tumbler and acrobat, with a fearlessness that made Alice pale on occasion, and which she very much hoped would not appeal to Eddie beyond a merely useful degree.

Finn stopped hoeing for a moment, apparently giving Eddie advice about troop movements, and then he saw Alice and waved heartily. She knew that Finn was a little bit in love with her, which was endearing, although it was only one of many endearing things about the boy, who was honest and forthright to a fault. The summer afternoon was so serene, and the scene so idyllic, that Alice felt abruptly foolish to be carrying the gaff, and she regretted having abandoned the waders, which ran the risk of being stolen by the lurker in the wood.

"Did you catch him?" Finn asked

"I did not," Alice told him. "He stole my newly tied fly and nearly took my pole into the bargain. But I know where he lives now. He can't hide from me."

She greeted the children, who marveled at the pike in the creel, especially its enormous mouth and teeth. Eddie immediately saw its military potential as a counter to the elephant, but Alice closed the top of the creel, pointing out the fish's potential as supper, which failed to impress either of the children.

"I've built a parachute, Mother, in order to launch soldiers from an airship like the one Father is to have." Eddie showed her a spotted handkerchief, cut into an octagon, the corners tied with string, the bottom ends tied around the neck of a marine.

"It doesn't work," Cleo put in. "He's killed seven soldiers trying."

"I have not," Eddie said. "One's broken his leg, that's all. I set it with a splint."

He broke off, seeing that Cleo was again mobilizing the elephant, and Alice leaned her fishing rod against the corner of the veranda and carried the creel into the house, where she found her husband sitting on the big upholstered chair next to a sunny window in the drawing room, his long legs resting atop an ottoman, Hodge the cat stretched out asleep across his knees.

Alice had bought the chair and ottoman in London, courtesy of Aunt Agatha's estate. The chair was one of the new coil-spring affairs with a vast amount of padding. Most of the furnishings in the house had belonged to her aunt, and were in varying degrees ancient, including the watercolors of wild flowers and fish that hung on the walls. The room, with its Turkey carpets and polished wood-paneling, was somewhat beyond the fashion, which delighted Alice, who found these reflections of the past both comforting and beautiful.

St. Ives looked up from a copy of Benson's *Air Vessels of the Royal Navy*, just now aware that Alice had come in. He wore down-at-heel slippers and the disreputable waistcoat with embroidered orchids and flower petal buttons that he had apparently owned since he was a young man at the university, when he was something more of a Bohemian. It was much frayed and was rubbed through at the collar, but he generally put it on when he was in an expansive, cheerful mood. The carpet roundabout the chair was littered with drawings, books, and catalogues.

"One week!" he said to her happily.

"Until…?"

"Until the vessel is airworthy. Or so Keeble tells me." He picked up a letter from the table next to the chair and waved it at her. "It came in today's post. Keeble has laid out the particulars – the miniaturization, the motive power. It's a very nearly fabulous craft, Alice, perhaps the first of its type – a rigid skeleton, do you see, built of bent bamboo, with the skin stretched around it so that it maintains its shape even when it's idle. Hydrogen gas will fill the nose of the craft first, so that it'll be very nearly vertical at launch, with the interior of the gondola remaining level due to its being hung on a pendulum. We'll stow it in the barn. I'm devising a means by which to draw back a vast section of the roof in order to sail her straight up into the sky. Have I mentioned that?"

"Not above a dozen times," she said. "I think it's a grand idea. The family can flee the country at a moment's notice when Scotland Yard finds us out. I'll keep a bag packed and ready."

St. Ives laughed out loud. He was happy enough with his pending airship to be easily amused. "What do you have in the creel?" he asked. "Supper or something to hang on the wall?"

"Supper, I believe. It's been a baffling afternoon."

He set Hodge onto the ground, hauled his legs off the footstool, picked up a scattering of papers from the floor, and set them atop the upholstery. Alice ascertained that the bottom of the creel was dry before settling it on the papers.

"Baffling in what sense?" he asked, opening the creel. "Outwitted by a fish, were you?"

"Yes, but I expected that. He's a wise old fish." She told him about the man in the wood, the crying out, the battle of the weir, and the strange business of someone having meddled with the pike.

The kitchen door opened, and St. Ives's factotum, Hasbro, walked in carrying lemonade on a tray. He and St. Ives had been through so many adventures together that neither *factotum* nor *manservant* quite applied, although it had at one time. Hasbro kept up his old habits, though, which had come to define a small part of him. Alice took a glass gratefully. Fishing was thirsty work. St. Ives pushed aside a mechanical bat that sat on the table – an automaton, built by Lambert in Paris, which was so perfectly contrived that it looked stuffed. He set his glass down and then peered into the creel again.

"You say that someone not only opened this, but examined the fish? And he didn't simply pinch it?"

"Yes. It was the strangest thing, especially given the man hiding among the trees. I was never apparently in any danger, and the fish is comfortable enough, but someone had a highly suspicious interest in the creel and in my fishing. Absolutely nothing came of it, I'm happy to say, although I left my wading boots behind."

"Should I fetch the wading boots, ma'am?" Hasbro asked. "I'm taking my afternoon constitutional shortly. I'd as soon walk along the river as elsewhere."

"Thank you, Hasbro," Alice said to him. "If you don't mind. You won't need to search for them."

St. Ives had his head in the basket now, evidently smelling the fish. He looked up, frowning. "Do you detect an odor?" he asked Hasbro, holding out the creel. "Not the odor of pike, but something else, something musty? I don't believe it to be the moss. Something quite distinct."

Hasbro sniffed the open creel, thought for a moment and sniffed again. "Boiling parsnips," he said. "Certainly neither the moss nor the fish."

"Mouse filth, I was thinking, although parsnips emit the same odor."

"If I were to make a hasty judgment, sir, I'd guess devil's porridge."

"Yes, and almost certainly distilled, not conveniently dredged out of a nearby ditch. There's none of it mixed into the moss."

"Devil's porridge?" Alice asked. "You don't mean to say…"

"Yes," St. Ives told her. "Assuredly it's hemlock. The demise of Socrates distilled into a clear liquid. Look here. The villain has sliced the fish open with something very sharp – a carefully honed knife or perhaps a scalpel – along the edge of the dorsal fin where the incision isn't apparent. He wanted to make sure that the poison invaded the flesh, you see. It's impossible to say how much he poured in or how potent the solution." He picked the fish up by the mouth and tail and turned it over. "No doubt he dumped some here on the gaff wound, also, poisoning the adjacent meat. If you'd simply given this to Mrs. Langley to stuff and poach, we'd all of us be dead by bedtime, Eddie and Cleo included."

"I'll just take a fowling piece with me along to the river," Hasbro said.

"Would you like company?" St. Ives asked.

"The rifle is company enough, I should think. I fear he'll be far away by now."

"Indeed," said St. Ives. "An escaped lunatic, I'd warrant, except that he would have to be a tolerably careful chemist, not that chemists don't run mad as often as the next man. Rather more often, quite likely." He glanced at Alice, who was looking steadily at him.

"Shall I have Mr. Binger dispose of the fish, sir?"

"If you will, Hasbro. Ask him to hack it up and cover it with quicklime, then bury it deeply enough so that Hodge won't get at it."

FIVE

THE RETURN OF THE DEAD

The suggestion that the hemlock fancier had been an escaped lunatic had failed to impress Alice; St. Ives had seen as much in her face, although she hadn't confronted him with it. The crime was too devious, too well thought out, too purposeful. He could think of only one man who might do such a thing, but why that man should be lurking in the environs of north Kent was a mystery to him. The man, an evil genius who called himself Dr. Narbondo, was well acquainted with their previous residence in Chingford. Indeed, Hasbro had chased him from the premises a little under a year ago when he'd come around at night intent on stealing St. Ives's bathyscaphe, which, it had to be admitted, St. Ives had recently stolen from him. But their removal to Aylesford had been kept quiet – no fanfare at all – and in fact he and Alice still owned the farmhouse at Chingford-by-the-Tower, which they now leased to Tubby Frobisher. They weren't *hiding* in Aylesford, but they weren't conspicuous either.

St. Ives walked along the rows of hops, which reached above the top of his head now, his mind sorting through various possibilities. Idly he watched out for the long-winged flies and lice that were the bane of hops, but there was no evidence of such evils. He picked a leaf and crushed it between his fingers. It had a slightly bitter smell. He dropped it, brushing his fingers on his trousers. If the hemlock had simply been torn up and sprinkled onto the pike, he might convince himself that it had been a devilish prank, but this had been something more – the work of someone who had a decoction of hemlock about his person, a determined poisoner, not a prankish devil.

He strolled out into the wisteria alley, looking with satisfaction at the broad green lawn away to his right, where there stood a dozen or so hoppers' huts. They would see considerable activity come September, when the hops were harvested, the grounds becoming a literal fiddler's green during the celebration afterward.

In the distance now, Hasbro approached from the direction of the river, carrying the rifle and rubber waders. St. Ives walked out to meet him.

"Nothing out of the way?" he asked.

"A deepening of the mystery, perhaps." Hasbro reached into one of the waders and drew out a piece of an oak branch, half the length of a cricket bat and stained with blood. "There were two distinct sets of footprints in the soil of the path. I'm persuaded that two men had come down separately from the direction of the village, one stopping near the weir and the other going on to the river's edge where the missus had apparently submerged the creel with the pike in it. Then the single track – the man who poisoned the fish – reversed direction and returned toward the village again, running afoul of the man whom she saw lurking in the wood near where she fished. At that point there was an apparent struggle – a rhododendron trod nearly flat. The shout was almost certainly uttered by the man who was struck with this club. It has a considerable heft to it, and the bloody result argues that the attacker meant to do him a considerable mischief. There was evidence that the stricken man fled into the trees. I found his footprints again some distance away, doubling back toward Aylesford once more after he had eluded his attacker."

"But who struck whom?" asked St. Ives.

"The man who fled into the wood was evidently the same man who had poisoned the fish."

"Did his footprints put you in mind of Narbondo?"

"Quite possibly, or a man of similar size. Nothing certain in that, however."

St. Ives stood silently for a moment, listening to the buzzing of an unseen fly. He heard Eddie's laughter from the direction of the house. "The first man, the poisoner, might have been pursued surreptitiously by the second, I assume?"

"More likely it was mere happenstance," said Hasbro. "If the second man had followed the first with some fell purpose, he wouldn't have tarried near the weir, it would seem. His prey might simply have continued along the river and got away."

"There's no indication that they were companions?"

"No, sir, to the contrary. Their separate tracks led back to the village, where I discovered that they had started out by different routes – one of them from behind the Chequers Inn and the other from the path that runs up into what's known as Hereafter Farm, or so I'm told by the publican at the Chequers."

"Isn't that a spiritualist commune?"

"Indeed, sir. Owned by a woman named Mother Laswell, who, I gather, is widely considered to harbor dark secrets. She has apparently lived in Aylesford these past forty years and is known by everyone, largely because of her reputation for speaking to the dead, and also her public disapproval of the industrial debris created by the paper mills. She's considered to be 'the bane of industry,' according to our publican."

"So the man from Hereafter Farm followed the other?"

"In some sense of that word," said Hasbro. "I wonder if it's conceivable that he observed the other doctoring the pike and took offense to it."

"Knock the man on the head, but leave the poisoned fish lying in the creel?" asked St. Ives. "He would be a tolerably strange guardian angel."

"Indeed he would," Hasbro said. "We're none the wiser, I'm afraid. There's no evident motive for the poisoning, or for our man to be laid out with a stick."

"The lack of motive suggests Narbondo," St. Ives said. "And of course motives invariably exist. We'll find them out in due time, although it would suit me down to the ground if the whole business simply went away. I'm not keen on tumult, Hasbro. I've had too much of it lately. I'm content to live the life of the gentleman farmer and let the planets revolve as they will. Indeed, I've promised Alice as much. But we'll keep our eyes open, certainly."

The two men parted company, Hasbro toward the house

and St. Ives toward the barn. Ahead of him he saw the filled-in pit that Mr. Binger, the groundskeeper, had dug to bury the pike, the white quicklime visible in the dirt. His mind began to dwell on the poisoned fish once again, and he found that he was angry, despite the gentleman farmer talk. He had suppressed the anger in front of Alice, and just moments ago, when speaking to Hasbro, he had bid it disappear, but here it was again, returning with a vengeance. Anger, he was certain, was almost always a toxicant, worthy of being buried beneath quicklime. Still, he would know the identity of the poisoner before he was done, which possibly meant a visit to Hereafter Farm and a chat with Mother Laswell.

It was often the case that he saw things more clearly when his mind was occupied elsewhere, and he forced himself now to think about the hiatus in the barn roof – the combination of pulleys and line that he would design to draw back sections of roof along a greased track on behalf of the airship. The undertaking wouldn't be simple, regardless of what he had told Alice. Hasbro, however, had served in the Royal Navy in his youth and was a wizard of tackle. And St. Ives would call on Keeble to help, once the air vessel was fit to take aloft. Together, the three of them would prevail. It occurred to him now that it would require a considerable force to move the sections of roof, given the necessary size of the outlet. A steam engine would do, but he abhorred the noise and the vapors, and certainly it would poison the livestock in the enclosed barn. The inscrutable Mother Laswell would condemn him publicly.

A capstan, perhaps? Surely it would take no more power to shift a section of the roof than it would to lift a large anchor aboard a ship. Cleo's siege engine came into his mind, and he pictured an elephant hauling on the capstan bars, the roof sliding open effortlessly. He let the image stay there, taking a good look at it, and he found that he was attracted to the idea despite its superficial gaudiness. Keeble could no doubt fabricate an automaton, an immense reproduction of Cleo's elephant, but it would cost them the farm to have it built. It occurred to him then that Finn Conrad had grown up in the circus and claimed experience in the training of pachyderms. Finn Conrad, it was true, claimed a number of things, some of them moderately implausible, but in the time that St. Ives had known the boy, he had seen no actual evidence that Finn exaggerated. He would no doubt be overjoyed to train an elephant. The barn would easily accommodate the creature and with room to spare, and, unlike a steam engine, an elephant's vapors would be harmless. Its dung, in fact, might be efficacious as a fertilizer. Eddie and Cleo could ride into Aylesford atop it as if it were a pony.

St. Ives pictured Alice's likely response to the idea, and his smile waned. Convincing Alice to approve of the elephant might be more complicated than engineering the opening of the roof. Perhaps if the elephant weren't mentioned until the work was finished? But that would be a variety of untruth. Alice would see that immediately. She had solid ideas about right behavior, and if St. Ives flew in the face of those ideas, the elephant wouldn't materialize, and he would look like a scrub into the bargain.

It might be simple enough, he thought, if he took Finn into his confidence from the outset. Finn was effortlessly persuasive, sometimes dangerously so. St. Ives wouldn't have to coerce him into prevailing upon Alice; Finn would see the sense in the elephant himself. If St. Ives could contrive a way to make it seem like the boy's idea from the outset…

The barn loomed in front of him now. The sun hung above the horizon, shining into the open door, which would have to be enlarged in order to admit the craft in the first place, since it would arrive long before they'd tackled the roof and found a convenient elephant. Tomorrow he would hire workmen to do the job if Alice had no objection. He walked into the interior, where it was nearly dark beyond the sunlit ground immediately inside the doorway. The dark hill of a haystack lay to his right, and to his left stood the wagon and the two-horse chaise. It was only recently that they had been able to set up in quite such a grand style, courtesy of Aunt Agatha again, who had been a generous old bird, seeing to the well-being of several nieces and nephews in her considerable will. Alice owed her passion for fishing to the old woman, who had claimed a kinship to Izaak Walton and who had traveled through Scotland and Ireland, often alone, relieving the streams of their burden of salmon and trout.

He stood still now, listening hard in the evening quiet and squinting into the deep shadows along the wall. He had seen something moving just now – a renegade sheep, perhaps, having come along home by itself…? He watched the darkness, seeing nothing for a long moment. Then there was firefly sort of flickering, a bit of witch light, dying away on the instant that he saw it, but leaving the shadow of what appeared to be a human image behind, which quickly evaporated into the darkness. It reoccurred, more brightly, the resulting shadow larger, taking on an even more decidedly human shape that was surrounded by an aura of soft, steady light. St. Ives took a tentative step forward, craning his neck to see, the hair standing up on the back of his neck. There was a boy – quite clearly a boy – sitting atop the vinegar keg. He was leaning forward, easily visible now, and no longer merely a shadow.

The sight of him, suffused in the orb of misty light, confounded St. Ives, who was apparently either suffering from impaired vision or some variety of swiftly moving madness. The boy – clearly not Finn Conrad, but more or less the same age – held a stick in his hand. Bent forward at the waist, he was apparently drawing or digging with the stick in the dirt of the barn floor. St. Ives realized with an unsettling shock that he was looking *through* the figure. He could see the slats in the barn wall behind him and the vinegar keg through the boy's legs.

There was no rational explanation for what he thought he saw, and St. Ives despised the irrational. A boy sat on the vinegar keg, right enough, he told himself, and his transparency was evidently an illusion contrived of sunlight and shadow, no doubt easily explainable, if only he could bring his mind to bear on the problem.

"Well, young sir," St. Ives began, finding his voice at last, but the boy did not apparently hear him, and instead of responding he began to fade away, evaporating like steam on a warm day. After a few seconds only a vague, boy-shaped aura remained, the stick evidently holding itself aloft, still marking in the dirt. Abruptly the aura vanished, and the stick fell to the ground.

St. Ives stood blinking, unable to accept what he had clearly seen. His mind denied it. It came to him that he had perhaps been poisoned by the hemlock after all, ingested it somehow, breathed a corruptive waft of the vapor that was only now making itself felt. What next? Paralysis, loss of speech, nausea, the mind remaining clear. He felt none of the symptoms except the clarity of mind. He stepped forward, intent on examining the stick, telling himself that it might yet be warm from the boy's grip – if there had been a boy, which there could not have been. The stick lay at the base of the keg. It hadn't been an illusion. He picked it up, but it told him nothing. It was neither warm nor cold. It was simply inert. He fetched a lantern from a hook in the wall, lit it, adjusted the wick, and held it over the keg. The name "Mary," was scratched very faintly into the hard-packed dirt of the floor.

He crushed his eyes closed, his mind revolving around useless explanations. He thought again of the hemlock, considering the possibility that in his poison-induced madness he himself had unconsciously wielded the stick, scratching the name in the dirt. He thought of women whom he knew with the name "Mary." Surely there were several of them, but he couldn't recall that any of them had passed through his mind in recent weeks or months. Why would he have written that particular name? Further madness?

His ignorance terrified him, and suddenly he very much wanted Alice's company. He turned his back on the vinegar barrel, squinting into the vast glow of the setting sun, which now filled the barn door. In the midst of that light stood the figure of a man, black as tar against the bright sunlight – a tall, narrow shadow with its arms to its sides. St. Ives stifled a surprised shout and stood gaping at the apparition in horror. The sun, blessedly, descended another fathom through the sky, lost a modicum of its brilliance, and the silhouette became a flesh and blood human being – a man whom St. Ives knew well enough, and he also knew that the man had been dead these eight years past.

SIX

THE RETURN OF BILL KRAKEN

"I've come back," the man in the doorway said in a living voice – the voice of Bill Kraken, an old friend.

"From the dead?" asked St. Ives, his mind still swimming from the ghostly figure on the vinegar barrel, trying to equate the phenomenon of the transparent boy with the ghost of Bill Kraken, but having no luck.

"That's not far off, sir. I've been good as dead six times over, and I despaired of coming home. But the fates is strange bedfellows, as they say, even when they're sober, which ain't often."

With an effort St. Ives yanked his mind back on course, forced some dignity into his demeanor, and stepped forward, putting out his hand. The hand that met his was solid enough. Kraken had aged, to be sure, but there was something steady about him now, not so much of the cockeyed slope to his features which had lent him the visage of a resident of Bedlam back in the days when he was selling peapods on the streets of London and was known as "Mad Bill." He was tall and narrow and walked with a tilt, his shock of hair angled away in the opposite direction.

"By God, I'm happy to see you, Bill," St. Ives said. "We thought you were lost to the Morecambe sands all those years ago. Jack and I found your wagon and your pony on the bottom of the bay just a year back."

"Old Stumpy!" Kraken said, clearly still lamenting the death of the pony. He shook his head sadly. "How did he look?"

"Tolerably skeletal, to tell you the truth. I was happy enough not to find your own skeleton still driving the wagon, in the employ of Davey Jones."

"It was a near-run thing, sir. I leapt clear of the wagon, do you see, onto a little rocky shingle that lay above the sands, but was nought but an island. I couldn't do a blessed thing but sit where I was while poor Stumpy went under, along with the device. It would have been death, pure and simple, to do ought else. I failed poor Stumpy, and I failed you, sir, and I've come to ask your forgiveness."

"There's no call for it, Bill. You're quite right about the sands. It would have been death for you to venture off your bit of solid ground. And as for the device, as you call it, we've fetched it home again, safe as it ever was, so there's no failing there, either."

The two men walked out of the deepening shadows of the barn, into the twilit evening. The air still carried the warmth of the afternoon, and there was the smell of blossom on the breeze. An owl flew past overhead, circled around, and landed on a branch of a nearby oak, regarding the two men openly. Kraken bowed to it – a little nod of the head, and the owl seemed to nod back, as if they were old friends.

"How did you win free in Morecambe, Bill, when the tide came up? And where have you been, for all that? We've often thought about you, Alice and I."

"I've been here and there, sir, more than anywhere else. I'd most given up, there on Morecambe Bay. I was safe enough from the Doctor, but I was surrounded by the quicksands and daren't move. When old Stumpy was gone I was alone and sad-like, thinking about him, and I made up my mind to shift, for better or worse. I'd either walk clear of the sands or follow old Stumpy down. But right then the tide come up raging – the Red Sea come again, sir, with no Moses at hand. The flood picked me up like a blessed leaf and bore me away. I nearly drowned four times a-sailing up the bay, and then I was caught up in some kind of river and was swept down again along the shoreline, going like billy-o, and it was all I could do to raise my head up into the blessed air and take a gulp before I was topsy-turvy again. I found myself in deep water by and by, out in Morecambe Bay proper, where I latched on to a drift log and floated half the night before I was picked up by a cutter out in the Irish Sea.

"It turned out she was a smuggler with a full hold, running for the Irish coast with a sloop hot behind, its guns loaded with grape, or so I was told. The captain was a God-fearing man, or he wouldn't have hove to and picked me up. They come around fast, fished me out with a hook, and were away again, with me wet and shivering and the seas coming in through the scuppers. It was the delay that cost them their liberty, for the sloop came upon us off what they call the Mountains of Mourne, when we were nearly ashore. They put a four-pound ball through the mainsail and we swung up into the wind, not being fond of death."

"The smugglers vouched for you, certainly?"

"Aye, they did, but damn-all good it did me. I was transported, and thank God I wasn't hanged."

"*Transported?*" St. Ives said. "That was given up years back."

"Tell that to the judge, sir. That's what them that spoke for me did. They told the Beak that I was flotsam that they'd fished out o' the drink, but the judge was a right devil, sir, set up in robes and a wig, and transported me is just what he did. No, sir – what's been given up and what ain't been given up is sometimes tolerably similar, if you follow me, depending on who's doing the giving and the taking. I was four years shearing sheep outside Port Jackson before I won free and set out for home again."

"And now you're living hereabouts? We're neighbors? It scarcely seems plausible."

"Yes, sir. I'm out on Hereafter Farm."

St. Ives found himself nearly speechless for a moment. "That would be Mother Laswell's community of spiritualists?"

"Right as rain, sir. When I run off from Port Jackson I took ship and worked my way back, but I was right worried about being taken up again, and so I slipped ashore by night at Allhallows and lived in the marshes for a time, looking after the flocks for a man named Spode. We didn't see eye to eye, though, and I made my way south afoot, down along the Medway, where I come upon Mother Laswell, whose horse had lost a shoe. She was sitting by her cart, all to seek, along with the boy Simonides, who was helpless. I lent a hand, seen her home to Hereafter, and stayed on."

"You've been there since?"

"Nigh onto three years now. The farm harbored some

bad sorts – I seen that straightaway – hangers on, you might say, taking and not giving, treating her shabby. 'Mother Laswell,' I told her, 'you need new fittings on the garden pump, but you need a tugboat and a pilot a sight worse than that.' Things had gone adrift on the Hereafter, you see, on account of her having a heart the size of a tub. Once she took someone in, she couldn't bear to put them out, and they knew it. I could bear it, though, and I set out to tidy things up with a broom and spittle, as they say. I found my sixth sense on account of Mother Laswell, who one fine day I mean to marry, if she'll have me."

"Your sixth sense?"

"I know that's not your way, sir, the mysteries of the spirits and suchlike, but I'll tell you plainly that you've had spirits hereabout, right there in the barn just now, or I'm a hedge pig. It was the boy, wasn't it, a-searching for his Mary?"

St. Ives gaped at Kraken now, every iota of his scientific soul screaming in protest. "How on *Earth* do you know that?" he asked. "You *saw* the figure of the boy, didn't you? Sitting on the keg? Surely you were standing in the doorway?"

"No, sir, I weren't. When I come up along the side of the barn I could *feel* him thereabouts, and quick enough I could see it in your face that you did, too. But I wasn't standing in no doorway until you saw me a-standing in it. How do I know it was the boy? Because his spirit's fluttering hereabouts, unsettled like. They're nought but moths, you see, spirits is, with no blessed place to go unless someone bottles them up and takes them away."

At that moment Alice appeared from around the side of the barn and stood looking at Kraken's back. Her face had turned ashen, and for a moment St. Ives thought she would faint, although fainting wasn't really in her nature. Kraken, seeing something in St. Ives's demeanor, turned slowly around, looked for a moment at Alice, and then took his hat off and bent his head.

"Bill Kraken, ma'am, in case you've forgot me."

"Of course I haven't forgotten you, Bill. Never in life." She stepped forward resolutely, took his hand, and looked hard at him. "It was *you* today, wasn't it, along by the river?"

"Yes, ma'am. It were."

St. Ives was aswim yet again. "By the river?" he asked Alice.

"The figure I saw in among the trees this afternoon, wearing that same green shirt."

"Of course!" St. Ives said, everything coming clear in a rush. "You were the one who came into the wood from Hereafter Farm. The man who wielded the club. My brain must be full of wool."

"That were me as well. I was coming along through the trees when I caught sight of the missus fishing the old weir. I scarce could credit it. I thought my senses had give out. I knew that Miss Agatha Walton was gone on to glory, and that someone had moved into the farmhouse, but I didn't know it was you. You was dug so far in at Chingford that I couldn't feature it, even when I saw Alice with my two eyes. I stood there a-watching her, and it made my heart glad as an oyster. Then I heard someone coming along the other way, and I stepped into the trees not wanting to be seen, and I weren't seen, although I myself seen well enough, and you can believe me when I say that had I been a carp, the sight would have took the scales off my forearm when I realized who he was. Your old enemy, sir.

"I picked up a stout piece of oak that lay there on the ground, stepped out onto the path, caught up with him in three strides, and laid him out. I thought I'd done for him, but he was up again and staggering. I could see that he was wondering whether he knew me. He'd seen me before, here and there. The last time it was the back of me he seen, driving that wagon over the sands at Morecambe Bay all them years back, but I didn't remind him of it. I raised the stick again, meaning to take his head off, but he bolted into the trees, bleeding like a pig in a butcher's yard. I would have made a job of it, too, I can tell you. My blood was up.

"I went back on up to Hereafter and my blood come down a fraction. I took to thinking that he might turn me in to the constabulary, which I couldn't afford, and I'd find myself in Newgate Prison this time, a-swinging from a gibbet and dreaming of Port Jackson after all. But then I got to thinking about Alice and about you, sir, and I was main happy that you was here in Aylesford, and I knew that I must seek you out and tell you about meeting the Doctor in the wood. I had some hope that you could mayhaps speak to Mother Laswell, too, and shed some light on the murder of Mary Eastman and this grave robbery, which give rise to poor Edward's ghost, God rest the boy's soul. And that's my tale, sir, first to last."

For the space of a long moment the evening was dead silent. Then the owl flew out of the oak tree, beating the air. Kraken waved his hand in a parting salute to the bird without taking his eyes from St. Ives's face.

"Narbondo, do you say?" St. Ives asked as the two men moved toward the house.

"It was him, sure enough – the creature who calls himself Narbondo."

"You're quite certain?"

"Aye, that I am, and it was him who murdered poor Mary Eastman and robbed his dead brother's grave of what they call the Aylesford Skull."

St. Ives could make nothing of this last part, but he knew that grave robbery and murder were nothing to an old hand like Narbondo, and it would have given the man vast pleasure to drench the pike in hemlock, knowing that Alice, whom he would recognize easily enough, would take it along home. St. Ives hadn't wanted to believe it, despite his suspicions. He had wanted their corner of the world to be at peace. Even now it came into his mind to hope that Narbondo had fled, that he would be anxious to put some distance between himself and the scenes of his various crimes.

He heard Cleo's laughter now, and the homely sound of Mrs. Langley working in the kitchen. Eddie stood atop the stepladder on the veranda, experimenting with his parachute, which caught the breeze now and very nearly worked. There was the smell of blossom on the breeze, which lent the summer evening a quality that might conceivably be matched in Heaven, but surely nowhere else. He wondered abruptly what Alice was thinking, but he could read nothing in her face.

"Is there evidence, Bill, that it was Narbondo who committed the crime?" he asked. "Certain enough to hang the man?"

"No, sir. Not so as to say 'evidence.' The law is a mortal

idiot when the fit's upon it. That's why I knocked him on the head with the stick when I saw my opportunity. Mother Laswell told me it was him, you see, come back home after all these years to finish what he fomentated as a boy. She saw the murder in the churchyard through the boy Edward's dead eyes. She woke up in the middle of the night with it. You'll tell me that it don't stand to reason, but that's the way with Mother Laswell. She don't care a groat for reason. When I caught sight of the Doctor a-sneaking along the path, I knew what she said was true as a piece of scripture."

"When was Mary Eastman murdered, Bill?" Alice asked.

"Last night, ma'am. After midnight it must have been, for Mary was seen walking in the village late, on her way to the rendezvous, no doubt. He cut her throat in the churchyard, pushed her into an open grave, and left her to bleed out. Murdered the sexton into the bargain."

"There you have it," St. Ives said to Alice, who couldn't keep the effect of Kraken's words out of her face. "We know who dosed the pike. Clearly he learned that we had settled here in Aylesford, and he saw it as his great good luck to be able to compound his crime. A happy coincidence from his point of view."

"He would do that?" Alice asked. "Poison children?"

"It would give him great pleasure," St. Ives told her. "And he has no love for you, not after the hard way you treated him at Eastbourne."

"My only regret is that we didn't shoot the man and cast his body from the cliff," Alice said in a dead-even voice.

Kraken gaped at Alice, as if not quite sure what to make of this pronouncement.

"Sorry to be so bloody minded, Bill," Alice told him, "but I've had my fill of this Dr. Narbondo. Hasbro has put up some lemonade, if you'd like a glass. And you can meet Eddie and Cleo, our children. You'll be Uncle William from this night on."

"I'd like that above all things, but would you come out to Hereafter, sir?" Kraken asked St. Ives. "Would you hear her out? Quick-like?"

"*Now*, Bill? There's perhaps no great hurry. The Doctor will have gone on his way, surely. No murderer tarries in the neighborhood of the crime, not a murderer as conspicuous as Narbondo at any rate."

"Meaning no disrespect, sir, but what you seen in the barn tells otherwise."

"Does it Bill?"

"Aye, it does. You know the Doctor better than any man alive, sir, better than Mother Laswell, despite that she raised him from a baby, and…"

"*Raised him from a baby?*" St. Ives was dumbfounded once again.

"Yes, sir. She was his own natural mother. She give him his Christian name, which he threw onto the rubbish heap along with his soul. He's been gone these thirty years, but now he's come back, and he's stolen the Aylesford Skull, the one object that he must not have, and Mother Laswell fears that it's the end of all things holy if he puts it to use. Come along and speak with her, sir. I've got no living right to ask anything of you, and I wouldn't ask it, neither. But for the sake of us all, I must."

A mule greeted them as they walked up the lamp-lit path to the rambling stone farmhouse occupied by Mother Laswell and her people.

"This is old Ned Ludd," Kraken said to St. Ives, who scratched the mule's forehead. The creature showed its enormous teeth in a wide grin.

"Named after the leader of the infamous Luddites, I take it," St. Ives said, thinking of Mother Laswell's grudge against industry.

"That he is. He's the guardian of the estate these last twenty years. Mother Laswell has taught him to count, and he knows his letters up to Q."

"He's a prodigy," said St. Ives.

"She trained up a talking chicken, too, although no one who didn't see it would credit it. One of the help cut its head off accidental like, more's the pity, and it was eaten with red wine and bacon, in the French manner."

Other buildings, many of their windows shining with the light of candles or lamps, stood nearby, and past the corner of one of them St. Ives could see the framed glass of an illuminated palm house in which a man nearly as old as poor Shorter worked over a bench of potted plants. Abruptly it seemed to St. Ives like weeks rather than days since he had returned from London, and Aylesford seemed positively like a holiday to him. One heard of lives changing on the instant, but he had always associated the change with tragedy – sudden blindness or a house burning – but this newfound homeliness that had settled upon him was a change of another sort, an unexpected boon.

Hereafter Farm appeared to be a wonder of productivity, with gardens laid out and fruit trees aplenty. Violin music emanated from one of the nearby cottages, played by someone with considerable talent. St. Ives was dumbfounded, although he couldn't quite say what he had expected to find aside from some caliber of lunacy, which might possibly coexist with its more Edenic virtues.

Kraken led him up onto the broad veranda and into the house, where they were observed by several children peeking out from behind a half-open door, beyond which St. Ives could see shelves of books. The children seemed to be dressed as gipsies, and they studied St. Ives as if he were an exotic species. There was the smell in the air of something baking, and St. Ives was reminded that he hadn't yet eaten supper. Kraken moved on into a vast, dimly lit sitting room, where a seven-sided table stood in the center of a densely patterned carpet, also seven-sided. If ever a table had levitational powers, thought St. Ives, this one clearly did. Atop it lay a Japanese magic mirror, its handle encased in woven bamboo. The ornamented backside faced upward, so that the several cryptic designs were visible. St. Ives was fond of the mysterious mirrors, as were his children, and in fact had several examples at home, with the oxy-hydrogen lamp set up in his study so that the patterns cast by the mirrors could be marveled at whenever the fit took them. He didn't count himself among the many who believed that the projections from such mirrors had mystical powers, however, and he very much hoped that he would not be called upon to argue the point tonight.

Around the table stood the requisite seven chairs, the legs carved into the semblance of dragons. The walls, painted a deep blue, were dotted with white stars. Overhead hung an ornate, seven-sided chandelier that must have held a hundred candles, of which twenty or so were lit. Save the chairs and table, there was no other furniture. It occurred to St. Ives that the room would have seen some curious things over the years.

A door opened opposite the one they'd entered, and a woman, no doubt Mother Laswell, swept through it, shutting the door behind her and stepping into the light. She was large and imposing, with a mass of red hair that belied her age, which St. Ives took to be somewhat past sixty. She wore a voluminous, indistinct garment that must have been cobbled together from several bolts of oriental silk. In her hand she held a jewel-studded lorgnette through which she regarded St. Ives, her head tilted back. She had a theatrical look about her, but a good face, St. Ives thought – one that had seen its share of troubles.

"This is the Professor, Mother Laswell," Kraken said to her. "Him what I told you about. Professor Langdon St. Ives, the great genius."

"Indeed," she said, moving spryly into the room. She took his hand, pressed it, and dropped it again. "I'm very pleased that you've come, Professor. What I have to say will take time in the telling, and I believe that you have family at home, so I'll get straight to the heart of the matter. William has informed me that you are familiar with the man who styles himself Dr. Ignacio Narbondo."

"Yes," St. Ives said. "I'm not certain that anyone is *familiar* with him, not in so many words. I'm not convinced that he entirely knows himself. But I've had...dealings with him over the years."

"*Dealings*," she said, as if she didn't half like the word. "I'd warrant they turned out badly. William told you that he was once my son?"

"I was astonished to hear it."

"Not many people *have* heard it, sir. I have no occasion to mention it. I myself put him out of my heart and mind thirty years ago, and in those years I haven't spoken of him save to one person, Mary Eastman, whom he murdered in the churchyard early this morning, although I assure you that there will be no evidence that he committed the crime. I pray that you won't judge me too harshly, Professor, or think me an unnatural mother. I loved him when he was a child, but by the time he was five years old he had ceased to be a child, and within a very few years he was scarcely human. A human devil, perhaps, and I use the term literally. Will you hear what I have to say?"

"I'd be quite willing. And I don't set up to judge anyone but myself, ma'am, although I make an exception for Dr. Narbondo. Your description of him is unfortunately accurate. I'm convinced, however, that he will go about his business and that you'll be quit of him for another thirty years. I'm not sure that I can be of any use to you."

"I'm not half so certain on either point. But if he has gone off, then the peril is even greater. A glass of sherry for you?"

"I can't think of anything that would suit me more, thank you."

She gestured at the table, and St. Ives pulled back one of the heavy chairs and sat down. Almost immediately a girl entered the room carrying a decanter and small glasses without apparently having been called upon to do so. *A hidden bell*, St. Ives thought. Then he saw that the girl was apparently blind, and yet she walked straight to the table without hesitation. Her left arm was awkwardly contorted, held out in front of her and bent sharply at the elbow. She set the tray onto the table, and then, her elbow aimed sharply downward, she poured sherry evenly into the three glasses, her milky eyes staring dead ahead. St. Ives wondered whether the milkiness was caused by some sort of covering – circles of very fine oiled silk, perhaps, or milk glass lenses.

"Thank you, Clara," Mother Laswell said. The girl curtsied, turned, and walked back out again, straight toward the door, her arm bent in front of her, the tip of her elbow seeming to draw her forcibly along.

"*She sees with her elber*," Kraken whispered heavily to St. Ives. "I've seen her do monstrous strange things for a blind girl. She can play at cards, sir, one handed of course, and shoot a fowling piece into a target. It don't stand to reason, but it's what she does."

Mother Laswell nodded ponderously. "At Hereafter

Farm we've got no grudge against reason, Professor, as long as it isn't the only star in the firmament. But there are other ways of seeing, elbows included. As a man of science, a rationalist, perhaps a materialist, you no doubt disagree, but that's the sort of strange company you've fallen in with this evening. I tell you this only because you will naturally have some fundamental doubts about what I have to say to you. I don't take offense to that. Belief that comes too easily is a shallow and often foolish thing. Stubborn disbelief is much the same."

"On that point we agree entirely," St. Ives said, discarding assumptions by the bucketful and wondering exactly what sort of company he *had* "fallen in with." Not entirely the company he had expected. "I'm anxious to hear you out, Mother Laswell. I have the highest opinion of Bill Kraken, and if Bill tells me that you've got something vital to say, I don't doubt it for an instant. I'm wholly at your service."

"Thank you, sir." She sipped the sherry, looking for a moment at St. Ives as if seeing into his soul, before setting her glass down and pointing at the magic mirror lying in the center of the table. "I assume that you recognize this object?"

"I believe it to be a Japanese magic mirror, madam. I've studied them somewhat. Wonderful toys. I myself possess several of the objects."

"And have you come to an understanding of them?"

"Not in so many words, no. I know that they're fabricated from a cast metal alloy, ground into a lens, and then coated with quicksilver, tin, and lead on the convex surface, which is then polished. How the images on the back of the mirror are projected, however, I can't quite say."

"There are those who believe that such a mirror has what might be referred to as spiritual powers."

"I'm not persuaded of any such thing," St. Ives said flatly.

"Good for you. Neither am I. And yet there exist objects contrived by man which might… open doors."

"Keys, for instance," St. Ives said, smiling at her.

"Just so." Mother Laswell smiled back at him. "Do you recall hearing of a man named John Mason? It's a common name, of course. He fabricated Japanese magic mirrors – this very mirror, in fact. Some fifteen years ago John Mason managed to blow himself to pieces when he purposefully detonated the dust in a grain silo."

"Indeed I do remember him, or at least I remember his demise. He was a colleague of Joseph Swann of incandescent lighting fame. His death was quite sensational."

"That's the man. Both of them were photographic chemists, you know. I believe that Swann severed ties with Mason a year or more before Mason's death. When the police searched Mason's house, they found a plethora of human skulls and dried bones. The skulls had been trepanned, the interior set with a mirror fabricated very much like the Japanese mirror you're familiar with, the backs of the mirrors etched with children's faces so lifelike that they could only have been reproduced from collodion negatives. It appeared as if Mason were attempting to construct a means of projecting an image through the eye sockets of the skull. It wasn't until the headless remains of several small children were exhumed from graves on Mason's property that he was revealed as a murderer and understood to be criminally insane."

"That charge would be difficult to contest," St. Ives said.

"There we disagree," Mother Laswell told him, "although certainly that depends on one's definitions of sanity. Certainly he was no more insane than my late husband, with whom he was acquainted, I'm very sorry to say. Such skulls, or mirrors, call them what you will, come into my story, but not until half the story is told. Here's the long and the short of it." She gazed up at the burning candles and squinted her eyes, collecting her thoughts, or perhaps seeing something in the soft haze of the light. The flames flickered on breezes through an open window in the far end of the room.

"The man who calls himself Dr. Ignacio Narbondo," she said, "is my only living son. His father, who fancied himself a man of science, disappeared out of our lives when the boy was two years old. His father often spoke of going into East India, and would talk about fabulous cities in the jungle as if he were longing to see them. Perhaps he did, in the end. In any event, the boy and I – I won't utter my son's actual name now that he has abandoned it himself – took a room in Limehouse after that, in a low court of the worst type, but there was little money to advance ourselves. After less than a year I married my husband's brother, only to discover too late what sort of a man he was. He brought me here to Aylesford, along with the boy, and I bore him a child whom we named Edward."

"The boy what you seen in the barn," Kraken said, nodding to Mother Laswell, who nodded in turn, as if this didn't surprise her in the least. "And if the boy's ghost lingers in Aylesford, Professor, so does the Doctor. That's certain.

He was somewhere nigh if Edward's spirit was in the barn."

"Certain?" St. Ives asked. "How so?"

"Because this Narbondo possesses the Aylesford Skull, do you see, which he took out of Edward's grave. It's the boy's abode – his unnatural home. Edward never moved on, never crossed over the river."

"And the Aylesford Skull, Mother Laswell, has been treated similarly to the skulls found in the home of John Mason?" St. Ives asked.

Mother Laswell's mind seemed at that moment to be adrift, unmoored by recollection. After a moment she sighed and said, "Yes, although it is a considerably more advanced example. The bottle stands by you, sir. I might take another glass for the sake of the humors. I don't fancy telling this story, and I haven't told it, except to Bill early this morning. I've kept it locked away, you see."

"But you can unburden yourself now," Kraken told her solicitously. "You're amongst friends. Share it out, and let us take up the weight of it in your stead."

St. Ives poured sherry into the glasses and then settled back in his chair, giving her room to breathe. She held her glass aloft and peered through it at the candlelight in the chandelier. Then she tasted it, set it down again, nodded, and went on.

"My sons grew up together, but not as brothers. The older one couldn't abide the sight of the younger. I saw him turn away from his... humanity, month by month, till I scarcely knew him. Perhaps the corruption was my husband's doing. He taught the boy what he knew of necromancy and vivisection. And the boy was a willing pupil, incredibly apt. I couldn't stop the thing that I could see growing within him, not with them both attracted to the same unnatural studies. My husband's laboratory stood at the top of the property, hidden among the trees. What they did there I can't say, and didn't want to know, and when fresh graves were dug up in the churchyard I turned a deaf ear, so to speak, to my shame, just as I suffered the crimes he did to me, and kept them secret. So time passed, until Edward was twelve years old and his brother nearly sixteen. Your Narbondo was completely foreign to me by this time, a hateful stranger, although he lived in this very house. Edward was fond of little Mary Eastman, and she of him, although both of them were children, really. This... Narbondo... fancied Mary Eastman himself, although I knew little of it until years later, when Mary took me into her confidence, for she was as guilt-ridden as I.

"To get to the heart of it, the man who calls himself Narbondo murdered his own brother in cold blood. He hanged him from the limb of a tree, endeavoring to make it seem that Edward was a self-destroyer. But fate is eccentric, Professor, and never more so than in this instance, for my late husband apparently found Edward still swinging from the branch, and Narbondo gawking at him, quite satisfied with himself, I'm sure.

"How do I know this, you're wondering. I can reveal that to you now, although I could not have yesterday, when Mary Eastman was still alive. Mary was a witness to the crime. Narbondo had the temerity to suggest that with Edward removed from the world, Mary might naturally favor himself, Narbondo, who was bound for glorious things, for power over life and death. Of course she spurned him. She saw quite clearly that he was a living horror, and she told him that she would see him hanged, an eye for an eye. And so he threatened her with the same fate, and she knew absolutely that he meant it. She fled, in fear for her life, but almost at once my late husband appeared, and she turned aside from the path and hid herself.

"They cut the body down, the two of them, and took it away. When Edward failed to come home that evening, there was a general hue and cry. A bloody knife was discovered, and marks of a body having been dragged to the edge of the river. It was spring, and the river was in flood, and it was assumed that Edward's body was somewhere downstream, tumbling toward the sea, and on that assumption the search ended.

"I understood the tale to be true, for what else was there for me to believe? Part of me suspected that Narbondo had wielded the knife; his demeanor, however, showed no trace of it. Years would pass before Mary Eastman told me the tale, although it was nearly beyond her powers to do so. The poor girl bore no blame, of course, for Edward was already dead, and she was afraid for her life. Narbondo sent her letters over the years, with clippings from the London papers, accounts of murders and mutilations, just to keep his threats fresh in her mind. She burned them, but they struck home in any event. She told me that she had never slept peacefully, although I pray that she does so now.

"What I tell you next is speculation, although much of it I heard from the mouth of my own shameless husband in the end. He spoke lightly of hellish things, as if there were no such place, if you take my meaning. He saw no virtue in sentiment. You believe yourself to be a rational man, Professor, but I tell you that there are depths of rationality that you haven't plumbed, and never will, for you don't have it in you to do so."

St. Ives looked out through the window at the moon that had risen above the treetops. It was quite dark outside, and he wondered abruptly what Alice and the children were doing while they waited for his return.

Mother Laswell poured another inch of sherry into the glasses, and studied his face. "You've a conscience," she said to him, "and you've compassion, and William tells me that you've done good in the world. I believe him, sir. But I tell you plainly that those three things are as irrational as any bed-sheet ghost. It's because of the scientist in you that you do not know who you are, or that you deny it."

EIGHT
CORPSE CANDLE

"Suddenly, out in the black night before us, and not two hundred yards away, we heard, at a moment when the wind was silent, the clear note of a human voice…"

Finn laid his magazine on the deal table next to his bed, his mind revolving on sunken galleons and drowned corpses awash on a wave-shattered coast. He wished mightily that he were on that very coast, watching the storm waves crash against the rocky shore and on the lookout for treasures cast up from the sea. He took a bite of the buttery shortcake that Mrs. Langley had brought over earlier today along with a pot of jam, which stood empty, the spoon still in it. He set what was left of the slice onto the oilcloth, carefully wiped his hands on his trousers, and studied the covers of his collection of *Cornhill Magazine*, eight copies in all so far. The Professor had passed them on to him, which sometimes meant within two or three days of the arrival of the magazine, the Professor being a prodigiously quick reader. Finn meant to tackle the stories one at a time, and he favored reading slowly, attending to the pictures along the way, looking back now and then to reread and savor a likely passage. He was in no hurry to finish good things, whether shortcakes or stories, and that was doubly true for "The Merry Men," which he had undertaken to read through this evening.

The lamp next to his bedside was smoking, and he turned the wick down a trifle, listening to the night breeze rustle the foliage beyond the window. Through the open curtain he could see that the lamps were still lit in the Professor's house, or, more rightly, in her house – Alice's house, Mrs. St. Ives – since it had belonged to her old aunt. Surely it wasn't respectable to think of her as Alice, but he relished the name and repeated it often to himself, and it had come to sound like a variety of beautiful flower to him.

A loneliness welled up within him now, although it was mixed with a draft of happiness, which led him to wonder at the strange good luck that had brought him here, this snug cottage being the first real home he could remember, discounting the wagon-roofed lorry in which he and his mother dwelt during their days traveling with Duffy's Circus. He thought about his mother, their happy days on the open road, his two threadbare years following her death, living hard in and around Billingsgate where he earned a few coins shucking oysters, as they called it, for Square Davey the oysterman, and summer nights sleeping beneath London Bridge, where he had discovered on a particularly dark evening that a short-bladed oyster knife might shuck the blood out of a man in short order if a person knew just where to put the blade. He had left the man lying in a crimson pool, black in the moon shadow, although whether dead or alive he couldn't say, because he hadn't lingered.

Remembering the man made him shudder, and he still

had nightmares of the face looming up before him, and the soft voice, "…Come with me now, boy," – just those five words, and the hand clutching his arm. He had wished the man dead more than once, if it weren't already so, although doubtless it was a sin to make such a wish. But that was in another lifetime, it seemed to him now, and he was happy to have got out of London and into the countryside. He still possessed the knife, which he kept sharp out of habit.

There was a scratching on the door – predictable old Hodge, wanting company. He stood up from his bed and slipped on his shoes. In the moment that he opened the door, Hodge flew in past his leg, leaping up onto the table and arching his back, looking keenly out into the night.

"What did you see, Hodge?" Finn asked. "It wasn't that old stoat out and about, was it?" Hodge didn't answer, but seemed soothed at the sound of Finn's voice and shifted his interest to the piece of shortcake that lay on the table. The light blinked out in the gallery windows of the big house opposite, the family settling down. Thinking to take in the night air, Finn stepped out through the door, closing it behind him, and stood listening to a nightingale singing in the trees nearby. The Professor had told him that it was only the male bird that sang at night, lonesome and without a mate. So it went for many things, or so his mother had told him. He saw that a fragment of moon rode in the sky, bright enough so that he could see a shifting in the shadows at the edge of the rose garden now – something solid, not a shadow at all. A deer, perhaps?

He walked in that direction as quietly as he could, the shape of the animal revealing itself as the distance shortened

– a red deer, right enough, a stag, enormous it seemed to Finn, with a broad set of antlers, eating the roses right off the stems, the scoundrel. It raised its head, looking at him indifferently. Finn picked up a stone and pitched it at the deer, hitting it on the flank. "Go on, sir!" Finn said to it. He had pruned those roses like old Binger had taught him, in such a way as to bring out the blooms. Precious few would be left by tomorrow if every animal in creation had its way with them. "Be off with you!" He shied another stone, a trifle harder, and the deer bolted up the alley in the direction of the road, but almost at once slowed down, walking at a leisurely gait, as if to have the last word on the matter.

Finn saw a strange shimmering light then, a faint glow moving among the shadows of the trees, perhaps a man with a muffled lantern...? The deer, seeming to see it also, abruptly skittered sideways, as if pushed by a heavy wind, and in the blink of an eye leapt into the undergrowth and disappeared. Finn realized that the night birds and crickets had fallen silent, although he couldn't say when it had happened, and he saw that the light wasn't apparently from a lantern at all, but had the look of moonlight – a circle of hovering mist, which was impossible on this warm, dry night, and there was no moonlight beneath the trees anyway.

Corpse candle, Finn thought. He had seen such a thing before, in the Erith Marshes – dead men abroad at night. He wasn't overly fond of dead men, or of any sort of ghost, but they were a curiosity, taken rightly, and not a thing to be feared, or so his mother had told him. And in fact his only memory of his grandmother was a memory of her ghost, which had appeared to them one night outside

Scarborough, where the circus had set up on a lea above the ocean. He remembered that his mother had wept to see the pale presence standing before them, although he was too young and frightened to understand quite why.

He watched the light, which shifted and changed shape, taking on the appearance of a human figure now, very small, like Tom Thumb adrift in the shadows. Then it expanded, and the figure of a young boy stood there, not quite solid, staring through coal black eyes into the distance, as if through a window that looked into an unseen land. The boy's mouth hung open, not as if he was speaking, but gaping open like a dead man's mouth, and his head was canted unnaturally to the side. He had been hanged. Finn could see a narrow band glowing brightly on his neck, where he had taken the weight of the rope. There was a whispering now – Finn heard it distinctly – although it sounded within his head, like a voice in a dream. He couldn't make out any words, just the whisper of a consciousness mingling with his own, and a sense of sorrow and of someone wandering in a vast darkness.

He heard the jingling of a horse's bell then, certainly out on the road, and the figure dimmed and disappeared along with the whispering. Finn was happy enough to see it go. Curious, he walked a few steps forward, wondering whether someone was out at night searching for the ghost and how they meant to catch it. He had seen a device once, a mirrored box that was baited with sweets as an attractant – Allsorts, being a favorite among ghosts. Once the ghost entered the box, the mirrors would keep it trapped.

There was the sound of the bell again, quite nearby,

but it stopped short this time, someone having silenced it. He took another step forward, hesitant to be seen. There it stood – a wagon, a man sitting in it, dressed in black, the horse also black, so that the wagon and the man and horse and all the trappings were nearly invisible against the darkness of the trees behind them.

The man saw him and nodded by way of greeting. "Come here, boy," he said in a low voice, gesturing Finn forward with the buggy whip. "Step out into the moonlight so that I can have a look at you."

Finn stood where he was, preferring the shadows. He could sense that the dead boy was still nearby, perhaps already in the possession of the dark man, who, Finn could see, had a distinct hunch on his back, although his cape and the darkness had hidden before now.

"I'm in a quandary," the man told him. "I'm looking for the London Road, quickest route. I fear I've lost my way in the darkness. I'm not too far out, I hope."

"No sir," Finn said, "not too far. There's a turning half a mile ahead that will take you into Wrotham Heath, and then it's the right fork and all the way into Greenwich. There's a coach inn at Wrotham Heath, sir, the Queen's Rest, which you might be wanting if you're looking for a room. It's a tolerable long shift into London starting as late as this."

It occurred to Finn that there was something off about the man, something bent, perhaps sinister, although it might be the lateness of the hour and the strange quiet that had swallowed the night. He heartily wished that he had stayed indoors with Hodge.

"A long shift is it? I'll take your word on that. You seem

to be a likely lad, answering so quick. I'll pay you a sovereign to see me to the inn, so that I don't miss the turning. You can sup there and be home well before dawn if you're not slow-footed. What do you say to that?"

"I say that I cannot, your honor."

"And why not?"

Because you have the face of Beelzebub, Finn thought, although he said nothing.

"Two sovereigns, then."

"No, sir, I cannot."

"Two sovereigns ain't enough for a lad like you, is it? Three then, and that's my best offer."

The offer was excessive. The man didn't want his help. He wanted something else, although God knew what. Did Finn know this man? There was something about him, in his features – something aside from his fell presence and the hump on his back. If the moon were a trifle brighter, perhaps it would come to him. He was certain he'd seen him, in London perhaps, along the docks.

"I'm wanted up at the house just now, sir. You can't miss the turning at Wrotham, though. The sign says 'Greenwich' clear enough."

The man gave him an ill look, as if he would just as soon run him over on the road. Then his face cleared abruptly and he said, "Then I'll be on my way, boy." With that he snapped the reins and the horse cantered away, the wagon fading almost at once into the darkness.

"God between us and all harm," Finn said aloud, crossing himself, and turned away. The ghostly presence had departed with the wagon, and the night birds took up their note in the trees and the crickets in the shrubbery. It came into his mind that he should speak to the Professor. It was tolerably doubtful that the man in the wagon had been idling on the road, contemplating the route to London – black mischief, more likely. As he walked back toward the cottage, however, he saw that the lower rooms of the house were dark, and only a solitary lamp burned upstairs in what was the Professor and Alice's bedchamber. He pushed open the door to his cottage and found that Hodge was asleep on his bed and the shortcake reduced to crumbs.

NINE

A LANE TO THE LAND OF THE DEAD

Mother Laswell looked slightly abashed, as if she had overreached herself. She turned the magic mirror on its base, the polished surface reflecting the candlelight. "I beg your forgiveness," she said. "I don't mean to speak slightingly of you."

"I find your words wholly complimentary," St. Ives said. "And perhaps no man can know himself entirely. Pray continue. Leave nothing out."

"Aye," Kraken said. "Speak your heart."

"I'm nearly through it, Professor, and just as well. I don't relish calling it up. It fell out that they took my Edward's body to the laboratory, where my husband... where my husband removed the head. It was then, or so I speculate, that he had Narbondo drag the corpse to the river to dispose of it, leaving the bloody knife as a piece of false evidence. Narbondo, clever boy that he was, disposed of the body in his own way. He wanted a corpse of his own to work on, you see, and the cost of a body as fresh as Edward's was too dear. He hid Edward's corpse in a garden shed and locked the door, visiting his brother in his spare moments thereafter, learning what he could of human anatomy. In the weeks that followed the murder, with Narbondo as a pupil, my husband fabricated a lamp from Edward's skull – the sort that John Mason had been at work on, but hadn't sufficient skill to contrive. My husband had taken photographs of Edward some time back. His aversion to sentimentality made me wonder at his motives at the time. He always had a motive, you see. He did nothing but with an eye toward gain.

"I became increasingly certain that he and his acolyte were responsible for Edward's death, and one afternoon, when I could stand it no longer, I made my way to the laboratory and surprised him at his work. It sounds insane for me to say that I knew my own son's skull when I saw it sitting atop a copper-sheathed table, but I *did* know it. It was no longer a mere skull, for he had completed his work upon it, to my horror. Beside it lay a notebook written out in my husband's clear hand. He had kept a record of his experimentations, as if he had been dissecting a cat.

"I confronted him with the murder, and he was quite bold in telling me to look to my own progeny if I needed a party to blame. The deformity, he told me, was in my own seed. I knew then that Edward had been murdered by his brother. My husband wasn't a timid man. He would happily have admitted to the crime if he had committed it. I gestured at Edward's skull, turned into God knew what. 'You would use him this way?' I asked my husband. 'Your own son?' 'He's no longer my son,' my husband said to me. 'He's dead. A mere corpse. And as for *using* him, my intention is to compel his ghost to remain among the living. You can thank me for that, for I believe that I've succeeded. I can summon him for you, if you'd like.'

"I was suddenly quite certain that he meant to murder me into the bargain, and I determined to impede his efforts now, since I had been dead in spirit for a very long time, and at that moment actual death seemed far more reasonable than life. I picked up a heavy glass cube with both hands and smashed it down onto my husband's head when he foolishly turned away, knocking him to the ground. And there he stayed, perhaps dead, although I scarcely believed it at the time. I snatched up Edward's skull and looked about for a place to hide it, because I meant to take it with me if I won free. It was a thing of horror, but it was all that was left to me. There was no place, however, that was safe, and so I pitched that glass cube through the window and the skull after it, watching as it rolled into the greenery on the banks of the little stream that runs down along the top of the farm. Then I snatched up the notebook and slipped it beneath my bodice. I began to smash things generally, then, caught up in a growing rage for what my husband had done, and in the smashing I knocked over a lamp, which cast burning oil on a heap of crates and papers and set the place alight. Good, I thought. I'll burn him to death.

"But luck wasn't with me. My husband staggered to his feet just then, not knowing whether to murder me or attend to the blaze, which had spread to the curtains. The old wooden boards in the wall caught fire, and the smoke drove us both out into the open air, my husband just then realizing that the skull had vanished from the tabletop. But he was scarcely in a position to mention it, for coming along toward us at a run was a group of men from the village, some of them carrying weapons. Among them was my own disgraced son. Aylesford still had a watchman in those days, and Narbondo had summoned him, having revealed that his own father was a vivisectionist and had murdered his brother Edward. The boy was clearly surprised to see me there, and watched in something like dismay as the laboratory burned. I knew what he regretted, and I was happy in my way for having deprived him of it, and for seeing the loss in his face. He had let his father complete his detestable work and then had betrayed him, intent upon taking the skull himself. Now it was lost to both of them.

"They dragged my husband away, and what they found beneath the charred floor of the laboratory was sufficient to hang him. At the trial Mary Eastman swore, no doubt at Narbondo's insistence and to her own undying shame, that she had seen my husband murder Edward, and so his fate was doubly sealed. There was no blame cast at me. I had long been considered an object of pity thereabouts, and when it was known that I had beaten my husband and set the laboratory alight, I was very nearly a heroine.

"Soon after, Narbondo disappeared from Aylesford and didn't return, there being nothing left for him here. He needed a larger stage on which to work his mischief. I'm aware that he searched for the skull in the ashes of the laboratory, knowing that several skulls had been found, each in a different state of ornamentation and blackened in the fire. I believe now that he suspected that I had it, but he never once accused me of it. Perhaps he was afraid of Mary Eastman, fearing that she would step forward if I came to harm at Narbondo's hand. He found my husband's notebook, however, and took it, although by then I had read it many times, and I knew the secret of Edward's skull, which I had retrieved from where it lay hidden along the stream. I buried my son's bones in the churchyard when they were discovered in that locked shed, but the skull I kept in my possession for thirty long years. I communed with Edward's spirit many, many times, Professor."

She fell silent then and St. Ives realized that she was weeping. Kraken put his hand on her arm, and she covered his hand with her own.

"Communed with his spirit?" St. Ives asked after an interval. "Do you mean literally?"

"Quite so," she said. "On nights when the fog rose off the fields I projected his… *features*, if you will, on the mists, and he appeared as he had been, as a boy, and with a semblance of life, or at least movement. He knew I was nearby, although I'm certain he couldn't see me, not in the sense that I can see you sitting before me now. He couldn't speak, of course, but his face betrayed his anguish, and I was haunted by the fear that I promoted his anguish each time I called him forth. There was a depravity on my part, too, which I very well knew. I resorted to laudanum in an effort to restore my sanity, but the drug magnified my longing, and soon I had two vices rather than just the one. Endeavoring to keep the dead alive is to murder oneself slowly, do you see? I knew I had to bury my Edward, and with William's help I finally did."

Kraken sat staring at the tabletop now, nodding silently. "Nearly a year ago, it was, sir – mid-July. We paid a visit to the churchyard, and with the sexton's help, we laid him to rest in his coffin."

"And now Narbondo has recovered it," St. Ives said. "He had only to murder Mary Eastman to complete his work."

Kraken stirred in his chair and cleared his throat. "Or to begin it, sir." And then to Mother Laswell he said, "The door, Mother. Tell the Professor about the door. It's the door, sir, that we're up against now."

She nodded, considered for a moment, and said, "It's here that we'll come a cropper, Professor. I don't ask you to believe what I'm about to reveal, but you must know that *I* believe it. My late husband had no interest in his son's ghost for its own sake. As was ever his way, he meant to make use of it. Spirits are misplaced in the world of the living. They long to move on, but for reasons beyond our ken, they sometimes do not. To put it into the simplest terms, John Mason had attempted to contrive a means to open a lane to the land of the dead, through which a ghost might pass on, and through which a man might follow, and might return through it again.

"I'm unaware of the particulars, sir, for the discussions in my late husband's notebook, when it referred to the opening of the gate, were mere sketches and implications, although there was some discussion of his affairs with John Mason, touching on Mason's inept work contriving the lamps, as he referred to them. My husband carried his own knowledge in his mind, for the most part, and his mind is closed to us now.

"It was open for a number of years to the youthful Narbondo, however. John Mason blew himself to pieces when he detonated the dust in a grain silo, attempting to project an earthbound spirit onto the suspended cloud before it exploded. Whether he was successful in opening a gate to the netherworld, if you will, God alone knows. I'm certain, however, that my husband was far more adept at necromancy than John Mason had been. My husband was a man of vast knowledge, Professor, arcane, evil knowledge, if you'll permit me to use the word, and he was very much feared in certain circles. Narbondo, however, had no fear of him, even as a boy, but used my husband to his own ends, just as my husband used others. Narbondo, we're certain, is in possession of what my husband referred to as the Aylesford Skull, simply to keep it distinct from others of its kind. He never for a moment thought of it as the skull of his only son, objects and people being merely more or less useful to him."

"You're worried that Narbondo will make use of the skull, as John Mason attempted to do?" St. Ives asked. "He means to open one of these fabled gates?"

"Exactly, sir, except that his goal, I fear, is to open the gate fully, and to leave it open."

"I don't quite follow you," St. Ives said.

Kraken tugged on his chin, widened his eyes, and said, "She means there'll be a-coming and going when he's finished, sir. That a man might walk across Piccadilly and into Hell as easy as kiss-my-hand and back out again with a bucket of brimstone and his hair afire, and so with them that dwells there, the dead and the living in a sort of hotchpotch, as the Scotsman said."

"Why would a man *desire* to bring about that end?" St. Ives asked.

"Bill's account is perhaps a bit fanciful," Mother Laswell

said, "but your question is well taken. Morbid curiosity, might answer, or an opportunity to travel where no man has traveled previously. It is quite possible that a man possessed by evil would be drawn to such an atrocity for reasons of his own, or perhaps in his narcissism he fancies himself a modern Virgil, who would lead people through the realms of the dead. We know nothing of the nature of the gate, Professor, or what lies beyond. We cannot say whether it leads to an actual, earthly place, or to the spirit world, or to both in some manner. But such questions are of secondary importance. It's the very *attempt* that we fear – the detonation, the spilling of human blood, perhaps on a massive scale."

St. Ives nodded. "I would *very* much like to see that notebook," he said. "No fragment of it remains?"

She shook her head decisively.

"And the laboratory? Perhaps the foundation still stands?"

"An oast house was built on the site."

"There's nothing then?"

"Nothing, Professor. What I know you now know. The only thing separating our mutual understanding has to do with belief."

St. Ives sat for a time in silence, and then said, "At the moment, Mother Laswell, I'm at a loss for a suitable response. You pay me a great compliment simply by taking me into your confidence, but I'm not certain that I can repay you in kind. Your story has a good deal to do with the ways in which a man's endeavors might betray the very things that he most loves, or should love – his wife and his children. Since you've been candid with me, I'll pay you in kind. At the moment my life is full of the duties I've mistakenly ignored to my own peril – my home and my wife and children. I'll consider what you've told me, and in fact won't be able to do otherwise, since the tale is compelling, but I tell you truthfully that I see no clear course of action, and, if I did, I'd be disinclined to pursue it. There's little profit in my speaking falsely here."

He stood up from the table as the clock was striking ten o'clock, and it came to him that Cleo and Eddie would be in bed by now, quite likely asleep, perhaps Alice also. He had meant to speak of air vessels and elephants to them tonight, simply to inform their dreams, but it would be too late for that. "Good evening, ma'am," he said, but Mother Laswell's eyes seemed to be focused on something that was a very great distance away, and his words apparently went unheard.

"I'll show you out, Professor," Kraken said in a low voice, leading the way toward the door. They passed through the entry hall and into the starlit night. Ned Ludd the mule was still abroad, as if standing sentinel until St. Ives had gone away and the imaginary drawbridge could be hoisted and secured. The sliver of moon shone in the sky in the direction of the river.

"I can find my way home, Bill. You remain with Mother Laswell. She needs some comfort."

"Aye, she's in a state, sir, and has been since the news of Mary Eastman's death this morning. As soon as she heard of the grave being dug up and the skull gone, she vowed to hunt Narbondo down. She brought him into the world, she said, and it was her bounden duty to take him out of it again and to put poor Edward to rest. She means to kill her own son, sir. I talked sense to her six to the dozen, but I don't have the words to make her see, and I was hoping that with your help she would…" He fell silent now, as if he had overreached himself.

"I honor you for it, Bill. And I envy your faith in both of us. I'm convinced that she will abandon any idea of killing Narbondo. She'll see things more clearly when the sun rises. Come round to meet Eddie and Cleo tomorrow. You'll understand me better, perhaps. A man changes over the years. We've had some adventures, you and I, but for me that season has passed away, or nearly so."

"Perhaps for the best, sir, if only you're in the right of it. Here now, Ned!" He stepped down off the porch and put his hand on the mule's neck. "Time for bed, old son." He nodded to St. Ives, deep worry visible in his face, then turned Ned Ludd around and headed in the direction of the barn, the shadowy outline of which St. Ives could see beyond the now-dark palm house.

TEN

WHAT DUTY REQUIRES

Alice sat in front of the mirror pinning up her hair, capturing and imprisoning wayward locks that would apparently much rather remain at liberty. St. Ives watched her happily. It was a Saturday morning, and they meant to breakfast on the veranda and then do very little. Alice would no doubt spend some time with her begonias, the new rhizomes already putting out leaves. As for him, he meant to set his mind to the problem of the barn, perhaps sketch his plans out again now that the elephant had complicated things.

"But what do *you* believe you should do?" Alice asked, turning to St. Ives. "In your heart of hearts? What does Duty require?"

"What do I *believe*? I believe that the entire business is nonsense. There's nothing nonsensical about the tragedy, of course. I don't mean that. Mother Laswell suffers a great deal of pain. But I don't for a moment believe that I can effect a cure for human misery. Perhaps time will answer in that regard, or perhaps Bill Kraken will answer. He seems wholly dedicated to her. As for Narbondo's anticipated depredations, you've said yourself that there's such a thing as the police. I have no regard for the lunatic idea that a man might open a lane to the land of the dead in this fabulous manner, although I have a high regard, if 'regard' is quite the right word, for Narbondo's capacity for evil. If I found him lurking hereabouts I'd be inclined to shoot him like a mad dog. But will I go out searching for him because I'm motivated by this wild notion of a gate to the afterlife? I will not."

"You sound quite certain."

"Never more so. I'm certain that Mother Laswell dearly wants her son's skull returned to her. She tells the truth. But I'm not persuaded that it's my business."

"I'm happy to hear it. It puts my mind at ease, and it cheers me that I don't have to beat you with a coal shovel. Poor Mother Laswell, though. I'll pay a visit to the farm and introduce myself."

St. Ives looked out the bedroom window, taking in the view. He could feel warmth through the glass. There was a tonic quality to the heat, a salutary tonic, and he found once again that he was quite happy. The children had indeed been asleep when he had returned last night, and the house quiet. Alice, however, had not been asleep, nor did either of them have any particular desire to sleep until quite late, or early, he reflected happily. They had got out of bed some time after midnight and gone downstairs together to tuck up the children. It being a warm night, Eddie and Cleo slept in what Aunt Agatha Walton had referred to as "the sleeping gallery," the windows covered with fine wire mesh against insects. As ever, when they tiptoed in they found Cleo's blankets on the floor and Eddie's virtually unmoved despite his being comfortably asleep beneath them. Mrs. Langley slept nearby in the adjacent scullery, which long years past had doubled as a maid's quarters. They had watched the sleeping children for the space of several minutes, listening to Mrs. Langley's soft snoring from beyond the door, and then had gone back up to bed, St. Ives falling instantly into a deep and grateful sleep.

It occurred to him now that Alice looked particularly radiant this morning, although she had only been a few minutes out of bed, and after a fairly short night. Her eyes very nearly sparkled. He thought again of Mother Laswell and her tribulations, and wondered if his own happiness was unnatural under the circumstances. It was not, he quickly decided.

"I'm thinking of running into the village today," he said.

"Consider having Logarithm pull you in the wagon," she told him, "unless you particularly want exercise."

"You're positively giddy," he said to her. "Perhaps you'd like to come along. I'm going to talk to Mr. Milford and his son about tripling the size of the barn door."

"On behalf of the airship?"

"Yes, indeed. It'll need a commodious great door. Simple to build, I believe, and Aunt Agatha's lumber room will answer for the materials."

"I'd be happy to go along. We'll take Eddie and Cleo, if that would suit you, and perhaps a picnic basket. I promised to show them where my nemesis the pike lives in the weir. The weir is a famous spot for newts and toads, you know, if you keep an eye out."

"Excellent. Cleo loves a newt." St. Ives nodded happily,

his mind shifting effortlessly from airships to toads and newts and then quite naturally on to the notion of elephants. Certainly there was no better moment to broach the subject with Alice, given her high spirits. "An idea came into my mind yesterday, my love."

"An *idea*," she said. "Treat it kindly, then; it finds itself in a tolerably strange place."

He laughed at the witticism. "You're right about that," he said, "more than you know, perhaps. I've come to the conclusion that we're in particular need of an elephant."

"What a perfectly wonderful idea, Langdon. One of your best, without a doubt. Perhaps we should have two of them?"

"I'm quite serious."

"As am I. They pine away without the company of fellow pachyderms, I understand."

Did he hear irony in her tone? There was nothing in her face to suggest it. "Finn Conrad has a sizeable knowledge of the creatures," he said, shouldering on. "I intend to put Finn in charge of it. We've got plenty of room in the barn, and…"

"You're *serious*?" she said.

"Quite. It will provide the motive power needed to shift the barn roof, do you see?"

"Don't elephants go on rampages? Tread people flat?"

"Only when provoked. None of us are in the business of provoking animals. This place breeds serenity, Alice. You can feel it in the air this morning. The lion lies down with the lamb even as we speak."

"An army of newts wouldn't serve to open the roof?"

He smiled at her and was relieved when she smiled back. "Think on it," he said. "We'll speak to Finn together in order to get an educated opinion. Certainly there's no tearing hurry."

There sounded a pounding from downstairs, an urgent pounding – on the front door, perhaps. They listened for a moment, assuming that Mrs. Langley would answer it. Hasbro would have gone off early on his usual Saturday morning errands. The pounding started up again, accompanied by a muffled shouting. Alice was first through the door, and St. Ives followed, both of them taking the stairs two at a time, and hurrying into the drawing room. It wasn't the front door at all. They found the gallery empty, the beds slept in but the children not in them. The pounding was coming from the scullery door. A chair was jammed beneath the door latch. St. Ives yanked it away, the door flew open, and Mrs. Langley staggered out, apparently mystified and angry.

"Where are the children?" Alice asked.

"I'm sure I don't know, ma'am. I woke up a moment ago and found myself locked into the scullery. Perhaps Finn…"

"Finn wouldn't have locked you into the scullery, Mrs. Langley," St. Ives said, a morbid fear rising in him. "I suggest that you two search the house. I'll find Finn." He realized that it was more a certainty than a fear, or the two together, feeding each other. Before he was out the door, however, there came a second pounding. He heard crying – almost certainly Cleo – in the coat closet. The key was in the lock, but was turned – no need for a chair to keep the door shut. He unlocked it and let her out. She dragged her blanket behind her, evidently fuddled with sleep. As soon as she saw her mother she burst into tears, trying to speak but without any success. Alice picked her up, comforting her, walking her back and forth until she was sensible. St. Ives watched, his heart pounding, praying that this was one of Eddie's games, although the chair against the scullery door...

"Did your brother lock you in?" Alice asked.

Cleo shook her head. "The man came," she said between sobs. "He took Eddie. He put me in the closet and I mustn't make a sound or he would hurt Eddie."

"When did the man come?" St. Ives asked. "Was it dark outside, Cleo?"

She nodded.

"And did you fall asleep in the closet after?" Alice asked her, and she nodded again.

Alice looked evenly at St. Ives. "*The man,*" she said flatly.

"I'll just speak to Finn now," St. Ives said, pushing through the gallery door and down the several stairs. How much had he told Alice about the skulls when he had recounted his conversation with Mother Laswell – surely not that they were commonly taken from children? He hoped fervently that he had left the details out. As he sprinted to Finn's cottage the idea came to him that he would tell Alice to be on the lookout for a ransom demand: there was hope in a ransom, after all. Surely that's what Narbondo intended...

He knocked on Finn's door, which opened immediately, Finn disheveled from sleep and holding a magazine open in his hand. "I was lying abed, sir, it being Saturday."

"Good for you, Finn, but there's trouble. Eddie's been taken."

"Taken, sir?"

"Kidnapped, I fear. Did you see anything odd early

this morning? Hear anything? You haven't seen Eddie up and about?"

Finn stared at him blankly, and, it seemed to St. Ives, turned pale. "No, sir. But last night, there was a man on the road. I didn't think…"

"What did he look like? A dark-haired smallish man? With a hump on his back?"

"Yes, sir. That's him. I was out looking at a deer that had got into the roses. I seen a corpse candle near the road, and walked down the wisteria alley, and there at the crossing your man sat in the wagon. He asked the way to the London Road, and so I told him."

"A corpse candle do you say?"

"Yes, sir. A spirit light, hovering nearby the wagon. It was the ghost of a boy; I could see that much. I didn't like the look on your man's face, sir, but I can't rightly tell you why. It was a thing you could smell almost. I can't think of another way to put it. I made sure to stand in the shadows. He wanted me to get into the cart with him, but I wouldn't, and he drove away."

"I fear that he returned," St. Ives said, "after you'd gone back up to your cottage. He drove away only because you'd seen him."

"Who was he, sir?"

"His name is Ignacio Narbondo. If you see him again, Finn, don't speak to him. Don't go near him. Run. He's the king of liars."

"I've heard you speak of this Narbondo, sir. And Jack Owlesby told me about him when I stayed at the house on Jermyn Street. Narbondo was the one as caused the trouble at Morecambe Bay."

"Yes," said St. Ives. "The very man, come round again."

Finn stood staring for a moment, his hand at his forehead. "I should have come looking for you, sir, or Mrs. St. Ives. I knew it was long odds against anyone coming along to tell him of the London Road that time of night, but I didn't think... I didn't... I should have come up to the house."

"You couldn't have known, Finn. I knew that Narbondo had been lurking roundabout, and I neglected to tell *you*. The blame in that regard is my own."

Finn was staring at St. Ives's feet now, his face set. He touched his forehead again with trembling fingers, as if he couldn't keep his hands still. "I didn't know..." he said, as if trying to come to grips with his regret.

"Finn," St. Ives told him. "The guilt of the crime lies solely with Narbondo, and what's left over I'll take. Do you understand me?"

"Yes," Finn said, nodding his head too rapidly to be convincing.

"Good man," St. Ives said. "See to things, Finn, while I'm gone. I'll be traveling in to London again."

A wagon came rattling along the wisteria alley now – Hasbro come home, and none too soon. St. Ives pressed Finn's shoulder and turned away, running toward Hasbro, who reined up the horses.

"We leave for London in half an hour," St. Ives said without preamble. "Narbondo has taken Eddie."

ELEVEN
TO LONDON

Alice watched as the wagon moved away, dust rising from the wheels, carrying her husband from her yet again, his portmanteau sitting on the bed of the cart. He turned and waved one last time before the wagon flung itself up onto the road and flew out of sight, but she knew that his mind was already on London, and on the terrible need to make haste yet again. The last thing she said to him was, "Bring me his head." But she knew now that it was her very anger at Narbondo that instigated vicious thoughts within her – anger at the hold that he had upon all of them, and especially upon her husband.

He can save others, she thought, watching the dust settle, *but he cannot save himself*, the utterance of the Corinthian soldier coming into her mind unbidden.

Bitter thoughts followed – recriminations that she wished weren't there, that had been drawn from within her as out of a dark well. She cast them aside and thought of her own part in the crime. Better to be angry with herself. Why hadn't she awakened? Wasn't she supposed to have some instinctive bond with her children, whom she'd foolishly allowed to sleep alone in the gallery? Why *that*, of all things, when the devil was abroad in the neighborhood?

"Gone again," she said out loud, pushing the unanswerable questions aside and talking now to the empty afternoon.

What if, she wondered – what if years ago, Langdon had taken a different turning in the road, and Narbondo and he had never been put into each other's way? What then? Would some other tragedy or woe have stepped into the breach? It was apparently what the human multitudes were born for. That she might or might not have awakened in the night made little difference now. It was foolish to lament what had not happened any more than to worry about what might. There were a million possible alternatives that arose in a lifetime, and it had quite simply fallen out by dumb chance that she now had both a husband and a son to lose in a single stroke.

She found a kerchief in her pocket and wiped the tears from her cheeks. She knew absolutely that unless she forced herself to remain even, with her wits intact, she would begin to sob, and that the sobbing would not answer, but would shatter what little command she had left of herself, and she would be no good to anyone. Though come to that, what good was she now?

Her mind turned to Finn, and she looked toward his cottage, where for some reason the door stood half open. Langdon had told her that Finn blamed himself for Eddie's kidnapping, and would certainly torture himself with it. *And so the poison spreads*, she thought. At that moment a gust of wind banged the door fully open. It swung back again, but didn't shut, and it came to her that the cottage was empty.

She began to run. Surely the boy wouldn't do himself a mischief; he was steadier than that. She looked into the interior, not bothering to knock. "Finn!" she shouted, but there was no answer. Drawers stood open and clothes lay on the bed where they had apparently been tossed. He had been in a hurry. She saw then that the lamp on the table by his bedside rested atop a sheet of foolscap, apparently left as a message, and in an instant she had snatched it up and read it hastily.

I've gone into London to try my hand, the note said. *I'm used to its ways having lived rough there for a time. I'm main sorry to have played my part so bad, but I mean to put it right. Finn Conrad.*

"God help us," she said, sitting down hard on the bed and reading the note through again. Her breath caught in her throat, and her heart was fluttering, and for a moment she thought she would faint. She forced herself to breathe evenly, closed her eyes, and sat just so until something leapt onto the bed – Hodge, she discovered. The cat stared at her, as if to imply that there was more she should be doing.

She stood up then and went out, tucking the note into her pocket and calling Hodge to follow her. She scooped him up, shut Finn's door behind her, and turned toward the house, but she hadn't taken ten steps before she heard a shout, and saw Bill Kraken heading toward her at a lopsided run, just then coming out of the hops orchard from the direction of Hereafter Farm. He waved at her, and she waited for him, even at a distance seeing trouble in his hurrying stride and in his face.

Kraken bent over and clasped his knees with his hands,

breathing hard, and then caught up with himself, took his cap off, and said, "Begging your pardon, ma'am, but I've come for the Professor. There's a mort of trouble at the farm."

She felt a wave of something strangely like relief, the wild idea coming into her mind that Narbondo might still be lurking nearby. Eddie mightn't be in London at all. St. Ives had taken the pistols, but there was still the fowling piece, which she could aim as well as anyone she knew, save perhaps Hasbro…

She realized abruptly that Kraken was waiting for her, and she brought herself back from her own thoughts. "What trouble, Bill?"

"Mother Laswell's gone off to London a-looking for the Doctor. Bent on murder, she is. She's sailing under the black flag, ma'am. No quarter. She'll have his liver and lights on a plate or die a-trying, despite he's her own son, blackguard that he is."

"To London, Bill? Are you certain?"

"Yes, ma'am. She left me ashore, I don't know how long ago. Hours maybe, for I was up ere the sun. I set to working in the garden before the day hottened up, and later on come in for breakfast a-looking for her, but she weren't there. I looked whether she was still abed, for she had sat up half the night in a black fret, but the bed was empty and had been laid upon, but not *in*, if you follow me. She had laid there a-waiting, do you see, making up her mind like. Then in come Simonides, the hired boy, who said he took her to the train early-on in the dogcart, and was just then getting back. By then she was London bound, perhaps already in Tooley Street. The Professor will tell me what to do, I'm main certain of it."

"The Professor's gone to London himself, Bill, on the same mission. Narbondo broke into the house in the night and kidnapped Eddie. Heaven knows when, exactly, or where he's taken Eddie, but St. Ives and Hasbro are bound for London to look into it. They've been gone this past quarter hour by wagon, and wasting no time."

Kraken clapped a hand to his forehead and staggered backward like a drunken man. "*London*," he muttered. "Blimey." Abruptly he touched his hat, already turning away. He set out running again, back the way he had come, perhaps intending to run all the way into London. Alice stood speechless, watching him dwindle in the distance. The empty world seemed to be turning around her, and her mind revolved with it, unfixed on anything in particular.

After a moment it settled again, and she made her way homeward, walking back into the quiet house, where she found Mrs. Langley at work, her face drawn and desperately unhappy. "I'm at wit's end," Mrs. Langley said to her. "I scarcely know which way to turn."

"Nor do I, Mrs. Langley. You couldn't have anticipated any of this. It would be a great solace to me if you wouldn't think badly of yourself. There's the house and farm to see to, and just the two of us. Finn has gone into London. We'll carry this corner of the world on our shoulders, and with the grace of God we can take up where we left off within a few days' time."

"Into London? Finn?"

"It seems that he wants to help the Professor find Eddie," she told her, leaving out the hurtful details.

Mrs. Langley shook her head. "If I thought I could help, ma'am, I'd go into London myself."

"I know you would. I'm quite certain of it. But you and I must do our part at home, it seems."

Cleo, already recovered, was studiously setting up soldiers, the clockwork elephant prepared to mow them down again. The breeze blew in through the open windows, the day slightly cooler than it had been – perfect weather, really, on what had been going to be a perfect day. It still was a perfect day in some larger sense, Alice thought, the clockwork world spinning along on its axis with complete indifference, birds hatching, calves foaling, her pike lurking in the deep water of the weir as it had time out of mind.

Waiting wasn't going to be easy, she thought. "I wonder if you'd like to go newting," she said to Cleo, not really considering what she was asking until the words were out of her mouth, but realizing that she had made a decision. "Newting and frogging. We'll bring a picnic."

"With biscuits," Cleo said, marching the elephant up the hillside that had recently been the settee, but was now a mountain range. "Jam biscuits?"

"And sandwiches, I should think."

"I'll just put something up," said Mrs. Langley, visibly bucking up. "We've some beautiful strawberries, and perhaps peaches. And a piece of that lovely York ham and a nice Stilton cheese."

"Would there be anything left of the deviled pork?"

"Yes, ma'am. The pot's half full. It'll go bad soon enough if we don't attend to it."

"Then it's our duty to attend to it. You'll come along, Mrs.

Langley? Have you ever had your hands on a living newt?"

"Oh dear me, yes, ma'am. I grew up by Shag's Pond, in Derbyshire. The newts were fearsome thereabouts, with poisonous eyes, my old dad told me, but they'd flee away when they saw my sister and I coming along with nets and pails. Dear me, yes. But I don't mean to..."

"Nonsense. It's settled. We'll go on into Aylesford afterward for tea at the inn and supper after, with a nice bottle of wine to keep our spirits up. If we sit around like mopes we'll compound the crime, and I refuse to do it. We'll fight the dragon in our own way."

"What dragon?" Cleo asked. "The big fish?"

"Yes, Cleo, the big fish. Fetch the nets and a bucket from the shed, if you will, and I'll see how many pairs of waders and fishing poles we can muster."

Mrs. Langley and Cleo both disappeared, busy now. Alice thought of Eddie. She closed her eyes for a moment, listening to the clatter in the kitchen, and then she wiped away the tears and went out through the door to get on with the day.

TWELVE

THE QUEEN'S REST

St. Ives looked again at his pocket watch, and was surprised to see that only ten minutes had passed since he had last done the same thing. They were rattling shrewdly along the nearly empty road, and yet they seemed to be taking forever about it. Orchards of pears and cherries fell away behind them, while plantations of chestnut and ash rose up to take their place and fell away in turn. Strawberry fields came and went. There were hop orchards that made their own small holding seem negligible by comparison, but all of these things passed out of his mind as they passed out of sight, and he returned inwardly to a dismal mental vision of London in all its vastness, its thousands of dark streets and courtyards and gin shops and lodging houses, the turmoil and hurry – such a confounding puzzle that it bred futility in the shadows of his mind.

There was nothing confounding, it occurred to him morbidly, in a man taking his own life merely out of self-loathing, and he thought of Mother Laswell and the burden that she carried – one son dead, the other a murderer, and she unable and unwilling to forgive herself for having married a bad man. *I believe that the entire business is nonsense*: his words came back to him now, rekindling his regret, and he uttered a silent apology to the poor woman and a prayer for all of them, although it was cold comfort.

"We've both missed our breakfast, sir," Hasbro said, recalling St. Ives from his musings.

St. Ives nodded, but said nothing.

"I suggest stopping at the Queen's Rest just ahead, sir, in Wrotham Heath, near the Archbishop's manor. There's no value in arriving in London unfed. Old Logarithm will want something, too."

"A delay would… unsettle me," St. Ives said flatly.

"Indeed, sir, although the delay would be momentary. It's a coaching inn on the Greenwich Road, and in deference to travelers they put up food in parcels. Bread and cheese, meat pies, and bottled ale. I've availed myself of the fare on occasion, and it's quite substantial. We'll be happy to have it an hour from now."

"No doubt you're correct," St. Ives said. "I've got no appetite, but perhaps that's not a virtue."

"No, sir, perhaps it's not, if you'll pardon my saying so. We'll want our wits about us in London, and we'll move more decisively if we're carrying a hamper of food instead of an empty belly."

The Queen's Rest soon came into view ahead, its heavily carved and brightly painted sign glowing with sunlight. On any other day it would have been a welcome sight to St. Ives, but this morning it meant nothing. Hasbro drew up in front of it, and the ostler came out of the adjacent stable and took the reins as Hasbro and St. Ives climbed down. St.

Ives saw that a man was standing in the doorway of the inn. The man tipped his hat, and St. Ives nodded doubtfully in his direction, thinking that he had a suspicious look about him. He caught himself, realizing that he felt mean and low, stricken with a case of the dismals, as Tubby Frobisher would put it. His natural civility had abdicated along with his appetite and had left him with a vague stupidity and muddled thoughts.

"Water and oats," Hasbro said to the ostler. "We leave in ten minutes sharp."

The man nodded and led the horse and wagon in out of the sunlight. St. Ives and Hasbro entered the inn, the public house smelling heavily of hops and baking bread. Two men sat at a table with glasses of beer and a plate of cheese and pickled eggs in front of them. One of them was dark and had chiseled features – handsome, no doubt, in his day. But he had been horribly wounded some time in the past, and was missing an ear and had a long scar from his brow to his mouth, the blade having split open his nostril, which had been badly repaired. He would have been handsome otherwise. The other man, who moments ago had been standing in the doorway, was hatless now. He had a large round head, bald but for a dark halo of curls. He nodded again cheerfully at St. Ives, who forced himself to smile and nod a greeting back. The man was perhaps a bit dense, St. Ives thought, and yet his jolly demeanor improved the general quality of the morning – a useful lesson about the underrated duty of conveying an air of contentment.

The publican came out from the kitchen and at Hasbro's bidding drew two glasses of bitter from the tap, setting them down on the bar top. To Hasbro's question of food, he replied, "I have a cold saddle of mutton, gentlemen, turned out in curry and figs, in the Indian style, and a pasty of mushroom and chicken as can be put up quick and eaten in hand."

"The pasties, I should think," said Hasbro, "and bottled ale, if you've got it."

"They've brought us the new screw-cap bottles, sir, just a week back. Would you like six, or would a round half a dozen suit you?" With that the man burst into laughter with such enthusiasm that St. Ives abruptly felt improved yet again, and he found that he was grateful for his glass of bitter, from which he drank deeply now, his ears fixed on the conversation at the table behind him.

"He was a rum cove if ever I've seen one," one of the two men said loudly enough to be overheard, sounding like the cheerful man with the bald-pate. "I don't trust a bleeding hunchback, Fred."

"It's not the poor sod's fault that he's got the hunch, George. And who are you to be calling names, an ugly bloke like you with a head like a melon?"

"It was his face what told the tale, not the hump," George replied. "I half pity the boy, having an uncle with a face like that. Better to be an orphan than to fall in with Old Poger."

"You gentlemen speak of a boy and a hunchback," St. Ives said, turning around anxiously. "I don't mean to come it the Grand Inquisitor, but did you see these two recently?"

"An hour, perhaps, weren't it Fred?"

"Thereabouts. Not more. Below Wrothamhill, it was, if you know it, sir."

"On the Greenwich road?" asked St. Ives.

"No, sir. Gravesend road," George said. "There was a bridge out – what they call the Trelawney Bridge, after the old squire, built before your grandfather was born, sir. Shattered by an infernal device a week past. Your man the hunchback was set to go roundabout through Stanstead, a considerable delay, but we put him right – showed him the tail end of the old Pilgrims Road. He could fetch the highway again at Hook Green by way of Harvel. Beautiful country, sir, out that way, and a tolerably quick route to Gravesend, although it would surprise you to hear it."

"Describe the boy, if you please," St. Ives said. He found that his heart was racing, and it suddenly seemed as if the publican was taking an unfathomably long time.

"Small little fellow," George told him. "Four years old, roundabout. Dark hair. Needed feeding up. Not at all happy, says I when I saw him. He wore a nightshirt with a vest over top and a cap. The man was his uncle, like we said, taking him into London, and they'd set out early, when the boy was still abed."

"London by way of Gravesend, do you say?"

"Boat, sir," Fred told him. "Quick enough when the tide is making."

"You know the gentleman, perhaps?" asked George. "I beg your honor's pardon for scandalizing the man. I meant no disrespect."

"Then what *did* you mean, you dim-witted sod?" Fred asked him. "You talk out of turn and insult this gentleman's friend without so much as a by-your-leave. That's what I've been a-telling you. Measure twice, cut once, as the sawyer put it."

George looked at the table, considerably abashed.

"I am indeed acquainted with the gentleman," St. Ives told them. "I owe him a debt of some consequence, and I hoped to find him here at the inn."

"You might catch him yet, if you hurry," said George. He bit a pickled egg in half and chewed it up heartily. "The man's wagon had a wheel that was rickety-like. We told him it wanted grease, and to have it seen to before setting out, but he told us to see to our own damned business and let him see to his, begging your honor's pardon. Like as not he's sitting by the roadside as we speak, waiting on the kindness of strangers, which would serve him right."

"And the Pilgrims Road, it's nearby?" St. Ives asked, his heart leaping again. The publican returned at that moment with the hamper of food and drink, and suddenly time was galloping.

"Easiest way is to catch it *before* you get into Wrotham proper, sir, on your right-hand side," Fred told him. "Marked on a stone, it is. It's not much to look at, a path more than a road, but it soon opens up, and you'll find no one to impede you if it's speed you want."

"Another glass of mild for our two friends here," St. Ives said to the publican, "and a glass of something for you." He dropped several shillings on the bar top, snatched up the box of bottled ale, and followed Hasbro out the door, where the stable boy held the horse's reins. Within moments they were on their way again, double quick, not slowing until they were within hailing distance of Wrotham.

"There it is," said St. Ives, pointing at the road sign, which looked more than a little like a gravestone. "Pilgrims Road. It's long odds against running them down unless they've thrown a wheel, but we've got to try, by God. Stumbling upon Fred and George was a bit of luck. Not the last of our luck, I hope."

THIRTEEN
LOST OBJECTS FOUND

Mother Laswell labored across London Bridge in the pitiless sun, shaded by a silk and bamboo parasol, which, she was certain, was the only thing that kept her from dropping dead from the monumental heat. She wondered whether the press of people on either side of her would buoy her up and carry her along if she fell, or whether she would be trampled underfoot and kicked into the Thames. She had heard that thousands of people crossed the bridge every hour, a human river flowing north to south and south to north, the current ebbing at night but flowing heavily again before dawn. The water of the Thames moved west to east beneath the granite pillars, stodgy and filthy now at the turn of the tide. There was a low roar of human voices roundabout her, ships' bells clanging, a constant shouting from men on hundreds of busy decks, masts like a forest of leafless trees against the backdrop of waterfront buildings and docks, black smoke rising from the steam packets passing under the bridge, so that the still air was very nearly as murky as the water beneath it.

Mother Laswell had spent the better part of her life at

war with the filth and clamor of industry, but she feared that it was merely another tide that couldn't be turned back or spanned by a bridge. Coming into London felt like a defeat, and so she rarely made the journey from Aylesford, where Hereafter Farm was a sort of ark, riding above the turmoil, and indeed she sometimes felt as old and exhausted as Noah. *No wonder the old ark-builder had been a drunkard*, she thought.

And then she thought suddenly of poor Bill Kraken, who was a good man, as true and constant as the pole star, but with a mind given over to tolerably strange ideas. She regretted not having left him a note this morning, although it was true that he couldn't read. Still, the absence of a message must have left him miserable. But her business wasn't his affair; indeed, it was beyond his understanding. The debacle was hers and hers alone to deal with. It was she who had brought it about, and she who would finish it and fetch the remains of her boy Edward home again. She couldn't abide the idea of Bill coming to harm trying to lend a hand.

Her discussion with Professor St. Ives had called up fragments of unhappy memory that she had studiously kept buried over the long years. After he had taken his leave, she had lain sleepless atop her bed as the slow hours had passed away, afraid to close her eyes lest sleep conjure long-interred recollections in even more vivid forms. Sometime in the early morning she *had* fallen asleep, only to be visited by a nightmare.

In her dream she arose from her bed and went outside into the windy night, drawn to the moonlit pasture beyond which lay the deep wood that sheltered her husband's laboratory. She climbed the stile over the low wall and struck out across the pasture, intent on recovering the severed skull of her beloved Edward, but she saw that her way was hindered by a distant high wall of black stone. As she approached, an arched door in the wall swung open, revealing a room illuminated by a flickering, orange glow. A hooded figure, more a shadow than a thing of substance, moved out through the doorway and was silhouetted for an instant against the orange light. There was the smell of mown grass on the wind, and the sound of chimes as if from a thousand small bells. The figure beckoned to her, and then rose into the night like black smoke and disappeared into the branches of the trees overhead.

Despite a rising terror, she was drawn to the door. She entered the room, where a stairway led downward, the darkness of the passage illuminated by the light of leaping orange flames glowing in nether regions below. The sound of voices reached her, wafted upward from deep pits, voices murmuring and crying out, snatches of mad laughter, the urgent murmuring of unspeakable regret, damnation, and suffering. She descended the stairs despite the black horror that filled her chest. She saw a shadow rising to meet her – something or someone ascending the stairs. She thought of the shadow figure that had opened the door and beckoned to her. But it wasn't he, at least not in that guise; it was a black goat, ancient as the grave, its eyes glowing, its matted hair smelling of must and decay and brimstone. She had turned and fled, sensing pursuit, hearing the cloven hooves clattering on the stones. She was too terrified to look back, but ran back up the stairs until she emerged again into the night wind blowing across the pasture. The door creaked shut behind her, closing a door on the dream, and she found herself sitting upright on her divan, her heart hammering, the sounds and the sheer terror of the vision filling her mind.

She had arisen and roused out Simonides the scullery boy, who could drive the cart to the station. She would catch the first train into London. Simonides would ask no questions, unlike Bill Kraken, who would both ask and answer them. She couldn't afford to be hindered, although she realized now, caught up in her trek across the bridge, that she was happy that *someone* feared for her, that another human being on this vast, crawling planet had Mother Laswell's interests in his heart.

If somehow she won through and found her way back to Aylesford, she would marry Bill, if he would still have her. The real possibility of it had come into her mind just this past moment, when she had recalled the dream. She had already turned him down twice – she was too old, had always been unlucky in marriage, was used to living alone, and more such excuses – but it had been like trying to reason with Ned Ludd, the mule. Her words went into the man's ears – God knows they were capacious ears – but they didn't take hold. They blew through like autumn leaves and out the other side. She smiled at the thought. Bill had become the pilot of Hereafter Farm, as if he were born to it, as if the farm had been waiting these long years for his arrival. If she were called upon to descend into Hell, she thought, there was no one else she would rather have by her side than Bill Kraken. Leaving him in ignorance this morning made her feel shabby and low.

She was jostled hard, two swaggering young men pushing past her and down toward Pudding Lane. She was across the river now, and into the shadows of the buildings, the tremendous flow of people disappearing into the great city as a river into the sea. She stood quite still for a moment, out of the way of foot traffic, and listened carefully to the sounds within her mind – sounds, as it were, of another sort. Edward's presence had slipped into her consciousness as through an open door, and she knew that she heard his voice now, small and distant, like murmuring from a closed room. She was quite certain he was no great distance away, and that he sensed her presence in return.

She set out again at a determined pace, the Monument coming into view, its gilt summit aflame in the sunlight. She bought a meat pie from a down-at-heel coster-lad dressed in a heavy coat two sizes too large for him, no doubt intolerably hot, and he with no safe place to hang it save around his shoulders. He was just about Edward's age when Edward had...

She gave the boy two crowns and felt guilty for not giving him more and at the same time foolish to be so completely at the mercy of sentiment. She walked on, eating the miserable, gristly pie, leaving the boy happily stupefied on the footpath. The bells of St. Clement's Church chimed out the story of the oranges and lemons, and she recalled from her childhood that St. Clement himself had been pitched into the sea with an anchor knotted around his neck. *Well*, she thought, *there's worse things than being Harriet Laswell abroad in London*, and she reminded herself that it was better to look outward than inward. "It's a poor heart that never rejoices," she said out loud, and set her sights on Lime Street now, where her old friend Mabel Morningstar lived near the Ship Tavern. The thought of the tavern reminded her that she would want something refreshing before long, a pint, perhaps, in order to restore her blood to its natural fluidity, now that the sun had thickened it.

When she turned the corner, her destination in sight at last, she saw Mabel herself on the pavement beyond the door of the tavern, dressed in the Robe of the Starry Firmament, which Mother Laswell had given her these many years past. It was Mabel's summoning robe, scarcely the sort of thing to wear abroad. Three centuries back and she'd have been burnt as a witch at Smithfield for appearing in daylight in a summoning robe.

Mabel knows I've come, Mother Laswell thought suddenly, and a chill of relief came upon her. She needed Mabel's powers, and her need was so great that Mabel had sensed her approach, and had caparisoned herself in anticipation.

"You look done up, Harriet," Mabel said to her. "Like a banger in a hot pan. I've got a high window that's catching the breeze just now, and something to wet your whistle – a nice shandy, if you've a mind for it. We'll go up."

"I'd be most grateful," Mother Laswell told her. "I'm parched as a desert." She followed her friend through the street door, past a small sign that read, "Fortunes Told, Clairvoyance, Necromancy, Lost Objects Found." They exchanged pleasantries, catching each other up as they climbed the dim, narrow stairs, one flight after another, around a corner into a long hallway lit with gaslight, with doors on either side. There was another set of stairs beyond that, the last, but Mother Laswell stopped for a moment to catch her breath. "I'm fairly knackered," she said. "The tramp from Tooley Street just about finished me. I took heart just now, though, because it came to me that you knew I was coming; I can see that, Mabel. You've put on your robe."

"I felt you a way off, Harriet. I had the sure presentiment of a sail billowing overhead, carrying you toward me like a boat on a river, so I made ready. I knew this wasn't a pleasure call. Your mind is full of dread and hope in equal measure. That much is plain. I came down to the street when you drew near, and there you were, your umbrella unfurled on the mast."

Her tone was cheery but there was deep concern in her smile. She had the homely appearance of a solidly built innkeeper or cook, hearty rather than dumpy, with a frazzle of brown hair, not yet showing any gray despite her sixty-odd years. Mother Laswell found that her mind was growing easier now that she wasn't alone, her step more sure as they climbed the last flight of stairs and entered Mabel's quarters. The two of them, both with considerable powers, would see to this together, and would prevail.

A long row of windows in the surprisingly large room looked down onto Fenchurch Street, the casements standing open, letting in air and sunlight both, just as Mabel had promised. There were books in age-darkened bookcases against the walls and more books and manuscripts heaped on the floor. A long, low cabinet stood against one wall, with turned legs and a medieval scene painted in the arts-and-crafts style on the four hinged doors. A pitcher and basin sat atop it.

As she sipped her shandy Mother Laswell studied a

framed photograph of Mabel's dead husband. He wore a morning coat and looked quite young and distinguished, despite his eyes being crossed on account of holding still for the photograph. He had been dead these ten years past. Mother Laswell had always been a little jealous of Mabel and the luck she'd had finding a husband who wasn't some variety of husk. Now he was simply another memory hung on the wall, all things having the sad habit of passing away.

She thought of Bill Kraken again and realized that she wanted his company badly. She had been a fool to come into London alone. It was a sin to be always doing for others but not letting others do for her – a kind of betrayal, a pig-headed pride dressed up like a saint, useful for self-deception but not much else.

Mabel pulled open a curtain, revealing a dim, closeted space in one corner of the room, its opposite walls affixed with long mirrors in plain, dark frames. The third wall of the small room had a candle sconce hung above a small, oak wardrobe cabinet, the doors carved with the image of a face peering out from a cluster of leaves. On top of the cabinet sat a crystal ball on a copper ring, and next to that a barometer. There were two chairs at a square table, one covered in satin that was woven with stars and symbols, the other plain. Small spring-clamps were affixed to the four corners of the tabletop. The room was otherwise unadorned, no frippery at all. Mabel Morningstar was a purely practical woman when it came to the magical arts.

She opened the wardrobe and drew out a roll of heavy vellum from among other rolls, which she spread out on the tabletop, clamping the corners into place. Painted on it was a detailed street-map of London, stretching from Notting Hill Gate to the East India Dock, the more outlying streets and neighborhoods being slightly too distant for her inner sight to penetrate. Objects in the river, corpses included, had always been hidden from Mabel unless she possessed some fragment of the missing thing – a lock of hair, say, if the lost object were a human being. Sometimes a kerchief or a cap would do. Although she could easily have swindled anxious customers by overstating the distance that her mind could range over the city, she despised the idea of giving people false hopes.

There seemed to Mother Laswell to be an almost frightening intensity in the atmosphere of the room, generated by something that was akin to hope, although not quite hope – something related to it: heartache perhaps, the dwindling of hope. She was aware of a heavy vibration that seemed to jostle the air, felt rather than heard, and the quicksilver in the barometer glowed distinctly, as if the heavy liquid was agitated, although not by anything observable.

Mabel took a planchette from among several on the shelves within the cabinet, laid it atop the map, and closed the cabinet. "Let's begin, Harriet," she said, sitting down in the decorated chair. "If you'll just draw the curtain across beside you…" She adjusted the needle in the planchette – not a pencil, but a pointer with a sharp, conical tip the color of iron. Mabel sat bolt upright, summoning her particular powers, her eyes unfocused and staring. A single candle burned in the sconce, the quicksilver in the barometer equally bright. The small room was warm – warmer, it seemed to Mother Laswell, than the larger room without.

From the chair opposite, Mother Laswell could see her own face in the mirror, as well as Mabel's back, the images repeated until they bent away into infinity. She became slowly aware of a continuous musical note as if someone were dragging a bow across a violin in a distant room. Although she couldn't have said just how, she knew that it originated from within the air roundabout them and not from outside. She breathed rhythmically and gently closed her eyes, thus closing her mind to the turmoil of the world without. She pictured a brazier alight with a small flame, and she held the image in her mind, the flame flickering and flaring and then dying away for a moment before darting upward again. The musical note remained constant, lying beneath the sound of the blood moving through her veins.

There Mother Laswell's mind remained, unconscious of the passing of time, although time, or the semblance of time, was surely passing, for the flame at last began to grow indistinct, and in its place appeared Edward's face as it had been before he died, slowly swimming into focus, wavering as the flame had wavered. The room suddenly grew chilly. Edward's eyes seemed to be searching for her, and then, abruptly, to discover her. The effect so unnerved her that her mind nearly leapt back into darkness, his face losing its features as if hidden behind a veil. She held her mind and will steady, however, out of long practice, and after a moment the veil lifted, and Edward's face floated before her again. Very faintly she heard the planchette moving across the vellum on the table, Mabel's hands steadying it, Edward's guiding it.

Mother Laswell opened her eyes slowly as she drew

a breath. Edward's transparent face remained before her, Mabel's features visible through it. The mirror behind Mabel reflected a long corridor of identical images: the edge of the curtain drawn across the door, the angular corner of the wardrobe cabinet, the glow of the candle flame, the back of Mabel's head and Mother Laswell's face, all of it overlaid by Edward's floating visage.

The planchette moved. Mabel's hands seemed to hover above it, trembling just a little, keeping pace with it. Her breathing was labored, and there was something deeply unsettling, perhaps fearful, in her staring, sightless eyes. Mother Laswell compelled herself to focus solely on Edward, to summon memories of him, to call forth the decades-old joy that she had taken in his very existence. At the same time she could see that the reflection in the corridor of mirrors was subtly changing. The vertical line of the curtains and the lines that formed the corner of the wardrobe cabinet began to shift, until the reflections in the mirror lost the semblance of concrete objects and became sharply drawn geometric shapes, parallel and perpendicular lines intersecting on the silver-black plane of the mirrors.

The room was dead cold now. Edward's face was evidently unhappy, his eyes darting here and there, as if he labored to understand where he was. *You're with me, my darling*, Mother Laswell whispered in her mind, casting the thought out before her. It did little good, however, and she was possessed abruptly by a presentiment of danger. The intersecting lines in the mirror slowly rearranged themselves into the features of another dim room – a room that was not a reflection of their own.

A man sat before a table in that room, gazing forward. On the table itself sat Edward's skull. Mother Laswell fought to maintain her mindfulness as she stared at the profile of the man who called himself Ignacio Narbondo, the murderer who had once been her son. Edward's confused face hovered over the table before him. Narbondo reached out as if to touch it, his fingers brushing through it. Immediately it began to fade. Mother Laswell's breath caught in her throat, and she heard the rushing of blood in her ears and the abrasive noise of the moving planchette. Mabel's own breathing was labored and stuttering.

There was the sound of the scraping of chair legs as Narbondo pushed himself away from the table and slowly turned toward Mother Laswell, a puzzled frown appearing on his face, his head canting with curiosity. The frown bloomed into a smile, and although she wanted to turn away from that smile, she would not, and perhaps could not. The room within the mirror faded slowly to black, until Narbondo's disembodied head was the only thing visible in the darkness. Mother Laswell sat stupefied with horror, watching the visage as it grew in size, as if it moved toward them from a vast distance. After an incalculable space of time, it exited the mirror and hovered over the moving planchette as Edward's had done.

The needle rasped hard across the vellum, tearing a gash in it before coming to an abrupt stop. Mabel Morningstar uttered a soft moan, lurched forward in her chair, and slumped down onto the tabletop. Narbondo's image fled back into the mirror, the candle flame guttered and went out, and the room was loud with sounds echoing up from

Fenchurch Street and from the tavern below.

Mother Laswell was aware of a church bell tolling as she heaved herself to her feet by an effort of will. She cast the curtain aside and staggered to the decorated cabinet where she vomited into the basin.

FOURTEEN

ON THE PILGRIMS ROAD

As St. Ives had been warned, the road was nothing at first but an expanded footpath, just wide enough to accommodate the wagon and rutted by spring rains – hard on a bad wheel, certainly. St. Ives watched anxiously ahead, looking out for a sign that the road was "opening up." Although Narbondo was a fiend in human form, he told himself, he hadn't the power to make his wagon fly, nor could he be certain that he was pursued. They would have to be subtle, however. Narbondo wouldn't hesitate to harm Eddie.

St. Ives wondered exactly what he meant by the idea of subtlety. He could hope for no element of surprise if Narbondo's wagon were broken down on the side of the road. The man would either scurry off into the underbrush like a stoat, which wasn't likely, especially with Eddie in tow, or else he would threaten to kill Eddie, which he would do without hesitation, if only as a last, triumphant act. St. Ives would have to shoot him without preamble. It was far better to confront him in Gravesend, where they could hide in plain sight in the crowds.

The land along the roadside became more wooded, and they passed beneath enormous oaks and beeches, which gave them a few moments' grateful shade. Dense scrublands rose away on either side, with now and then an overgrown footpath angling away, but with no sign of human habitation. Away to their left, a kestrel hovered thirty feet above the ground, its underside a beautiful, spotted chestnut brown, its eye on a mouse or some other small creature. It plummeted suddenly, and in a moment flew skyward again and into a nearby copse.

The land grew hilly, and the occasional chance of seeing some distance ahead gave St. Ives a brief respite from the recurring, dark labors of his mind. There was little to see, however, aside from more hills and scrub and the empty road. He realized that Hasbro was endeavoring to interest him in a pasty now, but he waved it away. The hope and enthusiasm he had felt at the Queen's Rest had once again abdicated.

"Regret kills the appetite, I find," he said.

Hasbro nodded. "It was a wise thing that you told young Finn, sir, if you don't mind my saying so, when he carried his own measure of regret. Self-blame pays a shabby return."

"If there was wisdom in anything I told the boy," St. Ives said, "it was a pittance. I've lost any claim on that commodity. The boy was nearly unhinged, however. I saw it at once. If only he had come up to the house and awakened me! Things would have gone differently for all of us, I can tell you. But he did not, which decision I quite understand in both my mind and my heart, although that understanding is worth precious little. As for my part in it, I neglected to tell Finn that Narbondo was in the neighborhood, which is far the greater of the two crimes, an omission that I cannot forgive nor understand. My regret at leaving Eddie and Cleo unprotected is..." He shook his head and left the rest to silence.

There were more tracks leading away from the main road now, which was at last becoming a proper road, certainly smoother, although still dusty. The improvement would serve Narbondo equally well, of course. A partridge ambled out from one of the side paths, nearly under the wheels of the wagon, but then beat its wings and retreated again. There was the smell of vegetation, and the morning was quiet save for the sound of the wagon.

After a moment Hasbro said, "I've often found, sir, that grief and regret are much like the loaves and the fishes, although in a contrary sense, if you will. Those two humors reproduce themselves, sewing discord in the heart and mind."

"You're in the right of it there," St. Ives said.

"A well turned out pasty, sir, is worth a great deal more than an entire hamper of either."

St. Ives found himself smiling, and took the pasty from Hasbro, who, he knew, would carry on in this persuasive manner until he had his way. He bit into it, and was moderately happy with his decision.

"Look aloft!" he shouted, nearly flinging the pasty away into the brush in his excitement. Far overhead to the east, perhaps over the Thames itself, flew an airship, an immensely long cylindrical balloon, pointed on either end. St. Ives snatched the brass telescope from the open luggage behind him and brought it into focus. There was no gondola beneath, but rather a row of four swing-like seats hanging from netting draped over the entire ship. Four tiny figures sat in the seats, each of them rowing the air with long sweeps, although they seemed to make no headway at all. It appeared as if they were dwindling, in fact, making rapid leeway on a current of wind blowing out of the south, so that they were bound for Scotland although the nose was pointed toward Sheerness. He watched until the air vessel was a mere insect moving in the blue sky, a very beautiful insect indeed, although utterly inefficient. He longed to be aloft in a craft of his own, and would be soon enough. He imagined landing in the field at the farm, Alice and Cleo coming out onto the veranda and running toward them. He and Eddie stepping out onto the grass.

"They appear to lack motive power," Hasbro said.

"Indeed they do. One cannot swim through the air, although fools keep trying. I pray they can bring it down somewhere safely. They're badly in need of William Keeble and his miniaturized electric motor, if they want a truly dirigible balloon. I'll just help myself to another of these pasties."

He was swallowing the first mouthful when two men stepped out onto the road a good distance ahead, as if to block their progress.

"Hold up!" someone shouted in that same moment, in the voice of a sea captain out-hollering a storm. It was neither of the two ahead. St. Ives looked over his shoulder and discovered that two more men sat on horseback behind them. He recognized them immediately, even at a distance – Fred and George from the Queen's Rest. It occurred to him that they must have set out soon after he and Hasbro had departed. George waved cheerfully. For a moment St. Ives was confounded, and he very nearly waved a greeting back. Then he saw that Fred held a pistol, exhibiting it now for St. Ives's edification.

The muddle cleared and he understood: all had been a lie. They had been practiced upon, led down the garden path. He swiveled around and looked at the two men in the road ahead. One, a big man with long, unkempt hair, held a truncheon, and the other secreted his hand in his coat, which might or might not mean something. Their own pistols were in the portmanteau behind them. He added stupidity to the day's list of his manifold criminal offenses, noting that the big man must be close to seven feet tall – twenty stone if he weighed an ounce, his black hair hanging past his shoulders, his beard equally lengthy. Hasbro drove the wagon forward very slowly, the distance of their enemies shortening both before and behind, and no escape on either side, unless they meant to burrow into the shrubbery.

"It's Fred and George, from the Queen's Rest," St. Ives said. "We've been duped. The pistols?"

"On top the rest," Hasbro told him. "I took the liberty of loading them. I suggest that I endeavor to run the two ahead down, sir, so perhaps you'll attend to our friends along behind."

"Say the word," St. Ives said, as they moved into the shade of an oak that arched over the road like an immense umbrella.

"Now," Hasbro said, whipping up the horse at the same moment. St. Ives twisted on the seat, the lurching of the wagon nearly throwing him off, and clutched at the portmanteau, which he tore open, reaching inside and closing his hand upon the pistols, one of which he thrust into Hasbro's outstretched hand. There was a heavy thud on the bed of the wagon, and he was shocked to see a man crouching upon it, having dropped from a tree limb, his hat tied under his chin. The man was grinning at him, a knife in his hand, but trying to keep his balance on the moving wagon. St. Ives flung himself forward, onto the wagon bed, lunging straight at the man, who stepped forward, although off-balance with surprise.

St. Ives felt the wagon slow, Hasbro perhaps not keen on pitching him off into the gorse. Clutching the grip of his pistol with both hands, St. Ives fired a shot straight past the knife wielder's head in the direction of the two men on horseback, who, seeing him take hasty aim, reined in and yanked their horses aside from the path. Without pause he struck the man before him hard on the side of the face with his weighted fist, simultaneously blocking a knife thrust with his forearm. The man grunted audibly and slammed down onto his back, although he saved himself from tumbling off the rear of the wagon and held onto the knife. He was endeavoring to heave himself to a sitting position even as St. Ives grabbed the wagon's side for balance and hit him again on his open, leering mouth with the butt of the pistol, blood spraying, the force of the blow pitching the man over backward, knife flying, his upper body disappearing from sight behind the wagon, although he held on tenaciously with his knees to the low railing at the back of the bed.

St. Ives saw that George and Fred were riding up hard behind them again, Fred holding his own pistol aloft, trying to move in close in order to make the shot count, although George, not apparently a skilled horseman, was encumbering him. St. Ives grasped his assailant's foot, levered him upward, and dumped him onto the road, where he struck his head and sprawled out, bouncing once before being run down by George's horse, which stumbled and fell forward onto its knees, pitching George off into the scrub along the road. Fred came along gamely, his pistol held aloft, but turned shy and veered away down a side path when St. Ives found his balance again, leveled his own pistol at him, and blew the hat off his head.

There was a general shouting ahead of them now, and St. Ives heard a gunshot. He threw his arms in front of his face in the moment that the bullet blew a splinter of wood out of the edge of the wagon bed, the splinter tearing through his coat and shirtsleeve, taking flesh with it, although he scarcely felt the wound. He knelt on the wagon bed, seeing that his current assailant stood just ahead in the road with his legs spread, aiming his smoking pistol carefully. The big man stood farther on, the truncheon held in his grasp, his arm upraised. Clearly he meant to strike the horse if the wagon came on. The forward momentum would double the force of the blow. That would surely end it.

"Rein up!" St. Ives shouted at Hasbro, and he aimed the pistol at the giant, but then swung his arm slightly and shot the man with the gun, who slammed over backward onto the road, a lucky shot if ever there was one.

The wagon bounced over the body of the fallen man as St Ives turned back and fired a shot at Fred, who had ridden close upon them again, and who was half hidden in the rising dust. Fred instantly pulled back on the reins, clutching his shoulder, his pistol sailing away. The wagon bounced again, the body flopping down in a heap, and St. Ives turned to see the giant rushing upon them, the truncheon upraised, straight up the center of the road. His face was set with a blind rage, and he was roaring, his mouth wide.

Hasbro calmly and deliberately shot the man in the arm. The truncheon dropped onto the road, and yet the giant came on, his arm hanging uselessly. The sight of two pistols at close range apparently changed his thinking, and he crashed away into the bush and was gone. The road before was empty. Behind them the body of the man who had fallen out of the tree lay crumpled and still some distance back, as did the body of the man with the pistol who had traveled beneath the wheels. The horse that had stumbled and gone down, miraculously, was gone, as were both Fred and George. St. Ives was happy about the horse. The two men lying on the road didn't concern him overmuch.

He and Hasbro had the advantage for the moment, and by mutual unspoken consent they were underway again, moving ahead at a canter, through open country. St. Ives sat in the bed of the wagon, now, holding a pistol in his surprisingly bloody hand. The splinter of wood from the edge of the wagon bed had done its work, although there was still only middling pain. He set the pistol atop his open portmanteau, removed his coat, and pressed a kerchief to the wound, which, thank God, was shallow, the flow of blood deceptive and easily staunched. He fully expected the three survivors to make a second attempt, and he watched the road for a sign of them, ready to blow them to kingdom come this time without any ceremony. They were serious, determined men, which was troubling.

The minutes passed, and the road remained empty – no dust, no sound but the rattling and creak of the wagon and Logarithm's hooves as he cantered along. St. Ives's mind calmed now that the storm was past, and he clambered back onto his seat, leaving the portmanteau open.

"Narbondo is beyond our reach now," he said flatly.

"Indeed, sir, although I would wager that he was well beyond it as soon as we turned off the highway in Wrotham. He no doubt passed along the London Road as we first assumed."

Ahead of them lay a proper road now. When they came up to it they saw a sign at the juncture that read "Harvel," with an instructive arrow pointing west. They turned in that direction, bound once again for the Gravesend Road. Another wagon moved along ahead of them in the near distance, and there were farms on either side once again. They were safe from another surprise, but two hours out of the way now – a fact that St. Ives forced out of his mind.

"Fred and George needn't have followed us," he said to Hasbro. "That seems to be telling. We were doing well enough on our own once we had taken their advice."

"Precisely, sir. We were gone off on a fool's errand, and would have found ourselves in this very spot in any event."

"Which means that they intended to lure us into the countryside in order to murder us, not merely to slow us down."

"It would seem so."

"Narbondo is certainly capable of murdering us for mere sport," St. Ives said, "but it seems wasteful to send five men to accomplish it."

"I believe that you miscalculate, sir. His desire to murder

for pleasure is a weakness in the man. Certainly Narbondo has reason to hate the both of us, but I'm convinced that he fears us as well, or something like it. We've repeatedly interfered with him, and he was very nearly brought to bay at the Chalk Cliffs and was thwarted on Morecambe Bay. He must by now suspect that he overreached himself when he lingered dangerously in Aylesford. When he kidnapped Eddie, he put a spade through the hornets' nest, sir, and he knows it."

St. Ives thought again of his conversation with Mother Laswell, and his words to Alice came back to him. The entire business of the Aylesford Skull and the portal to the land of the dead might well *be* nonsense, as he had insisted – surely it was – but Narbondo did not see it as nonsense. He saw it as something considerably more dangerous than that – something worth sending five men to waylay them on the road. Hasbro was in the right of it again. This was something much more than old grudges. St. Ives had trivialized it to his own and his family's peril. But John Mason hadn't trivialized it, nor had Mother Laswell or her vivisectionist husband, nor did Narbondo. There was a trail of dead people down the years, and St. Ives and Hasbro had nearly joined their ranks, because St. Ives had compelled himself to see the entire business as tiresome nonsense.

As if he had just learned a useful lesson in the dangers of stupidity, easy assumptions, and shallow logic, he thought again of his ill-fated interlude two weeks ago in London – of the notebooks and their theft and the part he had played in the entire wretched business. The thing was clear to him suddenly, as if a shade had been drawn back. It had been a night-and-day swindle – the notebooks, their disappearance, and the botched attempt to buy back something that quite likely hadn't been worth a tinker's dam to begin with – a swindle that had ended in bloody death for a desperate man who was a mere pawn, and a cartful of regret for St. Ives.

The whole thing had the virtue of being a multifarious lesson, however, and, if nothing more, he knew now the place where they were bound in the great city of London, and how they might come to terms with the man they would find there after stabling their horse and wagon. It was the first sensible thing that had come into his mind since he had heard Mrs. Langley pounding away on the scullery door. It wasn't much of a victory, but he had been a damnably dull creature this past twenty-four hours, and even this small victory put an edge on him again.

FIFTEEN
THE GOAT AND CABBAGE

The fish and seaweed reek of Billingsgate Market hung in the warm air along the Thames, the stone walls of the vast fish market doing little to contain it. The smell filled Finn with memories, recalling the days that he had worked with Square Davey, the oyster dredger, and had spent his time on the river, or loitering along Lower Thames Street, watching the boats come into the Custom House or the sunset from London Bridge or the hundreds of tall ships in the Pool. At night there was Toole's Theatre, and Mr. Woodin's Carpet Bag Wheeze, Mr. Woodin diving into his bag in the disguise of Martha Mivens and climbing out moments later as Major Bluster, better than anything old Duffy had put up during Finn's years in Duffy's Circus. It had been easy enough to sneak into Toole's and save the odd penny, and he smiled at the memory of it, although it was not a thing he would readily tell Alice or the Professor. He wondered, though, what was playing at Toole's this evening and whether the old dodge would still serve. But there was no discovering it, no going back.

A score of oyster boats were moored along the wharf that

was commonly called "Oyster Street." Early this morning they would have been swarming with people looking to purchase oysters by the bushel basketful, dripping with sand and sludge, brought upriver from the Thames Estuary, the best from Whitsable and points farther south. Finn could easily picture the early morning crowds, the sailors taking their ease, the salesmen shouting, the baskets drawn dripping from the hold, the coffee houses serving out coffee and bread and butter.

By ten o'clock this morning, though, it would have been over, and it was late now – three in the afternoon, the market finished, the coffee houses nearly empty of custom. Davey's oyster boat lay among the others, its blue-and-red-checked stripe along the waterline making it easily visible. Davey wasn't aboard, not surprising given the hour. He hadn't been in Rodway's Coffee House, either, which meant that he was likely in the Goat and Cabbage, an old, ramshackle public house in Peach Alley, named not for the fruit, but because it had been a haunt of Judases. Guy Fawkes had been betrayed there for a handful of shillings, or so Finn had been told by Square Davey, who was a great man for spinning tales.

He stepped into the mouth of the narrow alley, the old buildings leaning in overhead to block out the sky, all but a ribbon of it. In the winter months it was either dusk or night in Peach Alley, and even now, in midsummer, the alley lay in shadow, the sun shining only on the top row of dirty, heavily mullioned windows. A dead, half-eaten cat lay in the gutter, which was aswim with filth. Finn stepped over it and made his way down the cobbles, wary of whom he might see, or who might see him. The carved wooden sign depicted a lewd-eyed, bearded goat with a cabbage leaf for a cap. The weathered door opened abruptly, and a man wearing a battered slouch hat staggered out, his red eyes weeping gin, his clothes stinking. He looked back angrily, said something hard, stumbled on the broken curb, and lurched away muttering. Finn felt the hilt of his oyster knife on his belt, well covered by his shirt, and he stepped inside, prepared to slip back out again if Square Davey wasn't at his usual table – and in that case he would have come to the end of things, with nothing for it but to step aboard Davey's boat in order to wait and to regret the time slipping away.

"Finn Conrad, as I live and breathe!" said a voice from the shadows, and he saw Davey sitting in the corner alone, a pint glass half full in front of him. There was a look of surprise on the man's face, which quickly turned to a smile, and he nodded broadly. As ever, he smoked a bulldog pipe, and the reek hovered in a small cloud over his head. He wasn't a tall man, but was broad shouldered and heavyset, and he had almost no neck, hence his nickname. His shock of hair was white, although he didn't have the appearance of being old. Finn had no notion of his age. He looked around for less welcoming faces, didn't see any, and made his way to the table, where Davey gestured at a chair.

"A pint of plain for the boy!" Davey shouted at the man behind the bar, who was surly looking and missing an eye. A patch would have made him less hideous, although he could do nothing about his teeth, which were mainly snags. Finn got up to fetch his own pint, which he had no taste for, and then sat back down again. There were two women, tarted up and older than they first appeared, sitting alone some distance away, both of them casting him lascivious looks. He nodded politely and looked away.

"Ham sandwich, son?" Davey asked. "There'll be a lad on the street with sandwiches made up fresh. It's coming on teatime."

"No, thank you, sir," Finn said. "I ate this past hour." The lie wasn't a grievous sin, and he could buy his own sandwich on the street. He was in a hurry, and all the more so as evening drew near.

Davey nodded his head, paused a moment, and said seriously, "I wondered were you dead, Finn. One day you were an oysterman and the next gone away without a word to old Davey. Now here you are, your own self. Come back to the oystering trade have you?"

"No, sir," Finn said. "But I miss it. I was just recollecting those spring mornings at Whitsable, sir, with the baskets heaped with oysters. I haven't forgot that – the dredge coming up so heavy the rig nearly snapped."

"Then come along with me in the morning. There's the boat for a kip tonight. It's snug enough."

"I wish I could, sir, and might one day. But I've got to look into something, and it can't wait. I wonder if you can tell me about a man. He used to be seen here, seemed to have his way with the place, a swart man to look at, although not in color, but dark in spirit, so to speak, and in his clothes and hair. So much evil in him that you could feel the wickedness if you were standing across the street. A hunchback, middling small, mayhaps in a black cape."

"Oh, aye," said Davey, lowering his voice and looking around carefully. There were two men drinking nearby, although one was asleep with his face on the table, and the other was dribbling a glass of gin into his mouth two-handed, one hand gripping the wrist of the other to steady and guide it. "Your man is known as the Doctor hereabouts, although no kind of real medical man, I'd warrant. A blackguard of the worst sort. Devil's spawn. What of it, Finn? You don't want nothing to do with the likes of him. You ain't looking for a situation? It ain't come to that? I know you were quick with your hands, but were always an honest boy, Finn, never a foist."

"No, sir. I learned what I know in the circus, for amusement. A man loves to have his pocket picked for show. Anyway, I don't need work, especially from old Scratch. I'm growing hops out in Kent. But there's a man – a friend of mine – whose son's been kidnapped by the Doctor, as you call him, and it came to me that the Doctor was thick with the man they call the Crumpet. You remember the Crumpet, sir?"

The old man stared at him for a moment, as if searching his face, then cast his voice even lower and hunched forward. "Someone nearly did for the Crumpet with a knife under the bridge, Finn, the night you run off. I tell you that plainly, for what it's worth. I'm not the only one as knows it, although no one's sorry for it."

"*Nearly*, do you say?"

"Aye, a near-run thing. They say he lay in a fever down the way from this very pub for a week. It was the Doctor who sewed him up and saved his worthless life. They were in some manner of business together, although I haven't seen neither one along the docks this past year. You remember

Spry Jack, the dim-witted boy who hauled rubbish out of the market? He disappeared one night some months after you left. He was seen with the Crumpet down in Spitalfields, Whitechapel Road, the two of them walking hand in hand like father and son. The Doctor lives thereabouts, or so I was told by old Benson, the whelk man, who had a natural fondness for the boy, unlike the Crumpet, whose fondness ain't natural by a long chalk. Benson looked around the rookery with half a dozen friends, but nothing came of it. No one knew the Crumpet nor the Doctor, you see. No one had seen anything nor knew anything. They live in main fear of the man. Jack never came back to the market, and yet he'd been born there, in among the whelk casks, and lived hereabouts his whole life, which means he's dead or been taken away. Someone will put an end to the Crumpet for good and all, Finn. He's past his due. Like as not he knows full well who put a knife in him under the bridge, and he'll serve that person out if he gets a chance. Do you ken what I say, boy?"

"I do, sir. And I thank you for saying it. Whitechapel Road?"

"Spitalfields. Just below Flower and Dean, which is a sort of Hell on Earth, Finn. But if Benson and his lot couldn't find the precious Doctor, then he doesn't want to be found. It'll do you no good to go into the rookery."

"It's murder he'll commit again if he can't be found, and my fault, sir. I tell you that plainly." Saying this out loud brought the truth of it back into his mind, along with a vision of Alice. He couldn't bear to face her after Eddie was gone. Her sadness was his doing, or close enough, and would be his undoing if he didn't shift himself. He pushed the thought away so that he could speak. Remorse was best saved for later, when damnation was certain.

"Then I'll go along with you, Finn," Davey said. "I'll just fetch Lobster Wilson and the two Gulleys. We'll tackle it tomorrow, but in the light of day."

"I guess not, Captain Davey. I have a way about me that makes me hard to see, sir, if I don't want to be seen. I'd best go alone."

Davey shrugged. "It's a fool's errand, son, but the Lord bless you. You were always game. You watch yourself with that lot, though. You'll want humble clothes in the rookery, not that finery you're wearing now. Rags and tatters is what you need, and your money in your crabshells, although not those as you've got on your feet. They'll put a knife in you for a pair of quality shoes. You won't find help if you need it, not there, and the worse you need it the less you'll find it. There's nought there but thieves and cutthroats. There ain't but one honest lodging house, and that's Smith's. Look it up first thing, and find shelter in it if you've got a need. They'll take you for a sneak straight away, but when they're a-giving you the bum's rush, ask for Mr. Sawyer. If he's in, and ain't too far gone in drink, tell him you're a friend of Square Davey, and he'll do you right. But don't go asking him about the Doctor or the Crumpet or anything else that'll put a knife in his back, or yours."

"All right. Sawyer it is. At Smith's."

"And one other thing. I can tell you that the Doctor's been seen on the river. Not much happens on the river that I don't hear of sooner or later. Could be he's turned pirate or smuggler or both down around Egypt Bay, back in the marsh. More than one boat's been lost out there on a black night this last six months, one just a few weeks back, or so says a boy who was fished out of the river. Two others who were fished out dead weren't so talkative."

SIXTEEN
SLOCUMB'S MILLINERY

"I wonder if your master is in," St. Ives said to the boy who was sweeping the footpath in front of Slocumb's Millinery in Cheapside. "I owe him a small debt. Perhaps you would step inside and tell Mr. Slocumb that Langdon St. Ives would like to settle up. Tell him it has to do with the business of the illustrations by Joseph Banks. Can you remember all that?" He handed the boy a shilling to cement his memory and then sent him inside. St. Ives made himself visible in the sunshine, so that Slocumb might glimpse him through the window. He wanted to put the wind up the man.

There were dozens of hats on display in the window, hung on wooden hooks and perched high on top of wooden heads. The shop was gaily painted and well kept: no dust, no dead flies behind the glass. The prices were genteel. From what St. Ives could see there were no customers in the shop, and he wondered whether the manufacture of hats turned any sort of profit, or whether Slocumb depended on more interesting pursuits. St. Ives studied his own reflection in the bright glass, not entirely happy with what he saw, but he assumed that Slocumb was also studying it, unhappy for other reasons entirely.

He heard footsteps approaching behind him, and he looked back into the surprised face of the very woman to whom he had given five crowns, whose husband was now a two-weeks-old memory. She stopped and stared at him, as if trying to make sense of his presence, just as he was trying to make sense of hers. And then she shifted her eyes and stepped past him and into Slocumb's without a word spoken, her presence both a mystery and a complication.

St. Ives had only a moment to contemplate this before there sounded a whistle from the back of the shop, and he set off at a run around the edge of the building, where he found Hasbro holding a resigned Slocumb by the collar some few feet from the rear door. Slocumb was a nondescript man, of medium height and build, the sort of man one might glance at but not really see – a useful anonymity if one were describing him to the police. He wore spectacles that were contrived to make him appear owlishly studious, worn low on his nose, which gave him an appearance of condescension. His demeanor changed again when he removed the spectacles, as he did now. It seemed to St. Ives that there was no fear about him, however, but something more like resignation.

"That wheeze with the notebooks fell out badly," Slocumb started to say, no denial in his face or tone, when the rear door of the shop flew open and the woman from the street came out with a heather broom, which she swung first at St. Ives, clipping him on the shoulder, before turning to Hasbro, who shifted on his feet so that it was Slocumb who took the blow on the side of his head. She descended again upon St. Ives again, who trod back toward the street, putting up his hands and managing to wrench the broom from her grasp. He pitched it over the wall behind him and stood his ground, hoping to God that she would come to her senses. It was Slocumb who rescued him. Hasbro had set him free, and the man put his hands on the woman's shoulders now, and guided her weeping back into the shop, shutting the door behind her and shaking his head sadly. St. Ives found that he was shaken by the woman's anger, which he not only understood, but admired and feared.

"She's here to pick up little Claire, sir," Slocumb told them. "They'll be off to gather up young James, who studies at Mr. Markham's Day School. He's a bright lad, is Jimmy, and Jenny's fixed on the idea that he'll come to something, and not have to pick up a living on the streets like his poor father. Perhaps you'd give me a moment to lock the street door behind her?"

"I could attend to the shop," Hasbro said, "and leave you gentlemen to discuss business. I worked in the trade, Mr. Slocumb, when I was a young man – Benson's Millinery off Euston Square."

"Old man Benson!" Slocumb said, momentarily cheered by the memory. "I was fond of Benson, although he was an eccentric of the first water. He died some few months back, I'm sorry to say. Well… Thank you, sir. I'd be grateful if you'd step in. It's best to keep regular hours. Nothing worse than customers fagging down here for nought."

Hasbro nodded and went in through the door. St. Ives listened for sounds of a confrontation, his own friends naturally being the woman's enemies. But there was nothing. If anyone could calm the waters, it would be Hasbro. *Jenny and Claire and Jimmy* – three names to go along with the faces. A few minutes ago, in front of the shop, the sight of the woman had brought that night on the street back into his mind with vivid clarity, and now the names finished the tale. He wished that Slocumb hadn't named the children, who might have remained indistinct shadows. Then he thought of Eddie and of the perils of indecision – nothing indistinct there.

"You say that the business went badly," he said to Slocumb, getting to the point. "That's coming at it a little mild, I should think."

"In that we agree. How did you know to find me? Not that I've any business putting questions to you." He stepped back into the shadow of the building, out of the remains of the day's sunlight, which was still quite warm.

"The unfortunate man who died that night," St. Ives said, "he knew me the instant he saw me, but it was just today the reason came into my mind. I had seen him at Merton's on two or three occasions, going out on deliveries. I remembered the limp as well as his face. The rest followed."

"That was my nephew, George, sir. I wondered why he had bolted that night. That wasn't his way. He could brass it out in front of Lucifer himself. I suspected that he twigged that something was amiss and ran, but I had no idea it was you. When Jenny just now told me the truth of it, seeing you on the street as she did, I bolted, just like George. I couldn't stand a stint in Newgate, sir, not at my age, and no one to take care of Jenny and the little ones now that George is dead."

"I assume that the notebooks were frauds," St. Ives said, "two sets of frauds, one perfectly believable and one flawed. Merton's contrived them both, no doubt."

"No, sir," Slocumb said. "Merton found the notebooks right enough in an old trunk at Banks's home in Lincolnshire, in the Abbey. They'd been stored away this last century. Miraculous discovery, but you know Merton. He hears a rumor from a crow's mouth and then follows the bird to its nest."

"The ubiquitous old trunk, you say? Forgive me, but it's always the old trunk. I've seen Merton's work. I've profited from it, in my way. I've looked through his workroom – old paper, doctored ink, chemicals of all sorts. He can work marvels with weak tea and garden soil. William Henry Ireland was an amateur compared to Merton. It stands to reason that he mugged up Banks's early work and fabricated the notebooks himself. I believe that you negotiated the sale to the Royal Society, not naming Merton. When the fraudulent work was authenticated you contrived to have the notebooks replaced with the second, inferior set. Merton recovered the first set that way along with the papers that authenticated them, and sued for the money that was owed him for the lost set, which wasn't lost at all, but was once again in his possession. And of course he could resell it in due time, with the authentication papers in order. The Royal Society had a reputation to protect, and admitting to the whole business would mean scandal, which eliminated the police, and thus I found myself involved in this ill-conceived plan to re-purchase the stolen notebooks. Whose idea was it to sell them *back* to the Royal Society, I wonder? That was brilliant – a swindle on top of a swindle."

Slocumb stared at him for a moment and then said, "That was mine, sir. Merton had nothing to do with that bit. It was me alone who put George in the way of that Hansom cab just as surely as if I had pushed him."

St. Ives took this in. "Your niece Jenny would say that same thing about me."

"Perhaps it was the fates that pushed him, sir. It's an ill wind that blows no good. But you've still got it wrong about the old trunk. The three notebooks were Joseph Banks's work right enough, like I said. There's no gain in my making that up. Merton got it into his head that he could devise a fair copy as good as the original, out of artistic pride, if you like, and he set out to do it. That was the copy I took to the Society. Merton's name was never mentioned, nor my own, of course. I was a Frenchman named Diderot that evening. If their experts saw through the notebooks, that was to be the end of it. I would be outraged or aggrieved, whichever suited the general atmosphere, and Merton not suspected at all."

"And Merton with nothing to show for his work?" St. Ives asked. "Strange that he would be happy with that."

"For Merton it's the art of it, do you see, not the profit? And come to that, he would still possess the original notebooks and could do with them as he pleased. That was worth nothing to me, though. And so it was I who talked Merton into giving me his working copies of the notebooks, as he called them, for my part in the drama. I could do with them what I would, he said, although he had no idea I would do what I did. A fellow I know – I won't tell you his name

– exchanged them for the fair copy, which was left lying on a desk by some pitiful fool. The exchange was discovered almost at once, and it was then that the Society prevailed upon you to play the role of unscrupulous collector in order to buy back what they assumed were the originals.

"Wheels within wheels, sir, but it all came apart when George ran for it, poor beggar, and him with a game leg. Would you credit it, sir, if I told you that his right leg was destroyed in his youth when he ran afoul of a wagon? It's long odds that it would happen twice, and that the second encounter would finish him, although perhaps it's the fates again. There but for fortune…" He shook his head sadly. "I've had my say, sir. Don't be too hard on Harry Merton. He fancied giving the money back to the Society as a variety of executory bequest, legally speaking, upon his death. That kind of largesse was good for the soul, he said, and of course he still had Banks's originals, the copies having been run over along with George. He saw the Society's money as a sort of loan, you see, that he would repay in due time."

"What of Jenny and her children?" St. Ives asked. "Who's to care for them with George gone?"

"That would be me, sir, in my way. There would perhaps be no need for it if it hadn't gone ill for George, but…" He shrugged.

A mongrel dog came around the corner of the shop now and stood staring at the two of them. It evidently recognized Slocumb, for it came forward eagerly, wagging its tail, and Slocumb brought a piece of biscuit out of his pocket and gave it to the creature, petting it absently on the head. It lay down in the shade, looking at St. Ives as if waiting for him to come to a decision. St. Ives wished for a morsel of Hasbro's always-excellent advice at that moment, but Hasbro was inside the shop, selling hats.

"The Royal Society were careful not to bring the police into the business," St. Ives said at last, "and I'll stand by them in that regard. The entire thing turns out to have been a travesty, or perhaps tragedy, the two being close cousins under the circumstances. Your secret is safe with me, Mr. Slocumb, on one condition, and I'll warn you that you are in a precarious position if you refuse. Think of Jenny and the children before you answer."

"Anything, sir, and I thank you very kindly."

"It's vital that I know the likely whereabouts of Dr. Ignacio Narbondo. He keeps rooms in London, but it's certain that he moves them from time to time for the sake of secrecy."

Slocumb stood staring at him, the doubtful look on his face making it perfectly clear that the thanks had gone out of him. "I can't say, sir."

"You mean you *won't* say. I know that Merton has done business with Narbondo on occasion. You, being Merton's agent, would know what Merton knows and more into the bargain. As with the notebooks, Merton would have remained in the background in his dealings with Narbondo, and wisely. Narbondo would have his way with Merton. Not long ago he very nearly did, when he sent someone around to the Merton's shop with a lead pipe. If ever Merton needed you as an intermediary, it would be in dealings with Narbondo."

"It's that lead pipe that commands my attention, sir.

Newgate Prison or a lead pipe – Morton's Fork, and no doubt about it. It would be the end of Miles Slocumb, with Jenny and the little ones faring for themselves."

"You have my word that they'll be cared for and given every opportunity, Mr. Slocumb. They'll never in life have to fare for themselves unless they choose to."

Slocumb nodded his head slowly, contemplating this. "Right enough," he said finally. "Something like a month back Merton did a bit of business with the Doctor – conveyance of foreign contraband – I don't know what, and don't want to know. Merton wasn't keen on any of this because of that lead pipe, if you see what I mean. But he agreed, for it was the Doctor asking it of him, which was persuasive. And there was the chance of profit in it, come to that. It was me who hired a steam launch to bring the goods into Gravesend, although it never arrived, and it was me who hired the crew. Merton arranged the rest."

"You say that the launch never returned with its cargo? Did Narbondo complain to Merton?"

"He wanted recompense. He had paid a quarter of what was due for the product in advance, but he asked for double his money back, for the trouble invested and the time wasted. The launch was a dead loss pending the insurance. But a claim against the insurance would mean Merton's revealing details of the cargo, including a bill of lading, which he couldn't provide. Merton will pay up in both directions if he don't want trouble."

"And the crew? How many men?"

"Six altogether, including the lighterman and the ship's boy, so to call him – fireman, really."

"*None* of them returned? Perhaps they simply played the pirate and sailed off with the launch?"

"Two corpses were found, sir, the pilot and one of the crew, pulled out of the river near the Old Steps by dredgers. I was told they'd come up with the tide, three or four days dead. Both of them shot dead, not drowned."

"Betrayed by the others, perhaps, who stole the cargo?"

"That don't seem likely, sir. They put into Margate on the return, and it seems strange that they'd cut this sort of caper so close to home instead of the middle of the Channel at midnight. It's a rough patch of river along the marshes, pirates still being common enough. The long and the short of it is that Harry Merton should have chosen a longer spoon, if you take my meaning. Now the Doctor has him backed into a corner, as does the owner of the launch, and no way out except to empty his purse. Wisdom often comes at a price. Better pounds sterling than pounds of flesh, though."

"Indeed," said St. Ives, the entire story resonating in his mind, although it suggested nothing specific. "I'll just ask you for the Doctor's whereabouts now, as close as is sensible, and then I'll leave you to your hats."

"Spitalfields, below Flower and Dean," Slocumb said without hesitation. "Do you know the area?"

"Nothing aside from its reputation."

"It's worse than that, sir. Take my word. It's tolerably close quarters, with the houses packed together, and each crowded with thieves and cutthroats. I didn't meet the Doctor at his lodgings, but near enough, in Angel Alley, above Whitechapel Road. We struck a bargain and he disappeared for a nonce while I stood waiting, although I had my eyes wide open for villainy. There was a courtyard with a broad stone wall across it, with an open arch and another courtyard beyond. I'm main certain that he went into a shabby-looking entryway under that arch, although when he found me again he came from farther off, out of George Yard, I'd warrant, which confounded me. I advise you to take several stalwart friends with you when you seek him out. By midnight, mark my words, the populace will be far gone in drink, and won't scruple to murder you, no matter how many of you there are. They'll set the dogs on you, which don't care a fig about a bullet. And as for the Doctor, he won't be found unless he wants to be found, and by then you'll be in it up to the withers, and no way out."

SEVENTEEN

MERTON'S RARITIES

Merton's Rarities, Thames Street, near London Bridge, was empty of trade and at first appeared to be closed for the evening except for a lamp glowing in the back of the shop, in what would be Merton's workroom. Merton had been a purchasing clerk in the British Museum in his youth, and had established connections to various purveyors of antiquities and curiosities that were out of the regular line. Hence the clientele of Rarities was an eccentric lot. The shop, standing near the London Docks, was much frequented by sailors returning to port from exotic lands, looking to sell rather than buy, knowing that Merton would pay ready money for a well-preserved whale's eyeball or stuffed ape, or better yet for something particularly out of the ordinary – clean human skeletons, well assembled, fetching upwards of sixty pounds these days and worth half that at wholesale.

St. Ives had heard that Merton did a fair trade in severed heads bought dearly from Paris, fresh from the guillotine and preserved in double-refined spirits. He rapped on the door now, loudly, peering inside past the skeleton of some variety of great ape – almost certainly an orangutan. To

St. Ives's certain knowledge, Merton was a cartographer, a forger, and a dealer in rare books as well as curiosities – in short, a good man to know under the right circumstances. A year ago Merton had passed on a valuable map to St. Ives, who had profited from it, and St. Ives was loathe to do him an injury now, or to confront him with anything having the odor of extortion. But time was short. Within the shop, all was silent and still. Behind them, a fog rose from the Thames, drifting inland.

If Merton weren't in, then it was even odds he was either at home with Mrs. Merton eating an early supper, or else in his second shop open only to "the trade" – several subterranean rooms accessible from the back of a haberdashery on Threadneedle Street, where he kept certain species of merchandise well hidden. It was there that he was visited by hangman's assistants trundling Saratoga trunks. St. Ives was determined to run him to ground tonight, and time was ticking away. He and Hasbro were meeting with two "stalwart friends" in a little over an hour at Billson's Half Toad Inn in Smithfield, for supper and a council of war. The business at Slocumb's had taken longer than he had hoped, but it had borne fruit, although whether pears or apples he couldn't yet say.

Merton didn't travel; he had told St. Ives proudly that he had never in his life been out of Greater London, except on occasion to visit various aunts and uncles in the Midlands, which scarcely counted as travel. The world came to *him*, Merton liked to say, rarely the other way around. St. Ives wondered whether to climb over the garden wall from the side street and force the rear door, the mountain coming to Merton, so to speak. Merton might easily be in hiding if he had got wind of St. Ives's part in the notebooks fraud.

No sooner than he conceived the idea, however, than a shadow passed in front of the lamp in the workroom and remained there. St. Ives could just make out the half circle of Merton's round face, looking out at them. The rest of him stood mostly hidden by the edge of the door. St. Ives waved at him, and after another moment Merton apparently identified them. He hurried forward, unlocked the door, and ushered them in, wiping his hands on a piece of towel and gesturing toward a little grouping of stuffed chairs and deal tables in an alcove in the front of the shop. His sparse hair stood up nearly straight on his head, a slump-shouldered man of perhaps fifty years. He wore thick spectacles, his eyesight the victim of the close work he did as a sometimes forger. His lab coat had once been white, but was a palette of colors now, and despite the towel his hands were stained from whatever task he had been up to in his workroom.

"Sorry to keep you gentlemen waiting," he said. "A man can't be too careful once the sun sets. Glass of something?"

"Nothing for me, thank you," St. Ives said. "I don't mean to turn down a pleasant offer, but we're rather in a hurry, I'm afraid, and I for one need my sensibilities intact. We've urgent business to transact before we have the luxury of rest."

Hasbro waved the offer away as well, at which Merton said that perhaps they wouldn't mind if he took a dram. He poured a measure of whisky into a cut glass snifter, tipped a bit of water into it from a nearby bottle, and took an appreciative swallow and sat down. "I needed an excuse to be quits with the day," he said, heaving a sigh. "How can I help you two?"

"We have business with Dr. Ignacio Narbondo," St. Ives said flatly.

The smile left Merton's face. He set the glass down on a table, sat back in his chair, pressed his hands together in front of his mouth and blew air through them. "I scarcely know the man," he said.

"His own mother said the same thing to me just last night," St. Ives said, "but you and I have both had dealings with him in one way and another."

"Not for a *good* long time," Merton said.

"We talked to Mr. Slocumb," Hasbro told him. "Looked him up directly we got into the City."

Merton blinked at him, considering this.

"He was of your same mind," St. Ives put in. "When it comes to Narbondo, the less said the better. I understand that fully. But I have no time for scruples, Harry. My son has been kidnapped by the Doctor, early this morning. We believe him to be somewhere in Spitalfields. We'll do our best to run him to ground tonight. You cannot help us there, of course, but I discovered at Slocumb's that the mystery is deeper than I had thought. Under coercion he revealed the business of the lost steam launch and the contraband you attempted to smuggle into London…"

"I deny it!" Merton cried. "Smuggling, forsooth! Slocumb has misinformed you. He was ever the ungrateful…"

"No, sir, he has not misinformed us, and he seems to me to be a singularly forthright man. I threatened him, do you see? I offered to reveal the details of the Joseph Banks fraud to the Royal Society. That would have finished him, and I believe it would finish you."

Merton looked at him in astonishment. "You're a difficult man, Professor. I had no idea that an old friend of your standing would fling such a threat in my face after…"

"His son has been kidnapped by a murderer, sir," Hasbro said, his voice like a sword thrust. "The boy's life hangs in the balance."

Merton seemed to catch his breath now, and he blinked heavily several times before picking up his glass and draining the contents at a gulp. "Just so," he said. "I quite understand. I meant no…"

"We're both in a difficult position," St. Ives told him, "and might both do better if we were allies in this. I assure you that I have no distaste for honest smuggling when the need arises. I might ask you to arrange some such thing for me some day. What was it that the Doctor wanted transported into London?"

"A round dozen barrels of coal, taken out of a Neolithic cave very near the Normandy coast."

"Coal? He could have purchased a hundredweight for a few shillings, delivered to his door."

"This was… out of the ordinary coal, you might say. Lignite coal, to be certain, but an admixture of carbon, sulfur, old human bones, and other organic debris. Ancient human bones, I might add, kept dry and well preserved by the atmosphere in the cave. There was great expense involved; you would scarcely credit it if I told you."

"*Your* expense, I understand, once the coal was lost, and not Narbondo's."

"Yes," he said unhappily. "The business will come close to ruining me before it's done."

"I believe that Narbondo swindled you, Harry. I don't know quite how, but I intend to find out before I'm through. Indeed, I believe that you and I are caught up in the same net. If I can save my son from his grasp, I'll see whether I can recover something for you into the bargain."

"Well," said Merton, helping himself to more whisky, "I would take that as a kind gesture, certainly I would."

"Good," said St. Ives. "Then tell me one last thing. Have you heard of an object known as the Aylesford Skull?"

"Heard of it, yes. I have no idea of its existence, though rumors have arisen over the years. I have my ear to the ground, you know, and I hear all manner of things. To the best of my knowledge the story of the skull is fabulous, although if it existed it would be worth a fortune, and not a small one. No one has seen it or admitted to possessing it. And there's never yet been a collector who didn't eventually boast about his treasures, especially something of that magnitude. Human vanity requires it. If it were in someone's collection, I would know."

"But something *like* it, perhaps?" St. Ives asked. "A different example of a skull-lamp, so to speak?"

"Yes, certainly. Such things have been in the hands of collectors for hundreds of years. I've heard that they change hands for monstrous sums. The skull of the Duke of Monmouth was so altered. His head, you'll recall, had been sewn back onto his body after his beheading in order for the corpse to sit for a portrait by Benson. It was removed again afterward and sent to France, where a renowned alchemist fashioned it into such a lamp at enormous expense, allegedly financed by some member of the family, possibly the Earl of

Doncaster, although that's mere rumor. It's true, however, that the French are particularly keen on them. Marie Antoinette's skull resides in a particular library in Paris, to my certain knowledge."

"To what uses are these put, then? Merely decorative?"

"In a sense, yes," said Merton. "They are so contrived as to project an image of the person the skull belonged to. It's the image that's decorative, if you follow my meaning."

"An image like that of a so-called magic mirror?"

"Considerably more interesting. A moving image, I'm told, much sought after by spiritualists and by people who study the demonic. I'm afraid they're rather out of my line, though – quite beyond my means despite being of varying quality. If they function at all – cast even a meager representation of a ghost – they had best be kept in a vault for fear of theft."

St. Ives nodded. "Answer one last question if you please. Would the skull of a child be more valuable to those who fabricate these lamps than that of an adult human being?"

"Your own son?" Merton asked.

"Just so."

He shook his head at the thought. "Childhood is a time of deep and changing emotion, great wonder, the spirit at its brightest. So, in a word, yes, although a head taken from any living body is similarly energized. It's a matter of degree, I suppose."

"A victim of the guillotine, perhaps?" Hasbro asked.

"Indeed," Merton said. "And I'll remind you that even a skilled fabricator is only occasionally successful. The reward is great, and there are many inept bunglers who hope one day to succeed. The traffic in potentially useful human skulls is vast, immense sums spent, the results for the most part coming to nothing."

"Thank you, Harry," St. Ives said. "I'm sorry to have threatened you. You can understand my need, however."

"Indeed," Merton said. "You might put your questions to our good friend William Keeble, by the way."

St. Ives looked at him with evident surprise. "William Keeble cannot *conceivably* have any dealings with the sort of people who collect or purvey such things."

"Oh, indeed not, Professor. I don't mean to blacken the man's reputation. But he successfully miniaturized what is referred to as a Ruhmkorff lamp. You're familiar with them, no doubt? I'm told that the tiny Keeble variation is one of the marvels of the age, although I haven't seen one myself. It's said to sit neatly in the palm of one's hand, and yet it projects an extraordinarily bright light."

"And so it might lie within the cranial cavity of these reprehensibly contrived skulls?"

"Just so. I was given to believe that the commission came from a highly placed personage, although there was no mention of names, as you can imagine. Keeble might easily have been ignorant of the use that the lamp would be put to. He's not a worldly man, Professor."

Hasbro rose from his chair now and nodded toward the street. St. Ives glanced out, but saw nothing of interest. The evening outside was busy enough, with people on foot and carriages passing along Lower Thames Street. Stepping away from their small circle of light into the dimness of the ill-lit shop, Hasbro moved off silently, Merton and St.

Ives watching as he made his way toward the shelter of an immense curio cabinet that cast a particularly dense shadow at the corner of the window. After a moment he retraced his steps, sat down in his chair, and said, "It's our old friend George, sir."

"You're certain?" St. Ives asked him. "The last we saw of him he was unhorsed and flying into the shrubbery."

"He's making no effort to conceal himself."

"Tenacious, bold fellow, our George. Alone, is he?"

"Yes, sir. Apparently, although it seems doubtful that he's as bold as that."

"He means to follow us, then, and not attack us, you mean?"

"Indeed – *has* been following us, obviously, since we lost sight of him on the Pilgrims Road."

Merton was blinking at both of them. "*Attack* you? I don't mean to hurry you away, but I'm late for an appointment. Oh my, yes, very late. Mrs. Merton will flay me alive with a serpent. I regret being inhospitable, but…"

"Quite right," St. Ives told him. "We're also on the wing."

"I'll just slip out the back," Hasbro said, "and over the wall. Perhaps we can collar our man and have an informative chat."

St. Ives nodded. "I'll go out through the front door in two minutes' time. We would be fools, however, to allow George to distract us as he has in the past. If we cannot collar him, we'll let him go about his business and we'll go about ours. We'll see him again, and soon, I believe." He watched as Hasbro disappeared toward the rear of the shop, and began mentally to count the seconds in the efficient manner he had learned as a schoolboy: *one elephant, two elephants, three elephants…*

Merton rose from his chair, bent over the back of it, and pulled out several painted sign-boards, choosing one from among them. "On Holiday," it read. "I wish you the greatest luck in finding your son, Professor, and forgive me for reminding you of the promise you made to me this evening in regard to the money that was, I'm certain, stolen from me. I'm fearful that I've once again put my head in the noose. I believe you know the whereabouts of my second establishment?"

"Unless it has moved locations in the past two years," said St. Ives, starting in on the second sixty elephants.

"No, sir, it has not. I would very much like to know the results of your endeavors. It would give me the greatest pleasure to learn that Narbondo has been knocked on the head."

"We're of a like mind," St. Ives said, shaking Merton's hand. He walked toward the door with twenty elephants to spare, preparing himself for the possible chase. George would find it curious, perhaps, that he was coming out alone, but if his curiosity gave him a moment's pause, St. Ives would take advantage of it.

He heard the key turn in the lock behind him as soon as he was through the door, and the "On Holiday" sign-board clacked against the glass. There stood George, right enough, lounging in a shadowy doorway opposite, half shrouded by fog. St. Ives saw Hasbro step out of the byway onto the street, and in that instant St. Ives sprinted hard toward the relevant doorway, dodging around a carriage and nearly knocking over a crossing sweeper who offered to rid the path of horse manure. George was already afoot, however, dashing east along the river toward the Old Swan Pier, disappearing up a narrow, fogbound alley. St. Ives and Hasbro, running side by side now, dodging pedestrians, gained the mouth of the alley and saw the moving shadow just then cutting out of sight between two buildings. They followed warily, listening to their own footfalls on the cobbles until they arrived at the recess between the buildings.

"Easy does it," a voice said, and they saw George's face lit by a match that he touched to the bowl of his pipe, drawing the flame downward. He leaned against the sweating bricks of a building, in no particular hurry now. His face had been torn open, probably when he had been thrown from his horse, and was patched with a strip of bloodstained sticking plaster. Nothing in his demeanor suggested the pleasant bumpkin from the Queen's Rest. He had been a consummate actor. "I was sent by the Doctor to parlay, gentlemen," he said, "since you weren't given to it on the road this morning."

"Weren't *given* to it?" St. Ives said, immediately angered. "It was more in the line of murder than a parlay."

"But who did the murdering? Poor Badger's dead after that caper in the tree, stupid sod, but it was you who knocked him straightaway off the back of the wagon."

"He held a knife in his hand, which meant that he badly wanted to be knocked off the wagon. And if memory serves, it was you who ran him down, and it was Fred who pointed a pistol at us."

"Meant for persuasion, not murder, but mayhaps you're in the right of it. I'd have done something the same if the Badger had dropped onto the back of my wagon. You're wondering what I'm doing now, though. I've got no knife in my hand."

"Your misfortune, perhaps," St. Ives said.

Hasbro put his hand under his coat and sidestepped two paces deeper into the passage so that George was between them, or near enough.

George whistled, and there were answering whistles from back the way they'd come, and from farther on into the gloom of the passageway. "I haven't come alone, guv'nor," he said. "I'm to deliver a message from the Doctor, and then go on my way. You're to think on it."

"Deliver it, then, and be gone."

"The Doctor humbly offers the life of your son for the sum of fifty thousand sovereigns. No negotiation permitted. You have until tomorrow morning to come to a decision."

"And if I do not?"

"You will, your honor. I know it to be true."

"On what authority?"

George took the pipe out of his mouth and banged it against the edge of his fist, the coal falling out onto the ground, where it continued to glow. He slid the pipe into the pocket of his trousers, dusted his hands together, and then whistled again, twice, which meant, possibly, that he knew he was in dangerous waters, at the edge of the maelstrom, and that he wanted his friends to know the same. Again the answering whistles, twice each. St. Ives held very still, listening for approaching footfalls, but heard little beyond the distant traffic from Thames Street and shipping along the river.

"On the authority that you want your son safe. And that you're not keen to make the wrong choice and then have to explain yourself to the missus. No, sir, you wouldn't want that. I'm a married man myself, who had a son of my own, and I know. That would be middling hard, it would indeed."

"Your wife would almost certainly be elated if I were to kill you where you stand."

He shrugged. "That's as may be. But I'm merely the messenger, sir, and my message is that little Eddie won't be safe unless you agree to the Doctor's terms."

"In what way not safe? Say what's in your mouth, sir, and keep my son's name out of it."

"Right. The Doctor said to tell you that he's got a customer who wants one of the skulls, sir, that casts ghosts. This man will pay the same sum as the Doctor is asking of you. But the Customer, so-called, doesn't care what little boy is the cat's paw, if you follow me. It needn't be your son. That's what the Doctor put into my mouth to say."

"The *Customer*," St. Ives said, the word being suddenly loathsome to him. He stared at the man, contemplating his death, and George, seeing it in his eyes, looked furtive, ready to bolt. St. Ives felt a hand on his arm – Hasbro, who shook his head meaningfully. The moment passed, St. Ives forcing his anger downward, out of his mind. "Tell the Doctor," he said at last, "that I'll consider his offer. Tomorrow morning, do you say? How am I to assemble that sum this evening? The thing is impossible."

"Eight o'clock sharp on the morrow. Corner of Thrawl Street and Brick Lane, Spitalfields. Bring a token sum – something serious, mind you – to put on the barrelhead."

"I'll have to see that my son is safe."

"Agreed. There'll be a man there who you won't know, and others you won't see. He'll wear a red kerchief. Follow him, and he'll tell you what you need to do. You'll have time to find the rest of the nuggets, if you're quick about it. Meanwhile, the lad's safe, eating rashers and eggs. And he'll *stay* safe – aye, and your little daughter, too, so says the Doctor – if you gather up the boy and go on your way, back to Kent, and out of the Doctor's purview, so to say."

He paused a moment, something coming into his face as if he were considering, and in a low voice he said, "I believe it's on the up and up – that the Doctor will do as he says."

He whistled three times sharp, and then turned on his heel and walked past Hasbro, away down the passage, where he was quickly swallowed by the darkness and fog.

There were no answering whistles now – no need for them; the thing was done. Hasbro and St. Ives stood alone in the darkness for another moment, and then walked briskly up to Cannon Street, where they hailed a hansom cab, bound for Smithfield.

EIGHTEEN
THE ROOKERY

The street market lay near Tower Hill, a hundred stalls more or less – cobblers and tea dealers and meat sellers and dealers in household objects, stationery, dry goods, walking sticks, spectacles, fruits and vegetables, hot chestnuts, and general whatnot – the stalls thrown up on the instant along the street, the doors standing open in adjacent shops. Because of the fog the booths were already lit by gas lamps or candles, or with the bloody red light of heavily smoking grease lamps. Tonight there were crowds afoot, looking for bargains and buying night-time suppers to eat out of hand. There was the sound of organ music on the air and a general shouting. A hat was mysteriously knocked off an old gentleman's head and snatched up by a boy of five or six, who ran off pell-mell through the crowds, carrying his prize. A man in a nearby stall shouted for someone to stop the boy, which Finn might easily have done as the thief raced past, but instead he watched in amusement as the boy disappeared in the murk down toward the river. He wasn't surprised to hear the man in the stall commiserating with the irritated, hatless old gentleman, offering to sell him a replacement at half price, a hat very much like the one he had lost, although of superior make, a prime article, worth three times what he was asking. Ten minutes from now the boy would return with the hat he had carried away, and the hat seller's stock would be perpetually renewed. It was an old dodge, but the bare-headed gentleman could afford a few shillings for a hat, Finn thought, whereas the boy needed some part of those shillings for his supper, if he were to have any supper at all.

Finn had wandered through most of the markets in Greater London in his time, and had no particular regard for the organized markets of Covent Garden or Portobello Road. What he wanted tonight was the lowest sort, particularly a stall selling worn out clothing, of which there were many stalls to choose from, one of them lit by a single candle thrust into a cored-out turnip. He considered a shabby frock coat made of threadbare velvet that had once been dark green. It still sported three mother of pearl buttons and had the honor of being hung in the stall on an ill-fashioned tailor's dummy contrived from sticks. The rest of the apparel that was recognizable as such was laid out on the street. Unrecognizable apparel was heaped up in piles and sold by the bundle.

Finn looked through the offerings, finding an elbowless shirt with frayed cuffs that would do, and an old balaclava that had perhaps been through a fire. There was a down-at-heel pair of shoes, middling small, but with the toe-ends conveniently lopped off or perhaps chewed off. He found a pair of leather trousers, out at the knees and precariously thin behind, and decided impulsively to buy the old frock coat, which was long enough for decorum if the trousers betrayed him. The coat reduced the overall effect of poverty just slightly, but wasn't flash enough to put him at particular risk. He bought two other shirts that he could tie up into a four-armed bundle and use to hold the clothes he was wearing. Square Davey would keep them safe for him, although he would have to be quick getting them back to Billingsgate, for the evening was wearing on.

Finn paid for the goods, the owner of the stall being a boy not much older than he, undersized and underfed, with a wide, pimpled face.

"Ball crackers, six the penny?" the boy asked him in a low voice, raising his eyebrows. "You won't find them this cheap till Guy Fawkes, I'll warrant."

"I'll take a dozen," Finn said, it seeming like a good idea for half-formed reasons, and left moments later with the clothing and a bag of crackers.

It was an hour later that he found himself in Spitalfields, carrying the balaclava, slouching up and down the byways and alleys, getting to know the place as best he could in the short time he had. Despite Davey's warnings about the rookery, Finn found that he had no real fear of the place. It was true that the narrow streets were populated with thieves and prostitutes, but he had lived among down-and-out people before, known some right hard cases, and he knew how to keep to himself. It was also true that the face of the Crumpet dwelt in the back of his mind. Although the knife had come into Finn's hand quick enough under the bridge that night, when he hadn't time to think, he had done a lot of thinking since, and he didn't relish using it in that way again. He was in a practical mood, and preferred running to fighting.

The fog was intermittent, although settling in now as if it meant to stay. He could scarcely be expected to find a man whom he couldn't see for the fog, and so he hurried now. He found Smith's Lodging House, which recommended itself only because of the even more hideous squalor of the lodgings on either side. He considered going in to ask about Sawyer, but he hadn't the time now, and he went on past instead, studying the building and the street while the night was clear so that he would know it again if there were trouble.

An alley opened on his right, from which sounded the vicious barking and growling of dogs and the shouts of unseen men. He stepped into it, looking down its length and seeing beyond it a courtyard milling with people. Overhead, he was surprised to see a bridge, built of three-or-four-inch line and boards, held steady with lengths of taut rope that acted as stays, the line affixed to rooftops and the sides of buildings. He couldn't make out where it led – or where it started, perhaps the same thing – but he liked the look of the bridge, standing high above the reek and turmoil of the street. He had been an acrobat in Duffy's Circus, and a wirewalker for a time, and there was something in the bridge's rigging that recalled those years to his mind.

Then it occurred to him that the bridge would provide a first-rate view of things, if only the fog didn't spoil that view, as it surely would quite soon. But the fog would hide him, too, if it came to that. It was slightly strange that the bridge stood empty: clearly it wasn't a well-traveled avenue.

The neighborhood was a moldering ruin, but the bridge, curiously, was newish, or appeared so from where he stood. He walked down the alley toward the courtyard, passing an open area where a dozen men surrounded a waist-high enclosure, shouting encouragement at a small, growling dog that was busy killing a rat. Other dogs stood waiting in kennels, and rats in cages. In the courtyard itself, people were strangely subdued, talking in low tones among themselves, many of them looking at an old pump that stood in a pool of filthy water. He wandered in among them as if he were at home, saying, "Four a penny crackers!"

"Here then," said a man, who held out a penny. Finn dug four out of his pocket and handed them over, noticing that there was an odd atmosphere in the yard, as if people were waiting for something to happen.

He noted an old woman sitting on an overturned zinc tub, an enormous black cat lying asleep in her lap. Behind her stood a tall, very thin boy, with a long face and teeth like a horse. His hair, startlingly white, stood up atop his head as if he'd been in a hurricane. He was younger than Finn by a year or two, and he eyed Finn with a look of vast surprise that made Finn look over his own shoulder to see if something were coming up behind him. He saw that there was a lopsided cast to the boy's eyes that had something of the village idiot in it.

"Good evening, grandmother," Finn said to the woman, who nodded at him pleasantly enough. He showed her the coin and said, "I've just found a lucky penny. Perhaps it would buy supper for your cat. He reminds me of a friend of mine, old Hodgepodge, who I hope to see again some day." He petted the cat, who didn't complain, but raised one eyelid and looked at him without much appreciation.

"I thank you, young sir," she said. "I'll take the penny, since you've asked so pleasantly. The cat's name is Lazarus. He'll have a bit of fish tomorrow with that penny." She dropped the coin into a pocket in her apron and gestured behind her with her thumb. "Allow me to introduce Newman, one of my boys."

Finn put his hand out, and Newman shook it, his own hand long and narrow, like his face. "Finn Conrad," Finn said, "at your service."

"It's a good name for a cat, is Lazarus," Newman said. "He was brought back from the dead, like the cove in the Bible. Drownded in the scuttle and dead as a pie."

"I don't doubt it," Finn said. "What is this place? I'm from down Jacob's Island way."

"Angel Alley, it's called," Newman told him. "There's a ghost afoot."

"I thought there was something in the air tonight."

"Aye," the old woman told him. "Newman speaks the truth. It was a ghost, clear as you're standing before me. Carried in on the fog, and carried off the same way. I saw him plainly there by the pump, as did many of us." She gestured in that direction, keeping an eye on the pump in case the ghost should return.

"A ghost, ma'am? In a winding sheet, like? Laden with chains, like the spirit in the play?"

"A boy, clothed in the old fashion, looking alive as you or me, although he'd been hanged."

"You could see the mark of the rope on his neck,"

Newman said, "Plain as you're a-standing here."

"Do you fancy a cracker?" Finn asked him, and when Newman nodded, Finn handed him four of them, holding on to four more – the last of the lot. "No charge among friends," he said. Newman stared at the four balls in his open palm as if they were gold sovereigns.

Finn looked up at the bridge overhead, seeing now that there was a sort of landing at one end, three stories up at the rear of a dimly lit room. The hanged ghost must be the same that he'd seen on the road last night, which meant that Dr. Narbondo lived hereabouts, perhaps making use of the bridge for his comings and goings. The farther end of the bridge still lay out of sight in the distance, where fog swirled through again.

"Can you tell me about that bridge, ma'am?" he asked.

She peered at him, smiling in a cagey manner now, as if he had revealed himself at last. "If it's lead you're be pinching from the roof, you'd best take your business elsewhere. Them there's the hunchbacked doctor's rooms. Perhaps you haven't heard of him out on Jacob's Island, so I'll warn you to give him no cause to hear of *you*."

"Not lead, ma'am. There's not enough money in it, and too much work unless it's left lying about."

"Are you a cracksman, then?"

"No, ma'am. I keep out of other people's houses. It don't seem decent to trespass, and the Bible recommends against it."

"What's your specialism, then?"

"The foist, mostly, but I gave it up when I left the island, unless it's necessary. I worked for a coiner for a time before that, but he was hanged. I'm here temporary-like, buying and selling, bound for Portsmouth, where my brother has a pub on the harbor, in what they call Milton." He held up his hand, showing her the penny that she had put into her apron pocket a minute ago. She reached into her pocket to make certain it was the same coin.

"Clever lad," she said, taking it from him again. "I might could find you work and a kip here in the alley. It's share and share alike among my lads. Newman here is a messenger, mainly. He has knowledge of every street and byway in London, can name them and tell you the buildings along either side and who lives in which, and what they look like and who bolted with whose Uncle Bob. And he can run, too, like a fox when the dogs are on him. You'd scarce credit it unless you'd seen it. He's what the Frenchman calls a savant. You're the same, Finn. You've been trained up to pursue a calling, is what I think. God gave it to you to pick pockets. Don't bury your talents under a basket. The Good Book recommends against that, too." She nodded at him, apparently believing her own words.

"I thank you for the offer, ma'am, but I've changed my ways for good and all."

"Well, they say that honest work is the ticket, if you can get it. I'll tell you plainly that without you've got protection hereabouts, it's best if you pass on through. This is a rough place when the night wears on."

"Yes, ma'am. It's been a pleasure speaking to both of you, and to old Lazarus."

"If you shed some of your scruples and need work, come back to me, Finn. It's not everyone can stand a regular situation. You might find that your brother's pub don't suit you, nor the pay."

"Yes, ma'am," he said. "A pleasure," he said to Newman, shaking the boy's limp hand, and he walked in the direction of Whitechapel, which lay some distance ahead in the fog. He looked up at the bridge again, which, he could see now, ended at a second landing some sixty or eighty feet farther down. Behind the door on the landing there would no doubt be stairs to the street, although either they would be well guarded or the door locked.

It wasn't always vital to make use of a door, however, and he studied the walls and roofs of the buildings roundabout. A three-story, outward leaning, rickety structure stood at the corner of the street beside a rubble-strewn patch of ground that had somehow avoided being built on. He saw an ancient down-spout along the edge of the building, and two windows, one above the other, with broad sills, one of them a casement that was swung open, the room beyond it dark. There was a bit of a balcony with a tottering rail. The damp fog swept in now, grainy with the filth of coal gas.

In the obscurity, which he knew mightn't last, Finn stepped to the edge of the building and leaped upward, grasping the down-spout and settling his right foot onto the jagged corner of a broken timber, throwing his weight onto his foot so as not to wrench the spout loose. He grasped the sill of the window above him with his fingers and cast himself upward, pushing off on his foot and levering his hand against the spout, his elbow braced against the wall, all of this in one sure movement once he had left the ground. He perched now for half a moment, his feet wedged against wooden battens, his left foot tearing away a rotted board as he pushed off again, scrambling onto the sill at the base of the open window. It came into his mind to drop into the apparently empty – or at least dark – room, but then he heard a woman's voice say something sharp from inside, and he reached upward and grasped the bracket that once held a pulley for heaving loads up from the street. It was held strongly to the wall, thank God, and in a trice he hauled himself far enough up to make a leap for the rope stay that secured the bridge. Then it was easy to pull himself upward through the rigging onto the bridge itself. He crouched on the boards now in what would be plain view if the fog cleared again. Behind him stood a door, recently reinforced with wooden cleats – made particularly sturdy.

He pulled his balaclava over his head, since it was no longer safe to be seen. It was a cumbersome, saggy object, which he arranged as best he could. He stepped softly forward to try the door, which was locked, just as he had expected. If it had a dead-latch inside, he had no chance of opening it. He slid the blade of his oyster knife past the doorstop and moved it upward until it stopped. Then he wiggled it, slipping the latch. He listened but heard nothing, and so he opened the door carefully, leaving it ajar. He turned and made his way out across the bridge through the mist now, back toward the vague light cast from the "hunchbacked doctor's rooms." The snarling and barking of the dogs sounded from below and forward, and he heard notes of conversation rising from the courtyard. He wondered whether the ghost had put in another appearance, although it didn't much matter to him. He had but the one goal, and no time to waste on amusement. If the Doctor was within, then so was Eddie. It stood to reason.

The fog was even thicker by the time he gained the opposite landing where he crouched in the heavy shadows, with a view of the room itself through the broad window that he had seen from the courtyard. Within the room stood a table with a curiously decorated skull atop it – the vessel that held the ghost, perhaps. There were empty chairs, two plates of food, and a half-full glass of red wine. A second window, identical to the one that he looked through, stood in the farther wall, so that the room had a view both north and south. Soon Dr. Narbondo appeared leading Eddie by the hand, and the two sat down. Finn couldn't catch all the words, but the Doctor seemed to be advising Eddie to eat. Eddie shook his head and crossed his arms, upon which the Doctor suggested that the alternative was to starve.

Finn realized that he himself was hungry, and he watched with envy as Eddie poked at the food without any interest. The Doctor, however, cut his own meat and forked it into his mouth with the avidity of a cannibal, scarcely chewing it, gravy running down his chin. A gobbet of something dribbled out of his open mouth, and he wiped it away with the back of his hand and drained half his glass before spearing a piece of potato. He said something out loud now, not addressed to Eddie, but to someone else, almost certainly in the room beyond. There was a reply, but muddled, and then Narbondo said, quite clearly, that he very much understood his part of the bargain, but was uncertain that his Lordship could say the same. There was a reply, during which Narbondo put down his fork, picked up a gravy-laden chop from his plate, and, gripping the bone, tore a piece off with his teeth.

Finn considered this second man – "his Lordship." Why would any sort of Lordship be lurking in the rookery, which was a dangerous place for a man with tuppence in his pocket? The man's presence would have to be taken into account, Finn thought, watching Narbondo's grotesque eating with something akin to amazement. He wondered whether the savage eating meant that the Doctor was particularly hungry and enjoying his meal, or whether he simply didn't care about food at all, and was shoveling it down in order to be done with it.

It was a pretty question, really, and he thought now about the old woman in the courtyard, wondering what sort of creature she was. She had offered to do him a kindness, in her way, although doing so would make a sinner of him. Did she mean well, or the opposite? Did she know her own mind and heart, or did she lie to herself and believe it? Human beings, he thought, could be a strangely confounded lot. Cats were typically more sensible…

A man with a round, bald head entered the room now from behind Narbondo. "She's coming along," he said. "Won't be a minute now." Then he went out. Narbondo mopped his face with a napkin and sent Eddie into the farther room where his Lordship was hidden away. Something seemed to be pending…

Finn had a clear run at the window. If he made a prodigious, headfirst leap and balled himself up tightly he could throw himself through. The hateful balaclava might protect his head and neck from broken glass. He pictured it: springing up beyond the table, making for the second room, confounding his Lordship with exploding crackers, and then back out through the window with Eddie and away across the bridge.

Narbondo fiddled with the skull now, which suddenly came alive, the eyes glowing brightly. The ghost of the hanged boy was reflected in the glass of the window opposite.

Conversation abruptly heightened in the courtyard below. Someone shouted, "It's him!" and someone else said, "Of course it is, you goddamn sod."

Finn couldn't see the ghost from his vantage point, but it was obvious to him that it must emanate from the skull on the table – the dead boy's skull, no doubt. Narbondo canted his head and narrowed his eyes, as if listening hard. Finn heard nothing at all aside from the chaos of noises below. After a moment Narbondo fiddled with the skull again. The ghost was drawn back into its prison, the skull fell dark, and Narbondo sat back in his chair looking tolerably satisfied.

NINETEEN

BILLSON'S HALF TOAD INN

The evening was wearing on when St. Ives and Hasbro found themselves walking through the door of Billson's Half Toad Inn on Fingal Street, Lambert Court, Smithfield, near enough to the top end of Shoe Lane so that Chatterton's unhappy ghost still haunted the neighborhood along with the ghosts of the Smithfield martyrs. They took a table in their accustomed corner, which was luckily empty and where an open window let in the evening breeze, the fog drifting past outside. William Billson himself served them an ewer of ale and then went back after two more empty glasses in anticipation of the appearance of Jack Owlesby and Tubby Frobisher, St. Ives's companions in arms. St. Ives hoped that they had received his hastily telegraphed message from Gravesend. If they hadn't, then he and Hasbro would go on alone into the rookery in Spitalfields within the hour.

"This business of a ransom might be an utter fraud, sir," Hasbro said to St. Ives. "Narbondo wouldn't scruple to murder a child while swearing that he was playing a fiddle – please forgive me for speaking plainly. Narbondo's word, such as it is, means nothing to him."

197

"Nor would he scruple to take my money into the bargain," St. Ives said. "And thank you for speaking plainly. This is no time to mince words out of a specious regard for euphemism. I agree with you utterly. Take the case of Mary Eastman. The woman was no real threat to Narbondo, but he murdered her anyway. He sprinkled hemlock on Alice's pike for no conceivable gain. He made a bargain with Harry Merton, and then took the first opportunity to betray him – to steal his money – and then to insist that Merton pay him for the ill treatment. Whoever suggested that there was honor among thieves knew precious few thieves."

St. Ives paused for a moment, contemplating, and then said. "That rather puts me in mind of our friend George. There was something about his demeanor there in the alley that was damnably strange. It came over him at the end of our conversation."

"Something tolerably close to honesty, it seemed to me," Hasbro said. "Perhaps regret. I can't make it out, unless George isn't entirely whom we take him for."

"Lord knows we've taken him for any number of things today. One thing's sure: he doesn't know Narbondo as we do – by his acts, as the Bible says. If it turns out George has a soul, he might find himself in deep water. I'll have no dealings with Narbondo in any event. I mean to strike tonight, for good or ill."

Hasbro nodded, took a contemplative drink of ale, and said, "There's some small chance that your agreeing on tomorrow morning's rendezvous will put them at their ease. Do you believe in the existence of this alleged Customer?"

"Probably the man who commissioned another of

these lamps from Keeble," St. Ives said. "That would be my guess. It's senseless as mere invention when the threat of murder is entirely enough to force my hand, given that it's Narbondo who's making the threat. There's no need for him to fabricate a more elaborate story. An actual customer would give a rational explanation to the kidnapping, a sensible motivation."

"His presence might perhaps lend us some time. Narbondo is certainly as avaricious as he is murderous. Merton suggested that the man was highly placed, but that's scarcely surprising, since wealth would seem to be a requirement, given the cost of the merchandise."

"Keeble might shed some light on the man's identity," St. Ives said.

At that point the door opened, and three men walked in, Jack Owlesby, Tubby Frobisher, and a third man, whom St. Ives didn't recognize – about Jack's own age, which is to say twenty-four or -five. He wore a heavy mustache and had a fit look about him, as if he spent his time on a rugby pitch. He looked around the room appreciatively, taking in the high, oak wainscot that had been put up half a century before Dr. Johnson had made his occasional visit to the inn, and a century and a half before William Billson would buy the inn and rename it the Half Toad. The place was a marvel of homely perfection: the candlelight, the paintings of sailing ships on the walls, the enormous joint roasting on the spit, the tap boy drawing pints of ale, the satisfied patrons stowing away vast quantities of food and drink, and Henrietta Billson moving cheerfully and efficiently among it all, as if conducting an orchestra.

St. Ives found the presence of the newcomer tedious, however, regardless of the man's sensible appreciation of the place in which he found himself. Surely Jack had understood from the nature of his message that there was perilous work to be done. St. Ives had no intention of entertaining strangers, tonight of all nights.

Tubby saw the two of them and angled toward their table, a dark look on his usually jovial face. He carried a heavy blackthorn stick, which gave him a rough and ready appearance. St. Ives was heartily glad to see him. Tubby's stick was a cudgel rather than a cane, and with the top hollowed out and filled with lead, a more deadly weapon, perhaps, than St. Ives's true Irish shillelagh, although St. Ives in his youth had learned to fight with it in the Irish manner, and he much preferred its length and weight – more versatile than a cudgel, and without the lethal appearance.

Jack, a comparatively young man, was sometimes frivolous in his speech and actions, and rather too inclined to be whimsical and hyperbolic, but was utterly dependable. He was an aspiring writer, who had sold pieces to *The Graphic* and *Cornhill Magazine*, several of them concerning the adventures of Langdon St. Ives, which were accurate enough, but contrived to sound like fiction. St. Ives had known him and his wife Dorothy – the daughter of William Keeble – for many years. Although it couldn't be said that he was fearless, St. Ives had never known Jack to hesitate in the face of danger. Banishing fear, St. Ives had always thought, was more remarkable than fearlessness, which was too often mere stupidity, and equally often deadly. Jack's loyalty to St. Ives was complete. He drew up before the table now, gesturing at his companion.

"I'd like to introduce the two of you to my particular friend," he said. "Arthur Doyle. He's a doctor, University of Edinburgh, with a new practice in Southend. He's also a literary man, in London to speak to his publishers. I met him today at the offices of the *Temple Bar*, where he managed to sell a story. I, however, did not. Doyle, meet Professor Langdon St. Ives, and his long-time friend Hasbro."

"Very pleased to meet you both," the man said, his Scottish accent moderate.

His illuminated smile and the evident pleasure in his eyes were genuine, St. Ives noted, and he wondered what kind of writerly swill Jack had been filling him with this afternoon – apocryphal tales of grand exploits, no doubt.

"I've long wanted to meet you, sir," Doyle said to St. Ives. "We have a mutual friend at the university. You know Joseph Bell, I believe. He speaks highly of you."

"I do indeed," said St. Ives with happy surprise. "I had the pleasure of meeting with him a year ago, when we were in your country, in Dundee, looking into the Tay Bridge disaster. We went considerably out of our way to consult with Dr. Bell, although to no avail, despite our concurring on the issue of Thomas Bouch's culpability. The rail bridge was indeed badly engineered, although not so badly that it collapsed without, shall we say, nefarious encouragement. Please, sit down. We're about to take some supper, although we haven't much time to enjoy it."

"Thank you, sir," he said, and the two seated themselves. Tubby had already sat down and was familiarizing himself with the ale. "I've heard of this Narbondo," Doyle continued.

"Highly interesting man, and I don't doubt but what he had a hand in the Tay Bridge disaster, and has the blood of those seventy-five passengers on his hands. He was briefly at Edinburgh, you know, although long before my time. I believe that he called himself by a different name then. He was sent down for practicing vivisection. Doctor Bell brought the charges against him."

"Is that true?" St. Ives said. "I had no idea."

"It was kept quiet, of course – hidden from the press lest it sully the reputation of the University."

The inn door opened just then and a newsboy entered, selling the *Daily Telegraph*. "Lord Moorgate cuts up rough!" the boy shouted. "Calls Gladstone a bloody anarchist!" He moved among the tables, collecting coins, and was given a bowl of plum duff by Henrietta Billson, who also paid for several copies of the paper, which she hung over a stick on the wall. The act was a kindness, it seemed to St. Ives, since the patrons who wanted the paper had already paid for it. Tubby Frobisher bought a copy as the boy headed toward the door.

"Lord Moorgate is an idiot," Tubby announced after looking at the front page.

"Moorgate has the Queen's ear," Doyle said. "Gladstone is once again on the outs."

"Aye, she's influenced by Moorgate," Tubby said, "but she can't believe that Gladstone is planting infernal devices around London, for God's sake. Moorgate hates the Irish and so hates Gladstone. To my mind it's a crying shame that Moorgate wasn't stabbed to death in Phoenix Park. A knife in the guts would have gone a long way toward civilizing the man."

"I dare say," Doyle said, looking in a wide-eyed way at Tubby.

"Tubby has the habit of speaking what's on his mind, Doyle, as soon as the thought enters it," Jack Owlesby said. "His thoughts are his children, you see, and he loves them all equally."

"What Jack says is true, Mr. Doyle," Tubby put in. "Jack, on the other hand, very often attempts to say what's *not* on his mind, which generally leads to a sad confusion. One time he was bold enough to sing 'The Highwayman's Lament' without ever having heard it. He filled in nine-tenths of the lyrics with ta-dum, ta-dum, ta-dum. It was such a fulsome endeavor that the audience had no need ever to hear it again, something they admitted to the last man, quite vehemently as I recall."

"Never mind him, Doyle," Jack said. "Certainly it's the ale speaking, and not the man, prodigious though he might be."

"It's high time we got down to business, gentlemen," St. Ives said, making an effort to hide his growing impatience.

"I hope it wasn't forward of me," Jack put in quickly, "but I took it upon myself to invite Doyle along on our little adventure tonight."

"Only if it's entirely convenient to you, sir," Doyle said. "If you need another hand, so to speak."

St. Ives regarded him openly and liked what he saw. The man had a forthright and honest face, and a look of great vigor about him. Still, the offer was very nearly senseless, taken all the way around, since Doyle could scarcely know what he was asking. "Thank you for the offer, Mr. Doyle. Aside from the mention of Ignacio Narbondo, did Jack reveal the nature of our business?"

"Not the details," Jack said.

"Just so. I can tell you, Mr. Doyle – and I adjure you to remain silent on this front – that we're working on the nether side of the law. It's odds-on that people will be injured, perhaps killed. I'm in a desperate way, you see, sailing under a black flag. I tell you that plainly. My own safety is of little consequence to me."

"Nor mine," said Tubby, who picked up his blackthorn and thumped it on the floorboards. "I intend to knock these people on the head and let Satan sort them out."

Hasbro said nothing, but his silence and the set look on his face seemed to reveal a like way of thinking.

Doyle looked from one to the other of them and nodded. "I'm with you," he said to St. Ives. "I've read of your exploits in *The Graphic*, sir, and for a number of reasons I would be pleased to be a part of one of them. I'm a fair boxer, and I've made a particular study of a human being's natural physical weaknesses. I'm unencumbered by a wife, and although it's true that I have a new practice in Southend, business can be optimistically described as slow, and at present a locum attends to my affairs. He'll be glad to have another few days' salary before I return. In short, I'm my own man, and I'm quite prepared to follow you, come what may."

"There's spirit for you, eh!" Tubby cried, reaching for his glass. "Let's drink to the unencumbered Mr. Doyle! We'll beard Narbondo in his den, and be damned to him."

"So be it," St. Ives said, dismissing caution and raising his own glass. "Now there are five of us. I prefer an odd number. Are you armed, Jack?"

Owlesby opened his coat, revealing a marlinspike slipped into a long, narrow pocket.

"And you, Mr. Doyle? We'll be going into the rookery, Flower and Dean Street, and it's odds on we'll have to fight our way out."

"I prefer to use my fists, sir, if it comes to it."

"More in keeping with the Oath, perhaps?"

"Yes, although I let my conscience guide me in that regard."

"Then I advise you to be prudent. No unnecessary heroics. We leave none of us behind, alive or dead, and so it's best for all of us if we walk out." To the entire company St. Ives said, "As for the police, if something goes awry, we'll want the same story – simply that we were set upon by a gang of thieves and undertook to defend ourselves. That should answer nicely, given the low neighborhood, although the police might wonder at our business there. Our adversaries will scarcely lodge a complaint in any event. Mr. Doyle, I'll reveal to you that Dr. Narbondo has kidnapped my son and is threatening his life. Our only advantage, as Hasbro was just pointing out to me when you three walked in, is that the Doctor is particularly avaricious, always on the lookout for means with which to carry out his schemes. He has demanded a considerable sum of money as ransom. We very much hope that simple greed will preserve the life of my son, giving us time to act."

The food arrived at the table – thick cuts of roast beef, boiled potatoes with butter, an immense turbot stuffed with an oyster hash, and a leek pastry with bacon. They fell to, eating with a will, St. Ives discovering that he was sharp set, that he relished the food and was vastly hungry, had rarely eaten better – a great contrast with his closed stomach earlier in the day. It was the pending battle that did it, the chance that it was a last meal, or perhaps simply some bodily demand for sustenance before going into dangerous territory.

"I strongly suspect that to Narbondo's mind this is merely the prelude to further villainy," St. Ives told them. "It's quite possible that he means to draw us in, murder us, and have a clear field. Narbondo is rumored to be engaged in some larger, infinitely evil scheme, which we will thwart if ever we can, although thwarting that scheme is secondary to me tonight. Hasbro and I will go in first. They'll be on the lookout for us, but they have no idea of the three of you. You'll take no unwarranted chances, but if you can find a way to come around behind them, then between the surprise of the thing and the weight of our attack, we can dispatch them quickly and beard Narbondo in his den."

"Quite so," Tubby said, hefting his stick. "If I can't lay them out like wheat before the scythe, I'm a damned humbug." He was nearly apoplectic with anticipation, and Doyle looked at him with an expression that was something between admiring wonder and professional concern.

"But we must keep in sight of each other," St. Ives said, "each looking out for the other." He talked around the food, telling them what news they had got from Slocumb – the alley, the arched passage, the possibility of multiple exits. The rest they would discover in Spitalfields, come what may.

"One thing, gentlemen," he said, when they were rising to leave. "If it is within my power to do so, I mean to end Narbondo's career this evening, by whatever means are necessary, even if we are successful in securing my son unharmed. I have cold-blooded murder in my mind; I tell you that plainly and with no compunctions. If you have any objections to that, then by all means go about your business now; it's far the more sensible course."

Tubby laughed out loud, which startled Doyle once again, although he hesitated only a moment before putting out his hand for St. Ives to shake. "One for all, and all for one, as the saying goes." He winked at Tubby, who slapped him manfully on the shoulder, hard enough to knock a smaller man out of his chair. St. Ives was heartened by the high spirits, but Eddie was ever on his mind, as was Alice, and his own spirits were something less than high. George had been dead right about one thing: St. Ives could not return to Aylesford and to Alice having failed again, not this time.

TWENTY

MOTHER AND SON

For an anxious time, Mother Laswell had thought that Mabel was dead – throttled by the immense psychic charge of Narbondo's presence in the room. When her friend had come to, she was physically exhausted, barely able to stagger to bed, where she fell instantly into a fitful sleep, sitting up wild-eyed from time to time as if she saw some horror right there in the room. Mother Laswell had sat with her throughout the day, listening to her feverish ramblings and sponging her brow, returning time and again to study the torn, vellum map. The planchette needle had plowed a furrow straight into Spitalfields, stopping directly above Whitechapel Road in what appeared to be a warren of unnamed courtyards and alleyways. She wished that it had somehow been more exacting, but it would have to be enough. She would depend upon her senses to lead her on once she was near her destination.

In the evening she persuaded Mabel to drink a cup of tea, after which her friend passed into a more natural slumber. Mother Laswell had left her then, along with a note that expressed her gratitude but said nothing of her intentions. Mabel needn't be a party to the pending horror, for a horror it would surely be. Mother Laswell had gone down the stairs, taking her parasol with her, unsure whether she would return, or whether her journey would simply end tonight.

A patchy fog hung in the dark streets now, the gas lamps glowing with a gauzy, yellow light, the buildings tolerably distinct close at hand, but ghostly across the road and vanishing utterly in the distances. The stones beneath her feet were solid enough, however. Figures loomed up out of the murk, their footfalls strangely loud for the space of a few moments and then passing away into silence. She recalled the bright sunlight of her morning trek across the bridge and the press of people going about their daily business, all of it seeming almost cheerful to her now. The city had been very much alive. There was a sinister quality to things tonight, though, and she wondered where it originated – whether it was mere atmospheric stagecraft, a product of fog and shadow, or was it the offspring of her own mind, made dark by what she had become and what she must accomplish? Perhaps it was a glamor of sorts, a spell emitted from the room in which Narbondo sat alone with the ghost of his brother, his mind drawing her along through the gloom, her own mind convinced of the dull-witted notion that it was she who acted out of rational necessity.

That Narbondo had been able to project himself, to intrude upon Mabel's conjuring, had been a vast surprise, although she saw now that it oughtn't to have been. Narbondo was her son, after all. She should have suspected that he had the gift. She should have warned Mabel so that

Mabel might have guarded against his intrusion. But she had not, and her friend had paid dearly for the oversight. And yet for all that, now that she herself was forewarned it did her little good. Narbondo could murder her if he chose, and would no doubt do just that if he knew what she intended. When she searched her heart for motherly emotions that might stay her hand, she found mere darkness.

Well, she thought, *so be it*. She came to herself and discovered that she stood on the corner of Commercial Street and Flower and Dean without quite knowing how she had got there. She walked south, picturing Mabel's vellum map in her mind, and, on impulse, turned the corner onto Wentworth Street, although Whitechapel lay another long stretch to the south. She abandoned the mental image of the map and pictured herself a living planchette, drawn forward now by a magnetic tugging in her second mind. Edward's spirit was abroad, or had been; she sensed it clearly.

She slowed her pace, feeling her way with her mind more than with her eyes. Although Commercial Street had been a broad thoroughfare, Wentworth Street was narrow and crowded, and with a deviant personality, if a street could be said to have such a thing. A window opened now in the murk, and for a moment moonlight allowed her a view of a narrow byway – "Angel Alley," a sign read – a street of mean lodging houses, the second and third stories jutting out over the first so that the street seemed narrower yet. A strumpet with a sweet face passed, clutching the arm of a sailor who was evidently drunk, the two of them entering a door that revealed a set of stairs in what was apparently a nameless lodging house. A sign in the window offered "couples beds" for eight pence. There was a reek of garbage and human filth and general decay roundabout now, but she went resolutely up the alley.

Ten steps farther on a group of four low men lounged in an alcove against a nearby wall, one of them fearsomely large and with black, lank hair and beard, his arm in a makeshift sling, another a man with a mutilated face. The filthy window beside the four appeared at first to look out from an empty house. The panes were filmed with dirt, several of them broken and stopped with rags or paper. But then she saw candlelight through the window, and the haggard, pale, slack face of an idiot child peering out. There was the sound of arguing within, something smashed against a wall, someone cried out, and there was a burst of high, drunken laughter. People moved about beyond the staring child like restless spirits in Hell.

It came to her that the squalid lanes and alleys of the rookery were densely populated despite the nearly empty streets. She felt the weight of thousands of dull, sorrowful, hopeless minds pressing in upon her own mind and soul like the fog itself. She sensed hunger and illness, avarice, too, and a grasping, roiling evil in the dark spirit of the place. She searched for hope, but found little, either within herself or in the gloom that surrounded her.

"Take a dram, mother?" one of the four men asked her, and she hurried away without answering, listening to the laughter behind her, clutching her bag beneath her cloak. No one with any sense would carry anything of value in such a place unless they wanted to be knocked on the head.

Mother, he had said... She glanced furtively back at the men. Coincidence, no doubt.

Her temples throbbed painfully, and it came to her that her son Edward's spirit haunted the air roundabout, as if he were standing nearby. "Edward?" she asked in a whisper, listening with her mind rather than her ears. There was a courtyard ahead, with fog swirling through it. She was drawn into it, seeing now an illuminated figure hovering within the mists, its outline coming into focus: Edward's ghost, fully formed. His three-dimensional semblance was made solid by the fog itself, almost as solid as if he were a living boy. He seemed to see her – she was certain he did. Her breath caught in her throat, and her heart felt a yearning that made her faint. She stepped forward, holding out her arms until she was bathed in his light – not the meager candle glow that had generated his ghost when she had possessed the skull, but a vivid, living illumination. Images flitted through her mind now like pictures on a screen, memories of Edward's time on earth: Mary Eastman as a girl, the books by his bedside, a fire in the hearth, a patch of ground with his shadow swinging across it, the shadow of the rope rising from behind his head…

A wave of pain and sorrow engulfed her, and she turned her back on his ghost and staggered into the darkness. When she looked back he was gone. She saw now that a long wall divided the courtyard she stood in from the courtyard beyond. Atop the wall stood a lighted room – the same room that she had seen in the mirror this morning when she had convened with Mabel Morningstar. Narbondo sat at the table, looking out at her, Edward's skull before him, its eyes dark. The very sight of it once again filled her with both horror and longing – emotions that should have been incompatible, but were not. She heard footfalls, and turned toward a man who stepped out of the shadows to her left. He wore a low hat with a rounded crown, which gave him the air of a country parson.

"I'm sent to convey the Doctor's wishes, ma'am." He swept his hat from his head and bowed theatrically. He was bald on top, his hair in ringlets like an illustration of Nero. "He beckons you up, ma'am – bids you to come freely, of your own accord."

"Do you know who I am?" she asked, damned if she would be cowed by the man. She was in unfamiliar territory here, but that was all the more reason to be forthright. Her communion with Edward's ghost had solidified her resolve.

"No, ma'am," he said. "Only that the Doctor would have a word with you. I've been waiting this past hour, since nightfall, and now you've come. I'm bound to do my duty and show you up the stairs."

"Good enough. I'm bound to do my duty and follow. I wonder, though. Did you see the ghost just now?"

"Plainly."

"It was the ghost of my son," she said. "What do you think of that?"

"It's not my business to think, ma'am. I leave that to the Doctor. Will you come up?"

"Only if I know your name."

"That would be George Kittering, ma'am, at your service."

"You can call me Mother Laswell. The man upstairs, whom you call the Doctor, once called me 'mother,' and it wasn't figurative, mind you. I am indeed his mother."

George nodded, considering this but apparently having nothing to say. He turned around, moving toward the arched passage in the wall that loomed before them, almost obscured by fog. She was aware of footfalls behind her now, and she glanced back, not surprised to see the man who had offered her a dram of gin, followed by his three companions, the largest of the three looming a full foot above the others. She knew now that they weren't a threat to her. Quite the contrary, they had no doubt been waiting for her, four of Narbondo's bullies on the lookout for her appearance, perhaps to guarantee her safe passage through the rookery.

It came to her that the night suddenly had a fateful quality to it, as if something that had been scripted long ago were coming to pass. She and her murderous son were strangely of a like mind. She came to him willingly, out of need. He invited her in willingly, but what was his need? She reminded herself that it lay within her to exert her will in order to alter the script. She was a free woman and she disbelieved in fate.

The wall before her was built of stone, stained black by years of grit. Further on lay the adjacent courtyard, which contained a warren of windowless shanties, what were called back-to-backs, leaning together around the perimeter like card houses, side by side and one atop the other, fading in the murk in either direction. The people dwelling in the depths must live in perpetual darkness, she thought – candles or lanterns day and night, although surely they could scarcely afford to buy either candles or lamp oil. Here and there windows were faintly aglow. A semblance of life was carried on within, entire families living in single rooms

– many hundreds of lives having come to a standstill here in this place of darkness that was a biscuit toss away from the Royal Mint. Mother Laswell turned away unhappily, reminding herself that she was but one old woman in a city of millions, and that she had made a hash of her own family, or hadn't prevented it from happening, and yet fortune had treated her well despite it, but leaving her with a deep sense of guilt that she wouldn't cast off this side of the grave.

George opened a heavy door in the stone beneath the arch, nodding her into a little vestibule where a gas lamp threw out a sputtering glow. She climbed the stairs with a heavy heart and a sense of doom, hearing the door shut behind her, counting the sixteen stair treads that wound around on themselves, and finding herself in a passage that was richly decorated in its gaudy way, a stark contrast to the poverty below. She saw that George hadn't followed, and was relieved.

Another door just ahead stood ajar, and she knew at once that it led into the room that overlooked the courtyard. Again it came into her mind that Narbondo had drawn her there: the men lounging in the street, George waiting to greet her, the door standing open before her now. The robbery of poor Edward's grave and Mary Eastman's murder had baited the trap, and now here she was, ten seconds from setting foot in it. If she walked away, she wondered, would he let her go?

But walking away wasn't in her. She had come too far. She pushed the door wide and stepped through boldly, purposefully ignoring Narbondo who sat in a chair regarding her. She took in the room at a glance – the crates of books, the heaps of papers, the mean furnishings, the bare walls, as if the abode were merely temporary, the books and papers residing in the wooden crates that they had arrived in, ready to be carried out on the instant. She saw that a second immense window with curtains hanging to either side stood in the rear wall, bowed inward, weak with age. A second door, barred with a timber, stood adjacent to it, the window and the door looking back toward the hovels in the farther courtyard. Through the window she could see in the hazy moonlight what appeared to be the first few yards of a narrow, wooden suspension bridge leading away across the rooftops, or perhaps into a distant building.

There was a second room beyond the one in which she stood. Through its open door part of a long workbench was just visible, the top littered with tools and pieces of equipment that conveyed nothing to her mind. There were more wooden packing crates disgorging excelsior, and the place had an odious chemical reek. She heard what sounded like footsteps from within the room, someone pacing, and she got a brief glimpse of a man who peered out at her for an instant. It seemed to her that he wore a wig, and that his chin whiskers were false.

On the table, in front of her only living son, lay two plates, covered in broken meat and bones, potatoes and congealed gravy. She regarded Narbondo openly now. She compelled her mind into a cold objectivity, closed against sentiment. She could see in his face very little of the boy she remembered, which was hidden by a malignancy that he had purchased dearly over the years. He exuded an unnaturally vile essence – not an odor, but something very much like it – a palpable, repellent evil.

Her eyes returned to the table. *Two* plates? The man in the farther room, perhaps?

"My small houseguest," Narbondo said to her, as if knowing what was in her mind. "I'll introduce the two of you. Edward!" he cried, in a sharp voice.

The name electrified her. From the room beyond there appeared a small boy, four or five years of age, dressed in a white nightgown and black vest. He stood in the doorway, clearly hesitant to come any closer. He was apparently unhappy, although she saw something in his face that might be hope when he looked into her own. He was pushed from behind just then – she saw the sleeve of a black coat, perhaps velvet – and he staggered out toward the table.

"This is my beloved mother," Narbondo said to the boy. "She hails from Aylesford, and is in fact a neighbor of yours. Say 'good evening' to her, Edward."

"Good evening," the boy said, and then, after staring at her for another moment, he turned sharply around and disappeared back into the other room.

"I was quite pleased when I discovered the boy's name," Narbondo said to her. "Not that the name Edward is in short supply. It's serendipitous, though. You'll agree with me there. Our own Edward come again, I thought when I learned of it."

She stared at him for a moment without speaking, her wits fuddled by the boy's being there at all. His presence changed things, and she made up her mind – remade it – abruptly. "What I think is of no concern to you," she told him. "I'll take the boy with me when I go. I won't allow you to keep him, if that's what you had in mind."

"Not at all what I had in mind, mother. He's not worth keeping. He's a dull boy, says almost nothing, can barely read, cannot amuse himself. He can eat, but then a fly or a mouse can eat, so there's nothing in it to recommend him."

"What do you mean that he's a neighbor of mine? Who is the child?"

"The son of a man called Professor Langdon St. Ives and his wife Alice, lately hailing from Aylesford, the old Walton estate. Both of them have long been treasured friends of mine, and so I've taken it upon myself to borrow their son. The Professor was at your house, I believe – what was once my house – on the evening of the night that I abducted the boy. He no doubt awoke to his loss in the morning. I very much wish I could have been there to witness it. There's nothing more amusing than the face of someone happening upon dire knowledge. It effects a change that is imprinted on one's features forever. My," he said, smiling broadly now, "this is indeed splendid. Do you realize, mother, that this is the first conversation we've enjoyed together in… How long has it been?"

She didn't answer, but set her parasol on the table and took her handbag from beneath her cloak. She reached into it calmly and drew out a pistol. It had belonged to her husband, and was many years old, although she had kept it clean and oiled so that the barrel wouldn't be corrupted, and had actually shot it twice after Bill had come to the farm. She had managed to hit a large sunflower at five paces, blowing it to bits in a hail of seeds and petals.

"A flintlock, by heavens!" Narbondo said with mock

approval. "*Very* fine filigree work. Primed and loaded, I suppose? Half cocked already, if my eyes don't deceive me. Capital. It's a foggy night, though, as you no doubt observed when my dear brother – your own Edward – put in his brief but entertaining appearance. You were wise to have stowed the weapon in out of the wet. Damp powder won't answer, you know, no matter how badly you wish to murder your only living son."

She said nothing, but kept her mind steady, concentrating on the thing she must do, reminding herself of the man's manifold crimes, the murder of Edward and of Mary Eastman. Certainly he also intended to murder the poor boy in the other room – to make use of him as he made use of Edward. God knew how many others had suffered at his hand. She felt her own hand shaking, the now-heavy pistol dragging itself downward, and she firmed her grip and raised it again.

"Do you know that I once wept for the loss of your love?" Narbondo said to her.

She stared at him, confounded.

"I recall it with great clarity. It was when Edward was three years old, his birthday, and had acquired some resemblance to a human being rather than a mewling little beast. I felt the turning within you that day, your heart drawn to him, and my share diminished."

"You imagined that, Clarence," she said, using his Christian name and watching for any effect that it might have. It apparently had none, except for a thin smile, as if this were a bit of theater to him. She went on doggedly. "It was your imagining that made it so. You see darkness where there is light, and you revel in it. You much prefer the darkness. Perhaps you always did."

"Those are hard words, Mother, coming from your mouth. I'm quite scandalized."

"Nonsense. I can see in your face that you're amused. You know that I speak the truth, and yet the truth is meaningless to you. You knew quite well what Edward's death would do to me, and it was that very knowledge that prompted you. Mary told me that you capered around that tree like a mad thing, gibbering with glee. She could scarcely find the voice to describe it."

"She could scarcely find the voice to say anything to anyone. Something put the fear into her, perhaps." He grinned at her openly.

She raised the pistol, pointing it at his face, her hand shaking so badly now that she clutched her wrist with her free hand. She had been wrong. She *could* see something of the boy who had been her first son, the shape of the face, the fine, straight hair, the evident intelligence in his eyes – a faculty that he had squandered on wickedness. In her mind she pictured the sunflower, blown asunder...

"Return to Aylesford," he said, the grin abruptly disappearing. "I have work to do. I grant you a boon. You're free to walk out of this room now despite your waving that pistol at me, although I warn you that you should make haste. You've had your audience. Take yourself off, if you please."

"As God is my witness I've come here to put an end to you before I walk out," she said. "But I'll do as you ask of me on the condition that I take the boy with me."

"*Take* the boy? Aye, you can take him if you will. I'll

extend the same offer to you that I offered the boy's father only this evening. You may purchase young Eddie for the sum of fifty thousand pounds. In that happy event he is yours to keep. You can negotiate with the boy's family then, and perhaps turn a tidy profit. No? I thought not. You'll put an end to nothing on Earth, Mother, not with a pistol. It isn't in you to murder. It takes a stronger hand to…"

"Forgive me," she muttered to God and to herself, cocked the pistol fully and pulled the trigger. Sparks flew from the gun's muzzle and more from the flash hole, the shocking noise of the report taking her unawares. Through the sparks and smoke she saw Narbondo throw himself from his chair in the same instant that the window blew outwards in a hail of glass and splintered mullions. The shot had gone wide. She stood gaping, her mind stunned and with no thought of trying to reload the pistol: she would have no time for it, although she had a paper of powder in her handbag.

She was aware now of a vast clatter and shouting in the courtyard, what sounded like fighting. There was a pistol shot from below, and then another. Narbondo was rising from the floor, looking back at the open door. She thought of the boy Eddie, no doubt cowering in the other room, but before she could so much as take a step in that direction, there was a blur of movement before her – someone somersaulting through the shattered window, rolling hard into the table leg, snapping it off, the table aslant now, dishes clattering to the floor. The intruder was up and moving, dashing toward the second room and shouting "Eddie!" at the top of his lungs. There was an explosion from within the room – another pistol shot? – and then another.

In her shocked surprise she flung her own useless pistol hard at Narbondo's face, clipping him over the eye, stunning him for the time it took for her to heave the canted table over into his path. He tripped over it and went down. She saw Edward's skull tumble away into the fallen dishes and cursed herself for her haste. She let it lie for the moment and picked up a wooden chair, which she raised over her head to deal Narbondo another blow, but George came in at a run through the open door just then, carrying a truncheon, his face running blood, his hat gone, his shirt ripped open. She flung the chair at his chest, but he knocked it heavily aside with his forearm.

The acrobatic intruder – surely a boy, his face hidden by a ragged balaclava – came out of the room at a run dragging Eddie by the hand. The man in the velvet jacket appeared briefly in the open doorway and snatched at Eddie's vest. He missed his mark, caught himself on the door casing with his free hand, and disappeared back into the room, as if he were too timid to come out.

The boy looked at George through the eyeholes in the balaclava, breaking toward the barred door and throwing something hard at the floor. There was the sound of an explosion, George reflexively falling into a crouch. Mother Laswell threw herself at George, her arms outstretched, the two going down heavily on top of Narbondo. She felt the hard corner of the table gouge into her side, a sharp pain in her ribs, George clawing his way out from under her while reaching for the fallen truncheon. She saw the boy unbar the door and fling it open. Along with Eddie he ran out onto the landing and was gone into the fog, all of it happening in the space of several seconds.

Mother Laswell snatched up the truncheon in the instant before George's hand closed on it. She rose to her knees, hammering Narbondo and George with a flurry of blows, the sprung handle of the truncheon making it awkward in her grip, as if it were alive. But she heard the grunts, the men throwing their arms up to take the blows, cringing away from her. She rose even as she pummeled them, stepping clear of the table and the tangle of limbs.

She snatched at Edward's skull, kicking it away as she did so, chagrined to see two teeth spin away from the open mouth as the skull rolled against the wall. A hand pawed at her foot, now, Narbondo shouting for help in an incoherent rage. She evaded him and went after the skull again, but George was there ahead of her, and she managed only to snatch up one of the teeth, spin on her heel, grab her parasol, and heave herself out through the now-open door with the last of her strength, intent on making away across the footbridge and into the dark safety of the blessedly foggy night.

TWENTY-ONE
ANGEL ALLEY

The fog was a godsend, if only it would hold steady. St. Ives and Hasbro walked along Wentworth Street, which had become a Jewry in the last year, now home to thousands of immigrants from across Europe, a world within the world that was London. They looked idly into the stalls and shops, while keeping up a steady pace, as if merely passing through. They weren't apparently being followed, however, and with the thickening fog they proceeded more boldly, endeavoring to fetch the top end of Angel Alley at the same moment that their companions, proceeding now along Whitechapel Road, fetched the bottom end.

St. Ives considered the difficult business before him, but found no reliable answers. Shyness would avail them nothing, but there was the danger that a bold, surprising stroke might cost Eddie his life. Narbondo, however, was not only avaricious, but was also inhumanely cool. His most likely response to a surprise attack would be to scuttle away, taking Eddie with him and disappearing into the rookery. There was the odd business of Mother Laswell's door to Hell to complicate the issue – to stay Narbondo's hand or to make him even more murderous – but that could have no influence on tonight's adventure, given that St. Ives had no understanding of its particulars. *Still and all*, he told himself, *nothing ventured, nothing gained*. Then the image of Eddie came into his mind, and the easy platitude was suddenly shameful.

He checked his pocket watch, a fine Swiss chronometer; Jack Owlesby carried a second, identical watch in his pocket. It was just short of the agreed upon moment when they entered the north end of the alley, departing the world of something like civil behavior for the stark criminality of the rookery. Both men had a hand beneath their coats where their pistols lay. There must be no doubt in anyone's mind that they meant to use the weapons if they were pressed, which he hoped to God they wouldn't be, not before he had discovered Narbondo's lair and contrived a way in.

Ahead of them sounded the growling and snarling of dogs and the loud voices of men involved in some low sport. Slocumb's comment about dogs having no fear of pistols came into his mind, and indeed he saw a stack of kennels now, a mastiff slamming into the iron bars as they drew near, anxious to have at them. The human noise of the rat baiting, the wagering and shouted encouragement, died away as they passed the knot of men who stood around a fenced ring. But no one threatened or insulted them. Most looked at them curiously. Several doffed their caps and winked. The whole thing was unnatural.

The two of them stopped at the corner of a courtyard where they were still hidden in the murky darkness, although the fog had thinned again, a breeze blowing up the alley from

Whitechapel Road. From behind them the sounds of the rat baiting arose again, relieving the comparative silence. The open space ahead was strangely empty of people aside from several shadows waiting beneath a stone arch – the arch Slocumb had mentioned, no doubt, dividing the yard neatly in two. St. Ives could hear the mutter of conversation from the knot of men, who, if they looked sharp, would no doubt make out him and Hasbro lurking there, pressed against the dank bricks. But lurk they must, for they wanted Jack and Tubby and Doyle to make them out, and no mistake.

"Something's amiss," St. Ives whispered. "There's been no offer either to rob or murder us."

"Perhaps they assume that we have business with Narbondo, and that stays their hand," Hasbro replied. "Their silence has telegraphed our arrival."

Three stories above the courtyard stood a tottering wooden structure with a steep roof and a broad, mullioned window, built atop the wall with the arch in it – a variety of wall, St. Ives saw now, for it had doors set in the stones, leading to stairs, perhaps, and interior passages. The penthouse atop it might have been a pub in the last century. Oil lamps lit the interior of the room, in which stood a tall, heavyset woman, looking down at someone hidden by her bulk. Her back was to the window, her face averted, but her garish scarf and red hair gave her away utterly.

"God help us, it's Mother Laswell," St. Ives whispered. "There in the window."

"Indeed?" Hasbro said. "Our neighbor from Hereafter Farm?"

"Herself. Clearly in conversation with her son." St.

Ives had refused to come to her aid, and this was the result – she had almost certainly come into London alone to murder Narbondo. Bill Kraken had warned him – just last night, although it seemed a week ago. He found to his own surprise that he was somewhat relieved. If Mother Laswell shot Narbondo stone dead, there would be an end to it.

He could hear her suddenly, her voice elevated. One of the men in the courtyard walked out into the open and looked up at the window – the ubiquitous George. He watched for a brief time and then walked back to where he had been, content to let his master contend with her, as was St. Ives, at least for the moment. But no sooner had he come to this conclusion than George shouted, "Look sharp!" for in that instant Tubby Frobisher, flanked by Jack Owlesby and Arthur Doyle, appeared out of the mist, running hard into the farther courtyard, their intentions made obvious both by their demeanor and by the fact that Tubby gripped his blackthorn cudgel halfway up the shaft and was even then raising it over his head in order to strike a running blow. St. Ives waited, counting the moments, watching the door beneath the arch, which surely led upstairs, a door which might not be locked, since the men were apparently guarding it.

The four of them scattered now in several directions, drawing out weapons, one of them coming up with a wicked-looking dirk with a long blade, and another – George – finding a truncheon under his coat. The piratical giant from the Pilgrims Road was there, his arm in a sling, thank God, although St. Ives clapped a stopper over his thankfulness when the man drew out a long-barreled pistol and aimed carefully at Tubby, not fifteen feet from him, suddenly rushing to his doom. St. Ives shouted a warning even as he was sprinting forward, Hasbro beside him. The giant half turned at the sound of their running feet, and Tubby, seeing his doom distracted, pitched the blackthorn like a missile, the lead-weighted root-knob on the top striking the giant on the temple with lethal accuracy. The man pitched over, his pistol skittering away across the stones. St. Ives smashed his stick down on the back of George's head, a glancing blow, and George turned, swinging his truncheon at the same time, although awkwardly, St. Ives blocking it with his stick and shocked to feel the weight of the truncheon, which jarred his arm heavily. St. Ives sprang toward George at once, ducking under a blow and snatching the man's coat to yank him forward, but managing only to rip the coat open as George lurched away, wiping blood from his eyes, apparently not anxious to put up a fight. St. Ives flung away two buttons and cracked George on the forearm, hearing him grunt with pain. Still holding the truncheon, George turned and ran straight toward the door in the arch, flinging it open and slamming it shut behind him, a set of stairs revealed in the brief moment that the door was open.

St. Ives pursued him, hearing the sound of running feet and seeing with a sinking heart that the odds had shifted, that four more men had swarmed into the courtyard, all of them bruisers, holding short bats and moving with no hesitation at all. St. Ives swung his stick, cutting the legs out from beneath one of them, the man's haste tumbling him forward so that he lay splayed out on the stones. St. Ives abruptly found himself on his knees, a shattering pain in his skull. He looked back, trying to stand, seeing that Jack grappled with the man who had hit him. St. Ives remained there on his knees, his head swimming, watching stupidly as Doyle batted the dirk out of his own opponent's hand, apparently cutting himself, the side of his palm instantly awash with blood. Doyle danced on his toes, striking the man hard in the face and stomach, the man turning away from the onslaught, Doyle stepping after him and striking him a vicious blow on the lower back, over the kidney. The man shouted with the pain of it and staggered forward, falling to his knees, at which point Hasbro laid him out with the butt of his pistol. Jack was down now, clubbed by one of the newcomers.

St. Ives heard the muffled sound of a pistol shot – distant, perhaps from the room above. There followed a hail of shattered glass and debris on the stones of the farther courtyard. He staggered to his feet and made his way toward the door, stepping over the legs of the fallen giant, whose arm shot out like a snake, grasping his ankle. He fell hard onto his knees again, writhing around and spearing the man in the face with his stick, seeing that Jack was up again, tottering, but still holding the marlinspike, striking the giant a glancing blow.

St. Ives was suddenly free, although there was a man between him and the door now, waiting for him. Another pistol shot sounded, and the man fell, and St. Ives looked back, seeing Hasbro's arm outstretched, his pistol smoking as he took aim at one of two men attacking Tubby, whose back was against the wall, moving nimbly given his great bulk, gamely waiting for his chance to swing the blackthorn.

Another pistol shot, and one of Tubby's attackers fell, the odds changing again as Tubby surged forward like a juggernaut, feinting with his cudgel and delivering the now-lone attacker a vicious butt with his forehead.

St. Ives took the door latch in his hand but found it locked. He rammed it with his shoulder, although encumbered by the man who had been shot and who was now half blocking the door. He stepped back, taking out his own pistol and shooting through the heavy oak boards, blasting the latch and locking mechanism through the back of the door. Still it held, barred from within, no doubt. A second entrance, surely...

But he was struck once again from behind, and in the same moment that he heard another pistol shot he collapsed onto the ground, the side of his face in a puddle of filthy water, and although he did not lose consciousness, he was too disoriented to do anything more than wonder at his failure, and what it might mean.

TWENTY-TWO

THE BEST-LAID PLANS

Mother Laswell saw the boy ahead, moving quickly, given that he was towing the child. The bridge shook and swayed, and she wasn't as sure-footed as she once had been. In a moment the two ahead of her would disappear into the mists, and she very much wanted to keep up with them, but she was knackered – little strength left in her, her ribs perhaps cracked, given the ache in her side. She wheezed like a bellows and felt old and done.

She realized that she was still carrying the truncheon. She wasn't constituted to beat anyone with such a thing. Her wrist pained her now, as if she had sprained it flailing away like that. But there was no saying what troubles would appear before they were through, and so she held onto it, seeing that the two ahead of her had stopped. The boy in the balaclava seemed to be studying the nearby rooftop now, both hands on the heavy line that served as a rail of sorts. He bounced on his toes, perhaps taking the measure of the gap that separated the bridge from the roof tiles. She had seen him fly in through the window. He didn't want for courage.

The bridge began to sway even more perilously on

its ropes, then, and the boards rose and fell sickeningly beneath her feet. She looked behind her, seeing that George was coming along briskly. The bridge ended some distance farther on. She could make out a door there, a door that was swinging open. Two men appeared and headed toward them from that direction, slow but determined, wary of the swaying bridge, which sagged now as their combined weight bore them downward. In a matter of moments she and the boy and Eddie would simply be rounded up. Mother Laswell waded forward again, calling out to the boy, who picked Eddie up and hefted him. It occurred to her abruptly that the boy meant to pitch Eddie across the void and onto the roof of the nearer building. The stones of the courtyard lay far below: a fall would kill him.

"You dasn't!" Mother Laswell shouted out. "Leave him. I'll do what I can for him." She staggered up to him and put her hand on Eddie's shoulder. "Killing the boy wouldn't serve."

She spoke the evident truth, and the boy saw it. "I'll find you," he said, his voice muffled. He pushed Eddie into Mother Laswell's arms and looked into her face for a moment as if to make certain that he would know her again. He took one last look at the two men – ten feet away now – and then vaulted up onto the taut rope, dipped his weight twice, and launched himself upward and forward, latching onto an iron vent pipe protruding through the roof and scrabbling for a moment against the tiles with his feet. The bridge reeled backward despite the stays, swinging like a hammock, and Mother Laswell fell to her knees, clutching Eddie with one arm, holding onto the line with her free hand. The boy was up and moving, over the peak of the roof and disappearing down the other side.

The men closed in on her, in no hurry now. The bridge steadied itself. They couldn't follow the marvelous boy. He was safe, at least for the moment. She had an ally in London, and that was worth something. Eddie, alas, was not safe, nor was she, although she cared little for herself at this juncture. George bowed to her, betraying no emotion at all, certainly not anger. With a backhanded fling she sent his truncheon cartwheeling away across the rooftops.

"We'll need to make haste, Mother," he said. The blood had dried on his face now, one of his eyes blackened. "There's been a mort of gunfire, and there's no telling what might come of it if we linger. Down through the passage now, lads, we're finished here." His two silent cohorts, one of them handsome enough to be on the stage if it weren't for a shockingly disfigured face, turned and set out toward the door that yawned open fifty feet away. The other man was pear-shaped and appeared to be dim-witted.

Mother Laswell looked back toward the penthouse above the arch, but the lamps had been put out, all but one. Two shadows passed behind the broken window, carrying what appeared to be crates. A night breeze had sprung up out of the east, and the fog had cleared away, the stars shining overhead, roundabout the tired moon. She considered screaming at the top of her lungs as she shepherded Eddie along before her, just in case George's fears were correct, and her screaming would fetch the police. But George might be compelled to silence her – surely he wouldn't hesitate to do so – and there was Eddie to think of, along with everything else. Alive and healthy she might yet do some good.

An oil lamp, emitting greasy smoke, lit the stairs spiraling downward, the stairwell so narrow that her shoulders nearly brushed the walls and she was compelled to let Eddie go on ahead of her, although he clutched her hand fiercely. She was happy for the solid footing. They came out into the courtyard, which was filling with people again, bending out from within their homes, such as they were, now that the mayhem was apparently over.

A small, weasel-faced man, flashily dressed, walked up to them, bent over, and chucked Eddie under the chin. "What have we here?" he asked, grinning falsely. Eddie trod backward, pressing into Mother Laswell.

"Bugger off, Crumpet," George said to the man. "It's like you to show up when the jollification's over."

"Or just begun," Crumpet said, looking at Eddie rather than George. He thrust his tongue out and touched the tip of his own nose, and then winked. "But as for all that, I've got a job of work to do in the morning. I've been busy with the apparatus while you've been brawling."

"Then you and your apparatus can blow yourselves to damnation. You've got the Doctor's sanction for the moment, slipgibbet, but your time will come, mark my words," George said. To Mother Laswell he added, "I'll take charge of the lad now. That way leads to Whitechapel Road ma'am. You'd best be moving along now, while it's still early. Fred and Coker here will see you clear of the rookery. Bear south for the river and Tower Bridge. Perhaps there's a late train to Aylesford. The Doctor made it clear that we were to bring him the boy, but he said nothing about you, ma'am, and so you'd best be away before I'm told different. There's nought that you can do here now. For your own sake go home, and let the fates see to the future."

"The child is innocent," she said, looking hard into George's face. "I charge you with keeping him safe, for the sake of your mortal soul. It's not the fates that will see to your future. *You'll* see to it, sir. We all of us will, if we want to save ourselves from the fires of Hell. I don't believe it's in you to see a child hurt. I can tell that much in your face, although not in your friend's face." She nodded at the small man, who stood leering, but kept George's eye. "He's rubbish," she said, "but you're a better man than you know. Think on that."

"He's no friend of mine, ma'am. But you'd best move along. You can't change things here."

George didn't look away, but held her gaze, and she wondered if her words would have any effect. She turned abruptly and hurried off, Fred and Coker following close behind. Eddie cried out, but she was forced by circumstance to keep on, swearing to herself that she would return for him, although she had no idea what she meant or how she would do it.

Presently the broad thoroughfare of Whitechapel Road opened before her, and she found herself walking southward, as George had suggested. When she crossed Commercial Street through the traffic, she looked back. Fred and Coker had vanished, and she was alone, although not adrift. She had no notion of a late train to Aylesford. She had left Mabel to her own devices three hours ago, and would return to Lime Street now to look in on her. She wanted a friend, although she was unsure whether Mabel would especially want her back, given the trouble she had brought with her.

She hadn't gone twenty paces, however, when she saw a man whom she recognized coming along in the opposite direction across the street, his features clearly visible in the gaslight. He looked straight ahead and walked at a steady pace, as if he would be happy to quit the neighborhood as quickly as he could, but without attracting attention. He wore the chin whiskers, the wig, and the black coat of the man who had been hidden in the room with Eddie. But there was something else about him…

And then suddenly she knew him, beneath the disguise and despite his being much older than when she had last seen him. He had visited her husband several times at Hereafter Farm, not long before Edward's death. Now here he was closeted with Narbondo. After the scene in Narbondo's rooms, he would of course know her identity, but had he seen her here on the street, or did he suppose that she had gone on her way after being dismissed? *In for a penny*, she thought, and took six more steps before crossing the road, turning to follow him as he rounded the corner.

Mabel Morningstar felt very nearly human again. She had awakened famished – the pain in her forehead quite disappeared – and had gone downstairs to the tavern for a bowl of barley soup and some bread and cheese, which had set her up remarkably. Over dinner her mind and heart were caught up in considerations of her friend's sad state, the warring emotions and the maelstrom into which she was determined to fling herself. Mabel could think of nothing she could do to help; indeed, she scarcely understood Harriet Laswell's motivations or intentions. Rarely had she sensed a mind so terribly unsure of itself and yet so utterly compelled to act.

It was late when she returned to her rooms, carrying the uneaten portion of cheese and bread for the next morning's breakfast. Having slept away most of the day and evening, bed was out of the question, so she poured herself a glass of cognac, which, she considered, she heartily deserved, and sat down in her reading chair in the corner of the room, where there was the best light. *Northanger Abbey* lay on the table beside the chair – not her favorite of Miss Austen's novels, but by no means to be despised. When she tried to read it, however, she found that she couldn't attend to it.

She studied the ruined table map again, astonished anew at the long, straight tear in the vellum, recalling the terrible moment when her senses had been overpowered and she had lost consciousness. She mouthed a silent prayer for her friend: that Harriet come out of this with her wits about her and without regret, or at least no more regret than she could tolerate.

She heard footfalls on the stairs now – a man, from the sound of the heavy tread. She snatched up the paper knife without a thought, fear surging through her as the memory of that staring, slowly approaching face imposed itself upon her mind. At the same time she was astonished that the memory had returned with such potency. The footfalls stopped outside the door, and there was a long silence in which she composed herself, the fear having passed away as quickly as it had arrived. It came to her that this was a complete stranger, a customer, perhaps. She set down the paper knife, feeling slightly foolish. There was a hesitant knock, a shuffling of feet.

She arose and opened the door, bracing it with the toe of her shoe. A tall, lanky, haggard-looking man stood on the landing, twisting his cap in his hands. He had evidently taken two steps back from the door, so as not to impose himself upon her.

"I'm Bill Kraken, ma'am," he said. "You don't know the name, but I'm a friend of Mother Laswell, and I've come up to London to see her safe back home to Aylesford. I come here straightaway on the chance that she called upon you, you being her friend."

There was something about his demeanor that appealed to Mabel – a natural humility, certainly, and some sort of goodness that shone in his admittedly odd features. "She did indeed," Mabel said. "Will you come in?" She stood aside and gestured.

He entered hesitantly, as if it were beyond his station to do so. "I'm main desperate to find her," Kraken said. "She left Hereafter Farm this morning in a thundercloud. When I found out I most despaired of finding her once I got here, London being the behemoth of old. But it come to me to search for her logbook before I left, which is what she wrote in before supper. It took me most of an hour to find it. I come across your name in it, ma'am, and a mention of the Ship Tavern, what stands below on the street and what I knew well enough of old, and here I am, a-searching for lost things, like your sign says, and I mean to find her come what may."

"I'm very glad to meet you, Mr. Kraken," she said, "and

I'm happy to hear that she has a stalwart friend. Take a chair at the table and eat a morsel. You've had a long day of it."

He stood staring, still twisting his cap, which she took from him and laid on the sideboard before gesturing at a wooden chair by the dining table. "Right there, sir. You can take five minutes to collect yourself and eat some of this cheese and bread. I can offer you a glass of this capital French brandy or a bottle of ale, or both."

"Ale would go down most grateful, ma'am," Kraken said.

She set the plate in front of him and fetched the ale from her small kitchen. "Eat that, sir," she said. "Don't stand on ceremony. I'll tell you straightaway that Mother's gone into Spitalfields to find…"

"I know who she means to find and what she means to do to him," he said, talking from behind his hand as he chewed his food. "I mean to stop her, although I'm late in coming. It ain't right that she kill her own son, and no matter the reason. It would do for her, do you see? For good and all. I'll gladly take up the burden and…"

"*Kill her son?*"

"Yes, ma'am. She took her little flintlock pistol out of the case. She'll use it, too, if I don't find her, or else she'll come to harm trying. Spitalfields, you say?" He rose from the chair, draining half the bottle of ale at a gulp and apparently determined to be on his way, dinner or no.

She picked up the vellum map and handed it to him. "It's just here," she said, pointing at the endpoint of the tear. "Do you know the area? It's a Hell on Earth, the rookery is, so mind yourself." She picked up a napkin and loaded the bread and cheese into it, tying it up into a bundle.

"When I was a pea-pod man I knew it well enough, although it's nowhere for…" He shook his head darkly. "Ah, Christ," he said. "I thank you for your kindness ma'am, but I'd best be on my way. If she should return, you'd do her a service were you to lock her in."

With that Kraken snatched his hat from atop the sideboard, put it on, and took the bread and cheese in both hands. Mabel opened the door, and he loped away down the stairs clutching the torn map under his arm, his footfalls quickly fading. She stood for a minute looking down after him. In the many years she had known Mother Laswell, she had thought that both her sons were dead, but apparently she hadn't known her friend well at all. *The more a secret torments us*, she thought, *the more we keep it near, as if it were a precious stone and not a fragment of Hell.*

She closed the door and sat back down, taking another swallow of brandy, which she relished – a small good thing at a time like this. The clock on the sideboard chimed midnight, but sleep was even farther off than it had been fifteen minutes ago. She settled into her chair again, opened her book, and took up where she'd left off.

TWENTY-THREE

FLAMING SYLLABUB

Finn Conrad hunched across the rooftop, keeping out of sight as best he could. If he were seen he'd be taken for a thief, and although he could evade pursuit, he didn't want to be forced to do so. He contemplated a return to Angel Alley – and why not? – no one knew his face. He might have a second chance to find Eddie, the dawn being hours away yet. Finn knew that there had been desperate fighting in the courtyard, with several shots fired. If it had been the Professor and Hasbro, it might have changed everything. And yet if things had changed, he needed to know how. The fighting also meant that different lots of them were looking out for Eddie, if you counted the game old woman who had fired the pistol at Narbondo before following him out onto the bridge. She hadn't any idea of shooting, but he honored her for the attempt. He also wondered who she was. In any event, she couldn't help Eddie any more than she could help herself.

Crouching in the shadow of a chimney pot, he looked down at the alley and courtyard just west of Angel Alley, very nearly its twin, the same dozens of layabouts lounging

241

in the yard, gin served out of a keg, a trussed up pig just then being hauled down from a spit over an open fire, the process watched intently by a knot of men, the smoke blowing away on the breeze. There was a curious smell on the air – not the roasting pig – rising apparently from directly below him – the smell of rotten eggs mixed with the odor of pitch. Finn had smelled it before during his days in the circus. It was a memorable smell, nothing else quite like it, not in his experience, anyway. What he remembered was something called "flaming syllabub" by the man who concocted it in order to cast liquid fire on the Witch of Winter in an open field where Duffy's Circus was set up in Yorkshire. The man's face was burnt off when the siphon tube blew to pieces. They had buried the corpse, its head and upper body charred, no longer recognizably human, behind a hedgerow, along with the syllabub and the pressurized device for spraying it. It was quite the most awful thing that Finn had seen in his life, and the dreams had taken months to pass away.

He could see it below him now – a heavy iron pot lying atop a coal stove set out of the wind in a lamp-lit alcove. The pot had a lid on it, but thin smoke rose from the coals that heated the pot and from around the lid. In the light of a lamp hung on a peg, a bearded dwarf tended the fire beneath the kettle, which glowed with a raw white flame. He noted the dwarf's careful attention to it. The man was leery of getting too close, as if the pot might explode. Very nearby stood a coster's barrow, doctored up fancy. It had a polished metal bed, brass, apparently. It was long and narrow and with springs at the axles. Three kegs sat atop it. Finn took it at first to be a portable coffee stall, although soon enough he saw that he was wrong. The iron-bound kegs had no spigot. Instead, in one of them there appeared to be a bronze pipe set in the bung, with a flexible brass tube affixed to it, the excess coiled beside it on the bed, perhaps twenty feet of it. There was a nozzle on the end – the siphon, he thought, for spraying the syllabub. He saw the handle of a pump atop the keg, no doubt meant to pressurize it. The thing looked like a cross between a beer keg and a hubble-bubble, but he knew it was nothing as innocent as that. The long hose would allow a man to stand a good way off. A second keg with a funnel atop sat beside the first, an India-rubber hose with a broad-throated bellows connected to it, the bellows affixed flat to the wagon. A third keg, large enough to hold a couple of gallons sat alongside in a small heap of black dust.

He speculated over the apparatus for a moment, but couldn't puzzle it out, and it was none of his business anyway... unless it was. He made his way back to the peak of the roof and looked across toward Angel Alley, which was still mostly hidden by the warren of buildings. He could see the roof of Narbondo's apartment, directly opposite where he stood, which meant it was just opposite where the dwarf was cooking up syllabub. Were the buildings connected? Another way in and out, perhaps? He returned to his perch above the smoking kettle. Some distance away stood a convenient drainpipe that led downward to a lean-to roof that wasn't above eight feet off the ground – easy enough to climb down. He moved away in that direction, testing the strength of the drainpipe before making his way hand over hand until his feet stood on the lower roof. He leapt from there to the stones of the courtyard, knees bending to take the force of the drop, and then walked around the side of the lean-to toward where the dwarf worked at his oven. The best way was the bold way, when you were up to acrobatics.

"I've got a message from the Doctor," he said to the dwarf, who turned and looked Finn up and down as if he were a walking dustbin.

"You've got an ugly face, too," the dwarf said. "You can use them both for bum paper for all of me, and tell the bleeding Doctor I said so."

"You're to give me a ride down to Egypt Bay."

"Except I'm not a-going down to Egypt Bay, you little shit. Not till we're done with this here caper."

"Tomorrow," Finn said. "I don't mean tonight."

"Then tomorrow you wait here, sitting in plain sight. If the Crumpet says we're taking you to Egypt Bay, then that's just what we'll do."

Finn was suddenly at a loss for words, the name "Crumpet" catching in his throat along with his breath. A door began to open behind the barrow, and Finn turned away, trying to affect the air of someone naturally taking his leave. He heard the Crumpet's simpering, high-pitched voice say, "Do you want your bed sent out, dwarfy-dear? A nice nap, perhaps?"

"Shut your gob," said the dwarf, "where have you been this past two hours while I've been brewing up this stinking pitch?"

"Shepherding the night along," the Crumpet said. "Himself is in a pretty mood. Assassins everywhere, apparently."

"Now you're here, Crumpet, lend a hand. Clap on to that there tin and sort it out."

Finn angled toward the roast pig, being butchered now

on a board set up on two sawhorses, steaming chunks being handed out on sheets of newsprint. "I'll buy a portion, sir," Finn said, his voice husky, his heart beating hard.

"Take yourself off," a man said to him. "This ain't no public mess."

"Stow it, Tom," the man butchering the pig said. "It's my bleeding pig. The boy needs a bite of supper." He handed Finn a paper with a half-pound of dripping pork shank on it. "Keep your pennies," he said. "Duke Humphrey's treat."

Finn thanked him and stepped away into the shadows, making himself inconspicuous, wondering at the odd business of himself giving Newman the crackers for no reason other than it came into his head to do it. And now here he was eating first-rate pork that a man had given him that same way, one thing leading to another, or so he hoped. He liked the idea that a person might be served out for good deeds as well as bad. From the safety of his hiding place he held the newspaper in front of his face and blew on the hot meat while he watched the Crumpet struggle with a heap of folded tin, unhinging it into a four-sided box with no top or bottom. The dwarf used a pair of iron tongs to set the smoking pot of syllabub carefully onto the metal bed of the barrow, securing it with twisted wire, and then the two of them climbed onto upturned crates and slipped the tin sides down over the kegs, hiding them. Painted on the tin was the word "Pine-apples" with an ill-painted depiction of the fruit alongside.

The Crumpet took a step back, looked the cart over, took the lamp from its peg and hung it on a hook protruding from the barrow, and then cupped his hand over the chimney and blew out the flame. He closed the still-open door of the building behind him, and the two of them trudged away across the courtyard and up the alley toward Wentworth Street, the dwarf pushing the barrow and the Crumpet walking on ahead.

Finn gave them forty feet and then followed, soon stepping out onto Wentworth Street, past a sign on the wall: "George Yard," it read. Across Wentworth Street lay another narrow bystreet, toward which the two were evidently bound. There was a moderate crowd of people afoot, and the dwarf shouted, "Make a lane, there!" trying to push the barrow through the unheeding pedestrians.

Finn stood for a moment thinking, suddenly unsure whether to follow or to return to Angel Alley. The Crumpet was evidently going about Narbondo's dirty business, and it would be interesting to know what business that was. But Finn had no desire to put himself in the way of the Crumpet, or to leave Eddie behind if he could help it. The hot syllabub and siphon apparatus hidden in the barrow had an ominous air to it, although what it portended he couldn't begin to say – nothing so innocent as burning the Witch of Winter. There was little he could do about it anyway, he decided, and might likely get burnt to a cinder for trying.

Finn turned back toward Angel Alley, hurrying past the dog kennels now. His mention of Egypt Bay hadn't confounded the dwarf as he feared it might; it had gone straight home. He entered the yard with the pump where the ghost had appeared. The old woman and Lazarus were nowhere to be seen, but he spotted Newman standing in a ray of moonlight along a dangerously leaning wall of shacks built of ancient boards. The boy stood rigid, staring upward, as if at the moon itself, and Finn realized with a start that his eyes were rolled back into his head. He seemed to have petrified. His mouth was open. Perhaps he was asleep, standing up.

"Ahoy, Newman," Finn said, and then again louder when he got no response.

Newman's face changed, its slackness tightening, his mouth slowly drawing shut, his eyes reappearing. He swallowed heavily, his enormous Adam's apple bobbing. He stared at Finn for a moment before apparently recognizing him. "'Lo, Crackers," he said, blinking.

"Hello yourself," Finn said. "Do you know Jermyn Street?"

"Jermyn Street? Oh, aye. The length of it. There's Dunhill, where they sell the pipe tobacco, and Tarkenton's along past it, and…"

"I'm thinking about the far end. Near Green Park. Queen's Walk side."

"Oh, aye. There's…"

"A toymaker named Keeble has a shop there. I'll lay odds that you've looked into the window more than once."

A lamp switched on behind Newman's eyes. He nodded happily.

"There's a door just beyond that shop, at the far corner, the little cut-off piece of Jermyn, with a sign that says 'Scout's Rest.' Can you read?"

"Oh, aye. Somewhat, leastways."

"Look for the sign, then, right there on the corner, set into the bricks. Bang the knocker next to the sign. Hard, mind you. Wake the house. There's a speaking tube alongside.

When they answer, tell them that you've a message for Jack Owlesby, or Mrs. Owlesby, if she's in and he ain't."

"A message is it?" Newman asked, looking at him shrewdly now.

"You'll hear them through the speaking tube, just as clear as if they stood before you. Tell them, 'Finn Conrad says it's Egypt Bay, in the marsh.' Can you do that, say into the tube? Tell them that's where the Doctor's bound if he's bolted."

"Egypt Bay if the Doctor's bolted. In the marsh. Jack or the missus. Message from Finn Conrad to be shouted into the tube."

"That's it in a nut. Tell them Finn's gone on ahead as best he can. Can you go there now, to Jermyn Street? It's late, but... Here." Finn looked around hastily and, seeing no one evidently watching, he removed his toeless right shoe and took half a crown out of it before slipping the shoe back on. He pressed the coin into Newman's palm and closed his fingers around it. "Will you help me?" he asked.

Newman opened his hand and stared at the coin, then pocketed it. He nodded briskly.

"Don't tell anyone, not even old Lazarus," Finn started to say, but he said it to Newman's back, for the boy was already running, away up Angel Alley where he shortly disappeared from view. Finn followed him at a brisk pace, but by the time he got to Wentworth Street Newman had quite disappeared. To Finn's surprise, however, the Crumpet and the dwarf were still there, across the street now, communicating with someone inside a carriage – a five-glass landau, black and gold paint, very swank, luggage strapped onto the back atop a capacious rack, headlights shining into the night. The two horses stamped impatiently while the driver, an ugly, wrinkled gnome-like man in an ancient, enormously tall beaver top hat, waited on his seat beneath a gas lamp on a post. His boots, Finn saw, had two-inch-thick soles. He tapped his fingers against his knees as if keeping time to music that only he could hear.

Finn walked forward, as if to pass in front of the carriage, trying to get a look at the passenger. It was dim within the interior, but the silhouette of the hunchbacked man was clearly visible – Narbondo himself. The top of Eddie's head was just visible on the seat opposite. Finn studied the luggage rack, which was placed low to the ground on a sort of flying bridge at the level of the axels. There was ten inches or so between the narrow, strapped-down trunk and the back wall of the carriage.

The driver whipped up the horses now, and the coach moved away, the Crumpet and the dwarf setting out again. Finn took a running start, following the carriage as it gained speed, rocking on the rough pavement. As long as he kept tight to the rear corner, he would be out of sight of the driver. He ran faster, a measured distance from the moving vehicle. The two in the coach looked ahead. Abruptly he threw himself sideways and forward, pulling himself along the top of the trunk while pressing himself downward like a limpet, hanging tight to the straps to stop himself from falling off when the carriage took a sudden lurch. He pushed himself backward now, sliding down between the trunk and the stern of the carriage like a plate settling into a rack on the wall, sandwiched in tight and safe as a baby, although tolerably cramped, and with his nosed pressed to the trunk.

There was no hint of the landau slowing down, however, no calling out from people who might have seen him fling himself aboard, and soon they rounded onto a broad, smoothly metaled street, Finn safely hidden away.

After a time, he lifted himself carefully and craned his neck to see into the coach. He found himself looking past the back of Narbondo's head, and was surprised to see Eddie staring straight back at him. He put his finger to the side of his nose and the boy looked away. Finn settled down again, laid his head on his arm, and closed his eyes. He had long had the habit of falling asleep at will under rough circumstances, and that's what he did now, the coach jogging along through the midnight streets, bound for Egypt Bay.

TWENTY-FOUR
AFTER THE BATTLE

"Not much of a butcher's bill if you ask me," Tubby said, picking up a rasher of bacon from a platter in the middle of the table and folding it into his mouth. "Two of the villains dead, and four others off their feed for a month. Why thank you, Winnifred," he said to Mrs. Keeble, who set a plate of fried eggs and beans in front of him. "This is kindness personified."

William, Winnifred Keeble's inventor husband, snored in an upholstered chair, apparently indifferent to the promise of food. He was an early riser, up with the dawn, and was happily asleep by eight o'clock in the evening, which is to say, some four hours ago. Winnifred had driven him out of bed and compelled him to put on a dressing gown in deference to their late-arriving guests, but the effort hadn't really awakened him. Hasbro came out from the kitchen now with a steaming platter of chops and another of black pudding, followed by Jack Owlesby and his wife Dorothy, carrying pots of coffee and more plates of food.

"Vittles is up!" Tubby said, looking hard at his companions, who were still seated around the room.

St. Ives found it incredible that Tubby was unscathed. Given his reckless abandon in the melee he might have been murdered three times over. And a melee it had been, a wild brawl that had achieved considerably less than nothing. Doyle had pronounced St. Ives fit after sewing up a flap of scalp that had been laid open, but any of the blows that he had taken on the head might have knocked him permanently senseless. The aching in his forehead, although easing up some, was still a distraction, and he studiously kept his head very still. He thought of Alice and of her threat to beat him with a coal shovel – no need for that now, really. He wondered what she was doing, whether she was asleep or lying abed worrying. He pictured her in his mind, and his heart was filled with sadness at his failure. *"Christ, that my love were in my arms and I in my bed again,"* he thought, remembering the old poem that had affected him so strongly when he was a younger man. He was surprised that its effect was squared and cubed now that he was older and had lived some. It hadn't been but a day since he and Alice had parted, although it seemed like an eternity.

He thought about how full of optimism he had allowed himself to be just a few hours ago at the Half Toad, when they were at the beginning of things. That was too often the way of it – the fate of hopeful plans: inspired anticipation ending in unhappy regret. Certainly Narbondo had anticipated their arrival this evening and so had easily escaped, just as St. Ives had feared would happen. There was no point at all in returning to Thrawl Street in the morning on the pretense of carrying ransom money. They had been soundly beaten, no matter how many of the enemy they had brought down. That was the long and the short of it. The precious information they'd got from Slocumb about Narbondo's whereabouts was now yesterday's news, useful for wrapping up fried cod. They had come to a dead end.

Dorothy Owlesby, blond and pretty, fretted over her husband Jack, who had also been bandaged by an adept Arthur Doyle. Doyle's own left hand still oozed blood from the knife wound, which Doyle had stitched closed himself, sweating and grimacing, although St. Ives and Hasbro were both competent with a catgut suture. Doyle was apparently happy with the wound – a badge of honor – but clearly made an effort not to revel overmuch in the heroic nature of the part he had played in the episode. His evident bonhomie very nearly matched Tubby's. St. Ives rose from his armchair and took his place at the table, taking himself in hand and putting on a pleased face.

"I can't remember ever having eaten so well," Tubby said, shoveling eggs and beans into his mouth and then mopping his face with his napkin. "A skirmish does wonders for a man's appetite. Pass that beaker of coffee, if you will, and that jam pot."

"You say something of the same thing every time you sit down to sup," Jack said.

"There's nothing out of the ordinary about that," Tubby said. "There's scarcely a human being on earth who doesn't ask for the jam pot now and then. The jam pot is a philosophical item, Jack, much prized by the ancients. I beg you to consider that the Wildman of Borneo keeps a jam pot in his hollow tree, as does the Queen in her cupboard. Indeed, the jam pot is the homely object that puts us all on the side of the angels."

"Not the jam pot, you oaf," Jack said. "I mean that you insist absolutely that every meal is the best you've ever eaten. How can everything be the best of anything? If everything is the best, then it stands to reason that nothing is the best."

"I deny it," Tubby said. "The jam pot shows us the way. Every day it's filled afresh, you see – a new start, the world constantly turning toward the morning. We're blessed with a renewable appetite, and not just for food, mind you, but for the things of the world. That's the golden secret of the marmalade in the jam pot. Imagine if an appetite were like hair, that fell out as you grew older, and never grew back. You'd be in a sad way, Jack." He plucked a piece of toast out of the rack and slathered jam on it by way of illustration.

"I'm with you there," Doyle said. "A hearty appetite of any sort is synonymous with life itself. And as for the English breakfast, to my mind it's one of the wonders of the world. It seems to me that there's something particularly artistic in its being served at the stroke of midnight."

"Just so," St. Ives said, looking at his pocket watch. "It's already tomorrow, and I for one am heartily glad to see yesterday gone."

They ate in silence for a time, devouring the food, making inroads into the toast and cutlets, which seemed to be in never-ending supply.

"What's the state of this fabulous airship that Jack's been telling me about?" Doyle asked William Keeble.

Keeble, whose appetite had awakened, and he with it, was illuminated by the question and at once set out to answer it. The airship would fly, he told them. The decorative elements wanted gilt paint, and he contemplated a figurehead of some sort – something that wouldn't weigh it down too much by the nose. A pasteboard figure, perhaps, heavily varnished against the weather.

"We'll gild the lily in due time," St. Ives said. "Tomorrow we've got to be about our business, however, if only we know what it is. She's airworthy? You're certain of it?"

"Oh, yes. Quite certain. I spent the better part of the last two days on what might be called 'finishing touches.' Just this afternoon I fitted a fine brass periscope to a swivel on the craft's undercarriage, built on the design of Marié-Davy, which will reflect an image onto a lens in the gondola. The periscope can sweep the field of view, quite uninhibited. Farther astern sits a Ruhmkorff lamp that will cast a light for a hundred feet or so in the dead of night. Quite blindingly bright, if I do say so myself."

"Tell them about the perpetual motion you've invented, Father," Dorothy said. "It's phenomenally clever."

"It's not perpetual motion at all," Keeble said, smiling lovingly at his daughter, "although it's very like, I must say. And I did not invent it; I merely had my way with another man's invention – a giant of a man, so to speak, upon whose shoulders I stood. I've built a bladed weathervane, if you can picture it, a propeller, which swivels with the direction of the wind, so that the blades spin constantly, their motion turning the disks in what is known to science as a Wimshurst influence machine. The electrical charge produced by the machine flows into an array of simple Leyden jar batteries. Under the right conditions there's no reason the dirigible shouldn't circumnavigate the globe, providing its own motive power with the help of the wind."

"That's as perpetual as *anything*," Dorothy said.

"Indeed it is," Tubby put in. "It's the jam pot come again."

"The jam pot," Keeble said. "Just so. Of course." He blinked at Tubby several times, as if unable entirely to fathom the figure of the jam pot. "My men have begun the production of hydrogen, and the void has been filling for many hours."

"The *production* of hydrogen?" Tubby asked. "One hires an alchemist, perhaps, to conjure it out of the aether?"

"No indeed, sir. It's a simple business," Keeble said. "One asks one's apprentice to drip vitriol onto iron shavings. Hydrogen gas rises in the reek like a very phoenix, filling the body of the dirigible through an inverted funnel. In short order, the balloon is anxious to take flight, and will do so unless it's moored to the ground." He smiled at them over the rim of his coffee cup, very apparently happy with his revelations.

"My only… apprehension…" he said, "has to do with flying the craft in a lightning storm, which might lead to an explosive result."

"*Explosive?*" Tubby said. "It's a sort of floating squib, then?"

"After a fashion I suppose it is, although I've attached an experi-mental lightning rod of sorts that should draw away unwanted sparks or electrical charges."

"What's the nature of this rod?" asked Doyle. "It's not grounded, as they say. It cannot be, since the ship would be nowhere near the ground."

"The device consists of a solid glass ball mounted

on the end of the bowsprit," Keeble said, "much like the lightning inhibitors atop masts of ships at sea. It cannot be adequately tested without endangering the craft, of course, but theoretically everyone in the gondola should be as safe as babies. Nothing to worry about there, I assure you. Nothing at all. Perfectly safe."

Doyle nodded, perhaps out of a desire to be agreeable.

"We've been told that you've built a miniature example of this Ruhmkorff lamp," Hasbro said to Keeble.

"Oh, yes," Keeble said. "Wonderfully small, but throwing a prodigious bright beam. I built only the one example, although another man has recently commissioned a second. He seems to be quite anxious about it."

"Do you know the name of the man who commissioned the first?" St. Ives asked.

"A fellow named George Kittering. Very polite cove. Extraordinarily round head, it seemed to me."

"The ubiquitous George! Of course," St. Ives said. "We're well acquainted with George, chatted with him tonight, in fact. I'd be surprised if half London doesn't call him by name. This second commission – there was no apparent connection between it and the first? Not our man George again?"

"No, indeed. The second was a Dutchman named de Groot, the secretary of someone highly placed, or so he told me. Whom I can't say, and it scarcely seemed politic to ask. He was a stout man with short legs, who sweated profusely. Very florid all the way around, including his hair and beard, which were red as a newt."

St. Ives nodded. "There's the telling phrase again: 'highly placed.' Narbondo's nefarious *Customer*, I don't doubt. If we knew who this Dutchman was, we could perhaps make use of him – make him sweat a little more. But we do not know him. We're all to seek."

"What *do* we know in fact?" Doyle asked. "As a newcomer, it's perhaps none of my business, but…"

"It's entirely your business after the way in which you comported yourself tonight," St. Ives said. "We're considerably in your debt."

"Yes, indeed," Tubby put in. "That fellow with the dirk will be pissing blood for a week after…"

"For God's sake, man!" Jack said.

"Dreadfully sorry." Tubby looked abashed. "Perhaps another slice of that pudding?" he asked Winnifred.

"We'd best start at the beginning," St. Ives said, and he did his best to reveal the salient points of Mother Laswell's sad story, including the business of the Aylesford Skull, the alleged lane to the afterlife, and the likely reason for Narbondo's kidnapping Eddie.

Keeble sat with a look of startled horror on his face. "The fiends lied to me," he said. "I had no idea."

"Of course," St. Ives told him. "None of us knew anything at all until now. I still admit to finding elements of the problem little short of ludicrous, but it's clear that Narbondo does not, and so the immediate dangers are very real."

"I find it no such thing, sir, if I might state my opinion," Doyle said. "There's nothing necessarily ludicrous in it. I have a high regard for science, but an equally high regard for the thinking of your Mother Laswell. Indeed, science ignorantly deplores things of the spirit, so to speak, and at its own peril. Our highly placed personage – we suspect him of being in league with Narbondo?"

"Perhaps, but the evidence isn't persuasive," St. Ives said. "Narbondo famously keeps to himself, of course. I can't imagine that he would take on a partner or a confidante, not unless it was for his own immediate gain. If the two are connected, I suspect financial dealings – Narbondo making use of this person's money or power. And if that's the case, then the man treads on very thin ice."

St. Ives was suddenly weary. The food had done for him. It was past time to put an end to the day. "We'll give the airship a trial at first light then," he said.

Keeble looked askance at him. "Not *all* of you, certainly? Not at once?"

"No, William. Hasbro and I will take it aloft. You three," he said, addressing Jack, Doyle, and Tubby, "should go about your business. I thank you for your loyalty tonight, but I have no idea what tomorrow will bring, and I don't intend to keep you standing by. I intend to go to the police. Perhaps I should have done so immediately, although it would surely have impeded our own efforts tonight, perhaps for the better."

This pronouncement dampened all conversation, and there was a general silence again. The most voracious eating was over, and even Tubby merely toyed with his final piece of toast. "I for one will look in on Uncle Gilbert's bivouac down the river," Tubby said.

"Ah, the search for the elusive bustard," St. Ives put in. "I had forgotten. Give him my kindest regards, if you will."

"He'll be having a comfortable time of it," Tubby said. "He has something of the Arabian sultan in him, you know, when it comes to an encampment. I'll be nearby, Professor, if you've got any use for me, and I'll be on the lookout for your airship."

"Perhaps Doyle and I can make inquiries about this Dutchman named de Groot," Jack said, "if in fact that's his name."

"Happily," Doyle said. "I've no reason to return to Southend for another week."

"We've got beds already made up," Dorothy said. "You'll stay here tonight. You too, Tubby, unless you're keen on returning to Chingford. The lot of you, in fact. We'll make do."

"Thank you," St. Ives said, "but we'll just nip back over to the Half Toad as usual. Our dunnage is there. I'm done in, I'm afraid, so the sooner the better." He pushed his chair back from the table and Hasbro did the same, but before they had time to stand, the doorknocker downstairs hammered a half dozen times, leading to an absolute silence in the room. St. Ives was keenly alert. This would not be a social call, not at this late hour.

"I'll see to it," Jack said. He arose and went to the several speaking tubes moored to a wooden rack on the wall of the room. He plucked the first of them free and spoke into the funnel-like mouth of the thing. "Please to identify yourself," he said.

From the considerably larger funnel affixed to the wall nearby came a disembodied voice, a boy's voice, perhaps. "It's Newman, sir, at your service," the voice said.

"Do any of us know a *Newman*?" Jack asked the company, covering the speaking tube with his hand.

"Not any sort of Newman who would be knocking

at the door at this hour," Tubby said. "It's not the police, though, thank God."

"What do you want, Mr. Newman?" Jack asked into the mouthpiece. "State your business."

"Message for Mr. Owlesby or the missus if he ain't there," came the reply. "Finn Conrad sends word of the Doctor!"

St. Ives stood up out of his chair, a wave of pain cutting across his forehead and nearly staggering him. "*Finn Conrad!*" he shouted. "What on *Earth*...?" But he was already crossing the room to the door, Jack at his heels, the both of them hurrying down the stairs toward the street.

TWENTY-FIVE
LORD MOORGATE

Mother Laswell found herself crossing the mouth of Angel Alley again, following the disguised man. He headed up Whitechapel Road, and then very soon turned north onto Brick Lane, crossing Wentworth Street several streets east from where Mother Laswell had crossed it earlier in the evening. Abruptly she recalled his name: Nesbitt – Layton Nesbitt. She had a memory for names, especially names from the past, but she had to allow her mind to recover them by itself. If she actively sought them out, they'd stay hidden. There had been mention of Nesbitt in her husband's logbooks – several, if she remembered aright – that seemed to reveal his generally low opinion of the man, although a generally high regard for the man's money. Nesbitt had been a young man at the time.

The long day told on her joints, and she found she was limping on her right foot, her corns no doubt enflamed. She half expected Nesbitt to hail a hansom cab and disappear, leaving her to trudge back the way she'd come, a mile out of her way now, the entire adventure utterly pointless. Could she find her way back to Lime Street without entirely retracing her steps? Most of the street names meant little to her, but in her mind she could picture herself walking around the perimeter of a box. Currently they were moving dead away from the river. When he turned left again on a street called Hanbury, she was relieved to think that another left turn would take her in the general direction of Mabel's. If he turned right again, they would part company. She didn't have it in her to keep on at this pace.

Not long after this thought came into her mind, he turned abruptly into the shallow portico of a building with a bright-red door, hesitating for a moment while he fitted a key to the lock, then opened the door, and went in. She walked up to the building and stood looking at the facade. There was no sign of any sort – not an inn. A place, perhaps, where he kept rooms. Two windows fronted the street, hung with heavy velvet curtains. The interior was dimly lit. She peered past the curtain but could make little out, and she was acutely aware that she was merely loitering. She wondered what she meant to do. Beat on the door? What would she confront him with even if he answered?

It was long past midnight, and the street was very nearly empty. Two men hurried along down the footpath opposite, turning up an alley and disappearing. There was another man ambling along toward her, a few yards down. She felt perfectly aimless, like a top that had spun itself out under a chair. Had she gone about her business she would be at Mabel's by now, taking her ease.

The door opened, surprising her, and Nesbitt reappeared. He was accompanied now by a young woman who seemed to be half his age. He had removed the disguise, which had given him a comical air, and there was nothing comical about him now. He had steel gray hair and an angular face despite his heavy build. In the gaslight his eyes were the same color as his hair.

"Who cares that you lost your ring?" the woman said to him. "You can buy another."

"My *signet* ring," he told her, stopping on the footpath to pull on his gloves. "Of course I can buy another. Money is not the issue. I wouldn't want it found, do you see? Not where I've been tonight. The police would recognize it easily enough and wonder why I had been in that room."

"You should have kept it on your finger."

"I thank you for your advice. I found myself among strangers, actually, and so I put it into my pocket. Evidently it fell out. I wasn't at ease in that damned rookery, I can tell you. And I don't trust Narbondo. He's done nothing to demonstrate good faith. It's almost as if he's mocking me. He'll regret it if he is."

The two set out again, in Mother Laswell's direction, and in that moment Nesbitt looked straight at her. He blinked, as if in surprise, and then a slow, contemptuous smile formed on his face.

"You've followed me," he said. "How tenacious of you."

"You knew my late husband," she told him, "many years ago. You're Layton Nesbitt, I believe?"

"He's Lord Moorgate now," the woman said to her, a haughty look on her face. "You'd best curtsey, you old slattern."

"And you'd be wise to find more savory company, young lady. Your Lord Moorgate has dangerous friends, my son among them."

"Come now," Moorgate said, "*why* have you followed me?"

"I really cannot tell you," she said. "It was a sleeveless errand."

"You cannot, you say? You underestimate yourself, or perhaps you underestimate me. This is your second sleeveless errand of the evening, apparently. That seems uncannily thoughtless of you. I believe that you know something more than you say, or that you believe you do. How you know it is a mystery, but mysteries bore me. I'll just ask you to accompany us, ma'am, in order to come at a solution. We'll chat further, in the company of one or two of my dangerous friends."

"I will *not*, sir. I have no fear of you."

The woman grinned abruptly, as if finding this amusing, and Mother Laswell moved back a step, holding her parasol before her like a sword. She had a premonition of real danger now – from the woman, and not Nesbitt or Moorgate or whatever he called himself. Running wasn't in her, though. They would have her if they wanted her, no doubt about that, but perhaps she could poke one of them in the eye…

Moorgate lunged forward suddenly, taking three long steps and closing with her. He clutched her arm, wrenching the parasol out of her grasp and pitching it into the street. She attempted to twist away, but the woman came up beside her now and latched onto her other arm, and Mother Laswell found herself propelled forward, walking so as not to fall down. Quickly she decided that falling down was a better thing than going on, and so she slumped, her weight dragging her to the ground.

"I won't go another step," she said, sitting on the pavement. "I have nothing to say to you or your friends."

"I believe that you do," Lord Moorgate said, "and I believe that you will. Helen, convince her that I'm correct, if you don't mind. I'm weary of this."

The woman named Helen bent over in front of her and produced an ivory knitting needle from her sleeve. It had been filed to a sharp point, which she displayed for Mother Laswell's edification. "Upon my honor you'll come along willingly or I'll put this in your ear, my lady."

Mother Laswell stared into her face for a moment. *You've trod on a hornets' nest now, Mother*, she told herself. Having no choice in the matter she struggled to rise, neither of the two lending her any assistance. They were talking again. The woman laughed aloud. Mother Laswell heard a rush of footsteps behind her now – someone coming at a dead run – and she looked back in surprise, as did Moorgate and the woman named Helen.

Mother Laswell was confounded to see Bill Kraken six paces away running and not slowing down. Lord Moorgate set his feet to meet the onrush, but was simply mowed down, his hat flying away, Kraken banking off the nearby wall, catching himself, and leaping forward to kick Moorgate on the knee. Helen, knitting needle in her hand, lunged at Kraken as Moorgate fell, but Mother Laswell threw herself forward and grabbed a handful of Helen's dress and the woman tripped and went down, grunting audibly when her knee and hands struck the stones of the pavement, her knitting needle snapping in half. Mother Laswell leaned heavily against her as she got to her feet, stepping into the road to fetch her parasol, meaning to teach Helen a lesson in manners.

Moorgate leapt up and assumed a boxer's stance, he and Kraken circling Helen, who rolled up onto the footpath, shielding herself with her hands and arms. Moorgate feinted at Kraken, who ducked backward as his opponent took a wild swing at his jaw, Kraken knocking his fist away, Moorgate bobbing toward him again, lashing out and catching Kraken on the chin this time, knocking him backward.

With room to move now, Helen scrambled to her feet and turned toward Mother Laswell, who rushed in at her, pummeling her with the umbrella, thrusting it into her face, Helen windmilling her arms to fend it off and fleeing into the street. Mother Laswell followed, her blood up now, and took a wild swing with the umbrella at the back of Helen's head. The umbrella flew open, two of the ribs entangling themselves in Helen's hair and bringing her up short.

"Murder!" Helen began screaming. "Murder! Murder!"

Mother Laswell snatched the umbrella away with both hands, shouting, "We'll see who murders whom!" and starting forward again, but abruptly finding herself pulled backward. Behind them, Lord Moorgate lay face down on the pavement.

"We'd best take our leave," Kraken said, hurrying her along.

Suddenly energized, Mother Laswell found herself running, her corns be damned – something she hadn't done in years, the two of them rounding the corner and hastening south along Bishopsgate. When it was certain they weren't being followed, they slowed their pace and limped along, Kraken looking back every few yards, both of them laboring simply to breathe. No one followed. Lord Moorgate had given it up, apparently. Mother Laswell wondered if he were dead. More likely he would simply have gone on his way. He wouldn't want the police involved, not if he thought she knew something about his dealings, which he evidently *did* think, although he was dead wrong in that regard.

"We'd best keep on," Kraken said, gasping. "They'd jail me for certain, Mother, for laying into that gent."

"He's no gent," Mother Laswell said. "*You're* a gent, Bill, and I owe you an apology for running out on you this morning. Indeed, I owe you considerably more than that."

"Nobody owes me nothing, Mother, including you," Kraken said. "I don't hold with being owed. Who was he, then – him and the strumpet?"

"That was Lord Moorgate. You've savaged a Peer of the Realm, Bill. The woman was a vicious little adder. It's my great hope that we never meet them again. I've gone my entire life without brawling, and now twice in one night I've found myself in a rout. If you hadn't come along when you did, they'd have had their way with me." She took stock of her umbrella, which was flayed to pieces. A considerable hank of black hair was entangled in the bent ribs, and she saw with satisfaction that there was a bit of bloody skin attached.

The tooth! she thought, thrusting her hand into her pocket. With it, Mabel might once again locate Edward, even if Narbondo had moved him out of London. The tooth was still there, safe enough.

"Mabel Morningstar showed me the map," Kraken said, "and I been searching these last hours. It was dumb luck that I fell in with you when you were a-standing outside there on the street. When the two of them joined you, I held back till I seen what they were about. You didn't kill the Doctor, did you? I'm hopeful that you didn't. You couldn't of stood it, a woman with your heart."

"No, Bill. I didn't kill him, although I admit that I tried, or I think I did. I didn't have the spirit to do it for its own sake, but there was a boy there, and I plucked up the courage to use the pistol when it came into my mind to take the boy away."

"Eddie, his name is – the boy," Kraken said.

"Yes. How did you know?"

"The missus told me. Alice St. Ives – the Professor's missus, before I come into London."

"I'm bound to find that boy, Bill. I nearly brought him away with me, but I couldn't manage it. Narbondo will kill another child, do you see, and I can't have that. I couldn't stand having two on my conscience."

"No more can I, Mother. We're in it together, up to our necks. We've got a mort of seams to caulk, and no pitch hot, but we'll see it done, by God. Damn me if we won't."

"Nobody will damn you, Bill, ever. I don't deserve a friend such as you. I tell you that plainly."

"More than a friend, ma'am," Kraken mumbled. And then he nodded his head resolutely. "*More* than a friend." He said it clearly this time, his face looking both pleased and determined in the moonlight.

She gazed at him quizzically, a smile on her own face,

but he kept his eyes forward. She took his arm, happy enough not to press him, and he reached over and patted her hand.

TWENTY-SIX
SHADE HOUSE

It was very nearly dawn now, and Finn Conrad, still lying in his depression behind the coach, considered what he would do, because he would have to do it soon. His shoulder ached, his knee was bent at an unnatural angle, and the iron edge of the platform on which he lay dug into his elbow. He had no idea how long he had been rattling along, but it was too long, to his mind. Some time back, in St. Mary Hoo, where they had stopped for a time at an inn before leaving the pavement and driving into the wilds of the Cliffe Marshes, Finn had slipped off the back of the coach and hidden behind a hedgerow in order to keep from being discovered. Then he had leapt back on again when the coach got underway in the darkness, but not as nimbly as he had in London. In his diminished, cramped state he had nearly fallen. He should invent a tale right now, he told himself, and think it through in the time he had left. If they twigged to the lie, he would simply run away, if he weren't half crippled.

The coach was in among trees, rocking slowly along a rutted track. He could see the remnants of stars through the branches, and the bright moon, and in the eastern sky there was just the hint of dawn, the stars dimmed by it. He raised his head carefully and took a look in the direction of the distant, invisible Thames, where moonlight shone on a broad body of water: Egypt Bay, no doubt – the south shore along the Thames merely a line of shadow in the far distance. He thought of Square Davey, who was almost certainly on the river, possibly nearby. If he failed, he told himself, and something happened to Eddie, he would take Davey up on his offer to take up oystering again. Returning to Aylesford would be unthinkable. Thoughts of old Davey brought the Crumpet into his mind. The man would soon arrive in the Cliffe Marshes, and that would change everything on the instant. Finn must look for his chance to snatch Eddie away as soon as ever he could. If Newman had got his message through to the Professor, so much the better, but Finn couldn't depend on it and he couldn't wait for the Professor to play his hand.

The driver reined in the horses, and the coach drew to a stop before a run-down, ancient, three-story wooden structure, tilted where its north-facing wall had apparently sunk into the marshy ground over the years. Several windows looked out onto a weedy yard where there stood an enormous walnut tree, the upper limbs of which arched over the roof of the inn. A sign hanging on a post in the yard read 'Shade House,' the lamp above it throwing out enough radiance so that Finn drew his head in just a bit. Another lamp burned behind a downstairs shutter. Now the inn door opened and a man walked out and said something to the coachman, who climbed heavily down to the ground before muttering a reply. Finn recognized the newcomer from Narbondo's rooms on Angel Alley. He had thrown a cracker at the man just before fleeing through the door across the rope bridge with Eddie. He must have come along to the Bay immediately following the dust-up. His boots and trousers were brown with dirt, and he looked weary, his face bruised and cut. He opened the door of the coach now and helped Narbondo down, then lifted out the sleeping Eddie. He was delicate about it, and held the boy easily. There was something in the action that made Finn wonder whether the man had some variety of kindness in his heart, kindness that might be turned to advantage.

"See to the boy, George," Narbondo said in a low voice. "Put him in the lace bedroom and hang some bottles of champagne in the brook for Lord Moorgate. I suspect that he'll be along in a few hours, and we want to put him at his ease and play upon his pride. I mean to confound him come what may and let him rot, but he's too suspicious by half, and the longer we can keep him dancing the better."

With that Narbondo turned to the driver of the coach, and said, "Take your ease, Mr. Beaumont. George will see to the coach." He walked away then – not through the door of the Shade House, but around the side, disappearing into the darkness. Mr. Beaumont climbed stiffly down and went in through the open door of the inn.

George followed him, carrying Eddie, the night falling silent. Finn dragged himself off his perch and crept down to the ground, immediately setting in to shake himself limber and to push himself up on his toes to ease the cramping in his legs. A lamp came on behind one of the windows in the top floor now – Eddie being locked away, perhaps – near enough to the tree, Finn noticed, to climb up to it. He considered the succession of limbs both downward and upward, and whether Eddie might be induced to climb down, which was always more frightening and difficult than climbing up. *Doubtful*, he thought.

He settled his cap on his head and waited, reviewing his tale. Very shortly George came back out through the door, saw Finn standing there, and stopped in his tracks. Finn swept his cap from his head and bowed, thankful that he'd been wearing the balaclava earlier, which he had happily pitched into the street before they were out of London.

"Where in the devil's name did *you* come from?" George asked.

"St. Mary Hoo, sir, when this coach stopped for a time. I climbed up onto the back and rode along, hid by the baggage."

"Then you'll be able to find your way back to St. Mary Hoo afoot. Off with you." He jerked his head to underscore the command and pointed back down the road. "*Now*, boy. You don't want to linger – not here."

"I'm right anxious for a trial sir, if you'll have me. I was an ostler for two years in Yorkshire for Mr. Carnahan, and I can pick a man's pocket like it was nothing, if that suits your honor."

"I daresay you can. No doubt you picked Mr. Carnahan's pocket, whoever he is, which explains why you're no longer in his employ. And now you've skulked out of St. Mary Hoo in the dark of night. You've only just been breeched and already you're tearing along toward the gibbet like a devil in a red cap."

"I'm just trying to make my living, sir. If it please your honor to help me, I'd be grateful."

"It would not please me. I tell you to go home, wherever home is, before they put the rope around your neck. The noose is already tied, depend upon it. Better to look to the kindness of your mother, because there's little enough of that commodity you'll find in the world, nor here at Shade House, neither, for that matter."

"My mother's dead, sir, and my father's gone off. He left when I was a lad, and never came back. He was a drunk, sir, so I don't miss him. I took care of my little brother till he died of the bloody jack when he was only five years – not much older than the boy who come along in this coach just now. After that I left London and went north, where I worked in the cheesing line, Stilton mainly, and was scullery boy at the Bell Inn on the Great North Road, where I learned to butcher some. I can do a day's work, sir, no matter what. I don't peach, neither. Never have. I'd sooner stay here and work for my room and board, and no matter any pay. You won't be sorry for it."

George looked at him in silence, his head canted to the side so that he seemed to be inspecting him through the corner of his eye. The appraisal went on long enough so that Finn began to wonder whether the balaclava had done its work after all. He looked past George, into the trees, ready to bolt. Apparently making up his mind, George said, "Do you have a name, boy?"

"Newman, sir."

"Just Newman? No Christian name?"

"No, sir. I've always been Newman, your honor. Newman ain't Christian?"

"Some Newmans are and some aren't," George said. "When were you last in London?"

"Some time back," Finn said. "Six months, maybe."

"Not more recent?"

"No, sir."

"You're right certain of it?"

"Yes, sir."

George looked at him for a time again, saying nothing. A bird with a particularly mournful note called from the nearby wood, but otherwise the night was silent. *He knows*, Finn thought, looking out toward the dark trees, but in that moment George surprised him by nodding.

"Stable's around behind, Newman, near the Doctor's cottage, him whose carriage you rode in on uninvited. You stay out of the Doctor's way. He doesn't hold with senseless talk, nor with boys, neither. Thinks they're worthless, and he's probably right in that regard. I'm saying this for your own good. *Stay clear of the Doctor.* When you've curried the horses and put them up, find me in the kitchen. If you don't see me, ask for George. We'll see what you're made of and whether lying is on your list of talents. Be off with you now."

"Yes, sir," Finn said, and immediately climbed up onto the seat of the landau and picked up the reins, clicking the horses into a walk and following in Narbondo's wake around the side of the inn, looking sharp, since he had no idea whether Narbondo would recognize him from their conversation on the road in Aylesford two nights back. He was still half certain that George had seen through him – remembered the coat, maybe, from Angel Alley, although he would have seen it only briefly. But if he had recognized

276

Finn, then what was his game?

There was no sign of Narbondo, only the cottage, a mean, one-room shanty built of drift lumber hauled out of the bay. The window was propped open and the shutters pushed aside – easy enough to get in, although Finn could think of no good reason to do so, since Eddie wasn't there. A brook ran along behind the cottage, with a mill beside it farther down, the brook turning the wheel.

The stable stood nearby. Finn unhitched, fed, watered, and curried the horses, and then mucked out their stalls and pitched in clean straw before putting them away. He blew out the lanterns, walked out into the yard, discovering that it was morning outside, and he looked around one more time at the prospects for escape before walking in through the open back door of the inn. George was in the kitchen, as he had promised. It was a wide room, surprisingly clean and squared away. Finn took in the brick-and-iron ovens, the carving and breadboards, the hams and herbs and iron pots and pans hung on the walls and ceiling. A long window of bullseye glass let in the early morning light.

"All ship-shape in the stable, sir," Finn said, picking up a long knife and feeling the blade. "I'll just put an edge on this, if you'd like, and slice up that side of bacon, if it's bacon that's to be served out."

"You'll put the goddamned knife down," said a man who was just then coming into the kitchen, carrying an enormous sack of flour over his shoulder as if it were nothing and bending low to clear the top of the lintel above the door.

"Yes, sir," Finn said, and he put the knife down as he was told.

The man was big, immensely tall and heavy, dangerous looking. His black hair was long and his eyes sharp and smoldering. His left arm was put up in a sling that was dark brown with dried blood.

"This is Mr. McFee," George said. "He's particular in his ways, is Mr. McFee. I've told him you were to be given a trial in the kitchen, Newman. You'll do just as he tells you, if you've got any sense."

"If he had any sense he'd take himself off," McFee said, not looking at Finn. He set the flour down on the floor with his one good arm.

"I'll stay, sir, with your leave," Finn told him.

"Then put an edge on that knife if you can, boy," McFee told him. "We'll test the blade on your hand. If you ruin it, and I have to grind it again, it'll cost you an ear. We'll cook it with the chowder as a lark, like the French do with hens' ears. McFee's ear chowder, we'll call it."

Finn stared at him, wondering whether the man was practicing on him, but there was no humor in his face at all, something more like a simmering rage. Finn took up the knife, felt the edge again, and began to hone it carefully against the steel, wishing that he hadn't told George the nonsense about making cheeses. If McFee put him to work in that regard, Finn had best run, for he had no more notion of making cheese than of building chimneys. He handed over the knife, which McFee took from him, at the same time grasping Finn's wrist with the hand that was in the bloody sling.

"Open your fist, boy," he said. "When I say I'll do something, you'd best remember that I'll do it."

Finn did as he was told. It seemed to be the safest course, since running was out of the question. He kept his face utterly still as McFee ran the sharp blade lightly across his palm. A line of blood welled up. Reaching into a crockery jar that stood on the breadboard, McFee brought out a handful of black dust, which he held in front of Finn.

"This here's coal dust and human bone," McFee said, "ground up precious fine, which the Doctor takes with his vittles like another man takes salt. You'll mind yourself around the Doctor, boy, if you've got a head on you. Hear me now – you'll jump to it when I tell you to, or I'll slit your throat and feed you to the hogs." He sprinkled the coal dust liberally on Finn's sliced hand, rubbing it into the line of blood with his thumb. "That'll put paid to the bleeding, boy, and give you a gaudy mark into the bargain, permanent like. You've come into John McFee's kitchen. You're mine now. My mark's upon you."

TWENTY-SEVEN
ALOFT OVER LONDON

St. Ives had got perhaps four hours of real sleep, and in the middle of it had lurched awake from a nightmare that had filled him with a profound, breathless dread – a vision of Eddie and Alice disappearing into a black cleft in a stone wall, which had closed tightly behind them. Even so, he had fallen asleep again, and this morning his headache had quite disappeared, and he found that his mind was clear and sharp. He had no regard for the idea that dreams were prophetic. *No doubt they sometimes illustrated one's deepest fears*, he told himself, *but almost certainly in a manner that was merely symbolic.*

Almost certainly, he told himself again, and in any event, last night's blue devils had been consigned to Hell, where they could abide until he had some use for them, which wouldn't be soon. He had been shown the way by Finn Conrad, a boy alone in London and with precious few resources aside from his wits and his cleverness. The lesson might have been humbling rather than inspiring to any reasonably competent man. To St. Ives it was a tonic of the first water, to coin a somewhat ridiculous phrase, and so was the eastern horizon, which, seen now from their great height in the airship, glowed a magnificent orange, the sun coming up dripping out of the Dover Strait, and London laid out below them.

The gondola was a skeletal-looking, boat-built structure, very much like an enclosed launch, its keel tapering into a bowsprit in front. The gondola's wooden frame was stick-like, and scarcely seemed sturdy enough to bear the weight of the craft and its cargo. The plank floorboards creaked, and the breeze blew in through open ports – a potential irritation, perhaps, if St. Ives hadn't been wearing goggles. There were glass windows, in fact, hinged open at the moment, which might be closed in the case of rain, but it was Keeble's idea that the effect of the wind pushing against the gondola would be lessened if they remained open.

By now St. Ives felt safe enough, and was used to the movement of the spokes of the ship's wheel, which felt like a living thing beneath his hands. As soon as they had ascended above the rooftops his attention had been drawn to the miniature city laid out below them. He saw the dome of St. Paul's now, off the port bow, Queen Victoria Street and Blackfriars Bridge identifiable alongside, Hyde Park a leafy green acreage in the distance, everything small and neat. He took in the view of the shipping on the Thames, the first boats already plying back and forth to the Custom House or mooring at the Billingsgate docks. Smithfield Market lay dead ahead, with Billson's Half Toad Inn somewhere nearby, but he couldn't quite discern the inn among the many tiny buildings and streets, Lambert Court looking like any of a thousand other such courts from the air.

He had been aloft in balloons a number of times, but motive power made this something pleasingly different – a true, dirigible airship, not at the mercy of the winds, at least for the most part. He was a pilot rather than a passenger in that sense. Just as this thought came into his mind, however, a sudden gust shifted them bodily in the direction of the river, and for a moment he had precious little control of the craft as the nose quickly fell off course.

"She pays off to leeward prodigiously even in this moderate breeze," St. Ives said to Hasbro, who was peering intently into the periscope lens.

"Dizzyingly, I might add," Hasbro said, "what with the smaller view through the lens. One keeps losing perspective. I'm endeavoring to keep the St. Paul's in sight…" He looked out through the gondola window, then back into the lens, adjusting the periscope controls. "There, I've found it again."

First-rate practice, St. Ives thought. He moved the king-spoke of the ship's wheel to starboard, the airship turning slowly, heading back into the wind at an oblique angle and making tolerable headway against it. He intended to come completely around in a circle to starboard if he could, to see what the wind would do in all quarters. The controls were simple enough, the propeller providing surprising motive power, towing them rather than pushing. At twelve nautical miles an hour it was as fast as a sailing ship or a steam launch, although it didn't seem so, with the ground so far below and no visible wake or bow wave to judge by. He wondered what the effect of a thirty-knot headwind would be, or a quick downdraft, but he would have to wait until Aeolus provided him with useful examples of such things.

God willing it wouldn't mean disaster.

Keeble's clever electric engine hummed as they made their circuit, St. Ives keeping an eye on the compass needle, which traced the course. An imagined Aylesford swept past somewhere in the hazy distance, Alice and Cleo comfortably asleep, he hoped, and then, much farther away, the Channel and Beachy Head, with the coast of France beyond. They circled around farther, looking away west now, up the Thames, Wales lurking out there somewhere, and then very shortly what must be the Great North Road appeared below. Around they came into the east again, and a flock of birds flew past, out of the sun, which had crept higher into the sky, well clear of the sea, although the city was still largely in shadow. The blue lenses of St. Ives's goggles reduced the glare, but gave the world a strangely aquatic tinge, as if they sailed beneath a tropical ocean rather than through the sky. They were over Smithfield once again, back on course, although some distance west of where they had started their turn, no great time having elapsed in the experimental circuit.

"London is admirably quiet at this altitude," Hasbro said, not looking up from the periscope lens.

"Are people taking notice of us?" St. Ives asked, the idea appealing to him.

"Indeed. They come out into the street and point skyward. Some seem to be determined to follow, although our circuitous route has confounded their efforts."

"We'll drop down a few hundred feet," St. Ives said, "in order to give them a better view. See if you can pick out the Half Toad. I'd like to get several more absolute bearings before slanting away toward Greenwich."

When released by a foot pedal, an iron tiller with a ball atop tilted the propeller up and down, shifting the craft vertically. St. Ives pushed the tiller forward now, the ship descending toward the rooftops and leveling off when they were quite low.

"I believe I have Billson's in view," Hasbro said. "There lies the Smithfield Central Market and the top of Shoe Lane, if I'm not mistaken. Billson's must be one of the..."

There was a sudden, heavy concussion somewhere below them, a dull, muffled thud – an explosion, almost certainly. Abruptly the airship rushed upward nose first, was pushed as if from a great wind, the gondola sweeping downward on its pendulum to remain level. St. Ives had no control of the craft at all now, and it occurred to him that if the ship somersaulted, or came close to, the gondola might simply plunge into the rubberized skin of the craft and be engulfed. There was a terrible groaning noise, as if the bamboo struts that formed the skeleton of the craft were straining against their screws and rivets. Then the force lessened, and he eased forward on the tiller, depressing the nose, until they were level again. The ship answered the helm, the silence returned, and the engine hummed away as ever.

"A good deal of smoke seems to be issuing from the environs of the market," Hasbro said, "or very near – the Farringdon Street edge below Charterhouse Street. A great billowing now."

St. Ives could see it clearly as it rose into the sky ahead – black smoke, for the most part – and he was reminded of the Palm House at the Bayswater Club. He drew the tiller back, and the craft rose, passing over the leading edge of the cloud. People could be seen fleeing from the market, many running toward the grounds of St. Bartholomew the Less and others fleeing east along Charterhouse Street.

"My God," Hasbro said, his usual equanimity shattered. "They've blown a hole in the wall of the Fleet River, I believe. There's a torrent pouring out of the breach and washing down Farringdon Street, sweeping everything before it."

St. Ives craned his neck, watching the floodwaters rage along toward the Thames, carrying away wagons and horses that had been coming up toward the market. People fled away on every side, broken wagons washing up against the buildings along the street. The flood and debris must have been making a din, for people some distance ahead of the waters climbed up onto whatever high ground afforded itself, others ran east or west, if they were lucky enough to be near an intersection. St. Ives had rarely felt as useless, for there was nothing he could do to help except pray that people could find their way clear.

Blackfriars Bridge arched over the Thames ahead of them. Behind them the smoke had thinned, blowing away on the breeze. The flood showed no sign of abating, which was odd. In fact, now that St. Ives considered it, the flood itself was odd. It was true that the waters of the Fleet came down from high elevation in Hampstead Heath, as did most of the underground rivers, and that they were very near the surface in Smithfield, but even so, what explained their sudden issuance? The explosion alone wouldn't answer. The collapse of the tunnel, perhaps? – the Fleet simply blocked?

The papers would blame anarchists, as ever. It was

perilously simple to cast blame into the open pit of anarchy and have done with speculation. They crossed the river to the south shore, and then came around again, looking back toward Smithfield. The flow was diminished now, the river apparently having resumed its course after its ten minutes of wild freedom. But what had caused the cessation? The force of the waters might perhaps have cleared away the debris...

"The explosion in the Ranelagh Sewer was much the same," St. Ives said. "Too much the same to be mere coincidence, it seems to me."

"Your men got out along the embankment in that instance, I believe?"

"I'm fairly certain of it. Train the glass on the river's edge, if you will – there where the waters of the Fleet issue out. There seems to be activity there." The waters were much diminished, it seemed to St. Ives, although the flow was perhaps strengthening again.

"I have them in the lens now, sir. Two toshers, from the look of it, one of them a child. No, a dwarf, a bearded dwarf. There's a barred door in the face of the Embankment, but the gate stands open. The dwarf pushes a barrow with a lantern."

The blimp descended, St. Ives anxious to see the way of things. The two might easily be the same two who had effected the explosion at the Bayswater Club, especially given that they were trundling a barrow – an element too eccentric to be meaningless. It was possible, of course, that they were mere sewer hunters who had brought a cart along to haul their finds.

"They've taken an interest in us," Hasbro said.

St. Ives got a good look at the pair now, although he could tell nothing much from it. When he had gone into the Ranelagh Sewer beneath the Bayswater Club, he hadn't been able to see the face of his attacker. The dwarf was gesticulating, apparently arguing with his companion, pointing toward the airship. If they were mere toshers, illegally scavenging in the sewers, they would scarcely fear an airship, which could do damn-all to inconvenience them. They weren't dressed like toshers, either. The thin man wore a bright-blue flannel coat, gaudy shoes, and a straw boater, as if he were spending a holiday at the seaside.

Suddenly the dwarf leapt forward and pushed his barrow along the embankment toward the cover of the bridge, the thing bouncing and swerving. He glanced back at the airship, and was evidently fleeing. The barrow gave a leap, skidded sideways, and fell, the front panel of the enclosure popping upward. What appeared to be an iron kettle bounded off and rolled toward the Thames, bouncing once and then flying in an arc from the lower terrace. Its lid flew off as it described a short arc out over the river before plunging in. A whiff of white vapor ascended at the point where the waters closed over the kettle, and immediately there was a pool of liquid fire floating on the surface of the river in the shadow of the bridge. The dwarf's companion caught up with him now and cuffed him about the head, the dwarf warding off the blows. They soon gave it up, righted the barrow, and went on their hurried way, disappearing beneath the bridge.

The airship passed over, hundreds of people atop the bridge pointing skyward now. The two men and their barrow were nowhere to be seen, and they could easily skulk away into London from the shelter of the bridge. There was nothing to be done about any of it. As for St. Ives and Hasbro, their way lay to the east, and the sooner the better. St. Ives shifted the wheel to port, the airship carrying them around the newly constructed Cathedral of the Oxford Martyrs. From the air it appeared to be a preciously slender cast-iron framework around plate-glass rectangles, less sturdily constructed, it seemed to St. Ives, than the gondola in which he sat. The structure was built in the manner of the Crystal Palace, although considerably smaller. To St. Ives it looked something like the head of an Aberdeen terrier, but without any of the dog's virtues. Although Gladstone had condemned the cathedral as a silly piece of egotistic rubbish, the papers touted it as a marvel of its type, another of the grand architectural achievements of Victoria's reign. It would officially open with great ceremony sometime soon – an event that failed to interest St. Ives in the least, as did the political squabbling of the Queen and her prime minister.

"Is it the same pair that attacked you?" Hasbro asked.

"I'm compelled to believe that it is. If not the same two, then two from the same mold, surely. Anarchists, perhaps, although with strangely complicated methods. I wonder at the substance that was burning on the water."

"Greek fire, I should think. It's easily produced, ferociously hot."

"But why go to the trouble of taking along so dangerous a substance?" St. Ives asked. "An infernal device is far easier to produce with mere gunpowder, and it creates its own explosion with a simple clockwork mechanism."

"True," Hasbro said. "Consider, however, that the bursting of the Fleet Sewer might be mere practice toward some greater end, where an infernal device wouldn't serve."

"Could it be coal dust that exploded?" St. Ives asked, the idea coming into his mind abruptly. "I know so little of coal dust, but Merton's contraband coal raises the possibility, if this is indeed Narbondo's handiwork."

"Gilbert Frobisher is acquainted with the dangers of coal dust, sir, given that he's made his fortune in smelting."

"We'll quiz the man when we have an opportunity. It seems quite possible that Narbondo is behind both explosions – weeks ago at the club and again today. Suppose they dispersed the dust into the air in a confined space and detonated it by casting Greek fire into its midst. Grain silos explode with tremendous force when a few pounds of suspended dust are empowered by a lucifer match. A palm house would go up in much the same manner, although I have no idea how much dust would be required. Could such a thing be done in a sewer, though?"

"Possibly," Hasbro said. "There are chambers built into the walls of the tunnels at intervals. A dam built of coffer-work might deflect water into one of the chambers near a point where the river is particularly close to the surface. That same coffer-work might be constructed to allow the blockage of the chamber altogether, allowing for the dust to accumulate in a sufficient volume if it were pumped in. Certainly they'd have to find a chamber with a perilously thin outer wall to avoid blowing themselves up into the bargain, and at a point where the waters were very near the surface. Dangerous work, sir, with a great deal of labor involved, no doubt – immense preparation. Keeping the work hidden from the flushers would be the greatest task, I should think. It would take practice to get it right, no doubt, as well as a close knowledge of the sewers, but such a thing could be done if one had sufficient time and resources – funds to bribe the right parties."

"*Practice to get it right,*" St. Ives said. "I'm with you there. But practice to what end? Something that justified the expense and labor." On a whim he brought the ship around in a circle again, in order to take another look at the glass cathedral. "It's impossible not to have heard of the coming ceremony at the cathedral, but I'm afraid I haven't paid sufficient attention. Fairly grand, is it?"

"Yes, sir," said Hasbro. "The Queen will be in attendance along with other dignitaries."

Below them, men moved about, both inside and out of the building, finishing the work, clearing things away, as visible as fish in a crystal bowl. St. Ives thought again of Mother Laswell's fears about the lane to the land of the dead, a half-baked absurdity that he hadn't shared with Hasbro. *What would it take,* he wondered, *to turn the glass cathedral itself into a vast infernal device, perhaps with the Queen herself sitting at the very heart of it?*

"If the explosions are Narbondo's handiwork, as you believe, then there's certainly a well-defined, lucrative motive," Hasbro said.

"I have an idea what might justify it," he said, "although you won't be able to credit it. Mere logic cannot be brought to bear on it."

By the time he was through with the tale, they had

passed over Greenwich, moving more quickly than ever now, with the wind at their back and the sky an endless pastel blue in front of them. The bent finger of water that was Egypt Bay was clearly visible in the near distance, the uneven green terrain of the Cliffe Marshes stretching away on three sides, cut with sheep trails and dotted with ponds and meadows and thickets.

"What I find unsettling," Hasbro said, "is that if Narbondo managed to shift the Fleet out of its brick-and-mortar banks today, then he's very far along in his plans."

TWENTY-EIGHT
THE CIPHER

Aside from what appeared to be several piles of rags sleeping in the shelter of a wall, Angel Alley was empty in the early morning, the sun low in the sky, when Jack Owlesby, Arthur Doyle, and Tubby Frobisher arrived. Last night's vagrants were comatose, no doubt, and there were no screeching rats or snarling dogs to be heard, only the morning noises out on Wentworth Street, which awakened early. They had seen the dirigible pass overhead a short time earlier, which seemed to them to be an auspicious sight, as if things were moving forward in some organized manner now that they knew the whereabouts of Narbondo and of Finn Conrad. Both Jack and Tubby understood Finn to be almost supernaturally competent, and his loyalty knew no bounds, which might easily mean the death of him if he undertook to engage Narbondo alone.

"The door stands open," Tubby said in a low voice. He pointed with his cudgel at the arched door that led into Narbondo's penthouse.

"They could be lying in wait," Jack said, "knowing

that we'd simply walk in. The open door is an invitation to an assault."

"Then we'll nail their ears to the breadboard and pitch the lot of them through the window," Tubby said. He pushed the door open and they peered into the dark stairwell. The oil lamps were burned out, and all was quiet above, although they listened for a moment longer before climbing the stairs and walking into the empty room with its crippled table. A broken chair lay on the floor along with shattered dinner plates and splinters of wood and glass from the smashed window, through which the wind blew.

"Take note of that rope bridge," Tubby said, nodding toward the window. "The door at the distant end stands open."

"For my money they've gone off with no idea of returning," Doyle said. "It's little we'll find here."

"Here's something curious," Jack said, gesturing at the unbroken window opposite, which looked down toward Wentworth Street. Costermongers and a few carriages went up and down among early morning pedestrians. Two blue-coated soldiers on horseback stood on the far side of the street, apparently looking in the direction of the penthouse, which lay largely in shadow, and so there must be precious little that the soldiers could see. Even so, the three men moved away toward the farther room, where they would be entirely out of sight.

"I recommend moderate haste," Doyle said, "and then away, perhaps across the very useful rope bridge."

In the back room stood a workbench scattered with odd bits and pieces of things. Two small human skulls, both of them yellow-brown, cracked, and evidently ancient sat at the back of the bench. Both had been trepanned, the circular openings splintered, the skulls useful, perhaps, to hold morbidly decorative candles on a theatre stage, but not for Narbondo's fell purposes, given St. Ives's description of the lamps. Alongside the skulls, in a scattering of excelsior, lay pieces of exposed glass photographic plates, small screws and bits of sheet copper, and – strangely – odds and ends of shell casings and lead bullets lying in a heap of what appeared to be gunpowder, as if someone had been loading cartridges.

"There's an odd smell here," Tubby said. "Rather like garlic."

"White phosphorous," Doyle said, pointing at a porcelain dish with a heap of white dust in it. "Extremely flammable. Highly regarded by anarchists these days, by the way. There are photographic chemicals here also." He picked up two green-glass, capped bottles and then set them down again. "Ferrous sulfate and potassium cyanide," he said. He held up a piece of one of the photographic plates and scrutinized it. "Here's the negative image of a boy's face in profile."

"I believe it's Eddie's likeness," Jack said, looking at it. "Why, though?"

"To make the ransom demand more tenable, perhaps," Doyle said. "They must have had a darkroom assembled, which of course they took away with them."

"Let's *pray* it's to make the ransom demand more tenable, and not for some other bloody purpose," Tubby said. "I don't like this business of the decorated skulls. St. Ives seemed to think that vast sums of money are involved, enough to make child murder seem like a trifle."

"Here now!" Jack said, reaching into the debris beneath the bench and picking up a small object. "A signet ring, by God. An eagle clutching the letter M in its paws. Highly stylized, but moderately plain for all that. It might belong to anyone."

Tubby nodded sagely. "One would suppose that all signet rings belong to someone, Jack. I'm going to guess that this particular ring was lost by a man whose name begins with the letter 'M.' That excludes our friend Dr. Narbondo. Keep it safe, however."

There was a clattering from the direction of Wentworth Street, and Tubby stepped out into the adjacent room again to have a look, leaving his two friends to continue their search. "A carriage has arrived," he said through the door, "accompanied by two more soldiers aboard horses. The door swings open. By God, it's Keeble's Dutchman from the look of it, our man de Groot. Tremendous large head with the eyes of a pig. He's evidently coming on alone. Why would the man do such a thing when he's brought four soldiers with him?" Tubby walked back into the room.

"I'll warrant he wants this very ring," Jack said. "He'll summon the soldiers quickly enough when he discovers we're here. Out the back, I say."

"Nonsense," Tubby said. "We'll parlay with the man. Certainly he's a reasonable creature. The Dutch are great thinkers, although I'm told that they make their shoes out of wood. You two go about your business. I'll play the man a bit of a prank when he arrives and then we'll engage him in edifying discussion."

Silence fell and then there was the sound of a door

closing – Tubby stepping outside onto the bridge landing so as not to be seen – and then, very shortly, footfalls on the stairs. De Groot, if he was indeed the man who had purchased the miniature lamp from William Keeble, strode into the room, saw Doyle and Jack looking back at him, and at once drew a small pistol from beneath his coat. He was indeed a heavy-bodied man, dressed in a sack coat and with a deerstalker cap perched on his round head. He wore side-whiskers but no mustache, and had a tiny, pointed beard at his chin. His hair was theatrically red.

"I'll relieve you of the ring you're clutching, sir," he said, looking at Jack's closed fist. "Immediately, or I'll have you taken up for trespass and theft. There are four soldiers waiting in the road. Come, what business do you have here?"

"By God I own this building, sir," Jack lied. "Who in the devil are you?"

"The man who has come to collect a signet ring that does not belong to you."

"Then to whom does it belong? There's been considerable deviltry here, and I'd like to have a word with any witnesses."

"It gives me great pleasure to tell you to mind your own business," de Groot said. "You lie copiously. Give me the ring immediately, or I'll summon my men."

Tubby walked silently in behind de Groot at this juncture and hammered him on the back of the head with the cudgel. Jack moved forward and caught the falling pistol nimbly, pocketed both the pistol and the ring, and then stepped back out of the way as de Groot slowly collapsed onto his side in a heap.

"What about the horsemen?" Doyle asked.

"Still waiting patiently, God bless them," Tubby said, "although their patience no doubt has its limits." He bent over and wrenched off de Groot's coat, the man's limp arms swinging upward and then flapping to the ground again. He moaned and turned onto his back, his eyes shut, breathing heavily. Doyle pulled one eye open with his thumb, exposing the white of the rolled-back eyeball. Tubby searched the coat pockets, drawing out a purse and a sheaf of papers bound up in ribbon before flinging the coat into the corner of the room. "What are we looking for?" he asked.

"We don't know," Jack said. "Bring the lot." Doyle stepped past them into the front room in order to take another look out of the window.

"We'll take his purse into the bargain," Tubby said to Jack. "I rather fancy the coat, too, but it's an ironclad rule of mine that I don't dress in my victim's clothing."

"One of the soldiers is climbing down from his horse," Doyle said to them. "He's pointing this way, having a word with the others. We'd best be off."

"Hell and damnation," Tubby said. "No time to drop our man headfirst into the courtyard?"

But de Groot was moaning where he lay and shuffling his feet, and Jack and Doyle were already heading toward the door that led out onto the bridge. Tubby followed, the three of them making their awkward way, high above the courtyard, the boards beneath their feet bobbing and swaying. Tubby lifted his hat to a young woman walking below, and then the three of them went through the open door and into the shadows, where they stopped for a moment to look back.

There was movement through the broken window of the penthouse, and the sound of someone calling out tentatively – the soldier quite possibly, not wanting to offend de Groot, perhaps, by bursting in unannounced.

Doyle led the way downward and out into the alley again, the three of them moving away to the west as hurriedly as they could without calling attention to themselves, out onto Whitechapel Road and away toward Smithfield.

"Lord Moorgate, certainly," Jack said, shuffling through the papers. "Mr. de Groot seems to be privy to the man's most particular business. But what the devil is Moorgate up to?"

"Skullduggery, I don't doubt," Tubby said. "I have nothing but respect for your typical politico, and very damned little of that. I wish Doyle would work his magic on that cipher. I'm clemmed. I could eat a cow. We'd best be on our way as soon as he translates it, and so I'm leery of waiting breakfast on the man. We might all go hungry, which would be criminal."

As if in answer, Henry Billson came out of the kitchen carrying a plate on which sat a stuffed pastry shaped like a circular Greek temple, with columns around the outside and a fleur-de-lis atop. It was baked to a golden brown, and the steam smelled of goose liver and bacon. Billson set it atop the table in front of Jack and Tubby and dusted his hands.

"Strasburg pie," he said, "and kickshaws just finishing in the oven – Welsh rabbit, curry tarts, and, as another remove, a plate of cold oysters that Henrietta brought back from Billingsgate just this instant. I figured that you gentlemen might be peckish, but perhaps I should wait on the kickshaws until Mr. Doyle returns, if I can keep 'em hot."

"God bless you, William," Tubby said, "but Mr. Doyle might be hours yet. And he'd sooner starve than abandon his work. Bring out the lot of it, along with a spoon, if you will, so that Mr. Doyle can scrape up the crumbs if he comes too late for the feast. And send poor Hopeful out with an ewer of the Half Toad's best ale, if you would. We've got a long day ahead, and we need sustenance. We're bound for the Cliffe Marshes to exterminate vermin."

When Billson had gone off to the kitchen, Jack said, "What I read in the news about Lord Moorgate leads me to believe that he's no good, but I don't know quite why. He seems a pompous ass to me, prating on about other people's faults as if he has none of his own, and with no apparent goal but to puff himself up at another's expense. He despises Gladstone; that much is evident."

"His brand of Whiggery can't tolerate Gladstone's concern for the Irish," Tubby said. "I know him from White's. He's a bottomless pit of stinking lucre. He once wagered three-thousand pounds that Morris Whitby, the Drury Lane agent, would be sick at the stomach within a quarter of an hour. Said he could tell from the pallor of the man's face and the look in his eye. Lord Bingham took the bet and lost it again before they'd sunk their first glass of champagne. Poor Whitby began to act the part of a cat puking up a hairball and then set in to spewing his guts. Disgusting business. Krakatoa ain't in it. I heard from Wickham that Moorgate had dosed Whitby's gin to set it up, although Moorgate denied it, all the time grinning like a devil. Whitby threatened to sue, but there was no evidence. I wouldn't play cards with the likes of Moorgate, but then he wouldn't play cards with the likes of me, I suppose. I can easily imagine him consorting with Narbondo, although it would be the end of his reputation if it were known."

The ale appeared, nearly a gallon of it, and they breakfasted on the Strasburg pie and made inroads into the heap of oysters, which were indeed cold, Billson having the wonderful habit of layering the shells atop foundations of chipped ice.

"Perhaps we can set about destroying Moorgate's reputation if there's something damning in the cipher, which there must be, given that it's signed 'Guido Fox,'" Tubby said. "'Guy Fawkes, 'twas his intent, to blow up the King and Parliament,'" he recited. "But they can't be serious about blowing up the King, because there ain't one."

"Even if there were something to implicate Moorgate in de Groot's papers, he would claim that the 'Guido Fox' signature was a mere lark. And in any event nothing means anything unless Moorgate is particularly identified in it, and if it's evidently criminal."

"The signature is too clever by half. The police love the clever ones, Jack. It's the plain, stable sort of criminal who confounds them – the cheerful gent who lives in a cottage by day and turns into a murderer by night. Clearly this bunch has explosives on the mind, however – anarchy, perhaps, or this fabulous scheme of Narbondo's to hobnob in Hell, if we can credit it."

"St. Ives credits it, or at least believes that some such

thing is coming to pass, and that's good enough for me."

"Then I'll celebrate your sagacity by sampling the tarts and the Welsh rabbit, if only to make sure that they're up to Billson's usual standard. I suppose it's only fair that we lay aside a crumb or two for poor Doyle, given that he's doing the real work."

"Here's our man now," Jack said, nodding in the direction of the stairs.

Tubby poured ale into Doyle's glass and said to him as he sat down, "Jack was hungry as a wolf, and I was forced to prevent him from swallowing the entire breakfast and then eating the table into the bargain. What did you discover?" He heaped food onto Doyle's plate and handed him his fork.

"It was a simple transposition cipher," Doyle said, giving each of them a sheet of foolscap with two paragraphs written out on it. "The letters were separated into five lines and were often mingled with musical notes, which was confounding at first, but they gave the business away when I realized that they must be transposed along a five-line staff, do you see, like a piece of music, and not the usual three-line arrangement."

"Fascinating," Tubby said. "Eat up, old man. Time is passing."

"The notes were superfluous to the meaning," he said, "meant to confuse, although I saw something in them, and I suspected that 'Guido Fox' was a little too proud of himself. The notes were transposed in a manner of their own, distinct from the verbiage, but when it was all shifted along the five-line staff, you could sing the result in the manner of the old Irish Guy Fawkes song, 'The Ballynure Ballad.'"

"I haven't had the pleasure of hearing it sung," Tubby said, "and I'm not sure I have the stomach to hear it sung now, so I'm happy you've written it out plain like this. Have one of these capital curry tarts, Mr. Doyle, and a glass of ale, and give us the gist of it."

"The gist of it," Doyle said, swallowing a mouthful of tart, "isn't plain. It was sketchy enough so that I can only guess at the meaning, although no doubt it's obvious to both Lord Moorgate and the person who sent it – this self-styled Guido Fox. They mean to cause an outrage, probably explosive, and not on the fifth of November. Soon, I believe. There's no mention of a date and we don't know when the cipher was composed, but there is a reference to a Tuesday, which, as both of you are aware, is the very day of the week that Guy Fawkes was to blow up the House of Lords."

"Tomorrow!" Jack said.

"If it's not next week," Tubby put in. "Tuesdays come along with some regularity."

"Here's a reference to a 'Colonel W.O.,'" Jack said, looking at the paper that he held in his hands. "What do we make of that? A man's initials, I suppose. He seems to have assured Mr. Fox that his men will see to the 'crowd's cooperation when the dust begins to fly, along with the martyrs,' and that the stated sum is acceptable."

"How many colonels with the initials W.O. can there be in London?" Tubby asked. "Seems to me that it would be impossible to run them all to ground in order to ask them if they're involved in a crime. Flying martyrs! Have another of these Welsh rabbits, Mr. Doyle."

As he shifted his plate so that Tubby could slide the

morsel onto it, Doyle said, "As Jack pointed out, the initials might mean anything: 'War Office,' for example. What that would tell us is that there are soldiers involved, and that they've been bribed."

"There were four with de Groot this morning," Jack pointed out.

"It's a restful day in London when no one's being bribed," Tubby said.

"Here at the end," Doyle said, "he writes, 'Gladstone will reap the whirlwind.' I suggest that they mean to shift the blame for the outrage to the prime minister, who, we'll remember, has had a rocky time of it. They'll make him out to be a Fenian and he'll be tarred with the brush of a dozen infernal devices."

"We should settle the bill if we mean to be on the river at nine o'clock in order to catch the ebb," Jack said.

Tubby reached into his coat and withdrew de Groot's purse, from which he took a sheaf of banknotes. "Narbondo has his Moorgate to supply the odd five bob," he said, "and we have our de Groot, who is a capital fellow, ha ha. Did you catch that, Jack? – *capital* fellow. He's investing in our dealings, do you see?"

"I *do* see," Jack said, "and I'm sensible to the brilliance of the wordplay. How much has the fellow contributed?"

"Ninety pounds sterling!" Tubby said.

"I for one cannot steal the man's money," Doyle objected.

Tubby stood up out of his chair and gave him an incredulous look. "Steal? Nor could we," he said. "I assure you. A gentleman wouldn't consider it, although I cannot speak for Jack. But the man's given it freely, or at least he gave no objection, which is much the same. And I'll remind you that none of us are wealthy men, and we've got to pay William Billson for this food and drink, and also the captain of the steam yacht who's waiting to take us downriver. And if we hurry we still have a moment to stop at Gleeson's Mercantile to lay in a hamper of food and drink, since we oughtn't to drop in on Uncle Gilbert like a parcel of beggars. What money's left over we'll give back to de Groot when we encounter him next, except we'll pay him in coin, a great lot of it delivered to the back of his skull by way of a leather bag. We'll do him the favor of knocking some sense into him in measured doses."

TWENTY-NINE
CLIFFE VILLAGE

"I had another of the dreams last night, Bill," Mother Laswell said, "and it put me off my feed." She watched the landscape of the Cliffe Marshes pass by the train window – grasslands and scrub and pond water, with here and there a copse of small trees or a line of forest in the distance. Sheep in plenty wandered the marsh along random trails and across meadows. This branch of the South Eastern Line was new, with debris left lying in heaps, already up in weeds and rust.

"The same dream, was it?" Kraken asked her.

"The same and different. The door was there, and the fire within, but it opened in the air above a city street. Full of brimstone and smoke. Things flew out, bats, worse things – the spawn of Hell."

"The black goat?"

"Yes."

"Then it was a vision of what we fear, a-coming to pass."

"Perhaps it was," Mother Laswell said. "It's what *I've* come to fear, in any event, and maybe I put it into the minds of others who have troubles enough as it is. I'm wondering,

Bill, was it me who put it in my *own* mind to fear it – to dream the dream? Or was it a true vision? A prophecy? That's the rub, isn't it? We all of us carry a portmanteau full of fears and hopes with us, lying loose on either side, and we open the satchel ourselves, Pandora-like, not knowing what will fly free, although it's soon enough that we find out."

Kraken apparently had no answer to this except to look unhappy, and it occurred to Mother Laswell that she was being both morbid and philosophical, when Bill was neither of these things.

"Just *listen* to me," she said. "I sound like a perfect little whiner. You know I don't half mean it, Bill." She patted Kraken on the knee and winked at him to show that she saw through her own nonsense, but it did little to cheer him. They passed a cement works, followed close on by a chalk quarry, both of them hideous blights on the countryside. Although the relentless ruination of the God-given beauty of the world did not make her long for death by any means, certainly it made death more palatable. Hereafter Farm was a biscuit-toss to the south – twelve miles in all from Cliffe Village. She could walk the distance and be home before dark. *Home before dark* – the phrase had a compelling but fearful ring to it. She missed the youngsters and Ned Ludd something terrible, and the peace of the farm as well.

"It's a gift you've got, Mother," Kraken told her in a voice that was moderately stern.

"I'd as soon return it sometimes, Bill. Little happiness it's brought me. Many a mountain I've made out of a molehill."

"You oughtn't to be so low, is what I'm a-saying. Keep your spirits up. That's your only man to ward off the humdudgeon. Clap on to the recollection that you gave them reptiles a thunderous great dose yesterday, and by God we'll do for them again today, maybe for good and all."

"You're right, of course. But I'll tell you plainly that I don't like staying behind. There's nought for me to do in Cliffe, but to stand and wait. It makes a body feeble to contemplate it."

"With them corns a-flaring up, Mother, you mayn't come along. You'll be a cripple before we're halfway there. I don't mean to take the easy route, neither. It'll be hard going – in and out, and me back with the boy before sundown, and all of it quick and quiet as a weasel. Then we can find the Professor and take stock of the dreams."

"Tossing the corns in my face doesn't mollify me, Bill. The long and short of it is that I'm to darn stockings while you're putting things right."

The thought of waiting uselessly made her think of the Professor's poor wife. She searched her mind for the name – Alice, Bill had said. She didn't know the woman, had never seen her that she was aware of, but, again according to Bill, she was a great beauty inside and out. The black door had opened before Alice, too, and had swallowed her only son. If it were in her power, Mother Laswell decided, she would get a message out to Alice St. Ives, bearing some small scrap of hopeful news. She could perhaps do nothing about the waiting, but she might about the wondering.

"I'm at loose ends, Bill, that's the gist of it. You're certain, then, about the marsh? I'll stay behind, but I must know your thinking. You came into London in my time of need, without asking my leave to do it, and I tell you plainly that I mean to do the same for you if my second mind tells me I must."

"I'm main certain of the marsh, as certain as a man can be without calling down fate for a braggart. I knew where they'd taken the boy as soon as Mabel Morningstar mentioned the place of shadows when she was a-feeling of the tooth. Shade House, they call it. I been there myself, when I was down and out and living hard, tending the flocks for Mr. Spode, and I didn't like it none at all. It's always been a place for low types – cutthroats, people who don't mean to be found. Last I heard it was abandoned, but like as not the Doctor has laid claim to it. I aim to get in and out quick-like, through the tunnels."

"Tunnels, Bill?" Mother Laswell asked. "In a marsh?"

"Smugglers' tunnels is what they are, cut through the chalk and the water drained off. They're still in use – and so they aren't safe. There's an entrance below the old rectory, hid in the scrub growing up in the limekilns. It'll lead you to the back edge of Egypt Bay if you follow it, always taking the right-hand fork. Ships would come up the river, and run up onto the mud, accidental-on-purpose, and toss the cargo overside into the boats that come out of the channels along the bank. If they was twigged, they'd claim to be lightening the load to float her off. Smugglers would haul the goods across the bay and into the tunnels; then out they'd come in a dozen places, and no one the wiser. That's how they did it in the old days, and I can tell you that the old days ain't gone away. Mind what I say, Mother. I know the marsh, and I know the turning that leads in beneath Shade House itself afore you fetch up to the bay. With luck it'll be empty, the tunnel will, and I'll bring the boy back with me. You don't need to come a-looking. If it's in me to do it, I'll bring home your Edward's skull along of the rest."

She looked at him for a moment, having come to a decision some distance back, when they were leaving London behind them. "My Edward is gone," she said. "I've accepted that now, Bill. He was gone these many years ago. It was me that kept him alive. The thing that my husband made, that's not Edward, nor ever has been. When we buried it, I told myself that he was at rest. I told the Professor as much. You heard it yourself. I saw my own heart and mind, and I knew what was false in it. And yet I came into London in secret, because I couldn't let it alone."

"You come into London for the good of us all," Kraken told her.

"So I told myself. Listen to me, Bill. You're not to risk yourself trying to recover it. I forbid it."

"The dreams, Mother…"

"The Professor's boy is our aim now, Bill. As for the dreams, we'll leave Heaven and Hell to sort themselves out."

The train slowed and stopped, and they stepped out onto the platform, Kraken carrying the satchel that Mabel Morningstar had lent Mother Laswell. At the end of the platform, beyond the stairs to the street, stood a shop in the old style, the long front window set with horizontal shutters, the top tilting upward to make for a bit of shade, and the bottom tilting downward to make a counter. There were pipes and tobacco and magazines for sale in the shop. A small sign advertised a lending library. Mother Laswell's spirits raised a notch at the sight of it. She dearly loved a lending library, which was a variety of Aladdin's cave, although, like so many things, it was often better in anticipation than in fact. If she were at loose ends today, she thought, she at least might have something to read.

"I'll just look into this shop, Bill," she said. "They've books to lend." She walked toward it, her eyes on the dim interior, which even from several feet away was redolent with the pleasant smell of cut tobacco. A man stood within, measuring something on a scale. Behind him, on the rear wall were several shelves of books – a tolerably small Aladdin's cave, to be sure.

"I'd like to borrow a book," she said to the man, who was small and vaguely amphibious. He wore heavy spectacles through which he blinked at her. "A novel," she said. "Something in the Gothic line."

Out of the corner of her eye she saw a man sitting on a nearby bench stand up and walk away, which was nothing remarkable in itself. And yet there was something about him that drew her attention. She was half certain that she knew him, but from where? Or did he know *her*? *Yes*, she thought; that was it. She had felt the very instant of recognition, like a random thought passing through her mind. He was utterly nondescript – medium height, neither fat nor thin, dark clothing slightly down at heel. He crossed the road now, looking straight ahead so that she could see nothing more of him than his back, and at the first opportunity he turned up between two buildings and disappeared. Perhaps she was wrong, she thought now. In any event, he was gone.

She brought her mind back to the shopkeeper, who was clearly waiting for her to attend to business, and after a brief exchange she settled for a dilapidated copy of Mrs. Gaskell's *Lois the Witch*. "Can you recommend an inn?" she asked him.

"Yes, ma'am. The Chalk Horse, just across the street. A coaching inn, ma'am, on the Strood road, which runs along behind. Comfortable, they tell me, and I can vouch for the food and drink."

She thanked him, rejoined Bill Kraken, and the two of them waited out a chaise and a slow-moving wagon before crossing the road to the inn, a pleasant place built of whitewashed stone. There was a deeply carved wooden sign out front depicting a white horse against a dark hillside, and on the broad porch stood monstrous great dahlias in pots, bright red and pink and yellow, the size of dinner plates. She took a room on the second floor, and after Kraken saw to food and drink and a basin of hot water to soak her feet, she sent him down again for foolscap, quill, and ink. When all was done, Kraken put on his cap and stepped to the door.

"I'm a-going on into the marsh," he said, "now that you're settled."

She nodded at him, recognizing the look in his eye – the same squint that he had worn when he was laying into Lord Moorgate with his fists, and although she admired his resolve, she feared it as well. She saw the pistol in his hand now, with a long barrel, a wicked looking thing. "You'll take care of yourself, Bill? You're no good to me nor anyone else if you're shot dead or if you're taken up for shooting someone else."

"I'm no good to myself if I don't do what I must, Mother." He stepped out into the hallway, then turned back to the room and said, "You're a good woman, and I'm main glad to have found you."

Before she could answer he shut the door quietly. She listened to his footsteps dwindle away down the hall. His words remained in her mind, however. There was something doomful about them, as if he had said what couldn't wait, because there mightn't be a chance to say it if he waited.

Here she sat, soaking her corns. Yesterday morning she had lain in the darkness in just this same condition, knowing that she must act, but not acting, as if she were a thing of clockwork that had wound down. Her goal had changed somewhat, but it was equally urgent. It was true that Kraken was now acting for her, and he was a capable man, but that didn't make the pill go down any easier.

She soaked her feet until the water grew cold, and then dried them, mopped up the floor with the towel, and pitched the cold water out the back window onto the lawn below, surprising two goats that were cropping grass. She saw the ostler at work near the stable, and thought of the coach into Strood and then on to Maidstone, which was next door to Aylesford, no great distance to the south.

Her corns felt tip-top now, all things considered, and she regretted having stayed behind. The wild idea came into her mind that she might catch up with Bill if she hurried – except that he had a half hour's start and would be moving quickly. Probably he was already making his way north through the tunnels that he had spoken of. She couldn't abide the idea of going into a tunnel at any rate – spiders and bats, no doubt, and eternal darkness. The very thought of it brought her dreams back into her mind, and she slammed the door on them.

Resigned to her fate, she took up the quill and turned

to the paper and ink, thinking hard about what she meant to write. Plain speaking was best – no false hope. *Language,* she thought, *was as often as not meant to deceive as to speak the truth, but there could be no deception here.* She wouldn't be guilty of the crime of euphemism.

Mrs. St. Ives, she wrote. *We've never met, and yet we're thrown together, perhaps by fate, if it's fate you believe in. I believe in something more than that, which is helping oneself, if only I can find a way. We both have a son named Edward, and the man that murdered my son is the same man who has taken yours. We have a bond, I mean to say, and I must share with you what I know. I'm writing to tell you that last night I saw your boy Eddie, and he was unhurt. He's still in the hands of the man you know as Narbondo, who is feeding him and treating him well for all I could see. I tried to take Eddie back and failed, and we're now looking for Narbondo in the Cliffe Marshes, where he's gone to ground, perhaps to further his schemes. It's my belief that he'll return to London, and soon. Bill Kraken is in the marsh now searching for him. You know Bill, I believe, and so you know he's a good man, who would die for any one of us. I was told that Professor St. Ives came into London, but I don't know his whereabouts. There's a very marvelous boy, too, who is doing his part and has the gumption to prevail. We're all of us hard at work, is what I mainly wanted to say, with saving your boy Eddie as our one contentious goal. If it comes into your mind to go into London, you can get word of me and what I've learned from my dear friend Mabel Morningstar, who lives above the Ship Tavern, Lime Street, the City.*

Your friend and neighbor, Harriet Laswell of Hereafter

Farm, writing from the Chalk Horse Inn, Cliffe Village.

She reread it, was satisfied with the missive, and went downstairs to ask the innkeeper about the post, thinking to buy a penny stamp and post the letter straight into Aylesford, to Hereafter Farm. "I'm in a great hurry," she told him.

He shook his head. "Aylesford, ma'am? Sure enough it's close by, but the post is roundabout, you see, what with the sorting and sending on. I doubt it'll reach Aylesford for days."

"That won't do," she said, disappointed. "It'll be of no consequence then."

"Send it with the coach, ma'am. It's due any moment. I don't mean to come it too high, but a few shillings might speed your letter on its way directly. It puts in at the Chequers in Aylesford, you know."

"Splendid," she said. "Can you lend me a slip of paper and a pen?"

"Certainly, ma'am." The man found the items and laid them on the countertop, where she jotted down a quick note, waved the ink dry, and folded it.

She brought out a half crown and two shillings from her purse and pushed the coins toward him. "If you could just ask the coachman to give the shillings to young Sweeney, at the Chequers. He's to run the letter and this note out to Hereafter Farm and pass it on to the boy Simonides. The half crown he's to keep for himself, with my thanks."

"That's generosity, ma'am. He'll do it happily enough, will old Bob."

Mother Laswell trudged back up the stairs to her room. With luck, and if Simonides did his part, Alice might play her hand yet, although God knew what cards she would come to hold. "A mother should know," Mother Laswell muttered, worried now that Alice might end up coming to harm. She frowned at the sudden doubt. Life was like a stage play, with something doomful waiting in the wings to put in its appearance on stage. "For good or ill," she told herself out loud, "a mother should know."

She settled herself in her chair and picked up Mrs. Gaskell, hearing the coach rattle into the yard before she'd read to the bottom of the second page. She laid the book down, distracted with anticipation over the letter, and went to the window, seeing that the goats were still engaged in their supper. A man and woman descended from within the coach, along with old Bob, the coachman, who walked in through the back door of the inn while the stable boy stood with the horses. Two minutes later she was happy to see the door open again. A man came out – a commercial traveler, from the look of him – followed by the coachman, who was apparently a slave to his pocket watch. The passenger climbed in through the door, held open by the stable boy, and the coachman climbed up onto his seat, and without any delay the coach rattled away down the road. It came into Mother Laswell's mind that she had saved a penny on the stamp, although at the cost of a crown and two shillings. She smiled at the thought, and at the relief of having accomplished something.

The back door of the inn opened again, and the innkeeper stepped out, followed by another man – the man who had been sitting on the bench next to the lending library. His back was to her again, and she willed him to turn around so that she could see his face. Instantly he did her bidding, or so it seemed, for he looked in the direction of the departed coach, and in that moment she knew him – the man Fred, he of the ravaged face, who along with his friend Coker had escorted her out of Angel Alley last night. He glanced upward now, as if he saw her watching, and she moved out of sight. Moments later she risked another look, but he was gone, and so was the innkeeper, the yard empty of life aside from the two insatiable goats.

THIRTY
THE BARRED WINDOW

Finn prevented himself from allowing the pain to show on his face.

"Slice that bacon, then – thick-like," McFee said to him. "Yarely now. There's men to feed. Stoke up the fire in the stove and fry the rashers on the iron plate. Do you know coffee?"

"Aye, sir," Finn said.

"Don't lie to me."

"No, sir. I do know coffee, sir. I made it regular for Square Davey the oysterman."

"Then roast them beans and grind them. The bag lies yonder. Don't stand there like a slow-belly. And if you waste the beans, mark me, I'll decorate your other hand, same as the first."

Finn nodded, took off his green velvet jacket and hung it on a hook, and then did as he was told, staying out of the man's way as best he could. When he had a chance he swabbed his hand with a wet cloth, and although coal dust stained the cloth, the wound remained black, and the flesh of his palm seemed to creep. McFee set him to cutting up a blood pudding next – fresh red blood, thickened with coal dust measured out a palm's worth at a time until it was more black than red. Time was passing, platters of food carried out by a one-eyed man with a game leg, who said nothing and had the appearance of a halfwit. Now and then Finn slipped a morsel of something into his mouth, but it did little to quell his hunger, and the smell of the fresh coffee nearly made him faint.

"Take this plate of food up to the Doctor's cottage, boy, along o' that pot of coffee," McFee said to him, and he handed Finn a broad, china plate: the blood pudding in a bowl, eggs and rashers of bacon. He sprinkled the pudding with ground coal as a finishing touch.

"George has asked me to find the piss pots and empty them, sir, when I'm done here."

"You can find your way to Hell for all of me," McFee said without looking up.

The lie would suffice, but for a limited time. Soon George or McFee would think of him again, and perhaps send someone to search him out. Finn set down the plate and the coffee pot, put on his coat, and descended the tilted wooden steps, looking around him and walking toward the cottage, the corner of which was visible beyond the stable. The sun was well up in the sky now. Men tramped around in the yard, and he saw through the open door that three were at work along the brook, the millwheel turning. It wasn't corn they were shoveling onto the grinder; it was coal, apparently. Finn had the distinct notion that some particular endeavor was underway, the coal being ground by the shovelful – far too much for the Doctor's breakfast.

He had known a man in Duffy's Circus who ate ground glass and roofing nails, but that man could do no other useful work that would pay him as much, which perhaps explained it. But what explained the ground coal, which was being bunged up into the kegs and loaded onto a cart?

He looked at his palm, at the coarse black line that bisected it, which seemed to him to be little more than recompense for the blunder that had caused Eddie's troubles in the first place. It would remind him of more than McFee suspected, and would continue to remind him for the rest of his life if he didn't save Eddie. But he didn't need further such lessons, and he vowed not to go back into the kitchen.

He became aware of a buzzing noise now, something like a beehive in a tall tree, but growing louder. He searched the grounds around him curiously, saw nothing, and realized abruptly that the sound was coming from the sky. There, drawing near from out of the west, an airship wafted along over the marsh, flying low. It was turning in a wide curve, perhaps bound for the river or thereabouts, perhaps descending; it was hard to say.

It's the Professor, Finn thought, his heart leaping. St. Ives had spoken of the airship at every opportunity for weeks now, and surely this must be selfsame ship. *Good old Newman*, he thought. He had delivered the message. If Newman wasn't a Christian name, it was something just as good. Finn raised the coffee pot in a sort of salute, then quickly recovered his wits and pretended that he was merely shading his eyes to get a better view, and in that moment he noticed that Narbondo's head was thrust through the open cottage window, and that he, too, was watching the airship. He disappeared back into the room without looking in Finn's direction.

Finn walked on now, around the side of the stable, heading boldly toward the cottage door carrying the plate and the coffee pot. He stepped up onto the wooden stoop and casually looked behind him and to either side, seeing no one. It occurred to him that someone might be watching through one of the inn windows, and so he mimicked knocking on the cottage door, listened for a moment, and then laid the plate and pot on the stoop and walked away, around the side of the cottage to where the window stood open, out of sight of the inn. He hazarded a glance over the top of the sill, seeing that the room was empty of people, the piece of carpet on the floor pushed aside and a trapdoor standing open. There was a chair in the room, a lamp on a small deal table, a narrow bed against the wall, and a scattering of books – rough living for a man who possessed such a great deal of power, but then Narbondo's lodgings in Angel Alley had been much the same. *Easy to abandon when there was trouble*, Finn thought.

The cottage stood atop a low hill, and Finn crept toward the bottom, moving silently and listening hard. If he were caught his guilt would be obvious. The hill had been cut back and leveled behind the cottage, forming a small landing outside the cellar door, sheltered by willow scrub. There was a barred window beside the door – more a grate than a window, since there was no glass in it. Farther below lay a stand of trees around a small pond, choked with reeds and lilies. A hay bale was set up, with a target for shooting, and nearby stood various pieces of junk furniture, burned to cinders.

Finn peered in at the window, immediately seeing Narbondo, who stood at a high table, perhaps eight feet long and half as wide, built like a butcher's block and heavily stained. On the table in front of him sat a human skull, although something had been done to it, for the top of it shone silver in the lamplight as if the bone had been removed and the skull had been crowned with metal. Finn was stricken with the same diabolical unease that he had felt when he was first in Narbondo's presence – something in his face? He had seen many faces more frightful by far. This was something else, something best not considered too particularly, lest he attract some sort of hellish attention. "Naming calls," his mother used to say, and Finn had no desire to call forth anything.

The room itself intensified the feeling. Ring-bolts had been set into the sides of the table, useful, no doubt, for strapping things down. The room was clearly a surgeon's cabinet, and held two wooden chairs and another small table with a basin and pitcher atop it. An ochre-stained coat hung on the wall along with dozens of surgical tools – clamps and bone saws and knives and a heavy butcher's cleaver, and other appalling instruments that Finn couldn't identify and didn't care to. Leather-covered chains, both long and short, hung among the rest. A human skeleton dangled from a hook in the low ceiling, its arms outstretched and fixed with slender iron rods as if it were crucified. On shelves stood a variety of human and animal skulls as well as organs floating in liquid-filled jars, one of which was half full of human eyeballs.

Narbondo stepped around behind the table now, blocking Finn's view. He bent over, evidently fiddling with the skull, from which an intense light shone forth. Finn felt abruptly as if he was being watched, and he looked around him, seeing no one. He recalled the corpse candle near the road two nights ago, how he had felt the living consciousness of the ghost of the hanged boy. This was something similar – not someone watching *him*, but some entity that had come into the room. He sensed a great sorrow and fear and anger, principally anger, not a child this time.

He deliberately moved his mind away from the fell presence and watched Narbondo, who had crossed the room to fetch a three-tiered, wheeled tea cart on which sat a glass box perhaps three-feet high and one-foot deep and wide, built of a framework of thin metal. Finn saw then that it was in fact two boxes, one inside the other. Narbondo pushed the cart into the path of the light emanating from the skull, and when he stepped away Finn saw the entity itself – the palely visible doll-sized ghost of a woman, its transparent image hovering within the glass boxes.

There was a large leather bellows affixed to the side of a wooden box on the middle shelf, the mouth of the bellows connected to a coiled tube that entered the boxes, running through the outer box and into the inner. Finn was reminded of the pineapple barrow in Angel Alley, except that the smell of hot syllabub was missing. A slender pole hanging from a ceiling beam held a broad glass lens in front of the boxes. Narbondo maneuvered the lens down into the light now, positioning it in order to peer through it at the glowing homunculus imprisoned within the glass walls.

Finn heard the noise of an approaching carriage now, very close by, and apparently Narbondo heard it also, for he set out up the stairs to the room above, leaving the trapdoor open behind him. He would find his breakfast, Finn thought, and someone would cop it for having left it there. That would perhaps start a general search, which would be the beginning of the end for Finn Conrad. He heard voices within the cottage now, and he saw Narbondo descend into the cellar again, followed by a man and a woman. Both stopped when they reached the floor, where they stood and stared, first at the glowing glass boxes with the image of the woman within them and then at the source of the light – the skull on the table.

The man wore a black top hat and was tall and imposing, with gray hair and a narrow face, his features reminding Finn of a bloody-minded weasel. The woman had raven hair beneath her hat, her face covered by a black veil. *It's him*, Finn thought suddenly, recognizing the man as the one who had been in Narbondo's rooms last night. He had worn chin whiskers and a pince-nez and an obvious wig, but it was his Lordship, to be certain, undisguised now – or so Narbondo had called him. Last night he had drawn back into the corner of the room when the crackers exploded, fearful of gunfire, and then had lunged at Finn and Eddie at the last moment, and might have had them if he hadn't been timid. Clearly the man hadn't wanted to be identified, nor had he been keen to involve himself in any sort of danger. *No wonder*, Finn thought: he had a face that might be recognized on the street easily enough – a public figure, involved in low deeds.

Being veiled, the woman's face was impossible to read, but his Lordship affected a look of tired indifference. He removed his top hat and set it on the table.

"Very interesting work," he said, taking in the entrapped ghost and the skull with a broad gesture.

"This particular skull inhabited the head of a common prostitute. I took it on loan." Narbondo smiled at them, but got no response. "But come," he said, "I promised you an assurance of my powers, and an assurance you shall have. It will cost me this valuable skull, over which I've toiled, but I believe that it will give you an idea of the impending calamity. You and your consortium – I believe that's the cant term – can be easy in your minds."

Narbondo drew the lens downward, peering through it again, and for a moment Finn had a clear view of the ghost's startling visage. There was an appearance of intense, raw loathing radiating from it that Finn could sense quite clearly – more clearly than he could see it. He saw Narbondo recoil from it, and then hurriedly draw the great lens downward so that the light from the skull shone through it. A ray of pure white light illuminated the two boxes now, and the ghost vanished within that light, the intensity of its fierce emotion diminishing. Narbondo pressed the handle of the bellows half a dozen times, and a dark powder – coal dust, Finn supposed – flew out of the hose and swirled within the inner box, the ghost suddenly reappearing, showing plainly now against the suspended dust, looking almost solid and apparently cognizant that it was trapped within a glass coffin.

"You'd be advised to step back," Narbondo said as the glow within the boxes intensified. There was a penetrating wail in the air roundabout now, the sound of a mourner keening for the dead, a high note at the very edge of apprehension. The glow formed itself into a tiny sun, which began to smoke. Narbondo ceased pressing the bellows and stepped away himself, putting out his arm to sweep the other two even farther back, nearly to the window beyond which Finn watched. If they had looked behind them now, they would have seen him, but there was no chance of that, for they watched intently as the light in the box redoubled in intensity and then redoubled again. The keening noise rose to a higher and higher pitch, and then the interior of the box flashed brightly.

There was the sound of a muffled explosion, very small to Finn's ear, and in that instant the ghost erupted into a mass of bright sparks that spun for a moment in the void, accompanied by the sound of an inhuman shriek. The sparks winked out, and for a moment the box appeared to have flattened, taking on the semblance of an open door, beyond which lay an infinite darkness, the shriek echoing away into the void.

Finn was compelled to look away, his heart hammering with a dark fear. He watched a white crane fly low above the pond, its neck outstretched, the gray-black feathers spread along the edges of the white wings. When it had disappeared from sight, Finn took in a deep breath and turned back to the window. The light from the skull had gone out. A wisp of smoke arose from it, and there was the smell of sulfur and burning metal on the air. Around the skull the wooden table was aflame, a small circle of white witch fire. Narbondo looked about himself, shrugged, picked up Lord Moorgate's top hat, and dropped it over the skull. He pushed the magnifying lens up toward the ceiling, rolled the tea cart back into its place, and lit a second Argand lamp on a shelf above it, casting a light on the glass boxes – or rather a single box now, for the interior box had been shattered in the explosion. The exterior box had contained the blast, although the very heavy glass in the front panel had cracked in half and opened outward like a clamshell now.

"And so the vitality of the skull has been consumed," Narbondo said, "and the soul whisked away to the netherworld. You felt the darkness of that place when the door opened, I'll warrant. I saw it in your face, Lord Moorgate."

"I felt something, yes, although nothing that warrants my driving out into this godforsaken marsh." Moorgate's voice, intended to be commanding, quavered slightly too much to be persuasive. "You meant for this display to be an example of your powers, sir, and you ask me to take it on faith that something similar will bring down the cathedral, which is many hundreds of times the size of your trifling glass boxes. Your powers are impressive, but on a very small scale – scarcely the sort of assurance we had in mind. The Bayswater Club and Fleet River debacles were entertaining, but comparatively simple."

Narbondo shrugged. "It pains me to have fallen out of your good graces, my lord. I'm desolated, I assure you."

"You see fit to jest. I'll put it to you simply. My associates and I have done our part at great expense. You promised us the skull of the boy in payment, fully realized. In anticipation I had de Groot purchase one of the miniaturized lamps at considerable expense. I paid out a substantial sum to further our project, including hiring a man to produce forged letters that will damn that traitor Gladstone for good and all, indeed, will hang him. I've another twenty-five thousand pounds promised to see the plan through till the end. Our friend in the War Office tells me that everything is arranged. My man de Groot will make a payment as soon as he hears from me, and will deliver another sum when the thing is finished. All he needs in order to carry it out is the money, which is laid by. I've risked my career, my very life, in other words, in order to further both our goals, but aside from this… display, this teapot tempest… you, sir, have done nothing but make empty promises."

"Your political aspirations bore me, Lord Moorgate," Narbondo said, "as does the phantom noose that encircles your hypothetical head. We both stand to profit by this venture, but only if it's successful. My cheating you would scarcely lead to its success."

"My thinking exactly. I've been given to understand that you've offered to ransom the boy to his father for a sum equal to what I've agreed to give to my man in the War Office. I don't make any accusations, but it seems to me uncommon possible that you've promised the boy to two different parties, standing to gain twice if only you can hold out another day or so. Last night you were in London. Today I find you in the marsh. Heaven knows where you'll be next week, after the deed has been done."

"Heaven keeps no track of my comings and goings, I can assure you. I'll remind you that I did you the favor of letting you know where I was bound, for here you both are. I could scarcely remain in the rookery."

Moorgate waved the statement away, as if it didn't signify. "I mean to say that time is short, as you very well know. You promised to contrive a lamp from the skull of the boy, but you haven't undertaken to do it. I'm compelled to believe that you keep the boy alive because you mean to play us false if you can find a way."

"You're a bold man, Lord Moorgate. Once again you've come into my domain and made unwarranted assertions. I've only to whistle, and ten bloodthirsty men will come running. Perhaps *you* would like a turn atop the table here, my lord? Your own skull shows great promise." Narbondo gestured at the surgical instruments on the wall, his downturned face looking wantonly demonic.

It came into Finn's mind that nothing would serve his own endeavors more than immediate bloodshed in this underground room, if only to draw men away from the inn. He waited anxiously, watching Lord Moorgate's face, which was set like a stone mask, his hand under his coat now – a pistol, perhaps. The woman stood very still.

"I *jest*," Narbondo said after a desperately long moment. He smiled at the two. "I assure you that I had no intention of turning the boy over to his father. I merely hoped that the man would be foolhardy enough to bring me the ransom money, in which case I intended to relieve him of his life and his purse at one stroke. You'll agree that the scenario would have been monstrously comical. Come, tell me plainly what you want. Give me an opportunity to put things right. And you're free to remove your veil, my dear. I make it a habit of knowing my confederates. We all have our secrets, and so be it, but the veil carries things a trifle too far."

Moorgate reached out and snatched the woman's veil from her face, yanking off her hat in the process. He tore the veil from the hat, pitched the veil onto the floor, and then gave her the hat back. She restored it to the top of her head while fixing Moorgate with a hateful look.

"Meet Helen," Moorgate said to Narbondo. "Even I'm not certain it's her actual name, but you can trust her. I do, as far as it goes."

Narbondo bowed obsequiously. "Charmed," he said, looking at her intently, as if he saw something in her face.

"We've come to witness the boy's head separated from his body," Moorgate said. "Such a display would demonstrate your commitment to our joint endeavor. I applaud your attempt to profit by squeezing the boy's father, but now that the effort has failed, you've no reason to want the boy alive. I've promised you… head-money, as they say, and so I want my head. I want it now, and I want to see your own hands red with the boy's blood, and not his hypothetical blood. I'll have my way with this or I'll send to de Groot informing him to cease payment to the War Office and to call off Mr. Fox. He awaits my word."

"You've taken precautions. Good. I like a cautious man. And perhaps you've also got a small craving to see the operation transpire?" Narbondo leered at him.

"*I've* got such a craving," the woman said, the first words she'd spoken. "And then I'd like my breakfast."

"Excellent," Narbondo said, clapping his palms together as if he were quite pleased. "I'll send someone to fetch the boy."

Finn stood as if frozen, his mind comprehending this last exchange, but unable to resolve their words in any sensible way.

THIRTY-ONE
THE MESSAGE ARRIVES

Alice brushed another layer of Langdon's experimental fixative over the head of the pike. The mixture smelled of varnish and triple-refined spirits. She had done a neat job of severing the prodigious head, which was larger than she had anticipated. The pike had weighed over three stone, and it was unlikely that she would ever catch a larger. He had nearly foxed her again yesterday, running in under a hole in the bank half blocked with stones, but Alice had waded in after him, in order to keep the line straight and free. The battle had lasted twenty minutes, with Cleo and Mrs. Langley on the bank shouting advice.

The process of hardening the flesh required twelve coats of the varnish, inside and out, but because the varnish was so awfully hot, as Langdon had put it – chemically hot – it dried quickly, especially in the summer heat, and she had already applied the requisite number of coats to the inside of the scoured-out skull earlier today, which she had filled with a mixture of hide glue and smashed clinkers. She had thrust two bolts into it, which were now cemented tightly in place, and which would hold the head to its wooden plaque.

She had awakened before dawn this morning, unable to fall back to sleep, and had roused herself out of bed before her idle mind became active. She had set to work on the wooden table in the gallery, which had a view of the wisteria alley through the wire mesh over the windows. Now and then she pictured Langdon and Hasbro turning off the road and appearing beneath the wisteria, Eddie sitting between them on the seat of the wagon. She knew that picturing it wouldn't make it so, but it was a picture that was welcome in her mind, and which kept out other pictures not so welcome. She turned the pike's head to catch the sunlight coming in through the screen, wondering whether she had any glass eyes in her collection that would fit the empty sockets.

The door opened behind her now and Mrs. Langley entered, looking unhappily at the head of the pike. "The smell of that mixture is mortal!" she said. "You might perhaps take it outside, ma'am. We can set a table up in the open field, under a shade. It's a lovely day."

"You're right, of course," Alice told her. "I've become quite used to it, but now that you mention it my head is swimming." She capped the jar of varnish, put her brushes into a bowl of turpentine and followed Mrs. Langley into the kitchen, where Cleo stood on a chair, mixing something in a bowl with a long wooden spoon.

"We're making scones," Cleo said. "With bits of cherries."

"For a nice tea," Mrs. Langley put in. And then, in a lower voice, she said to Alice, "I inquired in the village this morning about Mr. Marchand, ma'am, the zookeeper. He's very much alive, apparently, although ancient. Living in

Maidstone, I'm told. His younger brother Bennett keeps the books at the paper mill on Hanley Road." She looked furtively at Cleo now, who was apparently paying no attention. "The younger Mr. Marchand has informed me that the… item of interest might indeed be purchased for a sum. A rather substantial sum, ma'am, but well within the stated limits."

"Splendid," Alice said. "You put our plan into motion, then?"

"I did. Are you certain it's… That it's quite… *reasonable*, ma'am?"

"No, indeed. It's utterly unreasonable, Mrs. Langley, and therein lies its attraction. I've come to suspect that reason is a much overrated commodity."

"Perhaps it is, ma'am. That's enough stirring, Cleo. They'll be leaden if they're over-beat."

There was a clattering outside, the unmistakable sound of a wagon rattling up the wisteria alley. Alice's heart leapt into her throat, and she rushed into the gallery again, her hand to her mouth, her heart beating, nearly unable to breathe. But it wasn't their wagon, and Langdon and Hasbro weren't driving it. A boy she didn't know sat on the seat. He reined up before the steps and climbed down, Alice already opening the door before he had a chance to knock.

"I'm Alice St. Ives," she said without preamble. "Have you news of my husband?" She had almost said, "my son," but caught herself, not wanting to tempt fate.

"No, ma'am," the boy said. "I've got a letter from Mother Laswell, what just came up with the coach from the village at Cliffe."

"*From Mother Laswell?* And who are you, then?"

"I'm Simonides, from Hereafter Farm," he said, plucking off his cap. "She said I was to find you mortal quick and give you this, and I'm to say that the wagon is yours to command. I'm to drive you out to Cliffe Village if you choose to go. Old Binion here is what's called a trotter, ma'am, bred up to it – tolerably fast and at your service."

He handed across an envelope. Mystified, Alice tore it open and read it, and then read it again. She looked up at the wisteria alley and then glanced across the lawn to where Finn's cottage stood empty in the sunshine, her mind revolving.

"Will you give me ten minutes?" she asked. "And then we must hurry."

"Ten minutes, ma'am, and we're off."

Alice came out through the door in nine, followed by Mrs. Langley, who held Cleo in her arms. She and Cleo would be fine, Mrs. Langley told her, along with sundry other bits and pieces of advice as Alice had thrown things into her bag, including clothing for Eddie. From her seat beside Simonides Alice promised to send word from Cliffe, promised any of a number of things to Mrs. Langley and Cleo both.

As the cart clattered away, she looked back at the two of them still standing on the veranda, in her mind seeing herself standing there the day before yesterday, filled with unhappiness, watching Langdon racing away from her. She was no longer standing and waiting, however, which had been her fervent wish, but she had no idea exactly what she *was* doing, only that she had an urgent need to find out.

THIRTY-TWO
THE TUNNEL BENEATH THE INN

Finn ran, his mind laboring to see a clear way before him. The front yard was blessedly empty – his good fortune, may it last. The walnut tree stood before him, and he was into the lower branches and climbing before he gave it another thought. No one cried out. The morning was still. He went straight to Eddie's window and looked in through the rippled, dirty glass. Eddie was asleep on the bed – no surprise in that. Finn knocked hard on the casement, but the boy didn't move. He knocked again. Still nothing. He yanked the sleeve of his velvet jacket up over his clenched fist and hit a windowpane fast and hard, the glass shattering. Eddie sat up, and Finn saw that the boy knew him instantly – no balaclava now. And there had been the wink and nod through the rear window of the coach. Eddie looked around wide-eyed and sprang out of bed, immediately putting on his slippers and vest, ready to bolt.

Finn slipped the latch on the window and pushed it open, and then slid over the sill and dropped to the floor. "They'll be after us," he said to Eddie. "Can you climb the tree?"

The boy shook his head, his face betraying his

334

unhappiness with the idea. *Cleo might have been game for it*, Finn thought, but Eddie was on the cautious side. Finn should have taught the boy to climb, of course, but it was too late to start now. He looked around the room, considering his options, of which there were none. He slipped the bolt high on the door and peered out: a long hallway leading away to the left, where there was a set of stairs; to the right a dead end. It was the stairs or nothing.

"Look here," Finn said to Eddie, crouching down so that he was something like the same height. "You and I are going to find our way out. I'm hellfire smart, but you're smarter than me by far. The two of us can do it together. The Professor – your father – is close by, down along the bay. If we can win free, you and I can find him easy as kiss-my-hand. He'll take the both of us home in his airship. Do you hear what I'm telling you?"

Eddie nodded.

"Then be ready to run. If they catch me, don't wait. You keep running. When you're outdoors, take to the trees and hide." He gripped Eddie's hand, said, "Now," and swung the door open, starting forward even as he saw that someone blocked the way – George, alone, his finger to his lips, his head shaking.

"As you value your life, do as I tell you," George said, his voice low. Finn nodded, and George said to him, "Follow me, then. You're leaving Shade House for good and all, and quickly. If we meet someone, you're my prisoner, do you see? Play your part, boy."

They descended the stairs at the end of the hall, sounds of loud talk and laughter below. Finn was happy to play his part, whatever it meant. He had been right about George, he thought, and he and Eddie were in luck that it was George sent to fetch them. There was no earthly reason for him to be playing them false. At the second floor he led them hurriedly down the hall, the noise from below diminishing. He swung open a door, closing it behind them, Finn still gripping Eddie's hand as they followed him readily across a broad room where there stood several tables and empty kegs. An open fireplace lay along one wall, big enough to walk a horse into. They passed into another room, this one with an oven, a coal scuttle alongside, an open arch behind, which led to a stairway where a dirty window of bullseye glass looked down at the millwheel.

They followed the stairs downward, Finn hearing what sounded like the rattling of a doorknob from somewhere above. George glanced back, evidently having heard it himself. At the base of the stairs stood two more doors, one of which George opened, hauling them through before barring it with a long timber, desperately quiet and cautious about it. He put his finger to his lips again, and tiptoed deeper into the room, where the three of them stood still, Eddie glancing at Finn, who winked at him and nodded.

After a moment of silence, someone tried the door, turning the knob, the door opening a quarter inch before jamming against the timber. The door shook heartily now. There was another silence – someone listening, perhaps – and then the receding footsteps of the person ascending the stairs. George let out a breath and nodded, and Finn felt a sense of relief for the first time that morning. Apparently they were in some sort of storeroom, given the sacks and crates haphazardly stacked on the flagstone floor. It came to him that they must be very near the kitchen, and indeed there was another low door. Perhaps McFee himself was in the room beyond.

"You're meant for the stage, boy," George said in a quiet voice, "with that tale of your poor brother dying of the bloody jack and you making cheeses. You'll do well in the world, if you don't find yourself murdered first. It was you in Spitalfields, wearing the balaclava, wasn't it, coming after the boy alone? I recalled the green of your coat when I saw it in the daylight."

"Yes, sir," Finn said. "That was me."

"You're main anxious to save the boy. Why? Perhaps he's kin?" He looked from one to the other of them.

"No, sir, nothing like that. I could have stopped him being taken by the Doctor in the first place, but I didn't do it. I'm trying to put it right."

George nodded. "I thought maybe you had scruples."

"What of you, sir?" Finn asked boldly. "You're in a right mess now."

"Not if they don't know it's me that's helped you. I'll think of something."

He glanced back at the door, and it seemed to Finn that the contrary was true. It had been George that Narbondo sent to fetch them. They would know it was George who helped them escape.

"You listen to what I tell you," George said. "There's tunnels beneath this inn. I'll show you to them, but you'll have to find your way through. This here's a bag with candles and matches. I keep it at the ready." He held out a leathern bag, and Finn took it. "If there's water running along the floor of the tunnel, follow it. You'll be descending, north toward the river. There'll come a time when there's a passage that leads up again, a dry passage. If you follow to the left, always to the left, mind, you'll come out near the bay. Take to the wood or whatever cover you can find, and make your way topside to the river. Do you ken what I'm telling you?"

"Yes," Finn said. "Water flows downward while we're getting clear, not when we're getting out, which is always to the left."

"That's it. If you take the wrong turning, then you might come out anywhere, so you follow a handy trail till you find yourself somewhere and know where you are. Do you have money?"

"In my shoe," Finn said.

"Good lad. Now, if it goes bad, and they catch you, you haven't seen old George and you don't know me. It was you who took the food and the candles out of the kitchen when McFee wasn't watching. Do you hear? It was you who barred the door, you who found your way to the tunnel. If they knew I was soft, they'd do for me. There'll be a hue and cry, and I'll be coming for you along with the rest. I doubt I can save you then without copping it."

"Yes, sir, and thank you, sir. We're grateful."

"Don't be grateful yet. You aren't clear of this place. Come."

He opened a door onto an empty closet – a strange thing in a storeroom. The entire floor, however, was cleverly hinged, which was evident only when George lifted it back. He nodded Eddie and Finn in before him, where a set of stairs led downward into the darkness. It came to Finn that everything had turned around on the instant. There had been no hope for escape from the room upstairs, and now the empty darkness before them was full of promise. The business of the tunnels was a mystery, but then everything in the world was a mystery until the mysteries were understood. A lucifer match and a candle would show them the way.

They found themselves in a dark, circular excavation now, roofed with timbers, a tiny stream flowing away downwards in the center of the dirty chalk floor, water seeping through the timbers above. The only light came from the open trap above them; the tunnel leading away was black and cool.

"Bon voyage, as the Frenchman would say. Light your candle." George tipped his hat, ascended the stairs, waited till the candle was lit, and then lowered the trap.

Finn took Eddie's hand and set out, hearing almost at once a scuffling noise above and behind them. He stopped and turned, supposing that George was coming back down through the trap, but no light appeared, and all was abruptly silent. They turned again into the tunnel and hurried onward, the candle throwing a very small circle of light around their feet and illuminating the flowing water, just as George had told them. It was dank, the air close and fetid, and the candle guttered, although there was no evident breeze. Eddie pressed close to Finn, but the boy was game enough. Finn considered the distance to the bay – not far, given what he'd seen from the coach earlier. But as soon as it entered his mind to be hopeful, a disembodied voice spoke out of the darkness somewhere in front of them.

"Hello, chicklets," it said. "Stop a moment."

The speaker opened the door of a dark-lantern. Finn looked at him in horror: the Crumpet, oily and grinning, dressed in the swank clothes that he had been wearing last night in the rookery, a blue waistcoat and black-and-white shoes with narrow toes. Chalk discolored the polished leather of his shoes. He wasn't much taller than Finn, now, but he was no less demonic than he had been that night under the bridge. He stood beaming at them, as if he were both pleased and surprised.

"Well, well, here we are," he said, winking at Finn. "Dame Fortune has smiled upon us, putting us in each other's company once again." His smile disappeared then, and he said, "Don't give it another thought, dearie, if it's your knife you're contemplating. I have one of my own, you see." He drew a long, narrow blade from under his coat. "Imagine my surprise when you cut me, boy, my guts pouring out through my belly. Before the sun sets today, we'll see what your own innards are made of; you have my word on it. The Doctor has promised you to me. The squeaker, however, is required upstairs, where his head is to be turned into a table ornament."

Finn flung the candle into the Crumpet's face and then turned and ran, hauling Eddie bodily along through the darkness, back toward the inn, splashing through the water, dragging his free hand along the wall and trying to calculate how far they had to run before slamming into the unseen stairway. It was close ahead, for certain. If the trap weren't locked...

"Help!" he shouted. "Christ! Help!" Hoping against all

odds that George might still be somewhere above and hear the cries.

And then they were there, and light appeared above, to his great relief, broadening as the trap was swung open. But it wasn't George who peered down at them and then descended the stairs. It was the dwarf from the rookery. He held a twin of the Crumpet's knife in his hand, the blade bloody brown and dripping in the half-light. They were trapped, fore and aft and walled in by the chalk walls on either side. Finn thought of his oyster knife, but skewering the Crumpet last time had been a matter of surprise as well as skill. There would be no surprising anyone now, and there was Eddie to think of.

"What of our good friend George, Sneed? Will he join us?" the Crumpet asked the dwarf.

"He run off."

"Then whose blood, I might ask, did you spill? Your dirk is awash with it."

"*George*, you mortal idiot. An awkward bastard, George, but I done him."

"You *done* him, Sneed? Do you mean you cut him, but you didn't *kill* him?"

"That's right, you bleeding sod," said the dwarf. "Under his rib, I cut him. Deep. He's bleeding like a hog to slaughter. He won't get far. McFee's after him."

The Crumpet nodded theatrically. "Very well. We've come to the bottom of it. Do you see what comes of what they call compassion?" he asked Finn, reaching forward and snatching the bag out of his hand. "A knife between the ribs. It's a difficult lesson, surely. I learned a similar lesson at your own hand – oh, yes, I remember it well. And many's the night I lay awake featuring how I'd teach it to you, turn and turn about, if I was lucky. And now here we are talking away like old friends, my luck come in at last. I'll be a mortally thorough teacher, young scamp. I promise you that. You'll sing before I'm through with the lesson."

He turned and set out back down the tunnel, and the dwarf pushed Finn, holding the knife up in his face as a warning. Finn thought unhappily of George, and the kindness that he'd done them. Kindness had meant the end of him. He held tightly to Eddie's hand, walking two steps behind the Crumpet. His oyster knife lay in its sheath in his coat pocket, and he had the urge to touch it, to make sure it was there, but he didn't dare. Instead he pictured how he would reach for it when the time came, unsheathe it, and strike with the curved blade, playing it over in his mind so that he would get it quick and right.

Last time, under London Bridge, there had been darkness, a ray of moonlight to see by. He had heard the Crumpet coming for him and was ready, a cold, black anger commanding his mind, drowning the fear. Afterward, when he was running, he knew what had happened only by the blood on his hand and clothing and the sharp intake of breath in the instant that the Crumpet had clutched his stomach and fallen. Finn had left the vision behind him when he left London for Kent, and the thought of poisoning his life and his dreams again sickened him. Even so, he had now become Eddie's keeper, to use the old phrase, and there was no turning your own cheek when it was your neighbor who was struck, or so his mother had taught him. If it was in him to do it, he would send the Crumpet to Hell.

They soon arrived at a door set into the wall of the tunnel, the chalk cut out to admit a timber frame and a long, heavy lintel overhead. The door stood open an inch, showing a line of light. The Crumpet pushed it open and gestured Finn and Eddie through, into the basement of Narbondo's cottage, the Crumpet standing behind him, the Crumpet's hand clamped onto Finn's arm. Narbondo stood before the wall full of surgical tools, regarding Finn curiously as soon as he appeared, and then smiling when he looked at Eddie. His two guests – Lord Moorgate and the woman, she wearing her veil again – stood nearby, Moorgate looking imperious, but the woman a mere mystery behind the veil.

"What of George?" Narbondo asked the dwarf.

"Don't you worry about George…" the dwarf started to say, holding up the bloody knife.

"Dead," the Crumpet said, "or as good as. McFee's seeing to him."

Narbondo shook his head. "Terrible shame," he said. "The man showed such promise, but he had a sentimental streak that he couldn't hide. Strap young Edward to the table, Sneed," he said to the dwarf, who slipped his knife into a scabbard attached to his ankle. "We'll catch his shrieks in Lord Moorgate's silk topper."

Finn looked around, calculating but seeing nothing – no way out, but aware in his mind of the sand flowing through the hourglass. There lay the door, fifteen feet away, and sunlight through the bars of the window, the wood beyond. But the door was shut, the window barred. Sneed hauled Eddie to the block, terror in the boy's eyes, and lifted him bodily, heaving him atop it. Finn heard Eddie speaking now, in a voice that was unnaturally normal. "Finn," he said, very low at first. And then louder: "Finn!"

"I'm here, Eddie," he said, hearing the uselessness in his words. "Your father's coming, Eddie, along with the others. Hold on!" Finn's mind was sharpened by his hatred of the evil in this room, by the things that had been done here, that had left their poison in the stones of the floor. No one was coming. It was just him and Eddie.

He felt the Crumpet's grip relax, and heard a high, barely discernible liquid mumbling coming from the man's mouth, which was near Finn's ear – strange endearments, pet names, a soft trilling sound that was an abomination. The Crumpet was standing very close behind, his hot breath on Finn's neck, and Finn felt saliva drip under his shirt collar. Once again he considered the knife in his pocket, wishing now that it had a longer blade. Eddie was incapable of helping himself. The boy could have no idea what fate awaited him, which was a small comfort, at least for the moment.

The room fell silent, aside from the Crumpet's loathsome mewling. Sneed let Eddie lie atop the table, turning to the implements on the wall. He stepped up onto one of the wooden chairs and fetched down two of the leather-covered chains, dumping them onto the ground before climbing down again, then bending over to pick one of them up, which he carried around to the other side of the block. Finn looked at his own open palm, at the coal-blackened line that crossed it.

Clenching his fist, he twisted suddenly and drove his elbow hard into the Crumpet's stomach, then slammed the heel of his shoe down onto his toe, wishing he'd worn boots. The Crumpet reeled back a step, a vicious and surprised look on his face now, still clutching the fabric of Finn's coat.

"Run!" Finn yelled hopefully, into the Crumpet's face. "Run, Eddie!" And before the Crumpet could react, Finn leaned forward and spat into his eye. The Crumpet's face contorted with surprise, and Finn lurched forward and jammed a thumb into his other eye, twisting and pressing it in, then yanking it out, slick with a bloody slime now, the Crumpet shrieking and releasing Finn's coat.

Finn whirled and ran just as Eddie rolled off the table, falling onto the floor and scrambling away, Sneed throwing himself across the table in an effort to grab him.

"The door!" Finn shouted, ducking past Lord Moorgate's stodgy effort to grab him. Eddie, not witless at all, but apparently keen on escape, leapt to the door and reached for the latch, but the woman in the veil was a step behind him, bolder than Moorgate, and Sneed right behind her.

The way was barred.

Finn snatched up a leather-covered chain now, some four feet in length, and swung it around his head, advancing on Narbondo, who had backed against the wall and was watching with amusement, but whose demeanor changed at the sight of Finn and the whirring chain. Narbondo was canny, and at once plucked up one of the wooden chairs, holding it in front of him with one hand, and reaching into his coat with the other, where his pistol no doubt lay. Finn spun away, angling to his right, rushing forward, and slinging the chain hard at the Crumpet's neck, holding tightly to the end as it frapped itself tight and fast. Finn yanked hard on it, the Crumpet pitching forward, his mouth open wide, his hands tearing at the chain. Finn rushed in and levered his foot against the Crumpet's back, wrenching on the chain, drawing hard on it, the Crumpet gagging.

"He's a dead man!" Finn shouted, but even as he did, he could see that it wouldn't do. The amusement had come back into Narbondo's face, and although his hand was still in his coat, he had set the chair down again. No one appeared to care greatly if the Crumpet lived or died, least of all Narbondo. The woman grasped Eddie tightly by the hair. Lord Moorgate held a pistol now, Sneed a knife. The Crumpet, coming to his senses, reached out and grasped Finn by the ankle, tripping him. Finn let go of the chain, and the Crumpet rolled clear. He struggled to stand, sucking air into his lungs, his left eye jammed shut, blood flowing down his cheek. He stared at Finn with a dead look in his good eye, something far beyond mere anger. His breath rasped in and out, and there were the marks of the chain on his neck, pressed right through the leather.

"Crumpet, when you're quite finished with your paroxysms," Narbondo said, "we'll continue. You'll be so kind as to wait your turn. It will come, I assure you."

There was a noise, then – the tunnel door rasping open across the ragstone floor, and into the room stepped a tall, gaunt man. His damp clothing was smeared with chalk, and his hair stood straight up on his head. His mouth was working, as if he were chewing something, and he looked from one to the other of them, one eye asquint, everyone in the room startled into surprised immobility, except for Narbondo, who bowed at the waist and swept his hand out.

"My old friend Bill Kraken!" Narbondo said. "I rather thought you'd pay us a visit. You're an acquaintance of my dear mother, I believe, and so you won't be surprised at my having anticipated you. She sent to tell us you were coming. I owe you a small debt, I believe, from our last meeting in Aylesford, which I intend to repay with interest. Come, join our little jollification."

Friend or foe? Finn wondered, looking at the stranger, whose face showed no reaction at all to Narbondo's chatter. Finn thought of the old woman who had tried to save Eddie in Angel Alley – the byway rightly named in that regard – and wondered if this were yet another angel, tolerably strange, to be sure, but welcome if it were so.

The man stared at Eddie and nodded, and then at the woman who gripped Eddie by the collar. From out of his coat he took a long pistol.

Narbondo's face underwent a change, although he recovered from it quickly. He had expected the man, Finn thought, but not the pistol, and was worried now that he had overreached himself. He must know, however, that Lord Moorgate possessed one of his own. Moorgate's right hand was held down along the seam of his trousers, hidden from Kraken's view.

Kraken's lips were pursed, and he looked from one to the other of them, as if contemplating whom to shoot first. He stopped when his gaze reached Narbondo once again – a gaze of intense loathing – and he nodded slowly, as if having decided. Finn braced himself, glancing again at the door. He would move fast when it started, with no goal but to take Eddie through the door, leaving the stranger to deal with the others. If it meant knocking the woman down, or worse, then so be it. He and Eddie were dead otherwise.

"You!" the stranger said to Narbondo, his voice shaking with anger. "The fiend that flieth by night! I'll see you in damnation. What I do here is in the memory of poor Mary Eastman, by God, and young Edward, your own brother. I been awaiting this day, and now it's upon us…"

Quit talking, Finn thought. *Do what you've come to do.*

Finn glanced at Lord Moorgate. Still no sign of the pistol, but he was ready. The stranger fell silent at last and took careful aim at Narbondo, a distance of maybe fifteen feet, Narbondo brassing it out like Satan.

Shoot him, Finn thought. Kraken steadied his hand, set his feet, squinted down the barrel, and Lord Moorgate shot him where he stood.

Kraken spun around, caught himself, staggered forward two steps, and looked with shocked surprise at Moorgate. The pistol was still in Kraken's hand, and he raised it again, aiming it at Moorgate now, who pulled the trigger of his own pistol a second time. The pistol misfired, and then misfired again. Now, as he fell, Kraken shot at Moorgate, blowing splinters out of the door beyond. He held onto the pistol, kneeling and looking around him, one hand pressed against his chest, blood flowing through his fingers. The woman flung the door open and ran out, Eddie shrugging away from her and running toward Finn. Narbondo and Moorgate followed the woman out of the cellar, Sneed in their wake. Eddie had pressed himself against the wall and put his hands in front of his face.

Someone slammed into Finn, knocking him down.

Finn rolled clear and sprang to his feet, throwing himself toward Eddie, Kraken's pistol ringing out right behind him. The Crumpet hurtled through the open door, looking back wildly with his one good eye.

"Go on!" Kraken said to Finn. "Take to the wood! I'll see to myself!" And with that Kraken staggered away into the darkness of the tunnel, pulling the door shut behind him.

Finn grabbed Eddie's hand and hauled him out into the sunshine. Ahead stood the pond, the Crumpet on the far shore by now. The others had disappeared, but everything would change as soon as it was perceived that Kraken was no longer a threat. There was shouting now from the direction of the unseen millwheel – a hue and cry – Narbondo no doubt rallying his men to face Kraken's pistol. The only real shelter was the wood, which lay to their left – southwest, given the position of the sun – and soon Finn and Eddie were running for all that they were worth in that direction, Eddie moving faster than Finn could credit.

They reached the brook that turned the millwheel, and followed it deeper into the wood along a narrow trail, Finn listening for sounds of pursuit. He slowed the pace. There was no use exhausting Eddie, and with any luck they would have a long way to travel before nightfall. The stream ran south, toward the Medway, toward home, and the trail was well enough traveled. It would take them somewhere without a doubt, and anywhere was better than where they had been.

"Follow this brook if you lose sight of me," Finn told Eddie. "Do you hear me?"

Eddie said, "Yes," and nodded his head, seeming to understand very well.

"Don't leave the path unless you must. If you follow the path you'll end up somewhere hopeful. Tell them you live at Agatha Walton's place, Aylesford." Despite Eddie's nodding again, Finn made him repeat the gist of it, just as George had done to him, but he felt a measure of futility.

The brook curved around toward the west and then straightened, again heading south. Aylesford lay below them, Finn thought: ten miles, twelve, maybe. They could walk it well enough in four hours if Eddie held up, or perhaps beg a ride from a willing farmer. He looked back and saw no one, but when he looked forward again, he nearly ran into Eddie, who had slowed down, peering ahead of him dubiously. There was a dead man lying across the path twenty feet farther on, his shoulders and head in the brook so that the water washed over his face. Finn didn't need to see the face, however, to know who it was – George, from the clothing and the bald head. He gestured Eddie forward, warning him not to look, although Finn had to, out of respect or so it seemed to him.

The back of George's coat was stained with blood – the work of Sneed's knife, no doubt. There were no other visible wounds, but there were footprints along the muddy bank of the brook, a mess of them, half of them perfectly enormous. George had put up a fight, but McFee – it had to be he – had apparently drowned him. There was nothing to do for him, and no time to dawdle in any event. They moved on at an even pace, Finn telling himself that George had done the right thing by helping them, although the thought was moderately cold comfort.

There was a noise then, off to the right – someone –

the Crumpet, running at a sort of gallop through the trees, angling across to cut them off, the tails of his blue coat flying up behind him. Eddie apparently saw him as well. He needed no encouragement, but ran like the wind up the trail, Finn behind him, pacing himself, glancing to the side in order to watch the Crumpet's approach. The man would cross their path forty or fifty feet ahead, where there was a clearing along the brook. The water was deep enough and rocky enough to slow him down, but it wouldn't stop him. Something else would have to stop him.

"Don't look back," Finn shouted breathlessly. "No matter what happens. Follow the trail, like I told you!"

And with that Finn leapt into the brook, landing atop a stone, leapt to another, and then across, running hard along the water's edge now, in packed sand and leaves, relieved to see that Eddie was flying up the trail some distance ahead. Who would the Crumpet want, Finn wondered, for he couldn't have the both of them.

The distance between them was closing fast. Finn took two half steps and threw himself into a tumble, rolling into a ball, straight into the Crumpet's path. He was struck hard, the Crumpet grunting and pitching forward, kicking Finn a glancing blow on the side of the head in passing. Finn was up onto his feet, his head reeling, seeing that the Crumpet was splayed out in the stream, struggling to rise. Eddie was out of sight, although the Crumpet would catch him easily enough once he was up and moving again. And so he was, almost at once, stumbling across the stream as if to follow Eddie, driven either by loyalty to Narbondo or by fear. It wouldn't do. Finn picked up a big stone with both hands and ran forward, pitching it at the Crumpet's head, striking him above the neck, so that his head jerked back, and he fell to his knees, coming down hard and shouting a curse when his knees struck.

He stood up again, turning toward Finn in a wild rage now. Finn had no intention of letting the man get near him, only to draw him away from Eddie. He picked up a smaller stone and threw it hard, the Crumpet shrugging aside as it flew past. He stood gazing at Finn now, his trouser legs torn open and water-soaked, his right knee bloody, his blue coat streaked with blood and filth. His face was dead calm, however, his one good eye unblinking, his other eye a closed, red weal. He drew out his knife and walked slowly toward Finn, picking his way back across the rocky stream as if he had time to spare after all. Finn backed away, thinking hard whether to chance more stones or to run.

In that moment Eddie appeared at a dead run. *Ah, no*, Finn thought, as Eddie picked up a small stone and threw it at the Crumpet, missing him by a wide margin. Eddie saw a tree branch, then, and picked it up, running toward the Crumpet's back, the Crumpet completely unaware. Eddie swung the branch at the back of the Crumpet's head, as hard as he could swing it. It glanced off, scraping down the Crumpet's ear and shoulder. Eddie turned and ran again, the Crumpet turning toward him. Finn picked up another heavy stone and ran toward the Crumpet, who feinted toward Eddie but then turned back toward Finn, dodging the stone easily, nearly getting hold of Finn's jacket. Eddie had vanished.

Finn broke and ran, back up the stream where he crossed to the path again, looking back to see the Crumpet coming on, not in a mad rush now, but with a calm determination, as if his life had narrowed to this one contentious goal. At least Eddie was safely out of sight, Finn thought, recalling his happy surprise when Eddie had picked up the branch. And then once again he was running.

THIRTY-THREE
THE KING OF THE DAFT

"Please, sir, no more of your histrionics," Lord Moorgate said. "I find them tedious in the extreme, and I'm anxious to be away. I came here desiring to bring some sensible conclusion to last night's abortive meeting. But now I find myself no further along and half a day wasted and having been shot at into the bargain. The boy has run off once again due to your stupidity, or something worse. You've failed me, Doctor, and I have half a mind to abandon you."

They stood in the cellar once again, Lord Moorgate, Helen, and Narbondo, the three of them alone, Narbondo's men dispersed – some of them searching the countryside, some of them loading barrels aboard the freshly painted steam launch.

"What's in the other half of your mind, Lord Moorgate? As is true of you and your associates, I have far too much invested in the project to see it abandoned now because of your suspicions and timidity."

"I warn you that you sail dangerously close to the wind when you accuse me of timidity, sir – a man to whom you owe your life, unless of course your life was never in danger in the first place. The lunatic with the pistol, after all, shot at me, not at you." He cocked his head and narrowed his eyes. "The salient point is that I'll find it impossible to explain to my business associates that the assurance I promised them has run away into the marsh. They're impatient men, Doctor, and quite unhappy to throw good money after bad. Your own head will be forfeit; depend upon it."

"What you explain to your business associates is of no concern to me," Narbondo said. He smiled at Helen, who seemed to be listening keenly. "Unless of course the beautiful Helen is one of those associates. In that case my concern is very nearly boundless."

"You jest once again, but to your own peril, sir. My suspicions are justified, I find. It's remarkable that you clearly anticipated the appearance of the lunatic with the pistol just now. As you no doubt know, that same man attacked me on the street last night after I left your apartment in Spitalfields. Now here he is again, like the ghost at the feast, but carrying a pistol. He threatens to murder you, but was that his intent?"

"I anticipated his arrival because one of my men intercepted a missive that revealed his approach. He shot at you, it seems to me, because you shot him. I have no idea why he attacked you in London. I don't care a groat for your suspicions."

"Then I'll come to the point. I'm willing to proceed, but on the condition that you supply the balance of the money that de Groot will pay to our man in the War Office. Then we're equally invested in the project's success. When you've finished your work with the boy's skull and demonstrate its effectiveness, we'll repay you. And don't pretend that you're not in funds, Doctor. I'm aware that you have a very deep purse."

Narbondo nodded. "You bargain like a Scotsman, sir. But answer me this: why shouldn't I cut your throat at once and take your money?"

"You're not daft enough to think that I have the money with me?"

"To the contrary, I'm the very king of the daft, sir. I wonder whether Helen knows where the money lies, and whether she would betray you."

"I might," Helen said promptly. "I will be the one to deliver the money to de Groot. Lord Moorgate intends to be in York tomorrow morning, innocently visiting his cousin."

"Which is entirely sensible," Moorgate said to Narbondo. He turned to Helen and said, "You'd be wise to remain silent, Helen. I tell you this for your own good."

"And what else has he promised you for your own good, my dear, now that your head is also in the noose? I don't say what has he *given* to you, because our Lord Moorgate seems to be a man of promises, which are very like wind, when you come to think of it. Look at this, my lady." Narbondo plucked a gold ring from the little finger of his right hand, displaying it in his open palm as he handed it to Helen, who gazed at it with evident appreciation and lust. It was an immense, jet-black pearl set in gold. The pearl had been hidden, turned backward in Narbondo's hand until this moment. "A token of my esteem," he said to her. "I possess another of the same, set in a necklace with diamonds."

"You waste your breath," Moorgate said. "Come, Helen, return the bauble to the Doctor. We're finished here."

Helen looked at Moorgate as if she weren't at all finished, her eyes as black as the pearls that Narbondo offered to her. In that instant, having made up his mind about her, Narbondo sprang forward, his knife in his hand, the same knife that had dispatched Mary Eastman, and others before her. He swept the blade across Moorgate's throat, and then at once fell back to avoid the spray of blood.

"Yes," he said, "finished indeed."

Moorgate's eyes remained wide open in surprise. His crimson breath bubbled out of his throat, which he touched now with a palsied hand, toppling to his knees, pressing his hand more forcefully, trying to breathe and to staunch the flow of blood.

"Keep the bauble or return it, as you wish," Narbondo said to Helen. "I have an entertaining suggestion, however, that will profit us both. You might want to hear it before you decide." He gestured at Lord Moorgate. "There is always a choice, you see."

THIRTY-FOUR
UNCLE GILBERT'S ENCAMPMENT

The airship floated some six feet above the flat, sandy sward near Gilbert Frobisher's vast Arabian tent – several tents, actually, as well as sun shades with their sides furled to let the sometimes considerable breeze slip through. The ship was moored fore and aft and along either side with heavy rope, long wooden stakes set deeply in the well-packed sand. A ladder made of rope and with wooden treads dangled from the open gondola door – more a gate than a door – the excess ladder piled on the ground.

A line of high dunes separated the encampment from the shore of Egypt Bay, the tent quite invisible from a boat on the water or from the track along the edge of the bay. St. Ives was inclined to think that this accounted for the fact that the extravagant and lonesome outpost hadn't been robbed and ravaged by Narbondo's men or other bands of river pirates and smugglers. The cooking smoke would have been visible, of course, but a single traveler with a simple campfire could account for cooking smoke.

St. Ives considered the company roundabout him as he sat drinking tea and eating toasted muffins and strawberries.

They were awaiting the arrival of Jack, Tubby, and Doyle, but the day was wearing on, St. Ives growing more anxious as the minutes passed, minutes that he kept track of by repeatedly conferring with his pocket watch. He had no right to ask it, but he badly wanted help with his likely assault on the surprisingly large company of cutthroats they'd seen from the airship when it passed over the infamous Shade House an hour back. Merton's map had named the inn, although unnecessarily, for its reputation as an old smugglers' outpost had been the stuff of legend.

Gilbert, who was the image of his nephew, easily as stout but with the hair gone from the top of his head and wearing heavy spectacles, had brought his valet with him, a man named Barlow, tall and fit and evidently competent, but with his ankle splinted and wrapped and propped on a settee. He had sprained it two days ago when he stepped into a rabbit hole. There was also an old birding acquaintance of Gilbert's named Mr. Hodgson, who was small and bandy-legged, although active, it appeared, for a man getting well along in years. He was taken up with the study of a surprisingly wide array of eggs and feathers and nests laid out upon tables, blue and pink and speckled eggs sitting comfortably in their requisite nests. He was so taken up with them, in fact, that he scarcely spoke, but was a slave to his collection, writing away in a notebook while sitting at a wide, wooden desk, leaping up to gaze at the particular construction of a nest or the shape of an egg and then returning to the notebook.

There was a cook, too, named Madame Leseur, a wide-bodied woman who spoke Frenchified English, and who worked her marvels within a kitchen enclosure that included an iron stove, broad chopping blocks, hencoops, and cabinets. She had heavily muscled arms and stout legs, as if she had spent her life carrying hod rather than cooking. Somehow she had contrived to bake bread, and several long loaves stood in a wire basket. A brace of pheasants hung overhead along with a ham, several wrapped cheeses, and bundles of herbs. She was filleting a fish at the moment with a wickedly thin knife, and there was a ragout of lamb in the oven that smelled good enough to draw boats in off the Thames. Wood smoke rose from the stovepipe, straight upward into the still air.

Gilbert had hired a company from Gravesend to transport the crated-up encampment, including books and spirits and feather beds and other civilized necessities, and to set the bivouac up, dig and enclose the privy, and return at three-day intervals with meat and green-stuff and fruit brought fresh from the orchards of Kent. Gilbert supplemented the stores with game, the pheasants being an example.

There was nothing wrong with shooting a bird now and then, Gilbert told St. Ives and Hasbro, showing them his new birding rifle. "An Anson and Deeley," he said proudly, "what they call a 'boxlock.' It's the very latest thing, Professor. Internal hammers, self-cocking. You flush the bird, bring up the gun, and pull the trigger on the instant as smoothly as kiss-my-hand. Scarcely sporting, you'll say, but if you had eaten Madame Leseur's cookery, you'd think differently."

Of the present company, only Barlow would have any business taking part in the sort of activity that St. Ives had planned – an all-out assault – but of course he could do no such thing laid up as he was. There would be no gainsaying

Uncle Gilbert, however, which was worrisome, since Gilbert was dangerously high-spirited and spontaneous. He had helped to save St. Ives's life some time back, and so St. Ives could not decently deny him a part in the coming raid, but he feared the result, the old man having Tubby's dangerous habit of putting himself in the way of trouble. Gilbert was given to a much higher pitch of excitement than his nephew, however, which tended to scatter the old man's wits.

St. Ives lost track of the substance of the conversation roundabout him, his mind adrift, and was visited suddenly by a clear, sun-lit vision of his home, as if he were standing in the wisteria alley – spring flowers in bloom, the hops growing, Eddie and Cleo's laughter on the breeze. He felt his heart beating heavily in his chest. Not trusting himself to speak, he stood up for the third time since they had arrived and walked out past the airship, carrying his telescope, up the side of the dune to where he had an overview of the bay. It was a glorious summer day in virtually every regard – the sun on the water, a living, nourishing warmth to the air, the sky a deep blue – and yet he cared nothing for it, and he could scarcely remember the quality of joy that he took in such things even a few days ago. He thought of Alice, missing her to an unsettling degree. He shut his eyes, shook his head, and made an effort to clear his mind of all sentiment, simply for the sake of his sanity. Opening his eyes again, he surveyed the expanse of water with his telescope, discovering that nothing had changed in the last half hour.

A swerve of shore hid much of the southern reaches of the bay, which was just as well; he and Narbondo were mutually invisible from each other. He looked out toward the inlet to the bay where the hilly ground blocked the view of the Thames and saw a line of smoke now that canted back upriver – a steam launch, almost certainly coming round into the bay, given the behavior of the smoke. He waited impatiently, and minutes later it was visible: a small launch heading straight toward him, damnably slowly, it seemed to St. Ives. The smoke from Madame Leseur's stove no doubt made their whereabouts clear. St. Ives hurried back into the encampment and announced the arrival, returning with Gilbert and Hasbro to the edge of the bay.

His three friends were ferried ashore in a scow that had been towing behind the launch. Their gear consisted mainly of two wooden crates with the stamp of Gleeson's Mercantile burned into the sides – Tubby's idea, no doubt, and very civilized of him, although it was coals to Newcastle, certainly, given Gilbert's provisions. St. Ives had no notion of remaining long enough to open a crate. He had rarely been so alive with the desire to act, and rarely so frustrated of the opportunity. The scow ran up onto the shore at last, Tubby handed a sum of money to the man at the oars, and the three companions stepped overside onto the sand. Hasbro and Jack carried away the larger crate between them, and Tubby manhandled the smaller, introducing Uncle Gilbert to Doyle, pointing out to his uncle that he already knew Jack, which lead to a riot of hand-shaking and recollection, and then Tubby walked away with his uncle, the two of them looking like the Tweedle brothers as they made their way up the dunes.

"We've made some small discoveries," Doyle said to St. Ives as they stood on the shore, the water lapping at their feet. "It's largely speculation and half-knowledge, but perhaps between the lot of us we can see the shape of things."

"Dinner is moments away, I should think," St. Ives said. "We'll talk as we eat, and either we'll get to the bottom of the business, or we will not. My own motive remains unaltered. I'm going to make another attempt to retrieve my son, as soon as I'm satisfied with what I know, or don't know, if it comes to it. I fear that Narbondo will effect an explosion in London soon, probably catastrophic."

"Tuesday, we believe," Jack said, having returned to them. He handed St. Ives the sheaf of papers they'd taken from de Groot. "Tomorrow, perhaps, or a week hence."

"Tomorrow, I'd guess, from the eagerness of their work," St. Ives said as they walked over the dunes. He wondered if, indeed, the day was at hand. If it were, then the two men they'd seen carrying Greek fire along the embankment this morning were only a small part of things. It was singularly impressive that they'd blown up the Fleet Sewer, but it must be a meager display indeed if Mother Laswell's fears were remotely sensible. Surely, he thought, there was no time for Narbondo to be contriving ornate new skulls for the Customer if in fact he looked forward to opening a door to the afterlife on the morrow. Narbondo already possessed the Aylesford Skull, his open sesame, as it were. Perhaps kidnapping Eddie had everything to do with revenge after all, revenge and profit – the attempt at extorting the heavy ransom from St. Ives, while taking fees from the Customer – playing them both false and luring St. Ives into the Cliffe Marshes into the bargain, thus getting him out of London. Any or all of this might be the case. Or none of it.

He studied de Groot's papers while awaiting dinner, neither surprised that Moorgate should be the infamous Customer, nor that he was working toward some nefarious political end. Regicide, however? Was the man so far gone in megalomania that he would dare to murder the Queen? Narbondo would seize at the chance to manipulate such a man.

Dinner appeared, arriving in several removes, the garlicky fish cooked in wine and herbs and finished with butter, the lamb ragout redolent with cloves and allspice and cinnamon, and bottles of India Pale Ale brewed by Uncle Gilbert's particular friend in East Sussex. Tubby and Gilbert mopped up the gravy with chunks of bread, Gilbert reporting on bustards, of which he had seen not a one, although they had recorded thirty-four other species of bird, having shot and eaten three of them. Their hopes were far from dashed, however, for they'd spoken to a man who claimed to have seen a fifty-pound bustard in an open meadow. The man hadn't been quite sober, perhaps, but liquor didn't turn a man into a liar by any means, Uncle Gilbert pointed out. The opposite was more often true. There was of course some chance that he had seen a particularly fat lamb...

Gilbert intended to stay through the summer, birding being his great passion, and the encampment having come to seem like a second home. St. Ives only half-listened, and as for the food, he ate but scarcely tasted it, his mind distant. He considered the mysterious Guido Fox, the business of the dust flying along with the martyrs. He thought of Shorter's palm house, the contraband coal, the phosphorous and gunpowder and lead bullets in Narbondo's lair in the rookery, the photographic plate with Eddie's image on it, which he swept out of his mind immediately now.

"What do you know of coal, sir?" he asked Uncle Gilbert, who had fallen silent while helping himself to another slice of fish.

"I know the price of it by the ton," he said, "and the relative merits of hard and soft varieties, but only when it comes to smelting. My firm manufactures railway iron, you know, near Blackboys. Not my firm any longer, of course, in any real sense of the word. I sold the vast majority of my shares in the spring. I'm a free man now."

"And a rich man," Tubby put in.

"Quite right," Gilbert said. "Buckets of the stuff. Croesus ain't in it. I enjoy my comforts, Professor."

"I'm quite enjoying them myself, sir. Dangerous, is it, coal? Flammable, of course; but explosive?"

"Can be. Depends on particle size and how it's treated."

"Doyle, you were telling us about your voyage aboard the *Mayumba* steamship," Jack said, "speaking of dangerous coal fires."

"We suffered a coal fire in a storage bunker," Doyle told them, leaning forward. "We were north of Madeira, coming home. The captain was opposed to flooding the bunker due to the weight of the water, which would make the ship unwieldy, what with the swell running high, so he elected to seal the bunker to reduce oxygen. The fire smoldered hot, though. At night the hull plates glowed red, and the boats were maintained at the ready. We had a cargo of palm oil aboard – highly explosive."

"There's a vast amount of dust in a coal bunker, of

course," said Gilbert, shaking his head, "and that's the problem, isn't it? If the bunker was opened and the ocean breeze allowed to suspend the dust, it might have gone very bad, sir, very bad indeed, no matter how many boats were readied."

"Tell me specifically about such explosions, if you please," St. Ives said.

"It's an elementary business, sir," Gilbert told him, "although I don't mean to come it the school teacher." He drank half a bottle of pale ale then, at a draft, and gasped afterward.

"I'm in need of a school teacher," St. Ives said. "Tell away."

"Well, sir. I'll tell you that five things are required to effect an explosion: a sufficiency of coal dust – less than you'd suppose – the suspension of the dust, along with oxygen, heat, and confinement. In the case of Mr. Doyle's ship, they were all on hand except the suspension. The coal would burn, low and hot, but without suspension there would be no explosion no matter the temperature. Hence the Captain's sealing of the bunker against the breeze. It reduced the oxygen, certainly, but the oxygen was far less dangerous than a gust of air."

"And all coal dust is equally explosive?" St. Ives asked.

"No, sir. Anthracite dust not at all. It's a matter of what they call the volatile ratio, do you see? Calculating it is a simple business, but suffice it to say that it must be bituminous coal or something softer to create a dust hazard, but only if the particle size is tolerably small."

"Lignite coal?"

"Quite explosive, especially if it's dry."

"The smaller the particle the more explosive, I take it."

"Just so, for two reasons. The small particles are of course easier to suspend, and the explosion requires less heat, which transfers far more quickly through fine dust." Gilbert took another hearty swallow of his ale, wiped his mouth with the back of his hand, and set the bottle down.

"It must take a great quantity of dust to set off an explosion of any consequence," Jack said. "Tubby pointed out to us that Guy Fawkes had hauled a dozen barrels of gunpowder into his basement beneath Parliament. Surely gunpowder is far more explosive than powdered coal?"

"Don't believe it for a minute, sir," Gilbert said. "Guy Fawkes was a fool, which is why he was hanged."

"Not hanged," Doyle said. "As I recall he leapt from the scaffold and broke his neck."

"My point is proven in either event," Gilbert said. "Here's the thing. If there was enough dust on the floor of this coal bunker so that footprints were clearly visible in it, there was enough dust for an explosion were the dust suddenly suspended, although perhaps not a terribly intense explosion. This is a matter of what the experts refer to as the 'minimum explosive concentration,' although it's not a fine science, sir, especially in a large structure. In a coal bunker it's much easier to calculate. To a point, the more dust, the greater the blast. Beyond a point, the dust has a smothering effect. If there was coal gas present also, as there often is, the result would be extraordinary." He thrust a piece of fish into his mouth at this juncture, immediately found a bone, and spat the bone and the piece of fish out into the grass. "Pardon me," he said, "that ain't manners. Come, what more do you need to know, Professor? I'm quite enjoying this, you

367

being the student and me the tutor, ha, ha."

"As for heat…" St. Ives began, thinking of Shorter's palm house, with the coal oil heaters and lamps.

"For dry, finely corned lignite coal, thoroughly suspended and in sufficient quantity," Gilbert said, anticipating him, "a mere spark might set it off. Certainly an open flame would bring about an explosion. The danger was very great in Mr. Doyle's ship, for there was no doubt red-hot dust on the floor. The mere act of suspension would have ignited it, the heat being already present."

St. Ives stood up and nodded his head, having made up his mind and feeling the day slipping away from him. "Gentlemen," he said, "I believe I see the way of it now. It's my belief that Narbondo and Lord Moorgate intend to create an atrocity at tomorrow's ceremony at the Cathedral of the Oxford Martyrs by pumping it full of suspended coal dust and igniting it, either with Greek fire or by some other source of heat. Hasbro tells me that the Queen will be on hand, along with no end of dignitaries and God knows how many thousands of onlookers. I doubt very much that we can stop it ourselves, and Narbondo's motivation – you'll have to take my oath on this – is so very implausible that it would be folly to attempt to persuade the police or the army to act. In order to avoid utter defeat I intend to attempt to rescue my son immediately, and let the devil take the hindmost. Once again, anyone who is with me is welcome. Duty to the Crown, however, would require that you leave for London post haste to attempt to prevent the debacle, if in fact I'm correct." St. Ives moved immediately to collect the weapons that he and Hasbro had brought along with them – the pistols that had served them well enough in Angel Alley, although their service had profited them little, except perhaps for saving their hides.

Gilbert sat blinking, looking around him as if perplexed, confounded by this wild speech and the sudden change in the weather of the conversation. "What's this *rescue* you speak of?" he asked. "I could see trouble in your face when you descended the ladder from your airship, Professor, but it was none of my damned business. Now that it's been spoken aloud, however…"

"Dr. Narbondo, whom you no doubt recall, has kidnapped my son."

The old man stood up, his face darkening. "Good God," he said. "The last we saw of that filthy reptile he was making away on his submarine boat like a frightened mole. Tubby, you remember that. I told you we should have shot the creature where he stood when we had the chance."

"We did what we could, Uncle, and you'll recall that we had no means of shooting him where he stood, much less when he was inside his ship."

"Aye, that was our downfall – insufficient weaponry. But I've got the means now, by God. The man is keen on revenge, no doubt, and this is his diabolic way of getting it."

"I believe you're in the right of it, sir. Revenge and more," St. Ives said.

"Can I be of service, then?" Gilbert asked. "I'd sooner shoot this Narbondo than to shoot a pheasant, although the pheasant would eat better, certainly."

"I thank you for the offer, sir," St. Ives told him.

Hasbro, Jack, Tubby, and Doyle were up and moving

now. There was no talk of London, just a silent preparation, and in moments they set out with St. Ives along the edge of the dunes, Egypt Bay invisible beyond. Uncle Gilbert carried his shotgun and wore his pith helmet against the sun.

"Don't dawdle on my account," he said. "I can keep up right enough. I'm an old man, perhaps, but I'm not a cripple. Hodgson assures me that he'll stand guard over the airship, Professor, along with Barlow. Can shoot a sparrow out of a tree at fifty feet with a pellet, can Hodgson, as long as he don't lose himself in his eggs and nests. And Barlow is a rare hand with a pistol. He's set up his chair and ottoman in the shade of the ship."

"I'm sorry to take you away from your bustards, sir," St. Ives said. "You didn't bargain for this."

Gilbert nodded sharply. "It's a child that's in need, sir, and what's more it's the son of a man I consider to be my friend, if I might be forward enough to say so. A child's life and happiness comes first for anyone who ain't a filthy Benthamite insect, and no disrespect meant to the Crown. But the Queen has the Guard to keep watch over her. It's their lookout, sir."

The track along the dunes was a weedy ribbon of sand and shell, and they made good time along it, soon finding themselves on a sheep path through a thicket that eventually turned into forest. They were utterly silent, having talked their way through a makeshift plan that seemed sensible, given what they had seen of the Shade House from the air. There was no point in further talk.

They trod on a carpet of leaves now, hearing the crying of gulls, a strengthening breeze soughing through the limbs overhead, and so they easily heard the footfalls of someone running, moments before Finn Conrad rounded a bend in the path ahead, looking back over his shoulder so that he slammed straight into St. Ives, who caught him, reeling back from the force. Looking up wildly, Finn tore himself away and took several steps toward the trees before he recognized them, at which sight he dropped to his knees, his chest heaving.

A man appeared then, clearly pursuing Finn, running hard, his face disfigured both by a vicious wound and an equally vicious appearance of demented rage. His mouth worked, his voice ululating something that approximated human speech. In his hand he held a long knife, not hesitating at the sight of the men ranged before him, but evidently set on murdering Finn.

"Cease!" Gilbert shouted, stepping forward, but yet the man came on in a mad rush as if the lot of them were invisible.

Gilbert brought up his shotgun and instantly blew the man over backward, a mass of birds flying upward from the trees as the report echoed through the wood.

THIRTY-FIVE

BLOODY BEEFSTEAK

Mother Laswell awoke in her chair at the sound of her book striking the ground. She was stricken with fear, her heart beating in her throat, the remnants of a dark dream evaporating in her mind like steam. She could still picture the dark house on the Thames and a nightmarish London veiled by cloud. The arched door of the house – the same door that had haunted other dreams – swung open, and standing within was Narbondo himself, holding Edward's skull before him. Then the skull was illuminated, and the twin lamps that were the eyes cast a vaporous light out over the city. There was the sound of chaos unleashed: the ground shook, buildings fell, and she had lurched awake.

She looked around her now and saw where she was – sitting in a chair in her room at the inn. The morning returned to her, and she looked at the clock on the wall, thinking that a great deal of time must have passed. But it wasn't so. She had been asleep for two hours, apparently, and she stood up now and poured herself a cup of now-cold tea from a pot on the sideboard. There were scones left, too, and so she ate one. When she had finished her cup and her scone, she found that she had no interest in her book. She thought of Alice. Surely the coach had arrived in Aylesford by now, although even if it had, Alice was still three or four hours away, depending on Simonides, where he was when the missive had arrived at Hereafter, and how quickly he had done his duty.

She stared at the clock, watching the pendulum move back and forth, seeming to mock her. *You don't need to come a-looking*, Bill had told her, but Bill had gone a-looking, hadn't he? No doubt he had been solicitous of her corns, which had regained their senses over the course of the morning. Sudden determination came into her mind, and she arose, thinking of leaving Bill a message with the innkeeper, but perhaps the innkeeper wasn't to be trusted. Or perhaps the man Fred was staying at this very inn, and his conversation with the innkeeper had been innocent. There was no telling, and so she decided to keep herself to herself, and went out into the street, asking after the old rectory of the man at the lending library.

She found the path easily enough, and very shortly she found herself alone in the quiet afternoon, the path winding around toward a distant wood. After she had walked for fifteen minutes, the rectory itself appeared ahead, built of black stone, apparently ancient and fallen into disrepair, the slate roof of the house overshadowed by great trees. A broad lawn surrounded the house, the lawn cut by a brook that ran out of the wood. She stood for a time looking into the clear water, at the smooth stones along the bottom, her mind disengaged by the idyllic scene before her. There was a path along the side of the brook, but where it went she didn't know, nor where the limekilns lay, with their mysterious smugglers' tunnels.

Abruptly there sounded a muted singing, apparently coming from within the rectory, and she saw now that a wagon stood behind the structure and that a horse was tethered nearby. She made her way toward the wagon, finding herself looking into the rectory through an open door at a very old man who was applying plaster to a decayed frieze on a wall. She watched him work for a time, seeing the care that he was putting into it, working with a number of small trowels and scrapers. He stood back to survey his work, taking a pipe and a pouch of tobacco out of his pocket. It was then that she knocked on the door.

He turned and said, "Hello, ma'am," cheerfully enough, and began packing tobacco into his pipe, shreds falling to the floor.

"Are you the caretaker?" she asked.

He shrugged. "After a fashion. The old place keeps falling down – bits and pieces of it – and I do what I can to put it back up. It's a scrimshaw, you might say – something like." He lit the pipe, drew on it, tamped it, and lit it again.

"It's very fine work to my mind," she told him. "The house appreciates it, you know. They develop something of a soul, houses do, over the years. I dare say this one's watched the centuries pass."

He smiled at her now. "That it has. I'm not fond of seeing good things in decline, you might say, although comes a time when a body can't stop it happening. If it's not drink and the devil, then it'll be something else that'll have done with us sooner or later. What might I do for you?"

"I'm looking for directions to an old inn, very notorious, called Shade House."

He shook his head. "You oughtn't to go near it, ma'am. It's far enough into the marsh to be isolated-like. It's got an evil reputation, and well deserved. If it has a soul, it's a black one. It's been damned these many long years."

"I'm not planning on walking the entire distance," she said. "Partway, that's all. I've been told the wood is very beautiful in summer. I might pick a mushroom if I see it. My Bill particularly fancies a mushroom."

"Ah," he said, apparently happy with this. "Look for the bloody beefsteak," he said. "Do you know it?"

"No. Sounds perfectly awful."

"None better, ma'am. Vast great thing, grows on the sides of oaks, the older the more succulent. You cut it and it bleeds, believe it or not. Fry it in butter, and you'll have something, you and Bill. For your own good, though, turn around and return after an hour's walking. You'll have seen what there is to see, and you'll be safe from the men who frequent Shade House – smugglers and pirates, the lot of them."

"I thank you for your concern, sir."

"Bob Mayhew, at your service." He took the pipe out of his mouth and tipped his hat.

"Harriet Laswell, at yours. People have called me *Mother* Laswell this last age. I'm pleased to meet you."

He nodded at her. "Easy enough to follow the stream, Mother. I've done it many a time. There's trout in the deeper pools that'll take a fly in the early morning."

"I'll just be on my way, then," she said. "It's good to have met you." He nodded again, and she left him to his work, setting out across the lawn again and into the shadow of the wood.

The path along the stream was covered with grass and moss, for the most part, although it was sometimes rocky, and now and then she had to push her way past encroaching bushes. She covered ground at a good pace despite that, however, and there was enough shade so that the warmth would have been pleasant enough, had she not been in such a hurry. She cast her mind roundabout her, opening it up to the chance that she might sense remnants of Bill's having passed this way, but nothing came to her except for a tolerably lonesome feeling.

Several hundred yards along the brook, she saw what appeared to be brickwork off through the trees – almost certainly old limekilns, apparently falling down, their arches half-hidden by willow and hazel. There was something both mysterious and morbid about the ruins, abandoned for so many years and now being reclaimed by the undergrowth. She walked toward them, looking for the tunnel mouth that Bill had told her about. There was a muddy, low area in front of the kilns, and she stopped before it, not wanting to foul her shoes merely out of curiosity. She saw, however, that someone had, for there was a line of footprints, half full of water, which led away into the midst of the kilns and brush. There was a patch of darkness beyond, perhaps the tunnel, perhaps dense shadow. She was quite certain that the footprints were Bill's, having seen their muddy image on the kitchen floor often enough at Hereafter Farm, and she suddenly wished that he hadn't gone alone into the tunnel, if in fact he had.

She hastened back to the path and set out again. She had a distinct presentiment of danger now, or if not danger, something amiss, something troubled, and she made an effort to clear her mind in order to let particulars into it, and although nothing more suggested itself, the presentiment didn't fade. She was aware that the sun was lower in the sky, and wondered how long she'd been afoot. She had no idea of turning back until she had reason to, but she didn't want to rush headlong into any foolishness, either. The path crossed the brook – not much of a ford, just a half dozen barely submerged stones. Immediately she slipped from one of them and plunged in with both feet, calf-deep. She slogged to the shore and went on, thinking that the cold water felt good on her tired feet, which were growing painful again. Bill had been right to leave her behind, she thought, because this trek would just about cripple her if she didn't turn back soon. But she was right in her way, too, and she was determined to go on. She listened hard for sounds besides her own footfalls, but heard only the splash of water, the calls of birds, and the wind sighing in the trees.

Very soon she stopped again. The presentiment had returned, doubly strong – troubling enough for her to move quickly off the path in order to hide behind a particularly broad trunk. Within moments a small boy appeared, hurrying along and looking back down the path. It scarcely seemed possible, but it was the boy Eddie. She called his name and stepped out from behind her tree, hoping that he would recognize her from their brief acquaintance in the alley last night. He stood stock-still and stared at her as she approached him. He had a wild look about him, and seemed ready to bolt, but he didn't. He took her hand right enough when she offered it, and she patted his head and hugged him to her. He sobbed once or twice, holding onto her dress, and then hiccupped and fell silent, looking back again, evident fear in his eyes.

"Are they following you?" she asked.

He shook his head, as if he didn't know, and she realized that it didn't matter. There wasn't a moment to lose if she wanted to gain something from her strange odyssey. She set off toward Cliffe Village again. She hadn't gone out looking for Eddie, but by the grace of God she had found him, and she wasn't going to let him slip away, not again. Then she thought of Bill and misgivings flooded in upon her. He was still out there somewhere – at the inn, wandering through the tunnels, perhaps injured. What would he say to her, though? He wouldn't risk the boy's life, not for a moment.

"If you weren't such a big lad, I'd carry you," she said. "Can you keep up?"

"I lost Finn," he told her. "The man chased us, and I ran."

"Lord protect us," she said under her breath, and then aloud she asked, "Did you see my Bill, Eddie? A tall, thin man, with hair like in a windstorm?"

"He was shot with a gun," Eddie said. "In the room where they do bad things."

She nearly fell, but caught herself and took in a deep breath, resisting the urge simply to sit down on the path. She found herself weeping silently, but she compelled herself to move on. Whatever else might have happened, she could have this small success; she would return Eddie to his mother and put an end to the woman's travails; her own were apparently endless.

On they went at an even pace, her mind spinning, until she recognized suddenly where they had got to, much more quickly than she would have thought possible. The limekilns lay away to their left. She could see the brick through the trees, but she didn't pay any of it more than a glance. She hadn't liked the idea of the tunnel from the start, and now that it was the bane of poor Bill Kraken, the most selfless man she had ever known, a man whom she had scorned, to her everlasting shame and regret…

She kicked something, and a stabbing pain lanced through her toe. She stopped and looked down, seeing that a bloody pistol lay on the path. It had been hidden in a weedy clump, where it had been dropped, but now it was shifted into plain sight, the barrel pointing like a compass needle up the path. She stared at it, unbelieving at first. It was Bill's pistol. She had seen it clearly at the Chalk Horse when he had gone out. The blood on it was fresh, bright red in the ray of filtered sunlight. Had it been there earlier? She swept it into the brook with the side of her foot, where it sank into a deep pool, glinting in the sunshine atop the dead leaves on the bottom. She grasped Eddie's hand again and hurried forward, the rectory coming into view far ahead. The way opened up, the lawn with its sheep…

Bob Mayhew was crouched beside his wagon, bent over the body of a man. She began to run in earnest, full of dread and hope, dragging Eddie along, knowing without any doubt that it was Bill who lay there.

"He come this far and pitched over," Mayhew said, "just

this past instant. I had my tools in the cart, and was set to leave, when I heard something behind me and I turned."

"He's my Bill," Mother Laswell said.

Mayhew looked at her, not quite comprehending.

"It wasn't the truth I told you," she said hurriedly, her hand to her forehead. "I wasn't looking for mushrooms. I was looking for two people, and I've found them both." She heaved a great sob now, which had come unbidden into her throat, and then shook her head to clear the emotions out of it. There was no time for sentiment.

"Better found than lost," Mayhew said. "But he's bled himself nearly white. We'll put him in the wagon and be off. There's a surgeon in the village, a good man. Saved my horse once, which was as good as dead."

"There's comfort in that," she said, and together they lifted Kraken onto the bed of the wagon, dragging and sliding him until he was entirely in. He muttered something, but Mother Laswell didn't catch what he said, and there was no time for conversation. She rinsed the gore from her hands in the stream water, and then, with Eddie between them on the rough wooden seat, Mayhew tossed the reins, and the horse set out at a trot. Soon they were in the village, the station and the bookman passing on the left and the Chalk Horse on the right. She would have to return *Lois the Witch*, before they set out, and she realized that she was already thinking of Hereafter Farm, hope having re-entered her being. There was fear in her, too, as she looked at Bill, pale and bloody, lying on his back, but she pushed the fear away, having had enough of it to last her for the rest of her life.

Mayhew drew up before a white cottage with a sign out front of a snake climbing a pole. He leapt down and hurried inside, and moments later he returned followed by a man in a stained white coat who was apparently a doctor. He bent over Kraken, felt his neck and wrist, and bade Mayhew to fetch Johnson from the smithy next door.

"Can you save him, Doctor?" Mother Laswell asked, holding onto Eddie, who was asleep now, and resting heavily against her.

"We'll see, ma'am," the doctor said. "He's bled some, but..."

The blacksmith arrived along with Mayhew, and together the three men plucked Kraken from the bed of the wagon and carried him inside the cottage, leaving Mother Laswell and Eddie alone. She sat for awhile in silence, letting the boy sleep, considering the strange way of things – her defeat yesterday when she had faced down Narbondo, her ignominious capture on the rope bridge in Spitalfields, and the elation she had felt when she realized that it was Bill Kraken who had come out of the night to fight Lord Moorgate and to save her from her otherwise inevitable fate. And now here she sat, having found a lost boy, her journey nearly at an end. She prayed that God would see fit to spare Bill, and anticipated bringing him home. *Yes*, she thought. They would return to Hereafter Farm as soon as ever they could. Bill would pull through. She was certain of it. Bill Kraken wasn't meant to die, not now, not after all this.

She saw a wagon rattling toward them from up the street – a wagon she knew. For a moment she was baffled, but then she saw with immense happiness that Simonides was holding the reins, a dark-haired woman sitting tall and straight on the seat beside him: Alice, of course! She had come at last. Simonides saw Mother Laswell and reined in the horses. Alice caught sight of Eddie and let out a small shriek, and then there was a great commotion, and Mother Laswell stood on the walkway that led into the doctor's quarters and watched the reuniting of mother and son.

"My race is run," Mother Laswell said to Alice. They sat in the inn parlor, drinking a glass of port, waiting for word of Bill. Eddie was fast asleep on a settee, dead tired and having consumed the better part of a meat pie with the avidity of a glutton. "I'm bound for Hereafter Farm, with Bill beside me, God willing. What will you do?"

"I'll take my son home," Alice said, "and pray for the safe return of my husband. Langdon told me something of your travails, your... search for your own son."

Mother Laswell nodded. "That's how I saw it for many and many a year, but this morning my mind changed. I woke up to a revelation. Since my boy died I've been searching for I don't know what – solace, no doubt, answers to questions I couldn't put into words. We both of us have something in common: we've both been searching, and we've both come to an end of it. I'm letting go of the past and setting my sights on the future, God willing that I've got Bill to spend it with."

Alice nodded. "I thank you for what you and Bill have done for Eddie. If there's any way to repay you, I'd do it willingly. I'm in your debt."

"Let's not speak of debt, ma'am. I'll ask this, however: when the Professor wins through, if he brings my Edward's remains home to Aylesford, you can ask him to undo the foul thing that my husband did so many years ago. That's all I ask."

The inn door opened and Mayhew walked in, his cap in his hands. "The doctor's sewed your Bill up. It was nip and tuck, and he's still precarious, but the bleeding's stopped, and the ball, which was beside the lung, is out now."

Mother Laswell wept, and Alice put her arm around her shoulders and waited her out.

THIRTY-SIX
THE BURNING

St. Ives stood looking at the dead man, at the bloody remnants of him, the shotgun blast ringing in his ears. There was a shocked silence among his companions. Finn had recovered from his exertions, but was looking away into the trees now, as if lost in thought. Uncle Gilbert stared at the fallen man, at what was left of his face, clearly surprised and aghast at the butchery that his weapon had wrought. St. Ives guessed that Gilbert hadn't meant to fire it, that the weapon had surprised him. If that was so, then it might have been any of them that lay dead on the ground – something that a man like Gilbert Frobisher would have a difficult time sorting out. A small gust of wind picked up dry leaves that went skittering away down the path, a reminder that the world was still turning.

"Leave some of these vermin for the rest of us, Uncle," Tubby said, attempting levity, but his uncle seemed shattered and simply worn out, and Tubby helped him to sit down on a fallen tree, where Gilbert mopped his face with a kerchief and shook his head.

Doyle stepped to his side, peering first into one eye

and then into the other and then feeling his pulse. "You've had a shock, sir," he said. "As a medical doctor I advise you to return to your camp. I tell you candidly to keep it in your mind that you stopped a man who was intent upon murdering a boy."

Gilbert nodded, although his face revealed no alteration.

"This was one of the two from out of the sewer near Blackfriars Bridge this morning," Hasbro said to St. Ives in a low voice. "I recognize his clothing."

"Pity he can't speak," St. Ives muttered. "We might have persuaded him to tell us something."

There were footsteps behind them now – old Hodgson, carrying his bird rifle and hurrying along. "I heard the report of a weapon," he said, "and I knew you weren't shooting partridge." Gilbert nodded at him without any enthusiasm, and Hodgson looked at the dead body and recoiled.

"Here's luck," said Doyle. "The two of you can go back together. A good bottle of wine will set you up again directly, Mr. Frobisher. Whisky might be more to the point."

"Just so," said Hodgson, evidently having come to an understanding of things. "And we've cataloguing to attend to. Buck up, old boy."

Tubby grasped the dead man by his ankles now and dragged him away, into the wood. He returned after a few minutes, dusting his hands. "I predict great celebration among the local vultures," he said.

"*Buteo buteo*," Gilbert muttered, stroking his chin now, his gaze unfocused.

Finn stepped across and put his hand on the old man's shoulder. "I'd like to thank you, sir," he said. "He meant to murder me, and worse, if you take my meaning. He swore to it, when he caught up with me back in the wood, and he would have had me, too, for I was worn out from running. You put an end to a right villain, sir. His name was the Crumpet, and he's had his hand in miseries of all variety. I learned just yesterday that he took a dull-witted boy named Spry Jack out of Billingsgate Market, and the boy never came back. All what he done with him, no one knows, nor wants to, but the Crumpet was a black-hearted devil, sir, and no mistake."

"I can vouch for it," St. Ives said. "He exploded an infernal device in London early this morning to our certain knowledge. Blew a hole in the wall of the Fleet River, quite likely murdering people in Smithfield. He attempted to murder *me* some weeks back after he blew up the palm house at the Bayswater Club and killed poor Shorter, the botanist. The world's a better place now that he's gone from it, and Narbondo has lost a lieutenant."

"Not *Jensen* Shorter of the Horticultural Society?" Gilbert asked. "We botanized together years ago. He was a great man for the lichens."

"That he was," St. Ives said. "You've avenged Shorter's murder into the bargain."

Gilbert shook his head sadly, the news of Shorter's death adding weight to his unhappiness, although it also added something like anger, which improved his demeanor, for there was less self-revulsion in it now. He looked at Finn and said, "We haven't met, young man. Gilbert Frobisher, at your service. I thank you for your kindness."

"This is Finn Conrad, Uncle," Tubby told him, "one of

the most sensible coves I know. He's got a good head on him, and is honest and brave to a fault."

"Is that so?" Gilbert said. "Well met, then. I'm happy to have done you a service, although I'll admit that it was rather abrupt."

"We'll just go along back, then," Hodgson said to Gilbert, taking him by the arm. "Doctor's orders, old man."

Gilbert arose, and without a word handed his shotgun and a pouch of shells to Tubby, who took the lot of it.

"You go with them, Finn," St. Ives said. "You've done your part and more."

"Pardon me, sir, but I have not," Finn said to him. "I know the trail where Eddie ran off, and I've been inside the inn and into the Doctor's murder room, where there's the tunnel door. You'll need me alongside you."

"I can't persuade you to take a rest?" St. Ives asked, knowing that he was defeated.

"No, sir, you cannot."

"So be it," St. Ives said, knowing from experience that Finn rarely said anything that he didn't mean. Unless he was tied into a chair, he would be commanded by his conscience.

"And I wanted to tell you about Eddie, sir," Finn said. "When the Crumpet came for me in the wood, Eddie was already escaped, far down the path and out of sight. But he came back, Eddie did, to try to save me from the Crumpet. He had a branch off a tree, big as he was, and he beat the Crumpet with it. It would have done your heart good, sir, to see it. He ran off then, like I told him to, and I struck the Crumpet with a big stone to distract him and to give me a chance to run off myself. The Crumpet followed me, thank

God, and not Eddie, but he was far enough behind so that I ran clear to this spot, where I found you. I'll never forget Eddie coming on with that branch, sir, to beat the Crumpet. Ever. Not as long as I live."

Finn stared at St. Ives for a moment, his chest heaving with the emotion of telling the story, but he turned away when he saw that St. Ives was weeping openly.

They set out again, the path leading back to the edge of the bay and around the swerve of the shore. Finn told them of the mill and the charcoal, of Narbondo eating it for breakfast, of Lord Moorgate and the woman named Helen, of George's kindness and his death at the hands of McFee and the dwarf Sneed, and of Bill Kraken's surprise appearance from the tunnel, leading to Finn's escape with Eddie. St. Ives was amazed, although he listened to all of it with growing unease: Kraken shot, but perhaps still alive, God save him, and Eddie alone in the wood with the big pirate abroad.

That Narbondo seemed to have anticipated Kraken's appearance was unsettling. The man was uncannily prescient. And the death of George struck him as particularly unfortunate – unfair, if there were any fairness in the world, which perhaps there was not. George had tried to redeem himself and was murdered for it. Certainly there was a lesson to be learned there, although it was an ugly one. He had brought violence down upon himself, but perhaps he had found an element of grace and an easier conscience in the end.

Perhaps they'd all of them find just deserts in the hereafter. At present, however, there was only the doing of things. St. Ives saw the inn through the trees now, the moment that Finn pointed it out. He heard nothing at all, however, no sounds of men at work, certainly not any sign of the industry that they'd viewed from the airship, only the cries of the gulls out over the bay.

From the old boathouse hidden in the trees a quarter mile away, there was a clear view of the path along the edge of the bay, which was nothing more than the low tide line, dried out in the sun. It was shrinking, however, with the incoming tide. Through his telescope, Narbondo watched the five men moving along the water's edge. The vile boy was alive, which meant that the Crumpet hadn't caught him, despite his spirited chase along the shore not thirty minutes past. The single gunshot that had sounded had quite possibly ended the Crumpet's career in mid-stride, which was not entirely an unfortunate thing, from Narbondo's point of view, since the Crumpet's depredations had begun to lead the man into stupidities. He had been amusing in his time, but if his time had passed, then so be it.

Narbondo saw that the fat man was armed. St. Ives and his factotum would no doubt possess the pistols that they had had with them last night. They were meddlesome men, and dangerous; he would give them that. He had underestimated St. Ives before, but this time St. Ives had underestimated Narbondo. It would be amusing to destroy St. Ives's airship as a parting gesture; it was a pity that they hadn't the time.

He nodded to McFee, who fired the boiler, and a short time later the very serviceable engine developed the pressure needed to propel the freshly painted launch out onto Egypt Bay. The casks of coal dust were lashed tightly together in the stern and covered with canvas, and the craft was full of men who would do what was asked of them if they were well paid. George, alas, had been a rare exception to the rule. If Narbondo was a man of sentiment, he might actually have had a fondness for George, but he had been exclusively fond of George's many talents, which the man had thrown away due to that feebleness of the mind known as kindness.

The narrow inlet of the bay lay dead ahead, the tide surging through it. He looked back across the expanse of water toward the aptly named Shade House, where he saw smoke rising above the trees. Of course. St. Ives and his cronies had burned the place. It was a futile gesture, mere anger at having once again come too late to the fair. The launch crossed into the moving water of the Thames now, and the narrow mouth of Egypt Bay closed behind them.

It was St. Ives and Tubby who entered the cellar room through the trapdoor in the cottage floor, Tubby lighting the Argand lamp in order to brighten the dim room. St. Ives saw the body lying on the table, the open door into a tunnel at their left, another door, this one shut, at their right, a barred window beside it through which the wind blew, carrying on it the smell of pond water and heather.

"Good Christ," Tubby said, looking at the man, who lay on his back on the table, strapped down with leather-covered chains across his chest and ankles, his dead eyes staring at the ceiling. His silk top hat sat behind his head.

The slit in his neck appeared to be a second gaping mouth, his chin and chest bathed in dried blood. His arms lay at his sides, although the hands had been severed at the wrists, and they gripped the chains that bound his chest. A calling card had been slid between two of the fingers. A prodigious quantity of blood had run out of his wrists as well as out of his throat. He had died there upon the table, St. Ives thought, his heart pumping out blood, although the wound in his neck had been delivered nearer to the door, where there was yet more blood on the stones of the floor. Someone had walked through it – a woman, clearly – who had gone out through the door. A bloody butcher's cleaver was fixed in the tabletop. Everything in the room argued that Narbondo practiced human vivisection. No mere anatomist needed to bind down a corpse, and certainly Narbondo was no surgeon. The debt St. Ives owed Finn and Bill Kraken couldn't be calculated.

Tubby plucked the calling card from the hand of the corpse and held it in the lamplight. "*Lord Moorgate*," he read aloud. "What does this mean, do you suppose?"

"A falling out, perhaps. Or perhaps that Narbondo has once again found it profitable to alter his plans."

St. Ives thought about this. Now that de Groot's identity was certain, it was clear that Lord Moorgate had purchased the miniaturized lamp from William Keeble. Moorgate was the Customer that George had mentioned, or had been, and no doubt about it. There was no evidence that Eddie had met with violence here. If Narbondo had carried out his threats to harm Eddie in order to profit from Moorgate, he wouldn't have scrupled to leave evidence of it for St. Ives to find. Indeed, it would give him great joy. Moorgate was dead and Eddie was not. Finn had saved Eddie's life. St. Ives scarcely allowed himself to believe it, but it seemed possible that Bill Kraken had done his part to turn the tide, that everything had changed when Bill had appeared and Finn and Eddie escaped into the wood.

"We're finished here," he said to Tubby.

"Almost," Tubby said, unscrewing the lid from the oil receptacle on top of the Argand lamp. He smelled it. "Whale oil, I believe," he said. And with that he upended it, pouring it over the edges of the table and onto the floor. "There lies a second lamp," he said, pointing at the Argand lamp that sat on the shelf above the glass boxes. "What do you make of that?" he asked.

St. Ives studied the broken glass box for a moment, having overlooked it in the darkness, and then having been distracted by the corpse. Now he noted the thin, bent pieces of lead came within the box, the shards of glass heaped on its floor, the bellows. It was dead clear what he was looking at: the results of a small coal dust explosion, contained within a double box, contrived, no doubt, to impress Moorgate, since Narbondo had proven the effectiveness of his methods often enough to be personally satisfied. Unless, of course, there was more to the trial than that. He studied the magnifying lens, pulling it down and peering through it. Gilbert had told them that a very moderate source of heat might set off the hovering dust. Greek fire might be necessary within the confines of the Fleet Sewer, but not at all necessary in a glass building. *Perhaps*, he thought, *it wasn't the explosion alone that was of interest…*

"Pity to waste this prime top hat," Tubby said picking it up from the table to inspect it.

On the table lay a human skull that had been hidden under the hat. St. Ives stepped across to look into it, relieved to see that it was from an adult human, not a child. It had been trepanned – a three-inch diameter hole. A litter of small screws lay within, along with bits of copper and silver, beneath which lay a small photographic plate, cracked in half. He drew out the pieces, fitted them together, and peered at it in front of the window. The image of a woman looked back at him, the details very finely rendered, the wisps of hair, her rather coarse complexion, her cheeks rouged – wet plate collodion photography, certainly. She had a look of suspicion on her face, heartlessness, perhaps, which showed through the rouge and powder and paint. Perhaps she was a Dean Street prostitute, St. Ives thought, an easy victim who would scarcely be missed were she to disappear.

"I take it this is one of the fabled skulls," Tubby said.

"Dismantled, yes. I believe that Narbondo called its ghost forth, if you'll allow me to use equally fabulous language, imprisoned it within the glass box, and blew it to pieces. I very much hope that its spirit was released from bondage, if that's the case."

"Sheer lunacy, it seems to me," Tubby said. "Do you have any objection to burning the entire lot of it?"

"None whatsoever," St. Ives said, dropping the pieces of photographic plate back into the skull.

Tubby laid the top hat back over it and emptied the

second receptacle, another quart of fresh oil over that which had by now soaked in.

St. Ives walked to the door and opened it, going out into the afternoon without a word. The place wanted badly to be burnt, and Lord Moorgate wouldn't object. Tubby followed him, smoke already swirling out through the window. They left the door standing open, found their companions, and followed Finn into the wood and along the creek. It came into St. Ives's mind to wonder how Lord Moorgate had found his way into the marsh. There had been no evidence of a coach, nor of a dead servant, had he brought one along. And the woman who had trodden through the blood? Was she the mysterious Helen? Clearly she had been safe from Narbondo's depredations. There were mysteries unsolved, he thought, but much had become clear to him.

Some distance up the path they found George's body in the brook, as Finn had described. There was no time to bury the man, and they could scarcely take the body along, for they were moving quickly now, bound for Cliffe Village, where Tubby, Jack, and Doyle would take the South Eastern Line back into London. In the village they could send someone to retrieve George's body. It was their good luck that the path followed the stream, for there were enough footprints in the soft soil to tell a coherent story, or at least parts of the story. The big pirate had murdered George, but hadn't gone on. The Crumpet's fate was well known to them. There were no other tracks save Eddie's for some little distance beyond where Finn and the Crumpet had turned back, but then Eddie had been met by someone coming along from the direction of the village – a woman. Who was she? Not the woman with the bloody shoes, surely. A stranger, then?

As for Narbondo, he had certainly removed himself and the coal to London. The emptiness of the inn, which had apparently been abandoned in haste, had spoken volumes. Finn had told them of a landau carriage in the barn, but the carriage and horses were gone. They had found a dead man in the tunnel. From the way the body lay, and from what Finn had told them, the man had almost certainly been shot while pursuing Kraken, which was heartening, unless there had been others involved in the pursuit who had been luckier than the dead man. Venturing deeper into the tunnel might have told the tale, but that wouldn't do. They hadn't the time. It was a difficult decision to make, since Bill might be lying in the darkness bleeding. The quicker they made their way into Cliffe Village, the quicker they could send someone into the tunnels to find him.

"Here now," said Jack. "Someone's joined. A man's boot-prints."

"A tall man," Doyle said, given the size. "And staggering, too. Wounded perhaps."

"Kraken!" St. Ives said, certain that he was right, yet worried that he would tempt fate with his certainty.

It took only a few minutes now to track him back to the tunnel in the limekilns, which settled the question. If these were the boot-prints of one of the pirates, the man would have gone off in the other direction, returning to the inn. Kraken was alive, or at least had been alive when he came out of the tunnel.

They hastened forward now, St. Ives calculating how

long it would take for him and Hasbro to return to Uncle Gilbert's bivouac for the airship. What they would find in London was uncertain. The only certainty was that speed was of the essence. If they were lucky, and Eddie were indeed safe, then they might do their part to stop the debacle at the cathedral. It suddenly seemed to St. Ives that his luck might perhaps be in again.

THIRTY-SEVEN

MRS. MARIGOLD

The very elegant coach, black lacquer and gold leaf, belonged to a Mrs. Marigold, whom Alice had met after Mother Laswell had gone off to the surgery to sit with Bill Kraken. The coach stood behind the inn, the horses apparently anxious to be away. Alice had put Eddie into the coach, the boy sleeping soundly again and likely to continue that way until they arrived in Aylesford. She stood in the sunshine, waiting for the driver and chatting with Mrs. Marigold, who was bound for Maidstone.

"Aylesford ain't out of the way at all, Mrs. St. Ives," the woman said to her. "Imagine having run into you by chance. My husband has spoken of Professor St. Ives on many occasions – very recently, I believe, when they were both in London, at the Bayswater Club. Mr. Marigold tried to interest him in becoming a member of the Piscatorial Society."

"Mr. Marigold is keen on fish, then?"

"Nearly a fanatic, you might say. Very keen on pike, although he's an enemy of the chub. He intends to rid the Medway of them, the poor dears. He's organized an anti-chub meeting today, in fact, in order to give them a general cursing." She smiled at Alice in a friendly way, and Alice smiled back. She rather liked the woman, although she had a hard appearance. In any event, Alice was happy not to spend the night in Cliffe Village waiting for the regular coach to appear in the morning.

"The chub has the habit of appearing where it's not wanted," Alice told her, "and of driving other species out."

"In that way it's not far removed from some women of my acquaintance. Here's my driver now."

An exceptionally small man with an immensely wrinkled, blackguardly face, wearing an old, high beaver hat, walked toward them. He touched his hat as he passed, and opened the door to the coach for them. Alice got in beside Eddie, Mrs. Marigold sitting across from them.

"Thank you Beaumont," Mrs. Marigold said, and the driver closed the door. Mrs. Marigold manipulated a locking mechanism, which clanked home solidly. "The door has the unfortunate habit of flying open, especially on an unpaved road," she said, "and Mr. Marigold understands the latch to be an effective deterrent to highwaymen, after that nasty incident at Bridgewood Gate."

"At Bridgewood Gate?" Alice said. "Not recently, I hope. I would have thought the roads safe enough from highwaymen these days."

"In the dark of night," Mrs. Marigold told her, smiling in an odd way, "there is no safe place."

The coach clattered out of the courtyard and away down the road at a good clip, running smoothly, the door making no effort to fly open. The two sat in silence for a time, Alice thinking of St. Ives, wondering where he was and wishing that she could tell him that Eddie was safe. It would be the one thing that he would pay a fortune to know. And she was horrified at the idea that Langdon might come to harm pointlessly, trying to save Eddie when he didn't want saving. She knew there was nothing further she could do about it, however. In Cliffe Village she had sent a telegraph message to Dorothy Owlesby. If Langdon were in London, Jack or Dorothy would surely find him and send him home. She set her mind to imagining their return to the farm – the look on Mrs. Langley's face.

Soon they were passing through Strood, where they would turn southeast toward Chatham, and then south again toward Aylesford and Maidstone. Alice had often enough come into Strood in the late summer with her Aunt Agatha to attend the Strood Fair, and they passed the site of the fair now, alongside the railway station, although it was too early yet for anything to be underway. She would bring Eddie and Cleo back in a month, she thought.

Eddie stirred now and sat up, rubbing his eyes and looking around, evidently having no idea where he was or how he had got there. He frowned, and then stared at Mrs. Marigold, who said, "Hello, child. I trust you slept well."

Eddie remained silent, looking around in a puzzled way. "Can you speak to Mrs. Marigold?" Alice asked him.

"This is the same coach," Eddie said, frowning now.

"The same as which, Eddie?" Alice asked, and in that moment Mrs. Marigold reached up and thumped twice on the ceiling for no conceivable reason except perhaps to signal the driver. They crossed an intersection, the signposts announcing a confluence of roads to Tonbridge, Gravesend,

Greenwich, Canterbury, and Maidstone. The driver whipped up the horses, and the coach sped up, rollicking along uphill now, along Watling Street, according to a street sign.

"I believe we've passed our turning," Alice said, feeling Eddie tug on her arm.

"I'm certain we haven't," Mrs. Marigold said to her evenly.

"I distinctly noted the signpost," Alice said. "We're on the Greenwich Road, toward London."

"Only temporarily, ma'am, I assure you."

"What is it, Eddie?" Alice asked.

"They *took* me in this coach," Eddie whispered.

"*Who* took you, dear? We're taking you now; is that what you mean?"

He shook his head, glancing furtively at Mrs. Marigold, then glancing away again. "The *Doctor*. They called him that."

"I see, dear," Alice said, suddenly deflated. In fact she *did* see, quite clearly now. She smiled woodenly at Mrs. Marigold, whoever she actually was, thinking to put her at ease, and then glanced at the door latch, the workings of which were not at all clear. She hadn't seen what the woman had done to lock it – a hidden mechanism, no doubt, designed to trap people inside.

Eddie gripped her arm tightly, and Alice looked up, still smiling. From out of her purse Mrs. Marigold had drawn a small but lethal-looking pistol. Her face was utterly blank now, and she held the pistol in her lap, aimed in Eddie's general direction. The coach was running downhill, into open country, the road to Maidstone and Aylesford falling away behind them.

* * *

In Cliffe Village, they found Bill Kraken easily enough. Everyone in the village knew that a man had been shot in the marsh, and that he lay close to death in the surgeon's house. The bullet had been awkwardly placed, very near his lung and an artery both, a miracle that Kraken had come all that way through the tunnels without bleeding to death. The doctor had dug it out, however, and it lay now on a metal tray next to the bed where Kraken lay sleeping. There was nothing to be done for him except to wait, which, Mother Laswell informed St. Ives, she was competent to do. She would wait forever, if that were what it took.

There was a train just leaving for London, and Doyle, Jack, Finn and Tubby hastened to catch it. Now that Eddie was safe, their duty was clear. St. Ives agreed that it was clear, at least for his friends. He was full of extreme joy to hear that Alice had taken Eddie home to Aylesford, and the idea of returning to London was very nearly unthinkable to him.

"They're long gone in the coach by now," Mother Laswell said. "No doubt already crossed over the Medway. You and Mr. Hasbro had best follow along, Professor. I intend to, as soon as Bill is fit to travel."

St. Ives nodded, once again thinking of his duties – to Alice and Eddie and Cleo on the one hand, and to the Crown and putting a stop to Narbondo on the other, if such a thing were possible. What had he told Alice? That he had no regard for the lunatic notion that a man might open a lane to the land of the dead. And yet even as he had said it,

401

he had known that he doubted himself: something in him, as irrational as it might be, had feared such things *might* be true. Denying it had merely been the simple thing to do under the circumstances. He and Alice had been caught up in a happy moment, after all, with a cheerful, carefree day laid out before them. One recollection led to another, and now he recalled his conversation with Alice on the night that he had returned home from London: *I don't want a dead husband,* she had told him, *and your children don't want a dead father. Can you grasp that?*

He had grasped it only superficially at the time, but he positively clung to it now as he weighed his duties, one against the other, wavering between them. There was the dirigible, of course, two hours away to the north. He and Hasbro would have to retrieve it. Hasbro had gone off to find a constable in order to tell him of the mysterious dead man they'd seen in the brook. Hasbro would go into London, he thought, and no doubt about it. Duty to the Crown would be paramount to all else, now that Eddie was safe.

St. Ives looked out of the window at the flower-strewn meadow that lay beyond the house, running downhill toward the edge of the wood. The sun shone on the flowers, a circus of yellow, purple and white blooms. He loved Alice with all his heart, and felt it keenly now. The poet Lovelace had recommended loving honor more, of course, but had been sent to Peterhouse Prison for his love of honor. Fear of dishonor, St. Ives thought, was often equally persuasive, although perhaps it was dishonorable to be persuaded by it.

"Hasbro and I had best be about our business," he said to Mother Laswell now. "Your predictions of an atrocity in

London are quite possibly coming to pass."

She nodded. "I've had dreams that revealed as much, Professor. I'll tell you, however, that I've changed my thinking in certain ways, now that Bill has made his feelings clear to me. The scales have fallen from my eyes, and I mean to see out my time on earth at Hereafter Farm. The shepherd is as vital as the soldier, Professor, and there's much to be said in favor of love."

"I believe that utterly," said St. Ives, "but I'll tell you plainly that our conversation two nights past has been very much on my mind. Last night I had a dream that seemed to me to be prophetic. I denied what it so clearly seemed to mean, but despite the denial I cannot rid myself of... a certain belief." He smiled at her, recalling her words to him when they sat around the seven-sided table in her astronomical seance parlor.

"We're masters of denial, Professor. I choose to deny nothing at present, but to act on my heart, since belief is tolerably multifarious. It seems to change with the seasons. But tell me, did your dream have to do with a door, sir? With a cave, perhaps, a cave of flames? Hell, to be more exacting, although surely that was something you would have inferred, something that you knew only through nameless dread?"

"Yes. That's it exactly."

"Then I can tell you that you and I have had the same dreams."

"A week ago that would have seemed to me to be mere coincidence."

"I'm not a great believer in coincidence," Mother Laswell said. "Bill found me on Hereafter Farm, adrift, you might say, and he found me in London last night in trouble once again. Both times he led me out of the desert. I won't deny him a third time, sir, and call it coincidence, but that's my business and not yours. I don't mean to know more than I know. I speak only for myself."

"Of course," St. Ives said.

"I, too, dreamt, this very afternoon. It was of the catastrophe. My son, Narbondo, if you will, inhabited a house on the Thames from which he projected Edward's image out over the city. The ground shook and buildings fell, as we hear will happen in end times. I can tell you that the house was shuttered, the windows and door arched, a bridge behind it spanning the river. I saw it clearly – a vision, I believe."

"Did you recognize the bridge, ma'am?" St. Ives asked, a query that wouldn't have found itself in his mouth only two days ago, when he had no faith in dreams.

She shook her head. "My knowledge of London doesn't stretch that far, I'm afraid."

The door opened at that juncture, and Hasbro stepped in. "I believe that if we make haste, sir, we can put down in Keeble's yard before the sun sets, although the wind is rising."

"Then we'd best be on our way."

"Will you do an old woman a kindness, Professor?" Mother Laswell asked him.

"Happily," he told her.

"If you find my son Edward's skull, and it's still… enlivened by that hellish machinery, will you dismantle it and bring it home to me? Don't for the love of God put yourself in any peril to do so. It's not worth injury, but I'd rest easier, as they say, if Edward were at rest."

"If ever I can," St. Ives said.

They met the doctor in the passage. "He's awake," the doctor said. "It's a miracle, to my mind, but he's asking after Mother Laswell. I hope that the shock of seeing her isn't too much for him."

"I believe it'll set him up like a tonic," St. Ives said, smiling broadly, and he and Hasbro looked in on Kraken, thanked him for his courage and loyalty, and went out into the late afternoon, striding toward the path through the wood and carrying Gilbert's shotgun in order to return it to him, the uneasy wind blowing in their faces until they were in the shelter of the trees.

THIRTY-EIGHT
CARRIED AWAY

"I t's blowing tolerably brisk," St. Ives said, when he and Hasbro had come within a quarter mile of the bivouac and could see the smoke from Madame Leseur's stove slanting out toward the Thames. They were in among the dunes, now, slowed by soft sand, and could occasionally gauge the breeze – which was out of the southwest – better than when they had been sheltered by trees. The sand wasn't flying yet, St. Ives noted, which was a positive sign.

"We'd best launch quickly if we launch at all," Hasbro said.

"Agreed. We'll ascend at once, to my mind, and not a moment to lose. In London we'll want the advantage of an aerial view. Hello, who the devil is this now…?"

Someone had appeared atop a distant dune and then disappeared again, certainly heading in their direction.

"I believe it to be Finn Conrad," Hasbro said.

"I'd say the same, except that the boy surely went into London with Jack, Tubby, and Doyle."

"That was his intention, certainly – or his orders, perhaps. I've often noted, however, that Finn has an independent spirit, which I quite admire."

"As do I," St. Ives said, "although I pray the boy survives it."

Finn appeared again, crossing another hill. When he saw the two of them he waved heartily and broke into a run. A minute later he rounded the edge of a dune and joined them, scarcely out of breath and quite cheerful, which St. Ives ascribed to Eddie's rescue.

"What a vast surprise it is to see you, Finn," St. Ives said as they went on their way again. "We rather thought you were bound for London."

"Yes, sir," Finn said. "I very nearly was, too. Uncle Gilbert sent me to tell you that he saw a steam launch put out from the far shore three hours back. It was Narbondo, and no doubt about it, seen clearly through the birding glasses. There was a right large crew, he said, and barrels stowed in the stern."

"Harry Merton's launch, no doubt," St. Ives said. "It'll be in London by now, carried up by the tide as well as by steam. If I had anticipated such a thing we could have had our companions mount a watch on Tower Bridge as soon as they arrived. The launch would have passed beneath, and they might have effected some sort of surprise on the docks."

"It rarely pays to look back," Hasbro said. "The only dividend is regret."

"That's the solemn truth," St. Ives said, "except perhaps in the curious case of Finn Conrad's not going into London."

"As for that," Finn said, "I took the liberty of changing the main plan when I learned that Jack was wary of my going into the sewers to thwart the pirates. I was to be stowed with Mrs. Owlesby and the Keebles until the trouble was past. It came into my mind as how there had better be three each of us, above ground and below, so to speak. There would be a sort of balance if I went along with the two of you. So I stepped off the train car before it was clear of the station, shouted my intentions at the open window, and set out along the path. I thought it best not to ask permission beforehand, for I had made up my mind and didn't want to seem to lack respect in the event that I was denied. That might be a sin. I know that, sir. But Square Davey used to tell me that without sin there can be no forgiveness, which is also a sin, and so it's much of a muchness, as the man said."

"I take your meaning," St. Ives said. "And it's just as well in any event. I quite agree with Jack. You're not going into the sewers, Finn. And as for coming along with Mr. Hasbro and I, it is quite impossible. The two of us make up the crew, do you see? The dirigible doesn't want the weight of a third hand, and there's certainly more danger in the air than beneath the streets of London."

"But I can't miss out on the fun, sir."

"You've saved Eddie's life, Finn, and I can scarcely repay you for that. But I won't put you in harm's way, not for King Solomon's treasure. If something were to happen to you... No," St. Ives said, shaking his head with utter finality, "the thing is impossible. If Gilbert Frobisher needs another hand in the bustard search, perhaps you can spend some idle time here – a sort of holiday, although Mrs. St. Ives would welcome you home, as would Cleo and Eddie."

Finn said nothing to this, and they tramped along in a heavy silence for the few minutes that it took to reach the camp. The dirigible rode at anchor as they had left it, but it shifted with the wind now, moving downward so that the mooring lines went slack, and then rising again on an updraft and straining against its tether like a living thing. From atop the sand hill that hid the ship from the bay, St. Ives saw a heavy line of purple clouds in the far distance – foul weather, without a doubt – and the air seemed to him to be laden with urgency, although it might as easily have been his mind.

Into one of the crates from Gleeson's Mercantile they loaded beakers of water and sandwiches and other delicacies from Uncle Gilbert's larder – things that could be eaten out of hand – hauling it straight down to the dirigible, where St. Ives ascended the ladder and climbed aboard. The deck beneath him shifted awkwardly on the billows of air, and he nearly pitched bodily through the open gate when he leaned out to pluck the crate from Hasbro's shoulder.

"Cast her loose!" St. Ives shouted, and he sat in the pilot's chair and focused his mind on the wheel and vertical tiller, reviewing the many things he had discovered during their earlier flight. With the wind up as it was, he would have little room for error, or at least that's how he would play it, and he was happy that they had taken the time to describe the great circle when they were over London this morning. He knew something of the way the airship would sail with the wind in various quarters, and it seemed to him that if they sailed fairly close to the wind they might slant round into London with some success.

Finn, Uncle Gilbert, and Madame Leseur, who were waiting to help with the unmooring, stood at three of the corners, Barlow with his game leg and Mr. Hodgson at the fourth, holding tightly to the various mooring lines, with orders to drop them rather than to be lifted off the ground. Hasbro appeared and disappeared below, releasing the knots from the wooden stakes, which they would leave behind, since the stakes were easily replaceable and would do them precious little good in London. One more stake and Hasbro could leave the rest to Uncle Gilbert's party and ascend the ladder himself.

The wind gusted now, and the airship fell alarmingly, St. Ives fully expecting the gondola to smash down onto the sward. He saw that Madame Leseur had dropped her line and thrown herself out of the way in order to avoid being hit, and he heard a general shouting break out, although it wasn't sensible. The nose of the ship ascended sharply now, the gondola swinging on its pendulum. The mooring lines at the bow snapped tight and then jerked loose with an audible twang. The gondola rose skyward, almost certainly unmoored. St. Ives heard incoherent shouting again, and he looked down through the open window beside him, where Madame Leseur sat in the grassy sand, Uncle Gilbert standing beside her, both of them pointing upward in amazement. He couldn't see Hasbro at all.

The ship was clearly unmoored, the wind blowing it out toward the Thames. St. Ives pushed down on the tiller, trying to land the craft along the shore of the bay, and he managed to turn into the wind enough to see the dunes receding behind him. His friends appeared to be quite small now, the lot of them looking upward, Madame Leseur and Hodgson helping Gilbert to his feet, Hasbro sprinting along in the wake of the ship, but powerless to do anything to stop it. There was no sign of Finn Conrad, and then St. Ives couldn't see them at all as the airship turned away in a gust of wind. He was helpless before the weather, aloft and alone and damn-all he could do about it.

The craft reacted strangely, dragged down at the stern, it seemed to St. Ives, but there was nothing to be done save to establish control over it. The gate swung closed on its hinge, but failed to latch, and then swung open hard again as the ship listed to port, tearing itself straight off the hinges and disappearing. St. Ives fervently hoped that it wasn't a sign of things to come, the ship falling apart piecemeal. Launching the airship had been a mistake, perhaps his last mistake. Already the encampment was some distance behind him, and it was clear that there was no going back. He thought of the obvious problem of landing and mooring the craft, wherever he ended up. The airship was pointed northwest now, and was straining against the wheel as St. Ives tried to force it farther around into the west.

He saw the Thames below, the ships and boats plying up and down in the dusk. There were stars visible on the western horizon, and the air was cool, with night coming on. The clouds he had seen from the dune were closer, the wind blowing them toward London, or so it seemed. He looked back toward the port side of the gondola to get a bearing along the shore of Egypt Bay before night hid it from him, but what he saw utterly baffled him. Finn Conrad stood in the open doorway, gripping the stanchions on either side, his hair blown back on his head. He nodded briskly and then turned to haul in the ladder.

"I grabbed hold of the ladder, sir," he said, catching his breath as he took the seat that Hasbro had occupied on the trip out. "I couldn't hold her back, though, and in a nonce I was swept aloft and too high to drop. Mr. Hasbro was holding onto one of the lines and dragging along the dunes, but the two of us didn't make an anchor, and he dropped off."

"Not from a height?"

"Not much of a one. He got up again, anyway, and for a moment I thought he would try to catch up to us, but it was no go."

"And you climbed the ladder when the ship was rising?" St. Ives said incredulously.

"No more trouble than standing atop a moving horse, sir. Less so, with my hands to grip. Can we make our way back to camp, then?"

"No, we cannot," St. Ives said. "Not in this wind."

"But what of Mr. Hasbro?"

"He must find his own way into London, which should be no great thing. It's the two of us that will be hard pressed to get there in time to be of use. Take a look through that lens there and try the controls of the telescope, Finn. It'll move opposite what seems right, but you'll see the way of it soon enough. We'll need to know where we are if we're to find our way. I'm damned glad to see you, I can tell you that."

Finn smiled at him, looking around the gondola now and nodding his head, as if he were happy with what he saw.

St. Ives realized that he himself meant what he said – heartily so. He had badly wanted a navigator, and now he had one. There was a look of profound joy on Finn's face, too, as he looked out over the patchwork of fields and meadows north of the river, still visible in the waning light, and it seemed to St. Ives that the boy's evident joy was worth a stack of ten-pound notes.

The Thames itself was some distance behind them now, a narrow black ribbon dotted with tiny, moving lights, and although they were making some headway, it wasn't enough. In the west lay the burnished gold remnants of the sunset above the Dover Strait. The sky, intensely purple overhead and deepening to black in the east, was already coming out in stars, the moon up, the evening having passed away in what seemed like minutes. God knows where they'd find themselves if they didn't soon put down in a cow pasture and abandon the airship – on the moon itself. St. Ives considered the possibility that the winds might diminish, or perhaps blow in some contrary direction at a higher altitude – something that would be useful to discover soon. He drew back on the tiller, and the airship canted upward, still drifting inexorably north. Eddie was safe, he told himself. His own fate, and that of Finn Conrad, must be given over to the eccentricities of moving air.

Alice watched the pistol uneasily as they covered the miles into London. She had no doubt that the woman would use the weapon if she were pressed, but probably not otherwise. Why Narbondo had set up this ruse was unclear, but certainly not simply to murder them in a moving coach. If murder were his goal, he would bring it about himself in some more loathsome and picturesque way.

"Mrs. Marigold," Alice said after half an hour of silence, "perhaps you would agree to point the pistol at the floor if I give you my assurance that we'll cooperate fully. We seem to have no choice in the matter, after all."

"My name is not in fact Marigold," the woman told her, "as you well know. And your assurances are worth nothing to me."

"You were *much* more pleasant when you *were* Mrs. Marigold. You could choose to be Mrs. Marigold again, you know, and improve the general condition of the world."

"The world can go to the devil, as can you. You will call me Helen."

"As you say," Alice said to her. Best to keep the peace, after all, what there was of it.

They traveled in silence again, the coach passing through Plumstead now and into Woolwich – familiar territory to Alice, for she had lived here as a girl – and she pointed out to Eddie the gate of the Royal Arsenal, where her father had worked as a mechanical engineer. He had taught her to hunt and shoot in the Plumstead Marshes, and her Aunt Agatha had taught her to fish in the ponds there and along the banks of the Thames. She had spent long afternoons tramping through Abbey Wood, often alone, carrying a novel or a book of poetry, and could recall the heavy scent of wildflowers on the spring air and the shocking explosions when cannon were tested at the arsenal – something that she had never quite got used to. Eddie listened to her attentively as they rattled through Greenwich and on into London, the road rolling up behind them, the stubborn Helen having nothing at all to say.

By now darkness had fallen, but the City of London was well lit with gas lamps, and Alice looked roundabout attentively, searching out street names, trying to get a sense of just where they were. What good it would do her she couldn't say, but surely it was better than not knowing.

The coach turned north, caught up in a crowd of pedestrians, omnibuses, carts, and wagons, all of which crossed the very beautiful Blackfriars Bridge in a great mass. Beyond it, rising skyward, its glass panels reflecting gas lamps and the shadowy movement of the city roundabout it, stood the newly built Cathedral of the Oxford Martyrs, which Alice pointed out to Eddie, although very shortly they lost sight of it when the coach turned up the carriageway along the Victoria Embankment.

Almost at once they drove through the gates of a dark courtyard at the rear of an equally dark, shuttered house of three stories, which appeared to be very old, a relic of London's past. The gates of the courtyard shut behind them, the carriage drew to a stop, and there was the sound of the driver climbing down from his seat. The door opened – its locking mechanism clearly meant to keep people in and not out – and Alice and Eddie were ushered from within at gunpoint.

The driver rang a bell at the rear door of the house, and Alice could see now that lamps burned inside. There was an answering ring, and they entered, Helen peering around, as though she had never been there before. The house felt utterly abandoned, as if in fact no one had occupied it for an age, and had perhaps just arrived. The furniture was Jacobean – massive and dark, with enormous, deeply carved sideboards and cupboards and straight-backed chairs with turned posts, the seats flat, no doubt monstrously uncomfortable to sit in. Heavy curtains covered the windows, but here and there the curtains were not quite closed, and still no light shone through the glass, as if the ground floor windows were perhaps shuttered. There was little dust and no sign of cobwebs, the house having been cleaned in anticipation of someone's arrival perhaps, or it might have been maintained that way for two or three centuries. The Turkey carpets, equally old from the look of them, and very rich, were apparently unworn.

There was the sound of a door shutting behind her, and

Alice realized that she and Eddie were alone in the room, perhaps in the house, the driver and Helen having gone out again. She heard the tinkle of bells and the sound of the coach leaving the courtyard.

But now there were footsteps somewhere above, and then a door closed followed by more footsteps, perhaps someone descending a stairway. She looked around for a weapon of any sort, but saw nothing useful, the room cluttered with the heavy furniture but almost empty of objects that might be thrown or brandished or broken to produce a cutting edge. She cursed her unthinking hurry when the boy Simonides had come for her. In her excitement she had lost her mind. A clasp knife might be worth a fortune now. Helen hadn't thought to search her bag, but if she had she would have found nothing but a hairbrush and a dressing case...

Alice hurriedly opened her traveling bag now and removed the dressing case, groping in the bottom of it, her hand closing on a bit of felt in which were enclosed three decorative hatpins. She removed the longest of the three, which had a piece of ivory affixed to it, carved in the shape of an elephant – a solid weight that she could grip in her hand. She returned the dressing case to the bag, which she set on a chair just as a panel in the wall whispered open and Dr. Narbondo bent through it.

He smiled at her and bowed. "Welcome to my home," he said heartily. "Your stay in London promises to be brief, but eventful. I believe I can guarantee that."

* * *

"Upon my honor, I have only the faintest idea why this new cathedral was built on that piece of ground," Harry Merton told Jack Owlesby. "But then it's scarcely the sort of thing that would be brought to my attention."

Jack, Tubby and Arthur Doyle stood in Merton's workroom – not in the Thames-side shop where St. Ives and Hasbro had found him, but in Merton's second shop, open by appointment only. Doyle had picked the lock on the alley door when Merton hadn't responded to their persistent knocking. The long bench or table at which he worked was covered in heavy paper and littered with inkpots and canisters containing strong reductions of tea and coffee, squid and sea hare inks, green algae and emulsions of garden soil, and dozens of other strange dyes and tints. There were brushes and quill pens and pieces of sponge lying about – all in all the stock in trade of a very advanced forger. Whatever Merton had been working on he had hastily slipped into a drawer when they stepped into the shop.

"We suspect that the cathedral is built on hallowed ground of some sort," Doyle said, "or perhaps cursed ground that needs to be sanctified or cleansed."

"Quite possibly," said Merton.

"Quite possibly which?" Tubby asked.

"It's true that it's built over an ancient pagan cemetery, the most ancient of those in London."

"I believe that the cemetery in Smithfield is the most ancient of the four *Roman* cemeteries," Doyle said. "It dates to the fourth century, unless I'm mistaken."

"You're correct, sir, as far as it goes. But there's an even more ancient burial ground, to my certain knowledge, that lies below Carmelite Street, stretching beneath the Temple itself, which predates the Roman cemeteries. It was not only pagan but was pre-Christian and pre-Roman, lost and forgotten centuries before Joseph of Arimathea carried the Grail to Glastonbury. It's very deeply situated, I'm told, part of a lost city, or so they say. Its existence is largely unknown except to the... cognoscenti."

"And Harry Merton knows it!" said Tubby. "You amaze me, sir."

"Not at all," said Merton, smiling at the compliment. Then the smile was replaced by a frown. "I deny that I *know* it. Not in so many words. It's mere rumor, no more. There were certain objects alleged to have been taken from there that made their way to the British Museum when I was a very young man. I had recently been promoted, you see, to the position of Associate Purchaser of Antiquities, quite the youngest employee ever so honored. But of course I would have nothing to do with the objects in question. Robbing the dead is an infamous business. I deplore it."

"All of us do," said Jack. "What variety of object?"

"Carvings, sir. Of soapstone and ivory. Representations of the heads of devils or gods, I believe, which amounts to the same thing, to my mind. Nasty looking items. Grotesques. I recall that one was tentacled, with a diabolical human face, much elongated and with sharpened incisors. It was meant to suggest cannibalism, without a doubt."

"And these were dug out of graves?" Doyle asked.

"I'm sure I don't know. But I would guess that they were taken from crypts."

"Is it conceivable that Ignacio Narbondo would be

aware of these catacombs? He certainly wouldn't scruple to rob graves."

"I would be most remarkably surprised if he were not aware of them," Merton said, "given that they exist at all. It was his nefarious stepfather who attempted to persuade me to traffic in the diabolical carvings. Of course I sent the man away. Would Narbondo have learned his stepfather's secrets? Assuredly. Depend upon it."

A bell tolled the hour somewhere beyond the walls of the shop, and Merton removed his apron, folded it, and hung it on a peg. "That was the bell of St. Mary Abchurch," he said. "Remarkable tone and accuracy, gentlemen. Correct to the minute. It informs me that it's time for me to lay down my work if I desire peace with Mrs. Merton."

"We'll need a map before you go," Tubby said. "Do you have such a thing, Harry? Not a common ordnance map, but something more arcane?"

"I might," Merton said. "Although it comes at a price. And I warn you that it's monstrously dangerous ground. The catacombs and their environs lie far beneath the Fleet River in a land of perpetual night. The door to that world was shut many years ago, according to all sources, hence the value of these detestable objects. There were only those few, you see. As collectible items, there is perhaps nothing rarer on Earth."

"We have no idea of seeking out these catacombs," Jack said. "A reliable map of the several underground rivers and their tributaries and access ways will do nicely. We mean to scour the area, Mr. Merton, but only the more modern passages, in order to head off an enormity contemplated by Dr. Narbondo."

"The man is my bane, gentlemen, as I told Professor St. Ives quite recently. I warn you that you take him far too lightly. How do you know that you were not followed here tonight?"

"We *were* followed," Tubby said, "but we knocked the man on the head and pitched his body into the river. We're the bane of Dr. Narbondo, sir. He won't survive us. We mean to pull his nose for him." He took de Groot's purse from his coat now and dumped the contents among the pots and jars and brushes on Merton's workbench.

Merton looked at the money and shook his head, as if he were suddenly weary and defeated – particularly weary of money. "Because you three are *particular* friends," he said, sweeping the bills and coins into an open drawer beneath the desk, "I'll help you. I'm doomed as it is, perpetually hunted down and taken to task. It's my lot in life, I suppose, to be victimized by my friends and enemies both."

He opened one of a series of wide, shallow drawers now and withdrew a map, and it occurred to Jack that five pounds would have purchased it as easily as fifty, for there was another apparently identical map beneath it. But it was another man's money that they were paying with, which was spent far more easily than one's own. "Might we have two?" Jack asked. "You seem to have a plethora of them, and we've two friends who are equally in need."

Merton widened his eyes, shrugged, and drew a second map out of the drawer. They wished him a good night and went out carrying their rolled-up maps, bound for Jermyn Street, supper, and sleep. Tomorrow would arrive tolerably early.

* * *

"It must be very like heaven, sir," Finn said. He had abandoned the telescope and stood next to St. Ives, looking intently out of the window of the airship.

St. Ives marveled at the fact that the boy apparently had no fear, that he was filled with wonder instead; the beauty of what lay beyond the windows of the gondola pushing any darkness from his mind. He searched his own mind for fear, but didn't find it. Perhaps it, too, was banished by the utter peace and great purity roundabout them. Passing below was a school of very low-flying gray clouds like great whales, the edges silver in the light of the moon, which shone brightly overhead, the sky awash with stars. Far below lay more stars – the lights of a small city, seeming to wink in the darkness. The clean air smelled like the air on a Scottish hillside or on the edge of the ocean, laden with moisture, it seemed to St. Ives, and the world aloft was almost silent, just the thrum of the wind in the rigging. He looked at his watch: three o'clock in the morning. Finn had slept for a time, and they had eaten most of the food that Madame Leseur had put by. St. Ives would have paid a good deal for hot coffee, or cold coffee, for that matter, but they had been in far too much of a hurry to think of it.

He tried to determine just *which* illuminated city lay below. Oxford, perhaps. Reading if they were lucky. Certainly not Swindon, he thought. God help them if they were that far out. They had been blown many miles off course to the northwest in the first hours, leaving the lights of London far behind. Finally, out of desperation, he had risen to two thousand feet, according to the clever Cailletet altimeter that Keeble had installed – high enough so that the black expanse of the North Sea was visible in the east. The altimeter was a very new invention, however, untested for the most part. Keeble had warned him about rising too high, for there was some risk of blowing up the airship like a penny squib because of the pressure of the expanding hydrogen gas. How high was too high? Keeble couldn't say. There were too many variables, mostly untested. A "test," it seemed to St. Ives, might likely prove fatal, and he wished he had studied the science of the craft more thoroughly, although of course he hadn't known that he himself would be tested in such a hellfire hurry.

The experiment of seeking the higher altitude had succeeded, however, for he had found a contrary wind, and they had made a wide circuit to the west and south, the North Sea disappearing below the horizon. Although they could not be said to be on course quite yet, they were in a fair way to run even farther south and west, drop down to a more sensible altitude, and make another attempt at London with a more favorable wind behind them.

Finn returned to the telescope, looking toward the horizon, the clouds having passed away for the moment. "I see darkness, sir, due south by the compass. The sea again, I believe, with towns along it."

"The Channel, I'd warrant," St. Ives said. "Fifty miles away, given our altitude. Perhaps sixty. The lights of Brighton and Eastbourne." There was some fair chance, then, that the city below them had been Reading – a piece of luck if it were so. He depressed the tiller, and the balloon canted downward, St. Ives turning the wheel to port, watching the compass and feeling the wind. It would be a bad business to hurry it out of anxiety, only to be blown back to the west, and have to rise to the higher altitude again in order to take another run at it. Dawn was three hours away.

They descended through scattered clouds, the gondola bouncing and jigging erratically, and then abruptly they were caught by the wind off the Channel – the same that had blown them so far off course hours ago. But it was their ally now that they were far enough southward, and St. Ives carefully brought the airship around farther, contemplating a sensible course for London. The starry sky overhead seemed to him to be darkening by degrees, and very soon the stars ahead of them disappeared behind massed clouds. The storm he had seen from his dune beside Egypt Bay would soon be upon them, for they were heading straight into it with the wind nearly at their back.

Rain began to fall, although they were running before it, for the most part, and for a time it spattered against the rear windows, which were already closed. Soon, however, drops began to sail in through the front windows also, falling onto the balloon above and washing down the sides. St. Ives closed them with the hinged frames of glass, his mind revolving on the general subject of windows, on the more sensible ports and portholes – whether the window was the hiatus itself, or the wood-and-glass barrier that filled it. It was a question that seemed philosophical, and he was on the verge either of coming at it or falling asleep when he realized that his vision was obscured by the rainwater coursing down the glass. He could perhaps fly by the compass…

"Can you see anything telling?" he asked Finn, the telescope being fit quite sensibly with a hood.

"I believe I see London, sir, in the far distance, away off to the right, off to starboard, I mean. A vast field of lights, and the river, I believe, snaking through it."

St. Ives felt a monumental relief. Their success wasn't assured by any means, but by God they had managed a bit of smart navigation. Some few minutes after that thought had receded from his mind, he saw the first bolts of lightning descend from the clouds ahead of them.

FORTY

MORNING

"Who would have thought that there were so many costers selling pineapples?" Jack asked. He and Tubby were standing under an awning out of the rain. "And at this early hour of the morning. We've got to look into every cart, I suppose, although I'm worried that we're wasting our time. One of Narbondo's people might be setting up shop a few yards away as we speak."

"Not a waste of time at all," Tubby told him. "One can never eat enough pineapple. And as for these fiends being a few yards away or half a mile, there's nothing we can do about it but continue to search. Perhaps Hasbro and Doyle are having better luck." He shoved the last of the slice into his mouth and chewed it up. "Uncle Gilbert spent some time in the Sandwich Isles, do you know, and grew very fond of the pineapple. He taught me to eat them as a boy, fried up in cane sugar of an afternoon, and served with a tot of brandy poured over and set alight. Those are glorious memories, Jack." He wiped the juice from his face with a kerchief.

"I don't doubt it for an instant, but here's another of the damned barrows," Jack said, "just now turning into the alley ahead. Two men this time, and a headlamp on the front of the barrow."

"By God that's one of *Merton's* alleys," Tubby said, as the two of them set out, Tubby carrying the dark-lantern. "'Carmelite Culvert,' it's called on the map. Look to your weapon, Jack. It's a dead end ahead. They'll fight like rats."

Jack was carrying de Groot's tiny pistol in his pocket, but he had never shot the thing, had never shot a pistol at all, let alone at a man. He had thought there would be some comfort in carrying it, but at the moment he felt nothing of the sort. The alley was empty when they reached it. Halfway down stood a deep, foul-smelling alcove an inch-deep in standing water. Several feet into the alcove stood a low, iron door, heavy with rust, not just quite tight.

"They're in a hurry," Tubby whispered. "Too much of a hurry to bother shutting the door, the fools."

"They mean to come back out this same way, no doubt," Jack said. He peered into the passage beyond the door, immediately seeing the lantern moving along some distance down – two lanterns, he saw now, one carried in a man's hand and the other the headlamp on the front of the cart, considerably brighter and showing far down the steeply descending tunnel.

Tubby set out, Jack following, pulling the door nearly shut behind them. The brick tunnel was thankfully dry – perhaps an access to the Fleet Sewer – and the loud creaking of the cart emboldened them to move even more hastily. Tubby carried his blackthorn raised across his chest for a backhand blow.

They were upon them quickly, apparently unheard

until the last few steps. The man carrying the lantern turned toward them, his illuminated face bearing a puzzled look. He flung the lantern into Tubby's face out of sheer surprise, and Tubby knocked it aside with his left forearm, the lantern clattering against the bricks on the opposite wall. Tubby struck with the blackthorn in the same moment, knocking the man sideways as Jack leapt past him, pursuing the one who pushed the cart, who was trundling along ever more rapidly down the decline, some distance ahead.

The man stopped abruptly, gripping the handle of the cart with one hand and skidding along for a moment on the soles of his boots. As momentum carried Jack helplessly forward, he saw the pistol come out of the man's coat. There was the crack of the weapon firing as Jack threw himself down, realizing even as he did so that the man had missed the hasty shot, and tumbled forward into the man's legs, bringing him down. His assailant hit him awkwardly on the side of the head, bit him on the hand, and then sprang up and sprinted down the tunnel in pursuit of the runaway cart, which careened away, bouncing on the uneven brick of the floor.

Jack followed at a run. The cart's headlight showed a turning in the wall dead ahead of it. The right-hand corner of the cart struck the wall at the turning and the cart caromed off the brick. Immediately the front wheels caught against something unseen, and the cart overturned, its tin sides flying off and its contents tumbling. The man pursuing it, too close to it to stop, pitched bodily over the top and into the waters of the Fleet River along with a smoking kettle that instantly threw a blanket of roaring flame over the waters.

Jack reached the fallen cart seconds later, Tubby following behind him now. They saw Narbondo's man rise from the flood entirely aflame, some ten feet down the river, the horror visible on his burning face. He tore at his clothing, yanking off his flaming jacket, wading downriver through the flood, shrieking inhumanly. He stumbled and went under, but when he rose he was once again covered with the burning sludge, and in another moment he fell and disappeared for good, the river carrying away the body and the flames together.

Tubby and Jack made their way back up the tunnel, silenced by what they had witnessed. Halfway along they passed the other of Narbondo's people, who had been shot through the back. Jack realized that the man had caught the hastily shot bullet meant for him, and was startled by the sight of the body, unhappily imagining his own body lying on the bricks, the life leaked out of him.

They went on without speaking until, near the alley door, they discerned the dark mouth of another tunnel, which they hadn't seen earlier, so intent had they been on their immediate task. Vague noises sounded from somewhere deep within.

From the centermost of the arched windows on the third floor of the old house, Narbondo watched with great satisfaction as the storm moved in over London. The sky was black to the distant horizon, and lightning flickered from the clouds, too distant yet for the sound of thunder to reach him. It was perfectly droll that it had appeared on this very day – life spectacularly imitating art – and it would add monumental impetus to the chaos he intended to provide for the city's amusement. People were gathering in the streets for the ceremony, dressed in capes and hoods and carrying umbrellas, costermongers threading through them despite the weather, selling hot potatoes and pea-pods and pies. Narbondo had seen a pineapple cart move through half an hour ago, pushed by Sneed the Dwarf accompanied by McFee, the two of them disappearing into an alley that led to the river and to the iron door that opened onto the Fleet Sewer, disused since a century past, when the Fleet was first arched over with brick and mortar and hidden from the sun. In the cart were kegs of coal dust, with several more already delivered and waiting below, along with the bellows device consisting of several pneumatic tubes of great circumference, powered by the steam engine from Merton's very useful launch and cleverly cooled by water drawn from the Fleet itself. Very soon the black dust would fly up, and it would begin.

He considered the myriad of tunnels that led away from the walls of the Fleet and the other underground rivers – the turnings, the double-backs, the hidden doors and iron ladders that went ever downward into the Stygian darkness. He had traveled those tunnels the first time as a sixteen-year-old boy, carrying rush-and-paraffin torches and lucifer matches of his own inventing, which had ignited for no good reason, burning him badly. Even then white phosphorous was known as "the devil's element," and perhaps that explained his attraction to it. His stepfather had regaled him with the legend of the ancient, long-buried world far beneath the London Temple, with its rumored access under Carmelite Street, and two days later Narbondo had betrayed his stepfather to the authorities. He had been on hand for his stepfather's hanging, and had watched gleefully as he swung out over the crowd, his eyes and tongue protruding, his neck having failed to break due to the hangman's ineptness. Narbondo had sold the body to resurrection men, and his stepfather's skeleton no doubt lived on in an anatomical theater now, perhaps at a great university.

A light rain began to fall, umbrellas blooming below him like black flowers. The time was drawing near, and Narbondo turned away to inspect the rifle that leaned against its stand next to the window, and the small but very flammable bullets that lay waiting in their copper tray. He found that he was in a state of high anticipation, which he despised in himself as weak, and for a moment he was tempted toward a dose of laudanum, but he rejected the idea. If ever there was a time for his faculties to be sharply honed, it was today.

A bell at the rear door rang now – two rings, followed by a pause, and then a third. He stepped to the wall and tugged on the bell rope, hearing the faint sound of its chime. In a few moments Beaumont appeared at the door, his beaver hat in his hand, ushering in the very enterprising Helen and a man whom Narbondo knew to be connected to the War Office, a colonel, apparently, and the man Lord Moorgate had insisted on calling Guido Fox. Beaumont disappeared, leaving the door open.

"The second part of the money is paid," Helen said without preamble.

"And what of de Groot?" Narbondo asked her.

"De Groot has warned the Queen's Guard very convincingly that there's the threat of a Fenian atrocity at the Cathedral. She'll remain in Buckingham Palace, today, although the crowd in the street doesn't know that. The letter implicating Gladstone and the Home Rule plot has been delivered surreptitiously, again by de Groot, to the newspapers as well as to the Palace."

"*Splendid*," Narbondo said. "That should further Lord Moorgate's political career enormously. A bold stroke indeed. I envy the man his foresight."

"And this is Mr. Guido Fox, who has accepted the second sum. I've assured him that the third and final payment will be made whether the endeavor succeeds or fails."

"Mr. Fox," Narbondo said, bowing deeply, "I bid you welcome." He looked at the man's neat mustaches, his military bearing, the supercilious cast in his eye, and hated him immensely. He served a purpose, however, there was no gainsaying it, and would have to be humored, although he seemed to be in no mood to be humored.

"Who is *this*?" Fox asked Helen angrily, jerking his thumb in Narbondo's direction. "Where's Lord Moorgate?"

"My name is Gobeline, Mr. Fox," Narbondo told him. "Phestus Gobeline. I'm Lord Moorgate's associate."

"Be damned to you, then. My business is with Lord Moorgate."

"As is mine, sir. Lord Moorgate is on holiday in York. He saw fit to remain at some distance from the… entertainment."

Fox stared at him for a moment. "He's gone off and we're to be in the thick of it?"

"You were paid to be in the thick of it, sir, by Lord Moorgate." He turned to Helen and said, "It's time to fetch Mrs. St. Ives and the boy, Helen. Beaumont is preparing to take the lot of you across to the cathedral. Time is of the essence, my dear."

Helen nodded and went out without a word.

"I suppose it's all one to me that Moorgate's cut and run," Fox said. "I don't care for the man, only for his money." He drew a cheroot out of his pocket and lit it, drawing deeply on it and blowing out a cloud of smoke.

"In that we agree entirely," said Narbondo, stepping back a pace.

"My men are pretending to search the interior of the cathedral for the device," Fox said. "The opening is postponed. The cathedral doors are locked, of course, and will remain so. Six of my men, the four searching the cathedral and the guards at the doors, have been purchased."

"*Purchased!* How very well put. The word has a ring of permanence to it. Think of it. When we're done with our morning's work, you can set up your carriage and retire for good and all. Here's the way of it: a short time after the arrival of the woman and her son, my man Beaumont will alert you to the fact that the undertaking has been so far successful by playing upon the cathedral organ. You'll have five minutes then – more than enough time – to make your way into the passage with your men and descend to safety beneath the street. The woman Helen will no doubt be quite anxious to accompany you, although I would rather that she remain within the cathedral to stand guard over Mrs. St. Ives, a most tenacious and dangerous woman."

"I'm to maroon her in the cathedral?"

"You'll be doing both of us a service if you do, Mr. Fox. We must consider the possibility that she means to extort money out of either or both of us. It would be a simple matter to close the door behind you and leave her to her fate."

"Done," Fox said, shrugging.

"And one last thing, sir. If the attempt is for any reason unsuccessful, you will please to return the two women and the boy to me through the passage again? Helen, in that case, might suffer a fall down the very steep stairs, since we'll have no more need of her services."

"Certainly she might," Fox said, looking steadily at Narbondo. "Now I'll have my little say. I warn you that if for a moment I believe that *I'm* being deceived, I'll walk out through the door into the street and name you as the anarchist. Moorgate won't contradict me, and no one on Earth would believe the word of an ugly hunchback over Lord Moorgate's, with my solemn testimony into the bargain. Keep that in mind, sir, and pay me the rightful balance when the deed is done. We'll part square that way, and may we never meet again on Earth."

Narbondo smiled and bowed in acquiescence. The man, certainly, would make an entertaining corpse.

FORTY-ONE

THE CATHEDRAL OF THE OXFORD MARTYRS

Alice had prepared herself, knowing they would come for her and Eddie at nine o'clock, Narbondo having had no reason to lie about it last night, when he had shown them to their room. She had prepared Eddie, too, choosing her words carefully, only to discover that he was surprisingly game, although he was perfectly aware that he had been threatened with murder just yesterday by the very man in whose house they were now held prisoner. He told her about how Finn Conrad had stowed away on the coach, and how Finn had shattered the glass and come through the inn window to fetch him, and how he and Finn had escaped from the cellar and beaten the man named the Crumpet. "I hit him with a great branch," he said.

"*Good* for you," Alice told him, "although it was a dangerous thing to do when you had already run away."

"I *know*," Eddie said, doubly happy, it seemed. He was perhaps a bit too anxious to engage the enemy again, and Alice explained to him about the virtues of prudence and living to fight again another day. But he wanted to know what the difference was between fighting today or tomorrow,

435

which seemed much the same to him.

"Best not to fight at all, if there's a way to avoid it honorably," she said. That led to further questions and further answers, which couldn't be resolved, but which passed the time agreeably – better than letting one's mind run, certainly.

There was the sound of a key in the lock, but when the door swung open it wasn't Narbondo holding the key; it was Helen, the familiar pistol in her hand. She ushered them through the house, in which direction Alice couldn't say, until they crossed before a window that looked out onto the Cathedral of the Oxford Martyrs. In the street below was a milling crowd, and she wondered whether Helen would try to take her and Eddie in among them. That would be Alice's opportunity, surely.

But no such opportunity came. Beaumont met them on the first floor, where he stood alongside the paneled wall of a vast staircase. He pushed on the edge of a panel in the wall, and it sprang inward and slid past the adjacent panel, opening a passageway beneath the stairs. Inside, on a shelf, sat an oil lamp and a tray of matches. Beaumont lit the wick of the lamp, adjusted it, and said, "Watch your step now, ma'am. Hold onto the boy. This here is a steep go." He proceeded down a set of stairs with stone treads, followed by Alice and Eddie and then Helen. Alice counted the narrow steps – twenty-six before they arrived at a landing, where the stairs jogged to the left. Another dozen steps down, and they reached a level passage again, this time with a floor of packed dirt, the low roof shored up with oak boards and posts, the wood still fresh enough so that Alice could smell the cut ends. She wondered how far beneath the street they were – thirty feet, given the number of stairs? She heard the sound of what must be a steam engine nearby, working steadily, its sound muffled. Where it was located she couldn't say.

"Do you hear it, ma'am?" Beaumont asked, holding his lantern aloft, and glancing back at Alice. "That's the wind, you know."

"It sounds very much like an engine."

"That it does, ma'am, an engine to drive the wind through the organ. The pipes want wind, do you see? I'm to play the instrument today – a vast great organ with a bellows the size of a four-horse wagon and a wind system that no one would believe without they saw it. Driven by steam, it is. I played the organ as a lad, in the old church in Brighton. I was the bellows boy for a time when my father played. It was a blessing to hear him, ma'am. When he was jailed they took pity on me and gave me a chance at it. But it didn't last, as they say, for I was taken up for selling clothes to the dolly shops and never went back to the organ. These here bellows in the Martyrs is too much for a man to push, though – too much for a dozen men, so as I say they use the steam. It's me that'll play the instrument, though."

"In the cathedral?" Alice asked. "Today?"

"It's the ceremony today, ma'am, where we're a-going now, with the Queen and all. Do you know Bach?"

"A passing familiarity. You're to play Bach, then?"

"The 'Fugue in G-Minor' – what they call the 'Little Fugue.'"

They began to ascend along the tunnel, and shortly

came upon a stairway leading upward. Still holding Eddie's hand, Alice glanced behind her as they went up, seeing that Helen was still at her station directly behind. It occurred to her that she might wheel around and kick Helen downstairs, although certainly it was better to wait until they reached the top. Then she thought of Beaumont, who was evidently loyal to Narbondo, and saw that nothing would come from kicking Helen downstairs, aside, perhaps, from momentary satisfaction.

They reached the top now, where there was a landing that stood before a closed door, which Beaumont opened with a key. A room lay beyond, empty but for a wicker basket with a nondescript metal vase lying in it. The room was paneled from floor to ceiling, a large wooden box with no apparent function except as a sort of way station meant to disguise the door, which was utterly hidden within the paneled wall when Beaumont shut it. The sound of the steam engine was louder now.

Beaumont manipulated one of the panels in the opposite wall, and it slid open quietly. Alice wondered how many of the panels in the cathedral walls were secret doors, and how Narbondo, and hence Beaumont, had come to understand them so thoroughly. Narbondo had evidently been at work here for a very long time, although it scarcely seemed possible that he had worked in secret. And to what end?

They stepped through the opening, into the interior of the Cathedral of the Oxford Martyrs, Alice holding tightly to Eddie's hand. A passage lay to the left, but they turned away from it, out into the nave, which was vaulted with lacey white arches that seemed far too delicate to support the immensely high glass ceiling, the transparent walls soaring away on three sides. The altar stood some distance away, gold and white, stretching across the great, raised transept, a half dozen broad stairs across the front of it. The altar itself was built of massively heavy stone and was easily thirty feet long and eight wide, supported by a low marble wall with arches that called an aqueduct to mind. Great chandeliers that must hold a thousand candles, as yet unlit, hung on golden chains above it.

The pews stretched away in either direction, delicately built, white-painted iron with golden cushions. Alice looked up into the heavens through the clear ceiling where a picturesque mass of clouds moved beyond the rain-washed glass. She heard steps trailing away – Beaumont hurrying along the passageway, his beaver hat bobbing atop his head.

Their being here made not one bit of sense to her, nor did the subterranean tunnel that connected the cathedral to Narbondo's lair. Simply walking across the street would have saved fifteen minutes, which meant, of course, that they ought not to be here, nearly alone in the cathedral, the doors closed to everyone else and guarded. She saw two soldiers inside the cathedral, thirty yards away, apparently searching for something. One looked back at her, stared for a moment, and went about his business again, which was strange.

Despite the rain there were hundreds of people on the street, standing about, the mob stretching away toward the Embankment and Blackfriars Bridge. Behind her stood the solid, fourth wall of the cathedral, the framed, wooden panels painted white and decorated with gilt filigree, the entire thing a backdrop for an enormous pipe organ on a scale that she wouldn't have believed possible – Beaumont's instrument, or the voice of it. The thousands of golden pipes stretched away twenty and thirty feet overhead, higher, possibly, the largest of the pipes being of massive circumference, like gilded smokestacks. The organ itself was invisible, its steam engine only barely discernable now, something she felt rather than heard.

She saw then that the organ itself stood on a dais with a domed roof hung high on the wall. Six marble columns supported the roof. On the floor below stood an identical domed portico, supported by the same marble colonnade. Beaumont appeared, very small and distant upon the dais. He looked out over the cathedral, bowed to an imaginary audience, and sat on the bench. His beaver hat was settled over his ears, and was visible over the waist-high parapet behind him.

"You'll take a seat, if you please," Helen said, "in this row of pews, here on the end with the boy beside you." Helen sat down on the pew behind them, gesturing with the pistol for Alice to do what was asked of her.

"As you say," Alice said, sitting down next to Eddie. She saw in the south wall a vast window of stained glass, depicting the execution of the Martyrs in Smithfield. Alice couldn't remember their names, but one, she recalled, had been the Archbishop of Canterbury, very nearly a neighbor since they had moved to Aylesford, although a few centuries removed. She recalled reading that the window had been designed by Millais.

"Pray tell me why we're here, if you'd be so kind, Helen," Alice asked now, turning to look at her. "Something to do with chub, perhaps?" Helen held the pistol in her lap. She could raise it easily enough, of course, but she seemed to have lost interest in it, as if something were on her mind. Alice slipped the hatpin out of her sleeve and held it tightly, hidden by her hand and wrist.

"The Cathedral is opening today with great fanfare," Helen said. "I'm told that the Queen was to attend, her first public appearance since her unfortunate fall on the stairway at Windsor Palace."

"*Was* to attend?"

"There was word of a plot against her, unfortunately – the work of unhappy Fenian anarchists funded by Gladstone himself. Almost unbelievable, isn't it? The several soldiers that you see milling about have been searching for an infernal device, but they're apparently failing to find such a thing, although the doors will remain locked until it's quite safe for the crowds to be let in. They'll be wet as seals by then, poor hens. I for one don't believe that there's a respectable Fenian between here and Hampstead Heath, not on a day like today, with such appalling weather."

As she said this there was a bolt of lightning in the sky, illuminating the interior of the dim cathedral, followed ten seconds later by a distant clap of thunder.

"What if I were to call on one of the soldiers, for assistance, then?" Alice asked. "Surely you can't shoot all of us."

"He'll prove to be mute, I do assure you. He's been given fifteen years' soldier's pay for taking part in Dr. Narbondo's little entertainment, as have his helpmates and the two standing guard outside the door. You, on the other hand, are given nothing. I ask you to bear in mind that I find your tone slightly too sardonic for my taste. I'll murder your son in an instant if you give me cause, and then, once you've seen him die, I'll murder you as well."

Hearing this, Alice instinctively grasped Eddie's hand, and Helen said to her, "Don't look appalled, my lady. I was given a great sum to play my part, and I'm to be given more when the curtain falls and the play is done, although I forfeit all if I make a blunder, and, I don't doubt, my life would be forfeit with it. Do you quite understand me?"

"*Understand* you?" Alice said. "Not at all, I assure you. It's not within my powers to understand you. If you ask me do I take your meaning, do I understand that you're a murderous, grasping wretch who has sold her soul for money, then, yes – I'm afraid I very much understand you in that regard."

Helen stared at Alice with intense hatred and began to utter another threat, but at that moment there sounded the rising shriek of the organ, Beaumont apparently finding his way around the keys. He struck out the first notes of the Fugue, paused, and started again, settling into it, the voice of the organ rising in volume as air filled the pipes. Alice was astonished by it – the very idea of Narbondo's coach driver playing the great organ was unimaginable, and yet it was so, the steady volume of sound filling the cathedral. Narbondo, she realized, had orchestrated the entire thing. Helen was a mere pawn.

And now, from out of the throats of the pipes – some very near the base, some near the top – issued what appeared to be black vapor, pouring out and rising into the air. Alice watched it curiously for a moment. An illusion? She had no sooner formed this question, however, when she was astonished to see, as if in a dream, the front of a building some distance up the street explode outward in a gush of smoke and debris, hurtling people before it.

FORTY-TWO
FROM THE ARCHED WINDOW

D r. Narbondo looked down the barrel of his rifle, a Martini-Henry, the solid brass cartridges loaded with .30 caliber bullets tipped with white phosphorous. They were crude, but he knew from experience that they were serviceable. He peered over the sight at a leaded, stained-glass window depicting the death of Thomas Cranmer, the bald-headed, heavily bearded martyr who had been Archbishop of Canterbury at the time of Queen Mary's reign, and who had tried to avoid being burned as a heretic by recanting his faith. When it was decided that he would burn anyway, he had recanted his recantation, no doubt facing immolation in a sad muddle. Narbondo had always found the archbishop's story one of the more amusing burning-at-the-stake tales.

The tip of the rifle barrel was steadied atop a tripod that stood in the window, and he aimed it now at Cranmer's left eye, which, when it blew out, would make for a round hole in the pane too small to release any troubling amount of coal dust. If his aim was off, and he shot Cranmer through the nose or the ear, or even the forehead, the result would be much the same, since the very glorious window – all the very glorious windows – would cease to exist within a few seconds of the flaming bullet passing through, given, of course, that there was enough suspended dust. He had a number of bullets, however, and the three martyrs had numerous, lead-encircled body parts, so in the end he would prevail.

He set the rifle on the floor, tilted against the wall. Nearby stood an assemblage of heavy gears operated by an iron lever. The mechanism opened a trapdoor in the floor, the door raised at the moment, standing ready. Within, built into a hollow in the walls in the floors below, was a long slide that led to the deep cellar, through which he could disappear beneath the city. Today, however, he intended merely to shield himself from danger, to be traveling downward when the inferno blew the cathedral apart, and away beneath the street and up again into the devastation.

Lower in the tripod he had fixed a triangular shelf, canted forward, on which sat the skull of his brother Edward, the boy's ghost entrapped within the bone and silver and crystal, longing to find its way into the afterlife. Narbondo would do his best to set the spirit free at last, for which the ghost would no doubt be grateful, if ghosts were capable of gratitude, which was doubtful.

He looked at his pocket watch, the minute hand just then finding its way to the top of the hour. He heard the organ commence. The rising sound of the Fugue muted by glass and distance, but distinguishable even so. The greatest of the pipes, thirty feet in length, had a deep base resonance that shook one's bones. Twenty seconds into the piece the counterpoint melody came in, and Narbondo smiled and nodded, moving his right hand as if conducting an orchestra and happy that he had allowed Beaumont to choose the piece. The man was bound for glory along with the cathedral.

Narbondo activated the lamp within the skull now. The beam could be detected only dimly in the rainy air, but he could see it quite clearly where it shone on the golden raiment of the pews. He also saw, to his intense happiness, coal dust pouring from the mouths of the organ pipes.

Suddenly there was a shattering explosion – not unexpected – on Tallis Street. It would be the Nabob Pub ceasing to exist, along with many of its patrons, the cellar having blown to pieces. He consulted his watch and then glanced out of the window to view the sudden madness that had infected the mob, people running and screaming, soldiers shouting and holding up their hands to stop the rout, swept aside by the fleeing crowds. London was in a sad state, cowed by the numerous anarchist atrocities of the past months and ready to flee at the sound of a sneeze.

He glanced at the watch again and counted slowly to five, at which point another explosion sounded, this one farther up the road, a boarding house that was almost certainly frequented by prostitutes, run by a woman who had sneered at Narbondo openly one afternoon. He was deeply pleased with himself, and he hung bodily out of the open window to see what havoc the second explosion had wrought. The crowd that had fled west had been turned back by it, and now, God help them, by a third explosion, which Narbondo witnessed quite clearly: north up Carpenter Street, the roof of a butcher's shop blowing off entire, disintegrating in the air and showering down onto the devastated shop and the buildings around it. He saw bodies on the pavement, some endeavoring to drag themselves away, people vaulting over them as they ran helter-skelter toward the river, impeding each other, pushing and shouting. There were flames, he saw happily, although the rain had begun to fall in earnest, as if the explosions had opened the skies.

He pulled back into the room, cursing the rain, looking upward as he did so and opening his mouth in surprise, his eyes wide. A quarter of a mile away to the northwest a dirigible airship flew beneath the lowering sky, a madman, certainly, aloft on such a day...

It came to him that it was Langdon St. Ives. Where did he suppose he would land the craft? The yard at The Temple, perhaps – the only open ground nearby. But landing an airship would be impossible in this weather, and The Temple lawn would be crowded with pedestrians. It was sheer madness. St. Ives had come too late to the fair, although he might perhaps sift through the wreckage of the cathedral later for fragments of his wife and son.

Narbondo laughed out loud, happy as a schoolboy as he watched the dirigible's gondola sway dangerously in the wind and rain, trailing half a dozen long pieces of what must be mooring line. The ship skimmed the dome of St. Paul's, coming steadily on. Was it angling down toward the cathedral itself? An idea came into his mind – a quite possibly *spectacular* idea – and he set the barrel of the rifle on its tripod and aimed it at the airship, imagining with great pleasure the result of an incendiary missile piercing the wall of the great, hydrogen-filled gasbag.

A lice tore herself away from the scene outside, realizing that Helen had disappeared, and that the black vapor pouring from the organ was indeed smoke or dust, heavy in the air now – not smoke: there was no smell of it. She glanced back in the direction of the hidden panel and caught a brief glimpse of Helen pounding and pushing on one of the panels, shouting at it. The soldiers would escape beneath the street, of course, *had* escaped. She grabbed Eddie's hand, surprised when he tugged it forcefully away.

"The airship!" Eddie shouted, pointing upward toward the dark, shifting sky.

She saw it then, the great balloon with its tiny gondola gliding over the dome of St. Paul's, evidently descending, but what in God's name…?

"It's Father!" Eddie shouted. "Finn told me Father would come in the airship!" He nodded his head with determination, as if the unlikely appearance of the ship had settled a bet.

She took his hand and ran now. Something was coming to pass, and swiftly. Helen stood at the panel, searching the seams with her fingers. "Open!" she barked, her voice breaking with fear.

Alice and Eddie ran toward the great altar now. The cloud of black dust that shrouded the interior seemed to be growing darker, raining down in a fine black grit over the golden pews. Alice could feel the grit in her throat, but she saw that the air was still comparatively clear in the transept.

"Climb beneath!" she shouted to Eddie, when they were still several paces away from the arched openings under the altar. He seemed to know full well what they were about, and he threw himself sideways across the marble, sliding on his hip beneath one of the arches and into the shadows. Alice scrambled in beside him, hauling in her skirts. When she looked out again, she saw Helen run back out along the pews, looking around wildly. She stopped, however, seeing something now, putting her hand to her mouth in evident surprise. Alice saw it too, now, and could scarcely believe her own eyes.

Hovering in the air over the pews was the illuminated image of a boy, quite large, perhaps a projection – an animated projection. He looked around, as if he could see his surroundings, and then gazed quite distinctly at his own out-held hands. Alice saw the fingers close, the black dust swirling around him, seeming to give him substance. The airship, she saw, was quite close, tilting and swaying in the wind, headed straight for the cathedral – too close, she saw, far too close to avoid disaster.

It came to her that they might get out of the cathedral altogether – find something heavy and throw it through one of the windows before Helen took it into her mind to shoot them. But when she turned her mind to the idea of escape, her ear was attuned to the shouting and screaming on the streets – utter chaos, certainly – and there was the sound of another explosion somewhere nearby, distinct from the sound of thunder.

She saw Helen hurrying toward them, the pistol held in front of her, a look of madness in her eyes. Sparks exploded from the muzzle of the weapon, and a chunk of marble blew out of the altar, cutting Alice's face, although she scarcely felt any pain. "Stay!" she said to Eddie, and slid out from under, clutching her hatpin, blood flowing into her eye as she stood up to meet Helen, who threw herself forward like a mad thing.

What do you see inside the cathedral, Finn?" St. Ives shouted above the noise. "People in the pews?"

"No, sir. Empty, what I can make of it, but there's much I can't see for the black dust."

They were dangerously close to the rooftops – had come within an ace of knocking the top off the bell tower of the Church of St. John the Baptist, but there were no more encumbrances now, only the wind, upon which they rose and fell and swerved sickeningly. But it was pushing them hard forward, which was good. St. Ives's intention, which he had revealed to Finn, was to look to the bowsprit with its heavy glass ball to save them by punching through the roof of the cathedral, smashing out enough glass to disperse the coal dust, and then to rise above it undamaged. He knew, as did Finn, that it would be precious close work, and that there was a good chance they were within minutes of death.

The cathedral appeared to be monumentally frail, and there was the possibility of the gondola simply knocking it completely to pieces. What if, St. Ives thought now, Narbondo had foxed him, perhaps intending to blow up the palm house at Kew Gardens instead, or to blow up nothing at all, but to coerce St. Ives into…

"The black dust rises from the organ pipes, sir! Can you hear the sound of it?"

"Yes," St. Ives said. He could indeed hear what must be a monstrous, steam-driven organ. He saw now that the streets and pavements roundabout the cathedral were full of people, from Fleet Street to the Embankment, with more pouring in from the north, perhaps ignorant of the explosion, although others ran frantically through them, out of the area, and there was great confusion. The Temple grounds, just to the east of the cathedral, were a-swarm, and people were thick again in the area of St. Andrew's Hill, making their way toward the cathedral beneath raised umbrellas. Soldiers appeared to be herding people away, but there were too few soldiers, and a general chaos seemed to be growing in fervor. He saw a fire brigade coming along Fleet Street, the horses hampered by the crowds. "Another minute, more or less," he said. "You'd best take your seat, Finn."

Finn gave up the telescope willingly and strapped himself in. Rain flew out of the sky in waves, obscuring everything, clearing again. There was a flash now, not lightning, but a small streaking flame that pierced the wall of the cathedral, leaving an orange trail as it flew through the black dust. The gondola swayed in the wind, the cathedral looming up before them – forty feet away, thirty, the ball at the tip of the bowsprit would strike the cathedral, and no avoiding it.

Yet another orange track cut through the dust, pinwheeling this time, throwing out a radiating circle of flame: *An incendiary bullet*, St. Ives thought. *Of course.* Much more sensible than Greek fire. But he had no sooner conceived the thought than there was yet another bullet, which struck the window of the gondola just to his right, the glass shattering, the spent projectile falling to the deck of the gondola. It dawned on him that Narbondo would achieve his end were he to send a bullet through the hide of the great balloon, and he considered the enormity of his own folly and the likely result of the explosions that would follow.

FORTY-THREE
THE GHOST'S REVENGE

A light shone ahead of them as Jack and Tubby moved toward what was apparently an outrage already in progress. They had proceeded for some distance in darkness, downhill again, before seeing the glow of a headlamp on the front of a barrow and the silhouettes of three men at work. One of them depressed a great bellows over and over, pumping coal dust into whatever building they had decided to destroy. Finn had told Jack of the flaming syllabub, and it seemed to him now that it was one thing to face a pistol, another to face a flood of burning vitriol.

They stood watching for a moment, taking stock. Tubby might try his luck with de Groot's pistol, but from this distance hitting one of them would be luck indeed, and would certainly announce their arrival. Would a bold stroke prevail? Success – survival, perhaps – would depend on the man with the syllabub nozzle being wary of the burning liquid, and of his not wanting to destroy his companions out of mere recklessness.

The Fleet River lay ahead of them, a bridge arching the

flood. They must be very near the outfall into the Thames. It would be on the bridge that they were exposed at the edge of the barrow light, still twenty feet away. It seemed madness to Jack, and he began to insist that Tubby remain sensible to the danger, but Tubby winked at him, uttered, "Death or glory, Jacky," hefted his blackthorn, and set out in a crouched run. Jack followed, the bridge dead ahead, the light growing around them, twinkling on the dark water.

Jack saw the man who worked the bellows step away, saw one of his companions pumping at a canister, no doubt pressurizing it. The third manipulated a lever on a hose that snaked away out of sight. Jack and Tubby leapt onto the bridge, now, their luck still with them. There was suddenly a heavy concussion, the wall of brick in front of the three men blowing outward, slamming them into the wall behind in a vast rush of flame and debris. In the sudden darkness Jack was flung into filthy water, deafened by the concussion and having no idea what had happened to Tubby. He struggled to keep his head above the current, paddling to steady himself and milling his feet in a search for the bottom, swept away down the subterranean river into utter darkness.

The ball plunged through a great square pane at the top of the cathedral wall, the roof tilting away above, shards of glass falling. St. Ives pulled steadily back on the tiller, and the gondola began to lift through the roof, which tilted away above them. They surged forward, shattering glass panels and tearing apart the thin, cast-iron framework of the roof.

The increasing wind, however, was far more powerful than Keeble's ingenious engine or St. Ives's mental encouragement, and it pressed the balloon and gondola downward. Abruptly the ship no longer answered the tiller, but scraped and shuddered another couple of yards before running aground, having caught fast. The gondola listed over and settled, the outer wall of the great balloon now visible out the starboard side, the fabric billowing. The wind fell off and there was a momentary quiet. St. Ives tried once again to lift the ship off, but there was no response at all, and he realized that he couldn't hear the hum of the engine.

He stood up, hearing now an odd whistling noise, which quickly gave way to a massive whooshing, like wind through a tunnel – the hydrogen gas escaping the balloon in a rush. He saw bamboo ribs tear through the fabric of the balloon, and realized that the airbag was breaking to pieces. The wind heightened again, tearing at the balloon's skin, opening great rents, pieces of fabric flying away into the air. Bamboo struts snapped and popped, screws tore free, and sections of bent bamboo rod twanged themselves straight. There was a constant groaning and creaking, the noise increasing by the moment, every sprung joint in the egg-shaped skeleton of the balloon weakening the entire structure.

"The ladder, Finn!" St. Ives yelled, but he saw that the boy had anticipated him, and was already dropping the length of the ladder out through the open door, hanging onto the doorframe with one hand, his hair blowing wildly.

Finn waved at St. Ives and shouted, "Don't look down, sir! Take a firm grip!" and then went over the side without hesitation, moving like a cat.

The ship listed further to port with Finn's weight on the ladder. St. Ives pressed himself against the farther wall, thinking to balance things, but the ship rocked ominously with the slightest movement. There was a sudden, vast, rending sound, and he was thrown forward onto his hands and knees. He looked back through the starboard window and saw that more than half the dirigible had flown to pieces and was simply gone, and that the rest, an immense eggshell-shaped kite, its lacework trellis of bamboo visible within, was being raised by the wind and was endeavoring to lift the gondola. He held on, prepared to be swept away into the sky. He heard lines snapping, and then the kite spun and broke free, sailing skyward on an up-rushing current of wind. A bolt of lightning struck it even as he watched, and the entire thing burst into flaming pieces that were beaten downward again by a monumental rain, littering the rooftops of London with the torn and broken remnants of Keeble's triumph.

There was a shattering crash, and both Alice and Helen looked up in shocked surprise, seeing the gondola plowing a furrow through the roof of the cathedral. Glass shards and iron bars rained down onto the pews, eighty or a hundred feet away. Helen had a look of utter confusion about her, and she set out toward the falling debris, changed her mind, and ran back toward Alice, looking hard at the altar now and possible safety. As Helen ran past, Alice tripped her, and Helen sprawled forward, the pistol flying from her hand, spinning away toward the altar. Eddie's hand shot out, grasped the pistol, and snaked back in.

Helen picked herself up, looking frantically around for the pistol. She apparently understood what had happened to it, and she crawled forward toward the altar. Alice grasped her by the ankles, pulling her back, Helen shrieking and struggling. She overturned herself suddenly, crossing her legs and kicking at Alice in a single motion, throwing her off. Alice slipped on the gritty marble and went down. Helen slithered in beneath the altar, Alice following, praying that Eddie wouldn't try to shoot the pistol, that he would pitch it away, that he would climb out from under the altar and run before Helen got to him.

In the twilight beneath the altar Alice saw Helen grasp Eddie's foot and yank him forward, snatching the pistol out of his hand and flinging herself back against the low wall. She pointed the pistol at Alice, who flinched away at the sight of it, the explosion immensely loud in the enclosed space.

J ack was swept along through the wild, rain-swollen torrent of water and sewage. He could see nothing of Tubby, although it seemed to him that Tubby had fallen in before him, and so must be somewhere ahead. He could get no purchase on the wall in order to slow himself down. A dead dog, immensely bloated, rose up out of the water and stared at him. Jack shouted in surprise, seeing Tubby in the dog's face for a demented instant and then realizing his error when the dog was drawn under again. A circle of light appeared ahead – the outlet into the Thames. It was unbroken by the lines of any sort of grate, and Jack was washed through the outlet into the rainy morning, the roiling flood dragging him helplessly down the embankment behind the dog, the current driving him over backward, so that he somersaulted the last five yards into the calm waters of the Thames, not ten feet from a moored steam yacht. A man in a badly crushed top hat stood on the deck holding a great long hook and smoking a pipe.

Jack saw that Tubby Frobisher was already aboard – they had no doubt been watching for Jack's issuance – and he sat with his back against the cabin looking half drowned. Jack waved and shouted at him happily, thinking of the bloated dog and whether the story of its appearance might be made more humorous than horrible.

Tubby struggled tiredly to his feet when he saw Jack, who turned to face the shore in order to give the hook some purchase. He was snared under the arms, hauled to the side, and dragged up onto the deck in a reek of tobacco smoke. Over the tops of the Thames-side buildings he could see plumes of smoke rising from the explosions. There was a mass of people and vehicles crossing Blackfriars Bridge, fleeing the terror. Standing high above the street, the gondola of the dirigible sat empty and impossibly alone atop the Cathedral of the Oxford Martyrs like a skeletal bird resting on a nest of twigs.

N arbondo cast away the rifle in a fit of anger and threw himself bodily down the chute, wondering where he had failed. The fault lay in the bullets, certainly, which meant that it lay within himself, since he had fashioned each and every one. He wasn't happy with failure unless it was within others. He flew along through the darkness now, sitting up very straight, holding tight to his coat where the wide-bore signal pistol, loaded with a heavy phosphorus charge, was secure in its holster. There would be no failure this time.

He sailed out into the cellar, spinning halfway around on the stone floor, before scrambling to his feet. He jogged into the landing of the underground passage where he grabbed the iron railing and leapt down the stairs, picturing what would come. He would have the element of surprise in his favor – the panel flying open, himself stepping out into the cathedral, his weapon drawn. The very look of the pistol would unnerve whoever thought of contesting with him.

He reached the cool air at the bottom of the tunnel, saw the iron door standing open where Fox and his men would have made their way into the sewers and hence to the street again, where they would help to quell the rout and to ensure that the cathedral remained locked. He could hear the laboring of the steam engine, now, McFee and Sneed earning their keep, and very faintly he heard the playing of the organ, Beaumont performing for no one. The stairs stretched away ahead of him, fifty or sixty feet up, and he forced himself to slow down, to take them one at a time, to hoard his energy and wits like a miser.

St. Ives slid across the steeply sloping gondola floor, jamming his feet against the doorframe to stop himself from bumping over the sill and hurtling into the void. He turned onto his stomach and let himself out into the open air, compelling himself not to think, but simply to act. The gondola tilted with his weight, and the rain pelted his body. He groped with his foot, wishing he had Finn's acrobatic skills, or perhaps his youth. Immediately he kicked a rung and discovered it to be strangely solid, as if the rope were being held tightly from below.

He found solid handholds and pushed farther out, the rung of the ladder taking his weight so that he was emboldened to grope with the other foot. In a trice he was firmly clamped to the ladder itself, both feet steady, and despite Finn's admonition, he chanced a look downward – a startling, breathtaking distance – and saw that Finn held the bottom rung of the ladder, hanging on it, his feet just touching the floor. The gondola shifted above him again, and he uttered a surprised shout as he dropped a heart-stopping two or three inches, and then began his downward climb without further hesitation, rung by slick rung, hanging tenaciously onto the wet rope until he felt Finn's hand slap his foot.

He descended until he was compelled to let go and drop to the floor, which was filthy with wet coal dust. He slipped, sprawled onto his breech, and stood up again, wiping his hands on his trousers. The cathedral appeared to be empty, filled only with the noise of the organ. Coal dust still gushed from the pipes, but was rising upward now, through the gaping hole in the roof and out into the open air.

Shading his face, he looked up to ascertain where the craft would fall, for fall it no doubt would, sooner or later. It was supported fore and aft by bent iron bars, but it was moving, the whole section of roof was moving, buffeted by the winds. There was a broad open section of the nave below it, with a vast, ornate compass rose inlaid in the marble floor, partly obscured by grit, long lines running out from it in the four points of the compass, the cathedral parallel with the east and west axis. He and Finn moved out of the area, out of the rain that fell through the hole in the roof, but stopped as one when they saw the glowing figure of Mother Laswell's son Edward hovering over the pews.

Even now, St. Ives's mind rebelled against the idea of the ghost's existence, of its being a living ghost in some sense of the phrase, and not an ingenious parlor trick. It spun very slowly, looking around itself with a semblance of consciousness in its eyes, as if it were gaining substance by the moment, perhaps contemplating its surroundings. Although much of the blowing coal dust had been dispersed or damped down by the rain, the ghost was strangely solid, translucent rather than transparent.

St. Ives followed the cone of projected light out through the high wall and saw the lamp itself, the Aylesford Skull, peering back at him through an arched window across the street, its eyes as bright as tiny silver suns. It was from that room – the room that Mother Laswell had seen so clearly in her dream – that Narbondo had fired his incendiary bullets, too hastily and too soon to effect an explosion, and ultimately too late once the dirigible had opened the roof. St. Ives felt a small but increasing satisfaction within him – that his suspicions had proven true, that he and Finn had arrived in time, that running the gondola through the roof of the cathedral hadn't turned out to be mere lunacy.

The organ abruptly lost its wind and played itself out, but the sudden silence lasted only a few moments before it was broken by the crack of a gunshot. St. Ives could still see no one in the cathedral, although in that moment Finn shouted, "It's her!" and sprinted toward the long, heavy altar sixty feet away in the raised transept that formed what would be the horizontal member of a cross.

A woman, disheveled, her clothes filthy with coal dust, stood before the altar now, apparently having crawled out from underneath. In her hand she held a heavy pistol, which she aimed haphazardly at Finn when she caught sight of him. St. Ives, several steps behind Finn, shouted a warning, but Finn apparently saw the pistol, for he threw himself forward, rolling up against the edge of the pews and disappearing down a row, confounding her aim. She pointed the weapon at St. Ives, her arms and cheeks bleeding from small wounds, her face twitching, her eyes utterly insane.

D oyle and Hasbro followed a small stream that coursed through a brick tunnel connecting the Fleet River to the Walbrook far below St. Martin Ludgate. There was the sound of what might be an engine, which grew louder as they moved west toward the Cathedral of the Oxford Martyrs. Soon they found the Fleet itself, raging with floodwaters from the storm, and they set out downriver in the direction of the cathedral.

Mingled with the noise of the engine now was the unmistakable sound of organ music. Hasbro drew his pistol, Doyle closed the shutter over the lantern, and they moved forward as quickly as they could, the Fleet flowing at their left hand. The engine abruptly fell silent, and the organ music dwindled. Hurried footfalls approached, and within moments two men appeared, coming along in a ring of lantern light – a giant of a man with a tangle of black hair, his arm in a sling, and a bearded dwarf. Neither carried weapons. Doyle opened the shutter on the lantern and Hasbro raised the pistol and stepped out to block the path. The dwarf turned and bolted into the darkness, but the giant rushed forward with a wild roar, heedless of the pistol. Hasbro calmly shot him in the chest. He staggered but came on again, his rage doubled, and Hasbro shot him a second time, the giant's body spinning around with the force of the bullet and toppling into the Fleet where it was drawn under the dark water.

*H*elen, St. Ives thought, the madwoman's name coming to him – almost certainly the woman who had walked through Lord Moorgate's blood after his throat was slit, who had only a moment ago shot the pistol that she gripped in a shaking hand. She looked away from St. Ives now, toward the paneled wall to her left, which slid open silently.

Dr. Narbondo himself stepped through it, dressed in a black, wide-belted Anglican cassock, looking around with satisfaction as if the cathedral were his own. In his arms he carried an open basket in which sat a black cone with the pointed end lopped off and capped with a thick, white wafer. It was clearly cast iron – an infernal machine, oddly shaped, certainly, but with an evil look about it.

Narbondo glanced around, nodding at St. Ives as if he accepted his presence there and wasn't at all concerned with it. Then he saw Helen and his expression grew wary. He took stock of her – watched the pistol in her hand. St. Ives saw Eddie appear behind the altar, under which he had no doubt been hiding. *Not now*, St. Ives thought. But Eddie looked about unhappily, saw his father, and dashed in his direction, as if his father's mere presence would protect him. St. Ives held his hand up in an attempt to wave him back. He saw Alice pull herself out from beneath the front of the altar now, and shout after Eddie, calling him to her. She tried to stand, but fell to the floor, her face running blood, the shoulder of her white blouse red with it.

Helen ran toward Narbondo, her mouth wide, spittle flying, knocking Eddie aside with her left forearm. She held the pistol out before her in her right hand. Narbondo set his basket down gingerly and in the same movement leapt forward to meet her. She shrieked in surprise and pulled the trigger, the recoil flinging her hand upward, the bullet flying wild. Narbondo snatched her wrist and yanked her around bodily. He grasped the hand that held the pistol, turned the pistol toward her, and shot her at close range through the throat, casting her mutilated body into St. Ives's path as he ran toward Eddie. Narbondo reached Eddie first, plucked him up, and threw him over his shoulder, Eddie kicking and pounding with his fists.

Narbondo stopped St. Ives in his tracks simply by pointing the pistol at Eddie's back and shaking his head with unmistakable meaning. St. Ives made a conscious effort to slow his breathing, to gain control of himself. He saw that Finn was kneeling next to Alice. She tried to sit up, succeeded. Narbondo glanced in their direction, aimed the pistol casually, and fired it, marble shards exploding from the corner of the altar.

"Calm yourself, Professor, as you value the lives of your wife and son," Narbondo said. "You tread on dangerous ground. If you'll just pick up that basket, we can be about our business. You have my word that your son is safe, although I'll keep him close for the time being."

St. Ives did as he was told. His mind, he discovered, was preternaturally clear now. He was aware that the storm had abated, or at least that the heavy rain and thunder had ceased. The canister in the basket, nestled in packed excelsior, was almost certainly a bomb. It was curiously shaped – a black iron vase.

"I'm reduced, as you see, to something cruder than coal dust, thanks to your grand heroics. What you carry is the ace in my sleeve, as the sharper says, although in this case it's a gelignite ace in a wicker basket. Its crown, simply put, is a thermal detonator. I warn you that the gelignite is somewhat sensitive to being dropped, so unless you wish to blow you and your son to flinders, I suggest that you take great care. Walk with me, now, sir." He gestured with the pistol and set out, carrying Eddie along the edge of the pews toward the open section of the nave, never taking his eyes from St. Ives's face.

"Place the basket on the pew, directly beneath Edward's revolving ghost," Narbondo said. "We'll send my mother's beloved son to kingdom come, where he longs to be."

St. Ives did as he was told and stepped away, looking up at the gondola, lodged in the roof. Now that the power of the storm had diminished, the gondola was still, held tight astern, the glass ball caught in the crotch of a bent iron strut.

"I want to make one last experiment," Narbondo said, "and it must be completed while the souls of the dead haunt the streets roundabout us. I assume that my mother told you about the door I mean to open when she summoned you to Hereafter Farm?"

"She did," said St. Ives evenly, his voice sounding mechanical in his ears. "The idea flies in the face of reason."

"My brother's ghost flies in the face of reason, Professor, and yet there he stands, undeniably. You're a man of great learning; surely you trust your own eyes not to lie."

The ghost was no longer spinning, but seemed to be looking down at them – or particularly at Eddie, St. Ives thought, if that were possible. Narbondo was correct. Everything about the phenomenon flew in the face of reason. St. Ives watched for his chance, some distraction, the creaking of the gondola or the shattering of a piece of falling glass. "Even if this door exists, how can you say that it be worth opening, or what lies beyond?"

"What care I for its worth? A door is but a convenient symbol for the way between here and there, a mere poetic figure until it's made real. We cannot begin to come at its worth until we see with our own eyes what lies beyond. I bid you, sir, to cast off the fetters that enslave your mind."

"There are a wide variety of fetters," St. Ives told him.

"Alas, you and I speak different languages, sir. I'll make myself clear, however. I am going to set young Eddie on the floor now, where he must sit passively like the swamis of old and contemplate the pending wonder. Do you hear me, boy? Will you sit on your backside and be still?"

"Yes," St. Ives said for him, recognizing the cast in Eddie's eye, the same cast that appeared there when his tin soldiers had had enough of his sister's mechanical elephant. St. Ives shook his head warningly.

Narbondo shoved the pistol into the belt around his cassock and drew a fat, pistol-like weapon out of his coat, a bulbous thing with a vastly wide bore, as if it was meant to shoot cricket balls as bullets. He pointed it at the wicker basket and pulled the trigger. A flaming orb of white fire blew out of the barrel, igniting the basket and the pew cushion and the white disk atop the device, which flared up brilliantly in the brief moment before an explosion ripped upward out of the iron cone in a burst of fire and smoke and flaming wad.

Edward's ghost disappeared within the flame and smoke, and in that moment St. Ives, half-deafened by the blast, threw himself forward, grabbed Eddie, and flung him across the dust-slick floor, Eddie sliding away as if he sat on a block of melting ice. A strange banshee wail arose in the air, finding its way through the ringing in St. Ives's ears, rising in pitch. Narbondo held his pistol again, having cast away the incendiary weapon.

"It wants a blood sacrifice," Narbondo shouted at him, cocking the pistol. "You'll do as well as the boy."

St. Ives threw himself forward, clipping Narbondo's legs out from under him. Narbondo slammed down onto his side atop the compass rose, rolled out from under St.

Ives and sprang into a crouch, aimed hurriedly downward, and pulled the trigger even as St. Ives was scrambling out of the way like a crab. The bullet punched into the marble floor, blasted-out fragments hammering St. Ives on the side of his head and face as he pushed himself to his knees, fully expecting to be shot with the second bullet.

Narbondo, however, was staring fixedly at the marble floor, which had split open along a seam defined by the north-south axis of the inlaid compass rose. The stones of the floor snapped and cracked, the fissure running outward in both directions from the flattened bullet, which was lodged in the center of the rose. Narbondo watched it fixedly, his face glowing with wonder and triumph.

St. Ives felt blood flowing into his collar and discovered that his ear was partly severed. What had begun as a banshee's wail was now a harmonic vibration that filled the cathedral with a single note, circling around them, seeming to emanate from all points of the compass and rising slowly in tone.

Narbondo raised the pistol and pointed it at St. Ives from six feet away – a fatal distance – but still he didn't shoot it. He nodded up at Edward's ghost, which still had a human shape but was composed entirely of swirling sparks. The crack in the floor was widening, more quickly now, dust and fragments of stone falling into it, soil visible below, the very ground itself opening. St. Ives looked for Eddie and saw him within the several pillars that held up the arched ceiling of the portico, well back toward the wall. Alice and Finn were coming along down the pews, both of them looking anxiously upward at the gondola.

The iron framework of the cathedral sang now. The glass panes vibrated visibly, like square pools of water into the centers of which stones had been dropped. The whirling, densely packed stars that filled the void that had been Edward's ghost glowed ever more brightly as the sound and vibration increased. Narbondo nodded with apparent satisfaction and cocked the pistol. Then, like the crest of a wave pitching over onto a beach, the swarm of stars fell out of the air and inundated him. He staggered forward, throwing his hands up. The pistol fell into the line-straight rift in the ground and flew out of sight. Narbondo, glowing within the whirling nebula of sparks, clutched at unseen things, his hands opening and closing spasmodically as he reeled at the edge of the chasm, several feet wide now. With an inhuman shriek he was dragged forward by the elemental particles of Edward's ghost and cast into the depths in a shower of sparks. St. Ives saw him strike the sloped bank of the fissure, making a failed attempt to stop himself and rolling pell-mell downward into the darkness. In the moments before they winked out, the descending sparks illuminated a geometric field of pale structures far, far below, appearing to St. Ives to be a subterranean graveyard, perhaps, or the ruins of an ancient subterranean city, which vanished a moment after he perceived it.

The rift was closing in on itself again. The harmonic vibration had reached a crescendo, awakening St. Ives from his rapt attention on the spectacle before him. Debris fell from above, the marble beneath his feet shuddered, and the panes of glass in the roof and walls shivered themselves to pieces as he turned and ran toward the portico, ducking under the domed roof as if out of a hailstorm. There sounded the screech of rending metal high overhead. The gondola fell nose-downward, hung for a moment by the stern, and then dropped, the glass orb in the bowsprit carrying it straight downward into the narrowing chasm, which closed on it with a vast exhalation of air, shattering the craft utterly, the rudder and propeller skittering away across the floor amid a confusion of broken sticks.

Within moments, the cathedral walls and roof had been reduced to an iron skeleton. The south wind blew across the floor, stirring up little whirlwinds of coal dust from beneath the pews. The great window depicting the death of the Oxford Martyrs still stood, however – perhaps the only glass remaining entire. Rays of light beamed through it in a myriad of colors, the morning sun showing in the heavens through broken clouds.

FORTY-FOUR
THE JAM POT

The afternoon weather was particularly fine – a warm breeze out of the west, perfect for eating outdoors. St. Ives contemplated birthdays, his own having come round again, time passing away. They'd had some shrewdly hard knocks, including a cool and bewildered acknowledgement from the Crown. There would be no recompense for the destroyed airship despite the arrest of Guido Fox, betrayed by de Groot along with Lord Moorgate, who was assumed to have fled.

But there was much to celebrate, most of it assembled before his eyes at this very moment. Eddie practiced throwing a boomerang that was a gift from Bill Kraken, who had carried it out of Port Jackson when he had fled Australia. He had given Cleo a kite decorated with a grinning moon face and with an immensely long tail. The kite rode above the broad lawn in front of the hopping huts, rising and swooping on the breeze, the sun high overhead and the sky a deep, luminous blue. Next week the huts would be full of workers, bringing in the harvest.

Eddie held his boomerang now, readying himself,

squinting toward a platoon of enemy soldiers that stood in neat ranks on a distant crate, threatening the peace of the quiet afternoon. He threw the boomerang smoothly, and instead of wheeling off into the roses and smashing blossoms as it had the habit of doing, it described a neat circle, rising and then dipping toward the ranked enemy troops, falling upon them soundlessly and destroying them. St. Ives applauded, shouted encouragement to Cleo, and then turned his attention to Gilbert Frobisher who was telling Alice that he had finally seen the great bustard, on the wing over the marsh just yesterday, the creature's body the size of a Smithfield ham. Hodgson had sought out the nest after seeing the bird take flight and had photographed a wonderful golden egg like something out of the Arabian Nights.

Mother Laswell and Mrs. Langley came out through the open door of the gallery now and down the several steps, carrying covered dishes toward three great tables set up on the broad lawn. Hasbro carried a tray bristling with bottles of French wine – Chateau Latour, which Gilbert and Tubby had brought from the marsh along with crates of Gilbert's pale ale, two vast pheasant-and-mushroom pies, and a tremendous treacle and cream pudding. Arthur Doyle and Jack Owlesby, seeing the train of food and drink crossing the lawn, gave off their game of Irish skittles and hurried forward. Dorothy had just knocked another pin out of the circle, and so accused them of abandoning the game from fear of losing to a woman.

St. Ives regarded the food and drink with an openly gluttonous look and thought of Tubby Frobisher's

signifying jam pot. Abruptly he wondered what had become of Finn Conrad, who had been away this past hour and a half on a mysterious errand. Hot food wanted eating, after all, but he didn't like the idea of sitting down to it without Finn in the company.

Cleo let out a sudden shriek, handed her roll of kite string to Bill Kraken, and set out at a run toward the wisteria alley, catching and passing her brother, who waved his boomerang as he ran. St. Ives heard Alice laugh, and he stood up, feeling her hand on his shoulder.

"Happy birthday, darling," she said to him.

Across the lawn, coming in from the direction of Aylesford, Finn rode atop an immense Indian elephant draped in scarlet and gold cloth decorated with bangles. It came into St. Ives's head that he was quite possibly dreaming, but Alice's touch and her happy laughter were far too real to be a figment. The beast skirted the rose garden with an admirable delicacy and walked placidly toward them, looking around with what appeared to be satisfaction on its wrinkled face before raising its trunk so that Finn Conrad could hand it a length of sugar cane.

ACKNOWLEDGMENTS

I'm immensely thankful to a number of people who helped bring this novel into being: Tim Powers, who generated ideas for the book over long lunches while I took frantic notes: a lot of pizzas under the bridge; my wife, Viki, who once again tirelessly and patiently corrected and commented on various drafts as yet another story came into being; and my friend Paul Buchanan, who read and reacted to early drafts and late drafts over plates of *juevos rancheros* at the Filling Station.

I'm especially thankful to John Berlyne, who put me up to writing this book in the first place.

ABOUT THE AUTHOR

James Paul Blaylock was born in Long Beach, California in 1950, and attended California State University, where he received an MA. He was befriended and mentored by Philip K. Dick, along with his contemporaries K.W. Jeter and Tim Powers, and is regarded – along with Powers and Jeter – as one of the founding fathers of the steampunk movement. Winner of two World Fantasy Awards and a Philip K. Dick Award, he is currently director of the Creative Writing Conservatory at the Orange County High School of the Arts, where Tim Powers is Writer in Residence. Blaylock lives in Orange CA with his wife, they have two sons.

BENEATH LONDON

James P. Blaylock

The collapse of the Victoria Embankment uncovers
a passage to an unknown realm beneath the city.
Langdon St. Ives sets out to explore it, not knowing
that a brilliant and wealthy psychopathic murderer is
working to keep the underworld's secrets hidden for
reasons of his own.

St. Ives and his stalwart friends investigate a string
of ghastly crimes: the gruesome death of a witch,
the kidnapping of a blind, psychic girl, and the grim
horrors of a secret hospital where experiments in
medical electricity and the development of human,
vampiric fungi, serve the strange, murderous ends of
perhaps St. Ives's most dangerous nemesis yet.

"Vividly imagined, as alive as any of the characters."
— The Book Bag

HOMUNCULUS

James P. Blaylock

It is the late 19th century and a mysterious airship orbits through the foggy skies. Its terrible secrets are sought by many, including the Royal Society, a fraudulent evangelist, a fiendish vivisectionist, an evil millionaire and an assorted group led by the scientist and explorer Professor Langdon St. Ives.

Can St. Ives keep the alien homunculus out of the claws of the villainous Ignacio Narbondo?

"The fastest, funniest, most colorful and grotesquely horrifying novel that could ever be written about Victorian London." — Tim Powers